SO YOU WANNA BE A POP STAR?

A CHOICES NOVEL

ZACHARY SERGI

RP | KIDS
PHILADELPHIA

DEDICATION:
TO BRITNY, LUCY, AMANDA,
AND KELLY (CLARKSON)

Running Press Teens
Hachette Book Group
1290 Avenue of the Americas, New York, NY 10104
www.runningpress.com/rpkids
@RP_Kids

Printed in the United States of America

First Edition: March 2023

Published by Running Press Teens, an imprint of Perseus Books, LLC, a subsidiary of Hachette Book Group, Inc. The Running Press Teens name and logo are trademarks of the Hachette Book Group.

The Hachette Speakers Bureau provides a wide range of authors for speaking events. To find out more, go to www.hachettespeakersbureau.com or email HachetteSpeakers@hbgusa.com.

Running Press books may be purchased in bulk for business, educational, or promotional use. For more information, please contact your local bookseller or the Hachette Book Group Special Markets Department at Special.Markets@hbgusa.com.

The publisher is not responsible for websites (or their content) that are not owned by the publisher.

Print book cover and interior design by Frances J. Soo Ping Chow

Library of Congress Cataloging-in-Publication Data has been applied for.

ISBNs: 9780762480821 (hardcover), 9780762480845 (ebook)

LSC-C

Printing 1, 2022

This novel was written for two kinds of readers:
Those who love control and those who love to lose control.

So, go ahead, read every page like a novel straight through if you want;
this was written with you in mind.

However, if you really want the full experience, follow the interactive
brick road and honor your choices while reading.

You might just find following the rules is the fastest way to break them . . .
Either way, this story now belongs to you.

INCLUDED IN THE BACK OF THE NOVEL IS A READING GUIDE TO help keep track of your most important decisions. You can easily read without using this guide, but it's there for you if you need it.

Once your Reading Guide is complete, you can also use it to compile two Character Personality Profiles. These determine what kind of reader you are and your signature song.

I encourage you to write in this book, but if you can't, a PDF copy of the Reading Guide can also be found online.

CHAPTER ONE

EVERLY

THE STAGE LIGHTS HIT ME AND I TRY TO SHINE JUST AS BRIGHT, even though I'm not sure what I'm doing up here anymore.

At least, for this final group performance, we're singing an original song I wrote. It might not be my best, but it's maybe saying something real about this experience? I figured if the five of us left in this competition are forced to perform together, we should try to sing something that might matter to us. And hopefully to someone out there listening.

"All that glitters isn't gold,

That's the line we're always sold."

It's deeply surreal to hear another artist sing a verse I wrote, especially in this setting. I'm still way more used to performing for bedroom ring lights and muted coffee shops, not under the blinding lights of a studio soundstage. Everywhere I look there's a different searing flash—white and green, red and purple. These lights currently bathe me in sapphire, same as the icy dress that wardrobe put me in.

I told myself when I entered *SO YOU WANNA BE A POP STAR? The Search for America's Next Teen Sensation* that I wouldn't sell out or do anything that felt inauthentic. But here I am wearing too much stage makeup, playing a heightened version of myself: the deep blue singer-songwriter who freezes up onstage. I guess it's all true, especially that last part. I still don't know what to do with my hands, standing here swaying awkwardly without a guitar or piano. Everything just feels so forced, including having to pretend that I vibe with *everyone* else onstage.

"Diamonds are a girl's best friend," CeCe keeps singing across the stage.

"Molds we fit to not offend."

At least I do genuinely adore CeCe. Hearing her sing the first verse, it feels almost worth giving away one of my songs to production. She inhabits the lyrics in a way I never could, breathing electric life into each phrase. She breaks forward in her ruby-lit track, her combat boots stomping and plaid shirt swinging. It's CeCe's personal mission to remind the world that Black women helped invent rock 'n' roll, and she is succeeding.

Watching CeCe, I'm heartened she feels so comfortable on a song of mine. She was actually the one to convince me I should even feature an original, after the producers asked me. We've been singing strictly covers, since we have to give up the rights to anything original performed on the show. This debut season of *SYWBAPS* hasn't exactly been a ratings smash, so it hasn't felt worth the sacrifice. But CeCe reminded me that I came here for exposure, no matter the size.

"You owe it to your fans," she said. "Just come up with something new for the situation. Don't overthink it."

It took one very sleepless night, but that's exactly what I did. Most of this other mainstream pop star stuff might not come easily to me, but I know I can always write a song. If I had more time with "Press Diamonds," I'd break apart the even syllable counts and strict rhyming structure, but then again, something about this mathematical evenness works for the song. It's way more bop-forward than my usual stuff. Blander, but somehow more flexible—which was the assignment.

"But these diamonds drip with blood,

Sweat and tears pooling to flood."

Hearing Vinny belt the pre-chorus next, I experience a rolling body chill. I can sing, but not like Vinny. The way he interprets my melody with all those R&B runs and minor key shifts, it's intimidating as hell. That said, Vinny does tend to swap diva power for nuanced feeling, so the lyrics take on an . . . unintended force. Vinny's voice quakes through every inch of space, seemingly supercharged by the purple-sequined blazer the stylists chose for him. "Royal colors for a queen," he joked earlier while we were waiting in the wings, his Italian New Yorker accent thick as ever.

"Your feed with shiny stories," Vinny keeps belting.

"Sure signs we'll edge your glories."

I snap myself back to reality as Vinny finishes, because we're all meant to sing the hopefully anthemic chorus together. As the driving beat builds, Vinny drops back to hit his mark, gleaming in deep amethyst. These different colors were the Executive Producers' idea, jewel-toned personas to show our different reflections of pop. It's a pretty literal interpretation of our genres and my song, but I have to admit, the effect does seem kind of dazzling from up here. I wonder if it translates to the audience at home.

"Put us in to pressure cook,

Forever pressed, unexpressed.

All the news that's fit to print,

Marathon we're forced to sprint."

I sing the first lines of the chorus, my voice blending smoothly with the others. We final five come from such different worlds, you'd expect us to clash. And I guess some of us do, offstage. But right now it's almost like we've been singing together for years.

"Live rent-free to mine our lonely islands," I sing, winding into the last line of the hook.

"But won't be turned into your press diamonds."

We hit the last two words with exaggerated orchestral hits. I suppose it doesn't take a genius to know what I wrote "Press Diamonds" about, but it did take a genius producer to make it sound so big. Usually my songs are much more intimate and acoustic. I've never heard one put through the pop-synthesizing machine before, so I've always been curious if it'd work. I'm happy to hear that it does, even if this song isn't one of my best.

Stepping back in line, I suppress a smile. I don't want to seem smug, especially given the lyrics I wrote specifically for the next contestant.

"Once before there lived pure coal,

Stripped it down with just one goal."

Dea's voice is the thinnest out of everyone left and, if we're being honest, pitch isn't always her best friend. But such mortal concerns are beneath Dea, who only ever drips with stage presence and star quality. Clad in a crystallized designer jumpsuit and sky-high boots, Dea is K-Pop perfection personified. Though I know she actually worships at the altar of brand-diversified solo artists like J.Lo and Dua Lipa. Watching Dea across the stage is like a master class in choreography, presence, and attitude. I refuse to admit that this sparks a pang of jealousy in my chest, so I instantly grind that emotion out. Months back in the semifinal rounds, Dea was the first genuine friend I made here.

But that was before.

"Upgrade, shift states 'til you break," Dea sings, punctuating each word with a dance move.

"A glittery, reflective, beautiful fake."

Dea steps back from her diamond-white light and turns to give me a megawatt smile. It projects pure charisma and gratitude, but I know Dea well enough to feel the invisible daggers she throws under the surface. *Thanks for those lyrics, Everly.*

I return the smile, radiating my own icy warmth. *You deserve every word, babe.*

"But these diamonds drip with blood,

Sweat and tears pooling to flood."

The pre-chorus then builds back up and occupies my full attention. Partially because I wish I spent more time finessing those lyrics, but mostly because they're sung by Stern Green. Stage-named for his ridiculously bright eyes, Stern is everything I thought I'd never want in a guy—a boy band F-boy supreme. I'm from the same LA valleys as HAIM and Billie Eilish; we're not supposed to crush on the blond, corn-fed pretty boys. Especially not the ones who slick up in LA to make it big. But there's something . . . different about Stern. An edge I can't quite grasp, bathed in emerald light.

It doesn't hurt to hear his liquid velvet voice wrap itself around my song. That also has a tightening effect on my chest that I'd rather not dwell on. Especially once Stern turns, projecting the full weight of his charms on Dea. Of course he'd flirt with *her* onstage.

I sing the second chorus on autopilot because right on cue, I start to feel lifted out of my body. My solo on the bridge is coming next. Even though I wrote this song, I already know my delivery will feel more wooden compared to the others, both for the studio audience and the cameras. I used to think I was a great performer in my bedroom, posting to social media, but that was before I landed on a stage with a million moving parts. I've made it this far in the competition twisting cover songs into interesting shapes and hiding behind an instrument, but I can tell the "will she conquer her stage fright" storyline lost its charm weeks ago. It's a miracle I survived the last round of eliminations.

I just don't understand how the others can make it look so effortless, living in the moment and shining the way they do. At least for this group performance I've been safe to hide in the background and reside in my thoughts. Because that's where I always live onstage: fully in my own head.

Like now, as my solo approaches. I try to decide whether to look at the audience or the judges. Then I think maybe I should look into the cameras, since this is a live TV show. But I never seem able to track which little red light is actively streaming, if I can even zero in on one of the many cameras swooping around the stage like hawks. Then I feel my hands stiffen, unsure what to do without a chord to play. Nerves burst through my veins like a million stinging insects, and I feel defeated before I even begin. I don't get it. I know I'm good at this whole music thing. I was born to do it.

So why is this part so impossible for me?

My chance to run offstage and vomit passes as the chorus recedes into the lullaby lilt I wrote for the bridge. My mouth instantly goes dry, but I lift the mic to my lips anyway, on autopilot. *Now or never, Everly,* I scream to myself. *Better show them what you're made of.*

Except as I step forward to sing my solo, the microphone somehow slips out of my sweaty palm. I watch in surreal slow motion as it crashes to the stage . . .

And promptly rolls away.

❖ Turn this into an impromptu performance piece. Undo the bun in my hair and **crawl** to the mic to show I'm no shiny diamond.
TURN TO PAGE 6

❖ Turn this into an impromptu duet. Cross the stage to share Stern's microphone, hoping he'll **harmonize** with me on the fly.
TURN TO PAGE 7

Before I know it, I'm untying my tight bun and letting my frizzy brown hair fall around my face. Then I drop to my knees, looking into the nearest camera. I don't really know what I'm doing, I just hope the fear in my eyes reads as something intentional.

Then I hear a voice riffing over my little show and realize CeCe is covering for me. As I begin to crawl forward toward the mic, I hear Vinny and Stern join in on the vocal cover. I have no idea if this looks as chaotic as it feels, but I just tell myself I'm trying to channel some unexpected Florence Welch energy.

I reach the mic just in time to start singing over the next section. This far down the stage and this close to the lights, I can't see much. I'm only vaguely aware of another camera rolling on its track around me.

"Diamonds are really just stones,

Falling ruins and building homes."

As I begin singing, I find my voice is less shaky than I expect. Wrapping itself around this melody I wrote, I can at least rely on my signature style. I keep passing my break, jumping between falsetto and my chest voice on the twisting progressions.

"Marking tombs and trapping rings,

Skipping lakes and breaking things."

By now I've stalked back to my spot on the stage, probably looking like some faerie princess gone feral. Figuring I might as well go with it, I find the closest camera and stare it down. I try to channel all my fear and nerves forward. Miraculously, it feels something like a release.

"Throw your stones to my witch death,

'Til stone coal is all that's left."

The spotlight shifts away from me as the final chorus refrains begin. I exhale between phrases, because I can't believe I just did that.

For once, I wasn't completely in my head onstage.

For once, I just operated on instinct.

But why did it take such an embarrassing mistake to finally get me there?

TURN TO PAGE 9

6

Operating on instinct, I cross the stage and stand beside Stern. He looks surprised, so I take one second to whisper in his ear as the next bar approaches.

"Harmonize."

I then turn toward Stern's microphone, forcing myself to ignore how he smells like the beach, all driftwood skin and ocean spray deodorant. I place my hand on his shoulder to steady myself, also ignoring the round curve of muscle there.

"Diamonds are really just stones,
Falling ruins and building homes."

As I begin singing, I find my voice is less shaky than I expect. Normally I'd pass my break, jumping between falsetto and my chest voice on the twisting melody, but I try to even out so Stern can follow.

"Marking tombs and trapping rings,
Skipping lakes and breaking things."

Stern manages to harmonize over the second line, hitting the fifth below my own high note. A ripple runs over my skin, and not from having my lips so close to Stern's. I get a full-body chill, because we sound *good* together.

Really good.

"Throw your stones to my witch death,
'Til stone coal is all that's left."

As Stern and I finish the last line, we both turn to look into each other's eyes. In the periphery, I can see an overhead camera swiveling on its track to capture the moment. I linger one second longer, feeling the electricity pass between us. For a moment, nothing has ever felt more real in my entire life.

Then the chorus refrain arrives. Stern turns back to hit his emerald mark and I see that someone from the crew has returned a microphone to my own sapphire mark. Hoping the cameras focus away from my scurrying, I return to my spot on the stage.

I start singing, immediately wondering where that surge of spontaneous confidence just came from. For that brief bridge, I was able to feel free onstage. But was that because of my mistake, or because I was singing with Stern? Was anything about what just happened real . . .

Or was it all just made for the cameras?

TURN TO PAGE 9

The final chorus begins and the backing music drops out. We planned to sing this last chorus a capella with a half-time feel, harmonizing as best we could in our one sound check rehearsal. Standing here now in our bejeweled spotlights, against all odds we sound kind of . . . incredible? If the cameras effectively capture half the feeling of this lifting vocal moment, you might even think the five of us have been singing together forever.

Then I remind myself what's really happening here. We aren't a unit. We're five relative strangers competing for the same solo record deal. Last week there were nine of us on this stage, and tomorrow only one of us will win. Blending isn't the point. So I push my voice up an octave, projecting louder to match the others on the last note. Only when the lights fade do I allow myself to breathe again.

The moment we finish, the studio audience erupts into cheers and applause. Once my eyes adjust, I think I see the panel of judges on their feet for a standing ovation.

Before I can really process any of this, a producer already signals us to leave the stage. They need to roll a package of the host giving out our information so viewers can vote for a winner before tomorrow's finale. Still, even after being ushered backstage and into a dressing room, we can hear the continued rumble of applause from the studio audience.

"Okay, did we just bring the house down?" Vinny asks first, vibrating.

"We were definitely good," CeCe agrees. "Almost as good as that song Everly wrote."

"I don't know how you created something that works for each of our styles," Stern then piles on, "but you're a genius, Everly."

I feel my cheeks flush. They're right; my song did kill it out there. But I'm just as surprised by the unexpected life it took on as everyone else. I'm not sure the credit really belongs with me, especially after my mic flub.

"You didn't have to drop your mic, you know," Dea cuts in, fanning herself. "We would have let you do that solo move if you asked first."

My cheeks flush again, but now for a different reason. Of course Dea would poke at the first thing I feel insecure about. Of course she'd rain on the one authentic performance moment I stepped into, even if it was completely by accident.

Well, I certainly don't need to explain myself to Dea Seo. Not anymore.

"When you write a song, you can take whatever artistic liberties you want," I return, knowing full well Dea has never written anything beyond a curated social media post. I sound harsher than I intend, but whatever. After tonight I never have to see Dea's perfect face again.

The room chills over for a moment, blistering from our cold snap.

"Well, I think we earned the right to celebrate tonight," Stern says, smiling big underneath a devilish glint in his eye. "The finale party is going to be epic!"

Everyone smiles back, including me. After all, we did make it to this finale together. And despite our significant differences, we managed to make something special tonight. We've earned one last celebration before everything changes tomorrow. Before the five of us go our separate ways . . .

And one of us wins a life-changing record deal.

CHAPTER TWO

EVERLY

THERE ARE TOO MANY SIGHTS TO TAKE IN AT THIS PARTY. IT'S ON a rooftop lounge in the heart of Hollywood and it's an unusually clear night, so I can see for miles in every direction: the darkened coastline, the glittering hills, the semi-urban sprawl stretching east. Heat lamps and fire pits and string lights glow everywhere, flickering reflections that catch in the ice cubes of dozens of drinks. The people holding these drinks are all dressed up, which can mean a hundred different things in LA.

This is my hometown, so I'm used to all of that. What I'm not used to is seeing a promotional poster of myself stretched eight feet high. Production set up five of these prints, one for each of us, side by side. I stare at my own and have a hard time connecting to it. Not just because the version of me who posed for that photo months ago had zero idea what I was in for—I had just turned eighteen, graduated high school, and convinced my dad to let me defer Berklee to pursue a solo career.

Really, this poster should give me a thrill. I've dreamed of something like this my entire life. But maybe I just hoped I was good enough to get a record deal without having to go on one of these cheesy shows? Yet I jumped in anyway, the moment the opportunity arose. Now I'm probably not even good enough to get a record deal *on* one of these shows.

I stare at this glossy version of myself on the poster. I see someone who knows in her bones she's a gifted songwriter, who promised herself she wouldn't do anything that felt inauthentic on this show. But this lanky Jewish girl, trying hard to seem effortless in a sundress and leather jacket, doesn't yet realize she's a dud on live stages. She might not have sold out, but I'm not sure she broke out, either—until that unexpected performance moment earlier.

How can I feel free like that again?

Then again, will it even matter if I lose the show tomorrow?

"Two chamomile teas with honey," CeCe announces, returning to our lounge corner.

I smile at CeCe. She looks awesome tonight in the clothes she got to pick for herself: a denim crop top, loose jeans, and an unbuttoned flannel. She also wears her hair natural in loose curls, letting it breathe from all the wigs and weaves the stylists have bombarded her with during filming.

I've taken tonight's production-free moment to wear my own favorite oversized linen trousers and fitted cream blazer, two vintage shop finds. I even wear my thick hair down to my shoulders, letting it frizz and tangle in all its highlighted glory. I've been forced into getting blowouts every day—not that I'm complaining. It's just nice to feel like myself for a few hours, instead of the most sharpened version of myself.

"It took the bartender ten minutes to figure out how to make tea at an event for underaged singers," CeCe begins. "But only thirty seconds for Stern to talk his way into a whiskey and Coke."

"That tracks," I reply.

CeCe scans for Stern and finds him across the roof, laughing loudly and high-fiving an actor I vaguely recognize. She rolls her eyes.

"Our small-town charmer sure does seem to operate just fine here, doesn't he?"

Looking over at Stern, I can tell what she means. His blond hair is gelled perfectly and he's styled within an inch of his life, looking like a manufactured teenage dream. Still, I don't see the same picture of Stern that CeCe does. Instead of a charming operator, I see someone working overtime to seem breezy. Instead of a slick artist wearing trendy accessories, I see someone sporting his father's class ring and his grandmother's rosary as a bracelet.

"That look," CeCe says, slapping the table. "Why didn't you tell me you have a thing for Stern?"

"Direct CeCe quote," I sigh. "'Stern represents everything wrong with America. And humanity.'"

CeCe shrugs. "Wrong is usually what makes people hot. I mean, I always go for the 'I just broke up with my boyfriend and hate men tonight' girls. Stern might glow with toxic patriarchal white privilege bullshit, but I would never judge anyone for who they love."

"That's generous," I reply. "But let's definitely refrain from calling it love?"

"Fine. But if you are going to hit on Stern, tonight is the perfect night."

"And why is that?"

"Because after tomorrow, you never have to see him again if you don't want to."

I open my mouth to argue, but then pause. CeCe has a point. I don't know if it makes me feel better or worse.

"I'm supposed to be the kind of girl who goes for artisanal paleo loafs, not buttered white bread," I say instead. "How can I be into Stern Green?"

"Because white bread is delicious," CeCe says. "Especially when you know it's bad for you. Besides, there's a reason the 'bad boy next door' thing usually works on you straight girls."

"And if it does work for me, will you never want to see me again after tomorrow too?"

I can't stand the thought of losing touch with CeCe. We didn't really get to bond until the most recent weeks, and I feel like I'm only just getting the chance to really know her.

"Nah, you're stuck with me," CeCe answers. "Just don't ignore my texts when I'm back in Atlanta and you're basking in your big win."

"Very funny," is all I can muster. Because if anyone is a lock to win this thing, it's Stern Green. Toxic patriarchal white privilege bullshit, indeed.

"Miss me?"

CeCe and I turn to find Vinny, a big grin on his face. Given the flushed color of his olive-tan cheeks, the tousled mess of his brown hair, and the rumple of his bomber jacket, we can tell exactly what he's been up to.

"We've barely been here a half hour," I begin. "How did you already find a guy to hook up with?"

"And where?" CeCe adds.

"A cater waiter from Grindr who watches the show, is into cubs, and has a van in the parking garage."

Vinny smiles from ear to ear, dripping in pride. His confidence is practically infectious.

"I thought you were a bear?" CeCe deadpans.

"I'm too young to be a bear. Though I have had a hairy chest since I was thirteen."

"Oh. Did you get his number?"

"Why would I do that?" Vinny returns, smiling wide as ever.

"I think you two just role-played a half century of male-female queer dating stereotypes in two questions flat," I interject, grinning.

"Aw, babe, didn't you hear? Binary is so last season," Vinny replies, plopping his elbows down on the table. "Now, who's taking bets on tomorrow's finale? My money is on you, Everly."

"Please," I react, my skin flushing. "I haven't even had the courage to open any of my socials since my literal mic drop."

"Oh, girl, you're fine," Vinny says. "Besides, that performance was maybe the best thing we've done all season, mic drop and all."

"Really?" CeCe jumps in. "Didn't Adam Lambert tweet at you after you covered him?"

"Yes, but according to the ratings, he is maybe the only singer watching our little show," Vinny sighs. "Still, that *was* a pretty stellar cover. Maybe I'll bet on myself to win?"

"Betting on yourself is always the right call."

The three of us turn to this new voice—and we all stiffen when we realize it belongs to one of the judges. Our first judge is a Disney star of the moment who never stays one second beyond filming. Our second judge is the iconic music manager Zahra Moon. But it's our third judge, Kree Duski, who stands before us now. *The* Kree Duski, as in songwriter supreme in league with the Bonnies and Caroles and Jonis of her generation.

Being in her presence still makes my knees go wobbly. We've gotten to spend some time on camera with the judges, but never in a casual setting like this.

"Mrs. Duski, it's an honor," CeCe says first.

"Please, I'm honored teenagers these days still know who I am," Kree laughs.

"Are you kidding?" I sputter. "My dad gave me his vinyl of your first album for my eleventh birthday."

"I'm also honored vinyl made a comeback," Kree smiles. "I'm on my way out, but I wanted to grab Everly here for a moment, if that's all right?"

"That is deeply all right," I gush.

I'm about to scope for a spot where we can talk, but CeCe and Vinny have already made themselves scarce. With a sudden flutter, I realize I really am going to miss those two.

"I just wanted to congratulate you on 'Press Diamonds,'" Kree begins once we're alone. "Especially since I heard you wrote it in one night."

"I did. But they handed it off to someone else for production, so I can't take all the credit."

"You absolutely can," Kree replies. "Can I ask, why did you write the song?"

That question obviously has a . . . complicated answer. Still, I tell myself to go with the most authentic version.

"Well, before the show I used to write songs and perform them on my social pages. That kind of connection with followers . . . or fans? Honestly, I don't love both of those words. The relationship feels much more like collaborators to me. I create something alone in my room, and then all these people breathe actual life into it. Anyway, it was a listener, one I hear from all the time, who encouraged me to try out for this show. I came on for listeners like her, and for the exposure—I only have a couple thousand followers. But any songs I release while I'm here belong to the show, so I haven't posted any new material in the past few months.

"So, to answer your question, I guess I wrote the song to remind everyone what I can do. But mostly, I wrote it as a thank-you to those original listeners. Because they give me as much as they say my music gives them."

I finish speaking, intimately aware of how long I just rambled to one of my idols. Who, come to think of it, has most likely experienced all of this herself a million times over.

"You know, I used to feel thankful social media wasn't around when I was eighteen," Kree begins. "But you've already learned a lot of lessons I wasn't even close to by your age."

"Coming from you, that means everything," I say. "But, uh, can I ask you a question?"

"Shoot."

"If I could just write songs and perform them in my bedroom, I think I'd be happiest. So how do you deal with all the other baggage of doing it as a career?"

Kree smiles. "If you figure that one out, be sure to let me know."

I laugh. Because . . . duh. I probably just summarized the plight of half the introverted artists in history.

"I *can* tell you what makes all the baggage worth carrying, though you seem to already know," Kree continues, leaning toward me like she's about to share a secret. "We artists have a duty, one that's easy to lose sight of in all the noise. If we're good at what we do and we're lucky, people out there start to depend on us to make sense of things for them. You might write to process your own emotions and experiences, but the art of translating that with gracefulness—it's an act of service. So that when listeners out there experience something or feel alone, they have something to hold on to. Your job is to keep doing that, to keep giving away chunks of your heart, without expecting anything in return."

Kree pauses, leaning in just a little closer. "But when you do get something back? That's the magic that makes it all worth it."

I listen to Kree's words like gospel delivered by a prophet of songwriting. I wish I had a pen so I could transcribe each word and read it to myself every morning. I open my mouth, my mind racing to try to properly express the impact of her advice.

"Mrs. Duski, I'm such a fan. Can I get a selfie for my socials?"

I turn to glimpse the person who has interrupted this sacred, life-changing exchange . . .

For a selfie.

Why am I not surprised to find Dea standing there, smiling sweetly with air-brushed perfection? She wears a floor-length dress, looking annoyingly chic and red carpet ready. Isn't there some other influencer she can go do a sponsored post with? Why in all nine rings of hell is Dea ruining a perfect moment with one of my idols?

"Of course," Kree says, turning toward Dea.

If Dea asks me to take this photo for her, I will throw her phone off the roof. Thankfully, she opts for a literal selfie, working her angles and posing like a model. Emotion flushes my body. I only hope I can contain it until Kree leaves.

"Well, I have to get home," Kree says next.

"Thank you so much for the photo. And the whole season," Dea says, grasping her phone between her thankful hands.

I don't speak. I know what will erupt when I do.

"And keep up the good work, Everly," Kree then says, winking at me. "I'll be watching."

I muster a grateful smile, thank goddess. I wish it were more, but I've never been very good at hiding my emotions. Once Kree turns to go, I finally direct the full force of my frustration at Dea in one look.

"Whoa. What? Did I interrupt something?" Dea asks, hands up.

Classic. She purposefully interrupts an obviously intimate moment, then feigns ignorance. Like I'm somehow now the bitchy one for reacting.

"Yes, you did. And you know it."

"Wow, Everly. Not everything is about you. But honestly, I did not intend to upset you."

"Oh, that line again?"

I turn to go. If I stay, I will explode at Dea. And I don't want to go there. Not here. Not tonight, when this is all so close to being over.

"What happened to us?" Dea then asks, calling after me.

I reel back around, hearing this absurd question. *Keep it together*, I shout somewhere in the recesses of my brain.

"It's like this every time, Dea. You do something cruel and selfish, then make me feel crazy for having a reaction."

Those awful, familiar emotions bubble back up—the exact ones I was hoping to avoid. Dea and I were inseparable when the show started. Until the top twenty, when she told a pop reporter she was "helping me learn to perform better because I didn't know how to yet." Then she showed a video the two of us made staying up late one night, with Dea trying to teach me some dance challenge.

It all seemed innocent enough, except for the fact that I asked Dea not to post that video. She came off looking like the polished pro while I looked like some gremlin rookie—literally, given the difference in our ideas of "pajamas." Worst of all, Dea did this right after the judges had critiqued her latest performance as robotic, but mine as an improvement. Yet after the public vote, guess who was safe and who saw her first drop into the bottom?

It wasn't even the impact on the competition that really hurt. What hurt was that Dea knew my lack of performance experience was my greatest insecurity; we had spent hours talking about it at our hotel sleepovers. Then, when she felt her own chances threatened, Dea weaponized that vulnerability against me. I didn't just feel betrayed—I felt *stupid* for ever trusting her. I felt so small, so exposed . . .

When I tried to tell Dea this, she shrugged the whole thing off. She said that she meant no harm and I was overreacting. I was shocked back then. But now I see Dea for what she really is: ruthless.

"I told you a hundred times," Dea responds. "If I hurt you, that wasn't my intention. I was trying to show everyone how authentic you can be."

I stare back at Dea, weighing her words.

✧ "I'm not spinning with you on this merry-go-round again," I **dismiss**, truly hoping to get away. Because I'm still not sure where the truth lies with Dea.

TURN TO PAGE 19

✧ "I don't need your help," I **engage**, not backing down. "I might suck at performing, but you do it so well to cover your lack of a voice. In every sense."

TURN TO PAGE 20

I turn away from Dea, hoping to finish this conversation that always ends the same. I truly don't know if she made a mistake like she claims—or like she claimed just now with Kree—but Dea just seems too smart for these digs not to be intentional. She's either purposefully attempting to be subtle while coming for me, or she's oblivious and self-centered enough not to notice.

Both scenarios boil my blood. How dare she treat me this way? I should rip into her, the way I know I can, but she doesn't even deserve my anger. Honestly, at this point, not even an earnest apology would make me trust her again. Now that she has proven her priorities, there's not enough fake eyelash glue in all of LA for Dea to put our friendship back together again.

"Wow. You really do think you're better than me."

Hearing Dea's words, spoken to my back, my mind flashes red. I spin to face her, my heartbeat now hammering in my chest. I open my mouth to react, because how dare she accuse me of being just as petty?

But what I see when I turn around catches me off guard. I don't find Dea standing defiantly, one manicured hand on her hip. I don't find her full of righteousness or narcissism. Instead, I see Dea with her eyes on the floor, looking a lot like a scared little girl.

The same exact way she made me feel.

It only sparks more fire. Dea's immaturity is so flawless, it makes me look like some unfeeling monster. If I open my mouth to say anything now, I will rip her to shreds. I will only validate the words she just threw at me. I refuse to give her the satisfaction.

But then another voice chimes in my head, like a pale-yellow light cutting through the crimson. *You don't speak because you're afraid of what the truth looks like.* I'm afraid of how genuine, how consuming this anger feels—of what it'll do if unleashed. I'm afraid I know where the roots of this rage really reach. I'm afraid of giving Dea any power in this situation because I'm afraid she'll only hurt me again. And I'm afraid that what Dea just said about me is probably fairly accurate.

So I don't say anything at all.

TURN TO PAGE 21

"Wow." Dea steps backward, like my blow hit her with actual force. "That was mean."

"At least I wear my mean on my sleeve," I keep on. "You hide yours under all *that*. But your filters don't fool me."

"Everly, always so clever." Dea looks away, folding her arms and tapping her foot.

And that's when I realize that she is . . . fighting back tears.

Shit.

I feel bad for one second, but then my anger returns with a flood. It's just like Dea to pick a fight she can't finish. It's just like her to poke at every one of my soft spots, then play the victim. This girl does nothing but expose my flaws, and she gets away with it flawlessly.

So I calm myself all the way down, trying to hide my hurt behind a cool, collected mask.

"You can deal with your jealousy on your own time, Dea," I say, slowly and deliberately. "But I'm done letting you waste my time with it."

TURN TO PAGE 21

Dea stares back at me, but it's hard to tell exactly what's going on behind her blue-colored contacts. Against my will, I flash back to the first night of the semifinals, when I first glimpsed her wearing the thickest glasses I'd ever seen. We were assigned hotel rooms next to each other, which was the start of our open-door sleepovers. I couldn't believe how many creams and serums Dea had packed. She offered to apply a special brew to my face, her eyes magnified behind those glass-bottle-thick lenses—the same ones she didn't happen to be wearing in that video of us she chose to share.

"Your natural eyes are way prettier than those fake contacts, you know," I said.

"Says the girl with perfect blue eyes," Dea replied. "Now don't talk or you'll crack this beauty mask."

I made up a stupid song then, "Beauty Mask," with the hook "Don't talk, you'll crack." Remembering this, I feel like *that* was the real Dea. The one with her beauty mask removed, being generous. So maybe—just maybe—I should cut her a break?

"Ah, did you two finally kiss and make up?" Stern's voice cuts in as he appears beside Dea. He smiles that beaming glow of his, looking between us. I can tell he knows we're definitely not made up, but he still tries to lighten the mood.

Stern then smiles directly at me, and it's almost enough to crack my own exterior.

"Let's just go, babe," Dea says, turning to Stern. "This will all be over tomorrow."

Dea then does the last thing I expect.

She leans forward and kisses Stern on the lips.

Dea holds there for a second, then she stops and turns back to look at me. Her eyes find mine just long enough to catch my unfiltered reaction.

Then Dea spins to leave, holding Stern's hand.

My blood feels like it vibrates out of my body, taking my draining heart with it.

◆ ◆ ◆

Through my daze, I somehow manage to find a solitary corner of the roof. From the cigarette butts lying on the ground, I'd guess this is some employee break space. I hope they don't mind me using it because a break is exactly what I need.

This corner of the roof faces west. Los Angeles stretches out beneath me, all twinkling lights and stopped cars and palm trees swaying in the wind. Behind all of it lies the midnight expanse of the Pacific Ocean, looming like some ominous cloud. What is it about staring at the ocean at night that makes it so terrifying? Is it the size, or the darkness, or the unknown? Is it how small that silent, churning water can make us feel?

Well, I certainly feel small and churning in this moment. I feel like someone has ripped a hole right in the center of my body and filled it with green acid. Stern and Dea. *Of course.* No one is supposed to know I have this annoying crush on Stern. But if CeCe could guess tonight, what are the chances Dea remains as clueless as she claims?

I try to breathe and let the view replace my thoughts. I try to freeze my insides into a crystal ball. I knew I should have stuffed a notebook in my purse tonight—I could really use it right now. Honestly, the only thing that makes everything bearable some days is knowing I can get a song out of it. The Notes app on my phone is a poor substitute, but it will have to do.

Ocean so dark, didn't see the wave 'til it crashed
Water so deep, can't tell swimming up from down

I feel a bit better, typing this out. It makes me wonder: Do other people feel their emotions this intensely, or is that part of what makes me an artist? If not, how does anyone survive anything when they're not an artist?

Then, suddenly, Kree's words smash into me way harder than anything Dea has done tonight. *You might write to process your own emotions and experiences, but the art of translating that with gracefulness—it's an act of service. So that when listeners out there experience something or feel alone, they have something to hold on to.*

That's how anyone survives.

With help.

"I thought you could use one of these."

I smell Stern before I register his presence: driftwood, whiskey, and laundry. I look down to see he holds out a tall ice-filled glass, bubbling and wedged with lemon.

"I took you for a gin and tonic kind of girl."

I turn to face Stern, finding that dopey grin on his full lips.

"Why's that?"

"Classic Hollywood," Stern tries. "Am I right?"

I can't help but break into a laugh. Stern does too.

"That's beyond cheesy."

"You'd think living in LA a while would've shaken all the small town out of me . . ."

I take the glass from Stern. I shouldn't drink tonight, but one sip won't hurt.

"For the record, I'm a Negroni kind of girl. But thank you anyway."

"Of course you are," Stern says, leaning up against the ledge to take in the view, his own whiskey and Coke in hand. "I can't believe you grew up here. It explains so much."

"Like what?"

"Like why you seem so cool, even though you're not trying to be."

Stern turns to face me and my breath catches in my throat. Despite making it this far on the show together, we haven't really gotten that much time to talk one-on-one. Most of our impressions have been from semi-afar, in passing. From this close, I can see the creases around Stern's eyes and the freckles across his exposed collarbone.

"All you LA people have that . . . thing. Self-possessed? I don't know. I'm not great with words."

"And how many LA natives do you know, mister small town?"

I regret the question the moment it leaves my lips, because Dea is from Glendora. More Inland Empire than LA proper, but still. Stern tenses up for a second too.

"So, when did you and Dea happen?" I ask.

"Very recently," he answers. "Wanna hear classic Hollywood? One of the producers said Dea had a crush on me, so I asked her out. She's way out of my league, though, if you ask me. They were actually gonna film our first date, but Dea insisted they didn't."

I try to absorb this information, but it's feeling difficult.

"How very Justin and Britney of you," I crack instead.

"Okay, I'm down with the millennial reference," Stern laughs. "But I like to think we're more like Shawn and Camila."

"I'm sure the fans will eat it up. Though that doesn't really leave the rest of us much of a fighting chance for tomorrow, does it?"

"Yeah, right," Stern laughs. Until he realizes I'm being serious. "Everly, you do realize you're going to win, right?"

Stern's words take me by surprise, yet again.

"Funny. I'd say the same exact thing to you."

"Well, you'd be wrong," Stern sighs. "Listen, I actually do like Dea. She's gorgeous and talented and we both want the same things. That's why we also agree being a couple is a good backup if we both lose. We decided to wait to announce the relationship until after the finale."

I can't help it. My eyes roll so hard that my nose crinkles up.

"Hey, I'm older than the rest of you," Stern says. "Not by much, but I've been in LA since graduating. And I've gotten nothing but doors slammed in my face for two years. This is my shot, finally. I'm not throwing it away."

Stern looks out at the ocean, like I just was. Feeling small, no doubt. But churning, still.

"Not all of us can play two instruments. Or nail our very first audition. Or write songs like casting spells by heart," Stern adds, slightly sullen.

I can literally hear it in his voice—the respect. And adoration. The jealousy and the vulnerability. Stern, Mr. Boy Band, Mr. Shoe-In, Mr. Easy Breezy . . .

He is convinced he doesn't live up to the hype.

So I remind him he's not alone.

❖ Earlier, I did that **crawl** to cover my mic drop.
TURN TO PAGE 25

❖ Earlier, I made us **harmonize** to cover my mic drop.
TURN TO PAGE 26

"At least you didn't drop your mic live on national television and crawl to pick it up," I offer.

"Are you kidding? That was just more magic, Everly."

"You do realize I am nowhere near as comfortable onstage as you. Or Vinny, or CeCe, or Dea. I'm the weakest link left for sure."

"Maybe. But you just started at that part, and you can learn how to perform. The other talents you have? Those can't be learned as easily."

Stern's words make my ears turn hot.

"Have you ever tried writing a song?" I ask.

"Me?" Stern laughs. "No."

"Why do you say that like it's a preposterous thought?"

"Because I'm the front man, the show man, the album cover," Stern answers. "I know what everyone expects from me."

"Except that sounds kind of like a chorus to me," I say, grinning.

"That's because you always hear songs in your head. Don't ever take that for granted," Stern says, serious as I've ever heard him. "I wish I could just stand onstage and sing an earnest song with a guitar."

"What's stopping you?"

"What's stopping you from performing like the pop star you are?" Stern returns.

"Please, I'm way more *folklore* than *Reputation*," I sigh. "My pop influences tend to perform at indie festivals, not stadiums."

"We all have our safe boxes, I guess," Stern sighs back. "Except we all also want to be seen differently, don't we?"

Stern goes soft once more, but this time I can tell he's not just talking about himself. He's talking about her.

Again.

"You know, you and Dea have a lot more in common than you think," Stern says next.

Yeah. I used to think that too.

"So do you and me, it turns out," I reply instead.

TURN TO PAGE 28

"Well, not all of us drop our mics on live national TV and need to be bailed out by the resident heartthrob."

Stern grins. "We did sound pretty good together, though, didn't we?"

"Seriously," I say. "You saved my butt today."

"And you wrote my favorite song I've gotten to sing all season. There's only so much one-man-boy-band a guy can take."

"I thought you loved singing that stuff?" I ask, surprised.

"Because I'm good at my job," Stern answers. "And I know what people want from me."

"And what's that?"

"'The resident heartthrob,'" Stern quotes, grinning wider.

"Touché," I reply.

"Don't get me wrong; my voice does sound best on that stuff. I just wish I knew what my first album should sound like, the way you already do."

Stern's words make my ears turn hot.

"Well, if you could sing anything, what would it be?" I ask.

"Whatever charts at number one," Stern answers, flashing that charming smile of his—the one that must usually get him off the hook.

"Fine. But what are your three favorite albums?" I push. "No thinking; just answer."

"*Traveller*, Chris Stapleton. *Divide*, Ed Sheeran. *Sweet Baby James*, James Taylor."

"Damn, that was fast," I react. "And those are really good answers, Stern."

"We're on a reality singing competition. Of course I have an answer to that question. You got asked in one of your interview packages. *Hotel Paper*, Michelle Branch; *Rumours*, Fleetwood Mac; and *folklore*, Taylor Swift."

"I can't believe you remember that," I say, trying not to blush.

"Of course I remember." Stern leans in close. "Especially because I get asked what my type of girl is and what my workout routine looks like—those kinds of things. But not one person has asked me that album question until you did just now."

Stern looks away again.

"No one has asked Dea either, for the record."

Suddenly, Stern's clarity takes on a sharpness. But I've had far more than enough of diamond edges for one night.

"She's the one who keeps antagonizing me, you know," I try.

"Maybe," Stern says, turning back to me with the full force of his green eyes. "But you're intimidating, Everly. And it's wild how little you seem to know it."

TURN TO PAGE 28

Stern leans closer to me, both of us staring at each other. Here, out on this ledge, the lights reflect in his bright eyes. I'd say it was from stars in the sky, but LA only has those on the ground.

For a moment, I consider kissing Stern. For a moment, every instinct in my body screams at me to jump in with him. For a moment, I convince myself that Stern sees me as clearly as I see him. For a moment, I can almost taste his whiskey on my lips.

But then another moment arrives, one that reminds me I barely know Stern. That if we kiss now, he might think it's about Dea, about revenge. And that kissing tonight would make cheaters out of both of us.

Then in the next moment, feeling Stern's full focus still on me, I decide if we ever do kiss, it will be real. It will be because there's a foundation under our feet, not a rooftop ledge.

"Good luck tomorrow," I say, forcing myself to pull away.

I walk toward the door that leads back to the party. Back toward the reality that this will be my last night on this show, and that soon I will return to my life and Stern will return to his. Sure, we might both stay in LA. But if this conversation has proven anything, it's that there are still whole worlds between us.

"Hey, can I ask a favor?" Stern calls out, catching me before I'm gone.

Despite my better judgment, I turn again.

"Whoever wins, can you write a song for my first album someday?" Stern asks.

I smile, nodding my head before I really walk away.

"Sure. But only if we write it together."

CHAPTER THREE

VINNY

FREEZING-COLD ICED COFFEE AND A SPLASH OF HALF-AND-
half. It's how I start every morning, but especially these production mornings with 6 a.m. wake-up calls. Like most teenage boys, I'm not an early riser. But for the stage, I'll do just about anything. That includes enduring the side-eye from our waiter after ordering my coffee with full-fat creamer and waffles with whipped cream. I used to think NYC and LA had a lot in common, but that was before the show flew me to this land where gluten and dairy are considered cardinal sins.

"The first thing I'm going to do is hug my dog, Alanis, and take her for the longest canyon hike of her life," Everly says, sipping her black coffee. "What about you, CeCe?"

"Eat a pound of my mom's lasagna," she replies. "If I have to eat one more kale salad I will scream."

"Can I get an amen?" I echo.

Everly, CeCe, and I have been playing a game of *What Will You Do When . . . ?* ever since I started this little breakfast club. There used to be four of us in the club, but Owen got voted off and shipped back to Florida weeks ago. We also usually convene at a more reasonable hour, but for finale day we have a full schedule of sound checks, fittings, press, and filming. So today the breakfast club had to meet at the hotel restaurant before our pickup for a game of *What Will You Do When Production Ends?*

"First, I am going to sleep as late as possible as often as possible," I begin. "Second, I'll binge all the episodes of *RuPaul's Drag Race* I'm behind on."

"I miss reality TV so much," CeCe adds. "Watching ten minutes on my phone before passing out doesn't count."

"Ha. The reality of reality. How meta," I say. "Wait, have you watched our show yet?"

"Vinny. I've watched every episode of every singing competition ever," CeCe answers. "Yes, I've watched our show. I also made my sisters promise to DVR it."

"Well, I haven't brought myself to watch most of it yet," Everly shares.

"I've seen bits and bobs," I say. "But hold up, CeCe, who still has a DVR?"

"Episodes disappear from streaming once there's a new season! I take my singing competition scholar duties very seriously."

"That's optimistic of you, thinking *SO YOU WANNA BE A POP STAR?* will get a new season, given the lack of ratings. See? More proof teens today don't use DVRs."

"I know," CeCe sighs. "But maybe our group performance last night helped? I haven't seen chemistry like that since Fifth Harmony was put together to sing 'Impossible.'"

"I know you love girl groups as much as these competition shows," Everly groans, "but please don't even put that idea out in the universe?"

"Look what it did for Normani and Camila Cabello," CeCe tries.

"Well, if nothing else, at least you can spend time with us in DVR form after this is all over," I offer, agreeing much more with Everly. Pop groups are a mess. I literally can't think of one that hasn't broken up, one way or another.

"It'll be nice to relive the experience before I go to Howard," CeCe says. "Making it this far has been surreal."

"One, don't talk like you've already lost," Everly replies. "And two, you still didn't defer your first year yet?"

"It's great your dad let you defer to try for a record deal," CeCe answers. "And this summer has been a real dream for me, but it has to end sometime."

"Girl, I know you have, like, eight siblings," I cut in, "but you're really going to have to get over this middle-child imposter syndrome. It's not cute. Especially because you're a badass biotch, and many people out there must see that for you to have made it to the finale."

"Don't get me wrong, I love doing this," CeCe says, fighting a rare blush. "But it doesn't take a scholar to know that even the winners of the biggest shows have a hard time making it. Let alone the runners-up on a small show like ours."

CeCe doesn't mean to, but her sentiment drops a bomb of truth on our bleary party. At least it's timed with the waiter arriving, giving us a minute to digest as he places down our respective waffle, omelet, and parfait plates.

"Sure, but there's a Jennifer Hudson or Tori Kelly every once in a while, right?" I try. Because, really, I need this competition to launch my life—probably more than any of the others.

Deferred or not, CeCe and Everly both have college as a fallback. All that's left for me back on the Lower East Side is my closet-sized room in Mom and Nona's rent-controlled apartment, along with all my friends having already left for college. I didn't really have a set plan for when I graduated, except to finally try getting a gig at a drag bar since I'd finally be old enough to perform. The dream was to make a name for myself and save enough coins to get on *RuPaul's Drag Race*. But then this competition, designed specifically for eighteen- to twenty-year-old singers, came along. Production claimed they were aiming for that particular teen superstar sweet spot, but it's probably more because they didn't have the budget to cast minors, given all the protective filming laws.

Whatever the real reason, I think every recent high school grad with a voice ditched their caps and gowns to run straight to the *SO YOU WANNA BE A POP STAR?* auditions. And ever since I made the first cut, I've dreamed about performing under that final shower of confetti.

❖ And if this were a straight-up singing competition about finding the best **voice**, I'd win for sure.
TURN TO PAGE 32

❖ And if I'd been allowed to perform in **drag** like I wanted, I'd win for sure.
TURN TO PAGE 34

I've always had the most powerful and acrobatic voice in the competition, serving the patron saints of Ariana, Christina, and Mariah. But we all know a blowout voice isn't enough to win one of these things—it takes a lot more than that to connect with an audience. Kind of like how if this were just a songwriting competition, Everly would win. Or just an emotional-delivery competition, CeCe. Or a dancing influencer competition, Dea.

But since this is indeed a pop star competition, I'm pretty sure Stern is going to win.

What chance do I stand against him, even with my voice? Stern is the American Dreamboat, while I'm a thicc and flamboyant queer kid from the Lower East Side. I suppose the world is changing every day—stranger things have happened than someone like me beating the resident normie heartthrob. But I'd bet all my nonexistent money that history decides to repeat itself here.

Though really, deep down, I know the biggest hurdle standing in my way: I don't quite know who I am as an artist yet. I've always loved performing, but I've never been able to narrow myself down to one lane. Drag felt like a good testing ground, but it requires time, money, and access I didn't have in high school. Instead, I performed in every single theater production I could, so I got good at filling roles. My first love isn't even musicals, I just enjoyed all the tests and challenges in stage productions, all the chances to explore and learn. It's why I was aiming for *Drag Race*, but then the chance to try out for this teen singing competition emerged.

I thought we'd get to explore different themes and genres every week like the other shows, but this one wanted us more fully formed. My vocal ability has carried me through, but I don't need to read the critics to know my song choices have been erratic at best and deeply derivative at worst. I've covered everyone from Justin to Kelly convincingly, but none of it adds up to a clear picture of who I am as a solo artist.

Basically, my greatest strength is also my greatest weakness. I might be able to sing everything, which makes my options endless—but that doesn't make finding my own point of view any easier. And every time I try, it just feels wrong. Too small, too specific. But maybe that's just another lame cover, hiding the fact I don't have an original artistic bone in my body?

TURN TO PAGE 36

A career in drag, the industry now booming thanks to Mama RuPaul, has always been the plan. Really, I just needed to wait until I was old enough to enter this bar-and-club-centric world. The fact that I was born with a limitless voice was always just going to be an extra feather in my wig cap. Thanks to the wonders of the internet and an excellent high school drama program, I have taught myself how to sew, design, style hair, and do makeup. I applied all these skills to my many leading roles in our school productions, even though I don't really adore musical theater. It was just the closest training grounds for drag I could find.

The only weapon I don't have in my arsenal is money, so I told myself I was delaying the debut of my own drag persona until I felt fully funded. It also doesn't help that I avoid social media like the plague, and half the job of any artist these days seems to be posting. Then I got cast on this show and kept advancing, round after round. Mostly I've sung big ballads from all my favorite divas and queer singers, but these covers have all been pretty paint-by-numbers. I'd like to think I could've turned this stage all the way out if I got to perform in drag, but that wasn't allowed by the producers or the network. It, quote, "wasn't the type of star they were looking for." Part of me wishes I had just said screw it, but as the Todrick Halls and Adore Delanos of *Idol* past have shown, these machines are sometimes hard to rage against.

And if I'm being honest, I know the real reason I accepted this drag ban. I know I have every ounce of the skill, personality, and talent it takes to be anything—but I have no actual idea what sets me apart as a performing artist. I mean, I haven't even been able to choose a drag name yet. What's my brand? My voice? My look? My sound?

I understand now why I've hidden away in my room honing my craft, why I've only slayed theater-acting roles, or only sang straight-up cover songs in this competition—and why I haven't pushed to debut a drag persona on this show . . .

It's because I don't know who that person should be yet. I kept waiting for that magic moment when something might click and feel perfectly right, but here we are at the finale. It turns out my greatest strength is also my greatest weakness—a cliché of all clichés. When your talents and passions are endless, how do you focus that down into one sharpened point?

TURN TO PAGE 36

My phone buzzes on the table and I fight the urge to groan out loud. Instead, I click the button to silence the call.

"Not even going to check who it is?" CeCe asks.

"It's my mom. She's already called like ten times this morning. She refuses to accept it's three hours earlier on this coast. So I refuse to answer my phone before 7 a.m."

"How do you know it's not an emergency?" Everly asks.

"We have a text code for that. Plus, if it were an emergency, my nona would pick up her landline and call. Trust me, I bet some Real Housewife got fired and my mom wants to talk conspiracy theories. I love her more than anyone, but my mom is deeply extra."

"Must be where you get it from," CeCe smirks.

"It certainly is," I say, taking another giant-sized bite of waffle. When we Vecchis do something, we do it big. Love, perform, fight, eat—the latter of which currently makes my stomach gurgle. I can already tell it's going to be one of those double Pepto dose kind of days. Today is too important to feel my usual tummy aches.

I've always ignored the fact that my gut hasn't ever been fully functional. Though after some significant badgering, my producer-handler here finally convinced me to go to her nutritionist for one of those food allergy inflammation blood tests. The results currently sit on my hotel room desk, and the nutritionist has been calling relentlessly, but I figure I should focus on today's finale first. Besides, I'm sure I'm just allergic to a couple things and will be fine once I cut those out. And really, who doesn't have a sensitive stomach these days? Plus, Mom would kill me if I suddenly couldn't eat her very-Italian cooking. I'd never, ever want to limit my ability to eat—food brings me way too much joy.

Being thicc has always been a virtue in our family anyway. I'm just thankful there's also a queer lane for my hairy curves. I pity those boomers and millennials conditioned to crave hairless six packs. I might have hated being bigger when I was younger, but that was before I realized there are entire categories of gay culture and dating—and more X-rated avenues—devoted to my body type. Why waste time working to be something I'm not by nature?

"How can you all still look so groggy?"

Dea appears at the head of the table, already in full makeup and her colored contacts. It makes me smile. Dea always declines my breakfast club invitations, instead using the time to beat that gorgeous mug of hers and live her pop star fantasy at all times. I'm sure she now also declines my invitations to avoid Everly, whose entire body clenches at the sight of Dea. That girl really cannot hide her emotions at all. I've tried to remain neutral in World War Deverly, because I don't think either is totally in the right. But when this is all over, I know Dea is the one I'll stay closest with. Since she and Everly fell out, Dea has become like my sister here—the same way Everly and CeCe have.

"Have none of you looked at your phones yet?" Dea tries again, seeming unusually exasperated.

"I keep my phone on silent most mornings," CeCe answers. "I'm on too many group texts. Especially with my siblings."

"I deleted the social media apps from my phone last night after the whole mic drop incident," Everly begins. "I promised myself I wouldn't re-download them until the dust settles tonight."

Dea would answer, but she seems too distracted by the sausage and bacon currently resting beside Everly's omelet. Dea is a vegan environmentalist, both genuinely and as part of her influencer persona. She clearly finds this meaty sight offensive—probably doubly so sitting in front of Everly.

"Well, I don't have any push notifications and I keep my phone on *Do Not Disturb* at all times," I add. "The only thing that breaks that blockade is my mother, obviously."

Dea looks at each of us with increasing alarm, like we're all from an alien species. "You need to open your favorite social app. Right now."

"Why?" Everly asks. "And shouldn't you be with your new boyfriend?"

Ouch. I guess this means Dea and Stern finally told Everly about their budding showmance. I guess it also means that didn't go particularly well. I've always suspected Everly had some secret eyes for Stern—and this reaction does nothing to convince me otherwise. The intrigue, darling!

"He's still sleeping," Dea replies. "And if you don't want to talk to me, I'll talk to Vinny. He's my best friend here."

She's got that right. Still, I have no desire to be dragged into the middle of Dea's drama. There might not be cameras following us around offstage, but this queen prefers to watch reality TV messiness, not live it.

"Dea, can't you just tell us—"

"Oh my god, just open an app!" she interrupts. "Trust me!"

My eyes bulge at Dea, but I do pick up my phone and swipe for Instagram—the only social I can remotely tolerate. The show has forced us to post once a day, either on their account or on our own, so I've been looking at these damn glossy snapshots far more often than I'd like. Though I know if I'm going to be any kind of public figure, I'd better learn to—

Suddenly, my thoughts scatter. I focus on the little red icon indicating new followers since I logged in yesterday. The number beside it reads *150K*. That can't be right.

"Wait, what?" CeCe speaks first. "My TikTok has two hundred thousand new followers. Overnight. How is that possible?"

"I picked up four hundred thousand followers across all platforms," Dea finally says, her voice vibrating. For an influencer, that's like depositing money in the bank. "It's our group performance from last night. If you look on YouTube, it has almost ten million views already. Then it went viral on TikTok. It even started a 'Press Diamonds' challenge."

That information has a hard time penetrating my brain. How can that be possible when our weekly episode ratings have never even come close to cracking a million? Then my eyes land on Everly, looking pale as a ghost in her chair. It clicks: her mic drop and her killer song. Whatever the rest of us are feeling, Everly must be feeling it times ten.

Just then, a spark of something ignites in my chest. I realize this must be why Mom has been calling nonstop. Even a social media nonfluencer like me understands what these unicorn numbers mean. Something fundamental might be about to shift in our lives. Was our performance really that good? I mean, it did feel different. Electric. Like a magical moment for sure. But would that be enough to break through like this?

"My TikTok has five hundred thousand new followers."

Everly says the words slowly, as if in a trance. All of our mouths collectively drop—especially Dea's. Social media is supposed to be her game, but it looks like Everly just pulled ahead without even trying. I decide I'll have to go back to Dea's room after this to keep her from stewing in her usual pit of repression.

Then that feeling in my chest begins to spread. As we all try to process this turn of events in silence, I'm sure one thought quakes through our minds:

What will this viral moment mean for the finale's winner?

And for the other four losers?

♦ ♦ ♦

Dea and I lie on our backs on her king-size bed. We should be getting ready for our impending pickup, but we both agreed that we required five minutes to absorb this situation.

"I really should post something," Dea says first. "But what do you post when your following doubles overnight? What will sound grateful and not braggy?"

"You're asking me?"

"Good point."

We both stare at the ceiling a little longer.

"Of course Everly got more followers than us," Dea sighs. "Do you think she's going to win tonight?"

I turn onto my side to face Dea, and she does the same.

"Have you checked how many new followers Stern has?" I ask.

Dea's extended eyelashes flutter as her eyes go wide. Pausing to scroll furiously, her jaw then drops again.

"He has seven hundred thousand followers on Instagram," Dea gasps. "He only had four thousand yesterday."

"I rest my case," I say, glancing down at Stern's profile. "I mean, the boy does love a shirtless photo with an inspirational quote caption."

Dea's face glazes over.

"Hey, that's your man now," I try. "Mis followers son sus followers?"

"Damnit, I'm going to have to stop reading the comments for a while once we announce we're a couple. Those get vicious for the girlfriends of heartthrobs."

"Girl, you're the heartthrob in this equation," I say. "But still, that's probably smart."

"If you tell me you never read your comments, I'm going to scream."

"I never read my comments."

Dea stares back at me, then proceeds to scream. I yelp in response out of pure surprise.

"Sorry, that felt necessary," Dea says. "Speaking of comments, Dame Gloves commented on the performance on TikTok. How wild is that?"

I laugh. I can't help it.

"Well, I went to high school with her back in New York," I explain.

"What? Really?" Dea shoots upright. "How have I never heard about this?"

"Because she was a few grades older; she barely knew who I was. Not that it stopped her from doing something awful to me," I answer. "I've tried my best to ignore her rise to pop superstardom ever since."

"Okay, if you think you can just casually mention that without telling me the story . . ." Dea begins. "Spill!"

"Ugh, fine," I sigh, even though I know this story usually slays, sad as it is. "Back then, she was the lead in the school play, *Guys and Dolls*, and I was just an extra. She was super popular and I was still a nobody, but I managed to hook up with her co-lead in the play. I wasn't out yet, so we met in secret when my mom and Nona were out at a doctor's appointment. Except he was so excited, he splooged all over my bedroom carpet. So there I was, buck naked, trying to scrub out the carpet before a stain could set in.

"Anyway, the next day at school, I don't just hear that I'm gay going around—I hear this story, about me on all fours scrubbing some nasty bubbles. And. I. Am. *Mortified*. I cried to one of my friends on the subway that afternoon, but you know what she told me? That I should confront this guy for telling everyone and outing me. So the next day at school, I did just that. I corner Mr. Carpet Destroyer and ask why he told everyone.

And you know what he says? That he didn't tell anyone—except the lead, Monica Stefania. And guess who then told the whole cast, who then told the whole school?

"Now, Monica was super talented and mega intimidating, so who was I to confront her as a lowly freshman? Besides, the damage was done. I honestly don't even know if Monica knew I wasn't out yet when she blabbed the latest hot goss, and the show must go on. My world didn't end, it was okay being gay, and Monica graduated. Just me and my sob story. Then I heard she had dropped out of the drama program at NYU and was singing in clubs, calling herself Dame Gloves. And I thought, ha, just what she deserves! A life of obscurity. Well, then 'Party Game' came out, and she became one of the biggest pop stars on the planet. So, in conclusion: yes, I was outed by *the* Dame Gloves in high school."

Dea blinks at me, her jaw still open. "Vinny, I'm so sorry. That's awful. Obviously, I no longer stan her." She then puts a hand on my shoulder. "But she'll remember your name now. Because I think we might be *famous*."

Dea leaps to her feet on the bed and says the last word in a whisper, like it's a dirty prayer. I leap to my feet to join her, ignoring the rumbles in my stomach—just like I ignore the emotions this story drudges up.

"Praise Britney Jean!" I yell back, jumping along.

Dea quickly scrolls to play "Piece of Me" on her phone. We go on like that for a minute, dancing and shouting on the bed, until we both collapse back down, panting and giddy. Dea lets the song play and while Britney continues to sing about the price of fame, I try to think about what comes next. Not just tonight, but after the show—win or lose.

"Maybe I'll stay in LA a while to see what happens?" I pose.

"You can come live with me as long as you want," Dea says without hesitation, as if it's nothing. "I use my second bedroom as a dressing room and shooting space, but I can clear my birds out of the third bedroom and move them into the primary."

I sit bolt upright.

"Wait a minute," I start. "You have a three-bedroom apartment all to yourself? How did you never mention that?"

"It's gross to brag," Dea answers. "And it's not like I earned it. I pay the monthly fees, but my parents bought it for me. They said it was a graduation present last summer, but it was just a way to get me out of their house and not feel guilty about never calling me. The shame . . . two doctors raising a pop-star-wannabe-influencer daughter."

Dea's face is all practiced calm as she speaks, but I can tell how much this stings her. A giant West Hollywood condo sounds amazing, but as the buzzing phone in my pocket reminds me, nothing replaces the love of a parent—even if that love is suffocatingly overinvolved.

I should know, since I've only got one parent left.

"I am going to get to the part where I thank you for literally offering me a place to live," I begin, trying to channel all the unspoken gratitude into my voice, because I know Dea hates anything too mushy-gushy. "But we need to talk about the fact that you have pet birds. How many?"

"Three. Madonna, Rihanna, and Selena," Dea answers. "And I'd only move them for you."

I fall back onto the bed, laughing and still feeling giddy.

"Well, it sounds like we'll have to get you a fourth bird," I say. "So we can add Dea, The Great One, to that list."

Dea falls beside me again just as the Britney song ends.

"Vinny. I don't think I'm going to win tonight."

"Neither do I."

We both lie here, trying to decide if that matters. I know what Dea must be thinking, comparing herself to Everly. The singer-songwriter versus the dancing queen. I can't imagine what the comments must say about them. And if any of the gossip rags catch wind of their little feud now, it will not be pretty.

Then I feel it bubble up from the underside of my brain. That familiar voice. The inner saboteur, as RuPaul calls it.

"Want to know why I never read the comments?" I ask next.

"Desperately."

Lying beside Dea, eyes on the ceiling, I wonder if speaking this saboteur's voice out loud will depower it, or just empower it. I guess there's only one way to find out.

"Because I already know what the trolls would say."

❖ "He **doesn't belong** here and he never will. It's why nothing good ever lasts too long for that fat femme queen."
TURN TO PAGE 44

❖ "That Vinny is such a **waste** of talent. He just copies everyone else because he can't pick a lane of his own."
TURN TO PAGE 45

I say the words and feel them flush through my body, taking on a life of their own. It's so much easier pushing the confident version of myself, the one who is funny and fun. The one who is secure in his queerness. The one who is a social butterfly, friend to everyone.

But that Vinny is always working, a chameleon constantly changing his colors. What's that saying? *A friend to all is a friend to none.* The truth is, I exert maximum effort to get everyone to like me, to charm my way from the outside in, to seem normal, to not be a burden to anyone . . . because I know no one would show up for me if I were any less.

If I could just *be*, I'd be alone.

"Vinny," Dea says, sitting up to face me. "Is that really what you think of yourself?"

There it is, I can see it in Dea's eyes—the panic. I've crossed a line, gotten too real, and now I'm going to lose her as a friend. Just like I'm going to lose this competition. Vinny: always too much and yet never quite enough.

Feeling all this, I suddenly have a craving for another full plate of waffles. But I push that down and away, as well.

"Don't get me wrong, I love myself and my body," I quickly cover. "I guess I just always dreamed of having that TV show friend group, the one that does everything together. In high school I kind of just floated all over, not really belonging anywhere. I wasn't unpopular or anything, but I didn't fit into any of the groups. Not even with the theater kids. I guess I'm afraid I'll just keep floating, even here. I guess I just want . . . some kind of anchor?"

Dea leans over and hugs me, squeezing me tight.

"Vinny. It would be my honor to be your LA anchor."

I squeeze Dea back. This means a lot to me—it really does. But I guess I've learned that actions speak louder than words. And if Dea were going to offer words, I wish she'd talk about the things that scare her too.

But hey, maybe we'll land there.

Or maybe we won't, forever floating.

TURN TO PAGE 47

I say the words and feel them flush through my body, taking on a life of their own. It's easy for me to flex my talents, and I'm grateful for that. I'm so thankful I can sing any song, I can replicate any look, I can perform any role. I'm proud of how hard I've worked to nurture these talents. But that Vinny is still a copycat, always emulating the greats. What's that saying? *A jack of all trades is a master of none.*

The truth is, I don't know who I am yet. A singer or a drag queen? Do I focus on vocals or makeup or hair or clothes or choreography? Deep down, I am good at playing the parts, but I don't know how to focus all my interests into one shiny package, like most of my peers. And because of that, I know I'm doomed to forever be the runner-up, to be overlooked—to be the one who comes close but doesn't win big.

"Vinny, you know that isn't true, right?" Dea says, sitting up to face me.

There it is, I can see it in Dea's eyes—the panic. I've crossed a line, gotten too real, and now I'm going to lose her as a friend. Just like I'm going to lose this competition. Vinny: always too much and yet never quite enough.

Feeling all this, I suddenly have a craving for another full plate of waffles. But I push that down and away, as well.

"Yeah, I know," I rebound. "It's just, the four of you have such clear points of view. You have these paths laid out for you, trailblazed by others. I guess I don't have that."

"That just means you'll blaze your own trail. The sky is the limit for you, Vinny."

I try to smile, but that's exactly the problem. My own options, my own pressure to be original—they only overwhelm me. But who wants to hear me complain about that? Certainly not someone who wishes their voice were stronger. I suddenly realize how insensitive I've been to Dea, just now. She has never said it out loud, but there's a reason she idolizes dancing divas with thriving lifestyle brands. She probably wishes, more than anything, that she could sing like me. In her mind, it might mean she'd have to work less to cover the gaps.

I lean over and hug Dea, giving her a squeeze.

"Maybe losing won't be the worst thing," I say, forcing myself to feel better for her. "Maybe it will just give us the freedom to do something even better?"

Dea gives me a weak smile in return.

Yeah. I also wish I believed winning didn't really matter.

TURN TO PAGE 47

CHAPTER FOUR
VINNY

STANDING ONSTAGE AT THE FINALE, I HAVE A HARD TIME PRO-cessing how I even got to this moment. Our intrepid host waits for the latest commercial break to end before she can finally announce the winner. The stage lights are dimmed, so I try to prepare myself.

Today has all been one big blur. I don't think any of us have had the chance to properly absorb our group performance going viral since this morning. It's been a nonstop grind of rehearsals and fittings and taping social media promos. Right now I stand onstage sweating profusely under the new lavender suit wardrobe insisted I wear. They made us all dress in our designated jewel tones from last night, since I guess people suddenly care about that. The Executive Producers even scrambled to have us professionally record our parts to "Press Diamonds" for a last-minute promo intro. The network is hoping the winning announcement will bring a ratings surge, so everyone is trying to ride the viral wave.

Honestly, all I can really think about in these last few moments is how much I wish Mom were here. Nona wouldn't be up to flying cross-country, but Mom could have easily made it if production had sprung for family to travel. Our little trio can't afford many bicoastal trips. Hell, pretty soon we're going to be completely priced out of the neighborhood where Mom grew up and where Nona moved after emigrating from Sicily. It's not lost on me that, if I win, the cash prize and record deal could change some of that for us.

I try to picture Mom and Nona huddled together in front of our TV back home, like they said they'd be when I finally called Mom back this morning. I know they probably feel just as nervous as I do, pouring way too many glasses of wine to cope. Then, inevitably, I think of Dad. His memory always pops up, but especially in these bigger moments. I'm not sure what he'd make of any of this, classic Italian man that he was. He died before I even understood I was queer, but he always loved hearing me sing—especially Celine Dion songs, of all things. Part of me believes he must have seen the real me all along. I just hope he'd be proud of me today, no matter what happens.

A producer finally cues the host, Stacie Mumba, a teen pop star of TRL-era fame. Lights roll across the stage as the enormous screen behind us plays the electronic *SO YOU WANNA BE A POP STAR?* theme music. As Stacie begins with her script about what an incredible journey this has been, my stomach flips over. Not because it's upset as usual, but from nerves. *This is it.* After months of nonstop eliminations and performances and filming, we're about to learn which one of us will win the hopefully life-changing prize.

I turn my head and my eyes find Dea, standing a few feet away from me on her mark. She looks like a true pop icon, dressed in another glittering Zuhair Murad jumpsuit. They've pulled her long black hair into a chignon, and her makeup is all dusted white. I'm obsessed with my own Alexander McQueen ensemble, but I must look like I'm attending prom next to full-glam Dea. Divas above, do I wish I could rock hair and makeup onstage like that, in full drag.

Then Dea turns and catches my eye. She winks at me, and the single gesture speaks every volume necessary. *Look where we are. No matter what, we got this.*

The spotlights then dim and Dea drops out of focus. I face forward again, looking out at the judges' panel and the faint outlines of the live studio audience. I take a deep breath. Then I feel one question bubbling, rising through my body.

Is it really possible I could win?

"The moment has finally arrived," Stacie announces into her microphone.

The underside of my dress shirt feels soaked through. I've always sweated more than the average human, especially when nervous.

Thankfully, the blazer covers any wet circles and I usually don't sweat as much from my face, so I put a confident smile on, masking my perspiration with inspiration. *Fake it 'til you make it.* Because you're definitely not supposed to see your favorite pop stars sweat, right?

"This whole season has been asking one constant question: *SO YOU WANNA BE A POP STAR?*" Stacie continues. "We've tested our finalists in every way, and I can confidently say that, yes, each one of these teens has shown they want to be a pop star. And if last night's stunning group performance is any indication—now at twenty million combined views and rising—I'm sure each of them will continue proving themselves beyond this show."

Oh, wow. That's a lot of views. I know the standard "everyone here is a superstar-to-be" routine is usually just hyperbole on these shows . . . but maybe each of us actually can turn this last-minute breakthrough into something, win or lose?

"So, shall we find out who is about to become America's next teen sensation?"

The lights shift again and suddenly I find myself bathed in purple. As the cameras track and roll to film each of us final five, I don't have to work too hard to put on my best *I hope I win* face. Because I really freaking hope that, against all odds, I win.

"The winner of season one of *SO YOU WANNA BE A POP STAR?* is . . ."

Stacie pauses and the cameras swivel to capture each of our dripping-in-nerves reactions, once again. I assumed they would count us down from fifth place to the winner for added suspense, but I'm happy they're just cutting to the chase after this hour-long broadcast. Any longer and I might faint.

The crowd roars over Stacie's extended pause, then hushes back down in anticipation. Everyone seems to be waiting on the edge of their seats as Stacie opens the results card in her manicured hands.

"Stern Green!"

I hear the name and my heart sinks all the way down to the stage floor. I may not be surprised about Stern winning, but I am surprised how much it suddenly stings. Always the runner-up, after all. I expect my purple spotlight to go out and wait for the stage to be bathed in green light and confetti.

But none of that happens.

"And Everly Brooks!" Stacie then announces, now shouting. "And Dea Seo! And CeCe Winnifred! And Vinny Vecchi!"

The entirety of my being freezes. What the mother-tucking what? We all win? How does that make any sense at all?

"After last night's unprecedented smash, our partner label, Unlimited Worldwide United, has decided the record deal isn't going to just *one* pop star," Stacie continues, still shouting as the backing track of "Press Diamonds" begins to play. "It's going to *all five* of them as the next pop supergroup! It is my honor to present to you officially for the first time, representing all the many colors of pop: Jeweltones!"

In the next instant, the audience erupts into a deafening roar of screams and applause. The stage lights go full power and suddenly I can't see anything. My heart threatens to leap out of my chest, but I feel numb at the same time. My brain can't process any of this fast enough. I won? No, not really. Do I even want to be in a group? Holy crap, did I just win a record deal? What does any of this mean?

And what in the world are the other four thinking, in this moment?

"America, I now give you Jeweltones! Everly, the clear-eyed sapphire artist," Stacie keeps shouting. Behind us, a screen begins populating our promo posters, sliced into fifths and encrusted with our bejeweled assignments. "CeCe, the beating ruby heart! Dea, the cutting diamond edge! Vinny, the diva amethyst queen! And Stern, the smooth emerald leader!"

Oh, hell no. Diva queen? I mean, accurate, but still. Plus, who died and made Stern a leader of anything? Wait, does this mean Stern is the one who really would have won if they had stuck to the original plan?

Just then, Stacie scurries offstage and "Press Diamonds" blares up from the background. Oh no. They want us to perform together? Right now?

Of course.

They just turned us into pop lightning rods, hoping a viral hit will strike twice.

I look across the stage and in the full lights, I can finally see the others clearly. Dea looks just as bewildered as me, but she still tries to keep up her polished façade. Everly looks like she's about to burst into tears, smash something, or maybe both. Stern just smiles and waves, tears of triumph streaming down his cheeks. Then a veritable monsoon of confetti begins raining down on us in our five-toned colors. I'm just barely able to spot CeCe through the falling cloud—but she looks ready. I guess if anyone is going to break us into this uncharted territory, it should be our resident reality-pop-group enthusiast. Hell, CeCe is probably even *excited* about this twist.

As she rips into the first verse of "Press Diamonds," I have no idea how I feel, so I force myself to remember one thing:

❖ Whatever this group is or isn't, I remind myself that I am the **voice** here.
TURN TO PAGE 52

❖ Whatever this group is or isn't, I'm taking this last chance to pull off a pre-planned **drag** stunt.
TURN TO PAGE 53

Last week, production had each of us choose a coronation song to perform if we won. Mine was going to be "The Show Must Go On" so I could channel my full Freddie Mercury fantasy—and deliver a message that this would only be the beginning. Well, I suppose the message of that song applies now more than ever. If they're going to coronate me Queen, then I'd better show them the crown fits just right.

I planned to blow the roof off with the final belting notes of that coronation song, but now I'll have to apply this showiness to my designated pre-chorus solo.

"But these diamonds drip with blood,

Sweat and tears pooling to flood."

I start by singing one full octave higher than I did yesterday. Instantly, the crowd explodes with cheers. The judges jump to their feet.

"Your feed with shiny stories,

Sure signs we'll edge your glories."

I pour every ounce of vocal firepower I possess into the building melody. Then, on the final word, I hit the highest note I know I'm capable of, in my falsetto.

As the other four break into the chorus across the stage, I hold out the high note, causing the audience to lose their minds.

Once I finish, my ears ring and my throat feels raw, but to hell with it.

They wanted a diva?

They're going to get one.

TURN TO PAGE 54

Last week, production had each of us choose a coronation song to perform if we won. Mine was going to be "The Show Must Go On" so I could channel my full Freddie Mercury fantasy—and deliver a message that this would only be the beginning. Well, I suppose the message of that song applies now more than ever. If they're going to coronate me Queen, then I'd better show them the crown fits just right.

If I won, I planned a stunt to pull in the last minutes of the live broadcast, before anyone could stop me. I suppose I should do this stunt now anyway, because in a way, I have won. But since I'll only get my one pre-chorus to shine solo, I'm going to have to make it count.

While CeCe sings the first verse, I reach into my blazer. Any true student of *RuPaul's Drag Race* knows you don't go to a finale without a few tricks up your sleeve—sometimes literally. I pull out the wig I stashed there, along with a pair of purple-stoned sunglasses. The wig is just a little jet-black bob, but it has survived my sleeve stashing with surprising grace.

CeCe's verse ends, and I step forward, taking my moment. The second the spotlight hits me in all my wigged-out glory, the crowd goes absolutely wild. As I sing my first line, I strut across the stage as best as I can in my dress shoes. I'd kill for a pair of thigh-high boots right about now, but I can still turn out a model walk with the best of them, even flat-footed.

Once I reach the end of the stage and my last pre-chorus note, I do the thing I pray will go well. I run back across the stage and spin into my mark, collapsing onto one back-bended leg for a half death drop.

As the others begin singing the chorus, I hear the screams and applause over the sound of every heaving breath.

A death drop will give them life—*every single time.*

TURN TO PAGE 54

I must black out a little from the adrenaline after that because the next thing I know, I find myself in a dressing room backstage with the others. A terrified-looking production assistant informs us our post-show press junket will start in ten minutes, then promptly disappears. The Executive Producers are nowhere to be seen, and why not? We're officially not their responsibility now that the show is over. Plus, who'd want to try managing the teenage hurricane that's probably about to rage?

"Can they even make us do this?" Dea asks first. "Did anyone else read the contracts?"

"You read the whole thing?" I ask, knowing this isn't really the point, but still.

"Most of it, along with my parents' lawyer," Dea answers. "I didn't remember it saying anything about groups."

"It doesn't matter," Everly says next, eerily calm. But, like, the *I'm about to murder someone in cold blood* kind of calm. "They can't force me—force us—into some fake group."

"Whoa, hold on," Stern jumps in. "I know it's a shock, but is this really such a bad thing? 'Press Diamonds' was the best thing any of us did all season. And clearly the world agrees."

"Stern, you're not actually our leader," Everly says. "Because we are *not a group*. I am a singer-songwriter. This is *not* me."

That drops some silence into the room.

I want to say something, but I don't know how to feel about any of this, either. Sure, I love me some Destiny's Child, but I always saw myself as a Beyoncé, which was probably obvious from the not-so-little solo stunt I just pulled onstage. Now that I've had a minute to think about it, that was deeply epic. But it was also probably not the best foot forward for a budding five-member group.

"Everly, you love Fleetwood Mac and HAIM," CeCe tries. "And some of the biggest music groups ever started as strangers. I mean, *X Factor* threw Fifth Harmony and One Direction together after they auditioned as solo artists. Little Mix too. Don't you love them, Vinny?"

I do love those divas. And CeCe might have a point . . .

"And all those TRL-era pop groups were made from open casting calls too: Spice Girls, Backstreet Boys, *NSYNC. Or the ones made on TV like Danity Kane and O-Town. And Dea, aren't you into BLACKPINK? They were strangers paired together during training bootcamps."

"I don't love BLACKPINK enough to throw away the solo branding I've worked so hard to build," Dea returns. "And I'm a trained dancer. Would we even do choreography? Does this mean that Everly never plays an instrument again? 'Press Diamonds' might have worked once, but we are from five different subgenres of pop. Not to mention, we're different genders. What is the end goal here? Is Everly going to write an entire album of songs that fit all of us just as well?"

"No, I will not be doing that," Everly says immediately. "I'm sorry, it's really not about you all. This is about staying authentic as an artist and a writer."

CeCe looks crushed. Maybe she was hoping we'd all be celebrating our joint win right now? Stern certainly looks that way, but he also looks weirdly . . . confident? He grins like he already knows this is going to work out, somehow. The delusion, darling.

"I'm sorry, CeCe, I know you love groups," Everly adds. "But one performance doesn't warrant an entire direction shift for our solo careers. This isn't what any of us signed up for."

"Actually, I'd venture this is exactly what you all signed up for."

We turn to this new voice and find none other than Zahra Moon, one of the judges and music manager supreme, standing in the doorway. Seeing her in the Balmain-suited, shimmery-brown flesh is still a thrill. I've followed her career because she reps a bunch of queer artists, but she has worked with many of the greats before that, Kree Duski included. I've also followed her as an out-and-proud transwoman, one of the few power-queers to make the Forbes list from behind the music industry scenes. Truth is, I'd follow Zahra into any trenches, so I'm dying to hear her take on this latest development.

"Figuratively speaking, you all came here to become stars," Zahra continues. "That group performance is trending, despite the odds. I don't think I have to tell you how rare it is for the music industry to pay attention to a reality show like this. The Kelly Clarkson and Carrie Underwood success stories are few and far between, but you all have s tumbled into a bit of a phenomenon. And when that happens, you strike while the iron is hot because, I guarantee you, it will go cold in the blink of an eye."

Zahra lets those words settle over us and not even Everly argues . . . at least for now.

"So now I'm asking, will you let me make you all stars together? This group win was my idea because I'd like to represent Jeweltones as your manager. But it's a package deal—all or nothing. And, before you say anything, I have something to show you."

Zahra closes the door and pulls out her phone. She opens some app I don't recognize and holds it up for us.

"This tracks the streaming and sales for industry insiders. 'Press Diamonds' just released alongside the group announcement. If all goes as expected, it's already on track to debut at number one on the charts that matter next week."

I lean in and can hardly believe my eyes. There it is on the screen in black and white: **"Press Diamonds" by Jeweltones**.

This is all . . . deeply surreal.

"Wait. You released that recording we did today as a single already?" Everly asks.

She looks so violated that I want to reach over and give her a hug. Except, *girl*. Your song—our song—is probably going to be number one? Everly needs a sobering shake instead. That is *beyond* amazing.

"Of course, and you should be thanking the label," Zahra answers. "UWU and the show own that song, but we'll talk about all the legalities soon. Right now, you only need to know one thing. You have fans, and they want you together. They already named their fandom the Gemstones today, before the finale even aired. And the moment you all get on your phones again, you'll see on your socials for yourselves. While you were busy preparing for tonight, your fans made this happen. So right now, you owe it to them to put on your happy faces and do the press junket as a unit. The rest, I promise you, we'll sort out together."

My mind spins. We have fans. Fans that love us so much together, they've already formed a community around us. Fans that are already making us hit artists. That are inspiring someone like Zahra Moon to put her considerable influence behind us. I might not know much right now, and I definitely don't know how I feel about joining a teen pop group, especially one as doomed-from-the-start as this one seems. But I do know a once-in-a-lifetime opportunity when it magically appears.

So it's about time I spoke my first real words on this group win.

❖ "Okay, team, it doesn't matter if we like it: this is our big break. So we suck it up and **fake it** tonight. Because, at the very least, we owe it to each other not to ruin this before we even give it a chance."
TURN TO PAGE 58

❖ "Zahra is right. I know this isn't what any of us planned, but this is the universe giving us exactly what we asked for. Maybe if we really come together and **compromise**, we can find a way to make everyone happy?"
TURN TO PAGE 60

"Listen, I know none of us wanted to be in a group," I continue before glancing at CeCe. "Well, none of us except CeCe maybe. And I know no one is probably happy about that solo stunt I pulled."

No one speaks up, which confirms this suspicion.

"I get it," I go on. "We all came here to launch solo careers, but maybe there's a reason that group performance broke through instead of any of our solo efforts all season long? I'm not going to stand here and name each of our strengths and weaknesses, but I will ask this: Who sees someone in this room whose strength covers their weaknesses as an artist? And who here wants to learn how someone else does what they do so well?"

I let that sink in a moment, because I certainly know I'd love to steal some skills from all four of these artists. Songwriting and emoting and serving and charming, oh my.

"If that doesn't work for you, then think of it this way," CeCe says, nodding at me. I'm thankful that she wants to keep the ball rolling. Besides, tough love is more her department. "We all share the same dream. Right now, for any of us to snag a piece of that dream, we have to do it this way. We rally and make it work, even if we're faking it like Vinny said. We're in show business, after all, so we put on a show. If we don't, I have a feeling we return to obscurity. Or worse, we invite hate and resentment. If music fans hate anyone, it's the Yokos, Zayns, and Ginger Spices of the pop world."

CeCe's words settle over the group, and to my surprise, no one immediately protests. CeCe gives me a quick smile, then we both turn to Zahra, who also nods—*good job*. Then, slowly, the other three nod along too. Even Everly. Good old-fashioned peer pressure with a touch of FOMO for the win.

Then, I think, *the crown is heavy, Stern darling. Best leave it with the real queens?*

"Fantastic. Tonight, we become Jeweltones," I say, not sure how I feel about that name yet, either. "And tomorrow, we figure out exactly what the hell that even means."

Surveying the group once more, everyone seems resigned to at least this much. None of us are here for it all, but we can all be here for this one moment.

After all, some people wait a lifetime for it.

TURN TO PAGE 62

"I know there's a lot to sort through," I continue. "And maybe once we have a moment to do that, we'll figure out this isn't going to work. But how can we throw away this chance when we've all fought so hard to get here?"

"Right, *compromise*," Everly says. "Coming from the guy who stole everyone's thunder onstage just minutes ago."

"You did the same thing yesterday, Everly," I reply.

"That was covering a mistake. What you did was obviously intentional, so please don't sell us on some all for one, one for all fantasy?"

I look to Dea to back me up, but she just turns away, folding in on herself.

Ouch.

"Fine. Vinny is the show-off stunt queen," CeCe jumps in, giving me a quick nod. "He can talk about that in our interviews. Everly, you should take the credit for writing the song. Stern, you'll play humble about your probable solo win, and I'll go full fan-girl-group at them. Then Dea . . ."

CeCe looks at Dea, trying to come up with her angle on the fly. But I can pick up the baton on his one.

"Dea is our influencer queen, so she can be the style-lead of the group."

Dea blinks at me, still not sure what to do with this turn of events.

"Right," CeCe jumps back in. "Tomorrow, we'll start to figure out how to turn this new fame into a business, whether that means doing it together or apart. But, at least for tonight, we agree to give the fans what they want from us?"

CeCe's words settle over the group, and to my surprise, no one immediately protests. CeCe turns and gives me a smile, then we both turn to Zahra, who also nods—*good job*. Slowly, the other three look at each other and then nod along. Even Everly. I breathe a sigh of relief. CeCe might have brought us home, but I kept us rolling. Queen of stunts, indeed.

"Fantastic. Tonight, we officially become Jeweltones," I say, not sure how I feel about that name yet, either. "And tomorrow, we figure out exactly what that even means."

Surveying the group once more, everyone seems resigned to at least this much.

It might be cliché, but leave it to the queers to turn a torrential rainstorm into a potential bejeweled rainbow.

TURN TO PAGE 62

CHAPTER FIVE

EVERLY

IT'S BEEN THREE DAYS SINCE THE FINALE, BUT THE PIT WEDGED in my stomach refuses to budge. Of course, the bland office where I sit doesn't help. It's nice enough, but I guess I expected something more inspiring from the music manager who represents some of my favorite indie singer-songwriters. I should be grateful to be here, but somehow all I feel is caged. The beige walls seem too dull, the posters and plaques feel too faded. Even the view, which overlooks the parking garage for the building next door, is dreary.

I turn my attention back to Benni D and the look on her face as she reads my *SO YOU WANNA BE A POP STAR?* contract only makes me feel worse. I know I shouldn't have, but I DMed her the night of the finale, back when my panic was at its height. Benni agreeing to meet with me felt like a glimmer of hope in this group cloud, helping me get through the last few days. However, that hope now feels dim.

"I'm afraid what Zahra told you was true, as far as I can tell," Benni says, looking up from the contract to meet my gaze. "There are very specific clauses written in for the prize winner. Like not being able to sign with anyone else in the music industry for one year after the release of your first album, which the label owns, and which you're contractually obligated to produce. While this language only applies to the winner, it doesn't specify that there could only be one winner. That said, it doesn't look like they planned on creating a group in advance, so there's a world where you hire a lawyer and fight to get out but . . . want my honest advice?"

"That's why I'm here," I answer. It was risky to take this solo manager meeting in the first place—it would not be a good look as my first move in this new group, internally or publicly. So I need to make this count.

"You all owe UWU your first album, and it's a pretty standard first record deal," Benni says. "Zahra is very good, and the label seems to be prioritizing Jeweltones, which bodes well for future promotional support. You said they rented you all a house in Beverly Hills?"

I nod, feeling my limbs go leaden. I already know where this is headed.

"Jeweltones is having a moment right now, like it or not. If I were your manager—which I legally cannot be, to be clear—I'd tell you to capitalize on this viral attention. You've struck gold. Plus, if the first album works, there's a clear path to launching your solo career in a few years. Which I'd be thrilled to talk about when the time comes."

I clench my jaw so tightly, my teeth ache. I release and try to take a breath. Even though it is deeply depressing to hear this, Benni's offer is also deeply meaningful.

"Okay, that's your business advice," I reply. "But I also came here because you represent real songwriters. What if I told you that I don't think I can make this work, artistically?"

"And why is that?" Benni asks. "These reality competitions put you in the same kind of creative boxes that this group will. And, from what I hear, you were very good at redecorating the inside."

"Thank you," I say, "but a few months on a show to break through is different than suddenly being pushed into a group that is supposed to produce original music. The competition felt like a compromise, but this feels like selling out."

Benni gives me a look. "I hate that phrase. *Selling out.* Look, there are working artists and there are amateurs. Working requires compromise; no one is immune to that. But I don't think that's what really worries you about this group, is it?"

I reach for the glass of water Benni offered me earlier and buy some time. She is right, but I am not pulling her into the interpersonal nonsense. "I guess I'm afraid I'll just fade into the background. Or if not, that I'll force myself into a different shape just so I fit in. I don't mind leaning into more mainstream synth-pop. I know my style could fit in with artists like Griff and Sigrid and Léon, or even small groups like MUNA or Aly & AJ. But they're still all in the same sonic space. Jeweltones has five different artists in totally different pop lanes. I want my songs to feel like a cobblestone street, not a freeway."

"And 'Press Diamonds' is a freeway?"

"Not necessarily, but it was meant to be a one-time experiment, not a song I'm expected to sing for the rest of my life. Besides, the others aren't going to want to do an entire album of 'Press Diamonds,' even if that *was* what I wanted."

I take another sip of water and I can tell I'm not really convincing Benni. I'm not even sure why it matters at this point, but I just need her to understand me.

"You represent singer-songwriters," I say, shifting gears. "Some of them have said the worst thing we can do as artists is be inauthentic. I just don't see how Jeweltones leaves room for any of us, not just me, to be fully authentic artists."

Benni watches me, thinking over her next words carefully.

"Look, I know this isn't how you envisioned your dreams coming true. But I encourage you to remember this really is dream-come-true stuff— and that no working artist is an island of pure authenticity. That said, if you really can't get there, I understand. In that case, you can quit, refuse your cut of the prize money, get out of the record deal, and wait one year to release your own music."

I feel my throat start to close. "Hold on. I can at least release new songs on social media, right?"

"Not if you want to retain ownership. If you refuse the prize, there's a clause that sidelines you for a year." Benni gives me a look and sighs. "You'd be starting from scratch again, after that."

I can't meet her gaze, because it starts to feel just like the sterilized staleness of this office. *Grow up. Be an adult. This is the business.*

It all makes me want to cry.

Benni tries to look sympathetic.

Walking to the elevator, I grab my headphones and scroll for one of my favorite security blanket albums. I've never been that close to my mom, as the product of her short-lived second marriage to my dad, but she has pretty good taste in music. On the rare weekends when I'd visit her, she'd give me access to her playlists. Dad is a classic vinyl album completist, but Mom loves putting together custom mixes of the latest pop.

I might not have worked out an answer to my Jeweltones conundrum yet, but there is one album that always manages to make me feel like myself, even on my worst days.

◈ Michelle Branch's ***Hotel Paper***, which Mom introduced to me. It's a collection of earnest songs written by a teen girl who stood out among the manufactured pop that surrounded her at the time.
TURN TO PAGE 66

◈ Fleetwood Mac's ***Rumours***, given to me by Dad. It's an innovative album forged from the fires of collaboration and fueled by passionate, opposing emotions.
TURN TO PAGE 68

Of all Mom's curated music, *Hotel Paper* always stood out to me. Maybe it was because, during the time of the millennial pop explosion, Michelle Branch was one of the original teen queens wielding a guitar pick and a sharp pen instead of a choreographed routine and a synthesized style. The album is also just full of gorgeously written songs from a perspective I've always understood.

I play the title track as I ride the elevator. It's one of my favorite songs of all time, since it inspired me to start writing and playing guitar. The song is about writing in lonely hotel rooms, about your dreams taking you away from other beloved things. As I listen now, I obviously begin to vibe with that emotion on a whole new level.

That's why I love songs so much. They have a way of walking you through life. They stay the same, but somehow also constantly evolve with you. Eight-year-old me could never have fathomed what this song would mean to eighteen-year-old me, leaving a dream meeting with nothing but bittersweet considerations. And what will twenty-eight-year-old me be feeling someday that I can't possibly fathom now, listening to this same song again?

I always promised myself I'd cover "Hotel Paper" on my own first album. Not just because Michelle Branch's legacy in country-folk song-writer-pop has been criminally underrated, but also because she covered everyone from Joni Mitchell to Radiohead on her albums, not to mention my second-favorite criminally underrated singer-songwriter of all time, Patty Griffin. Taylor Swift might have mega-popularized the sound I love so much, but in my humble opinion, Patty and Michelle walked so Taylor could run. I've always wanted to ask Taylor if she was inspired by Michelle and Patty the way she inspires me. Though, right now, there are about a million other questions I'd like to ask instead. What would any of these incredible women have done if they were put in this group position for their first album?

The idea that I could someday stand among these titans, that I could inspire the next generation of female songwriters . . . it's *the* dream. However, it's so unexpected that my doorway into this dream could be "Press Diamonds." I can live with that song, but I just can't figure out how to keep writing authentically while locked in this group, cast only in the part of the sapphire Jeweltone. I'm so much more than that. Besides, everyone knows that the longer the public sees you one way, the more impossible it becomes to pivot.

Of course, I could just walk away instead of making this potential compromise. But on the other hand, will I ever get as big a break as this again? The music industry isn't exactly forgiving, especially to young women. Not to mention my graduation deal with Dad, which would run out before I could release any new music anyway. Besides, how could I not release songs to my listeners for one whole year? The idea of writing in complete solitude and uncertainty for so long sounds unbearable.

Deep down I know this all pales in comparison to the most terrifying potential outcome of this scenario: What if I leave the group and they become iconic superstars while I'm left in the dust?

I mean, I should just be happy to get a big break at all.

So why do I feel like I would've rather lost and gotten to keep my freedom?

I can't stop these questions from plaguing me, so I crank up the volume, praying Michelle will deliver me an unexpected answer. Then it suddenly occurs to me: she did go on to form The Wreckers for her next album. While it was a duo with one singular sound, it still was a pivot from pop to country . . .

So maybe I'm meant to do something like that too?

TURN TO PAGE 70

I fell in love with this country-folk pop-rock album long before I learned the legend of the creative conditions it was written under. *Rumours* just inhabits so many soundscapes I still love to this day, from the upbeat bops like "Second Hand News" and "Go Your Own Way" to the lilting melancholia of "Dreams" and "Songbird," to the moody churn of "The Chain" and "Gold Dust Woman." It's an album that has always felt like a roadmap for my own journey as a country-folk-pop songwriter.

I suppose it's fitting, then, that Fleetwood Mac was on the verge of breaking up while making this iconic album. Somehow, the tension of heated disputes and crumbling divorce managed to create musical magic. Despite this, I really despise the stereotype that to make the best music, you have to be in the worst shape. Although, to be honest, I've already experienced the "whole greater than the sum of its parts" thing with Jeweltones, it seems.

I skip ahead to "Dreams" as I step into the elevator, feeling a pull to the message of that song. Am I meant to have my own Fleetwood Mac moment here just like Stevie Nicks? Is there a world where this pressure somehow continues to produce sonic diamonds? What Vinny and CeCe said before is true. I could stand to learn from the others, especially when it comes to performing. And I *did* feel so much safer in the group than performing solo . . . but what about my songwriting?

How can I get around diluting myself as a compromise to ensure the group succeeds? I could just embrace this opportunity and give up ownership of my first album, but do I really want to share those songs with four others forever? On the B-side, it probably wouldn't be any better to let a gallery of mega-producers craft Jeweltones some trendy, broad music of the moment. I watch the floor numbers drop and then suddenly think, *what if they force me to learn choreography?*

Really, it comes down to taking creative control or losing it . . .

Is there a way to do one without the other in this group?

I know these are questions I'd have to answer with the others, but if Fleetwood freaking Mac couldn't make it work, what chance do we really stand? At least they could agree on a general sound, but will Jeweltones be able to do even that much? Then there are the heaviest questions that sit in my stomach: If I walk away and get cast as the vindictive villain, will Jeweltones become an iconic act without me? Or, perhaps even worse, will we be just another one-hit wonder if I stay? Could my solo aspirations ever recover from either? The music industry is so fickle . . . and the only thing that ever endures is good music.

So, really, this all boils down to one question:

Will I write better music with or without Jeweltones?

I try to calm down, focusing on "Dreams" playing in my ears. I remind myself that music has always been a collaborative art. No artist ever makes music fully solo—it takes teams of musicians and engineers to produce at a professional level. Besides, some of my favorite Stevie Nicks songs from her own solo career have actually been duets. Sure, I might be kidding myself to think that a five-person group is the same as one artist taking control of a creative team . . .

But maybe I just need to give the collaborative compromise a chance to work before I shut it down?

TURN TO PAGE 70

As I exit the elevator and walk through the lobby, it feels like I might have arrived at my first answer. I stand to lose more by walking away than by giving Jeweltones a shot. I sigh out loud, feeling my brain begin to catch up with my heart in that gut instinct place. But even as this sobering creative realization settles, it only branches into a whole new fleet of concerns.

For months in the competition, we were told we needed to beat each other to make our dreams come true. Now we need to find some way to rely on each other to succeed? How am I going to trust these people who I've been fighting—and failing—to outperform until now?

I would at least be excited to work with CeCe. I know she'd challenge me in all the best ways. And Vinny is kind and flexible enough as an artist to work with, so maybe that wouldn't be too bad. I guess I could say the same about Stern, though that doesn't erase the complications of my crush—or change the fact that Stern and Dea are a couple now. I mean, finale night was supposed to be the end for Dea and me, not the beginning.

As the next song on the album plays, I open a ride-sharing app to get back to the Jeweltones house—no label-provided black SUVs for clandestine solo career meetings. The only reason I could safely get away in the first place was by telling everyone I had a gynecologist appointment. Thankfully, Dad is driving my car out from our place in the valley today, so maybe I'll finally get some freedom. Then again, I bet the label won't want its shiniest new jewel seen driving around LA in Jane Honda, my beloved-but-ancient high school car.

I only wait a minute before my ride arrives. Sliding into the backseat, I see that the young woman driving can't be more than a few years older than me.

"Oh my god, you're Everly from Jeweltones!" she suddenly shouts, looking back at me.

"Oh, wow. You're the first person to recognize me out in the world," I say, blushing.

"No way!" the driver yelps. "I promise I won't bother you the whole drive, you're just my first celebrity passenger!"

"Celebrity? Yeah, right."

"Seriously! All my friends are obsessed with 'Press Diamonds.' My little sister even used an app to rip your performances from YouTube and make them into singles. Oh crap, is that bad? We'll totally buy your stuff when it's official too. She's just such a huge fan. We both are."

I'm struck speechless.

This is . . . kind of everything I ever dreamed of.

"Think we could get a selfie, maybe, when I drop you off?" the driver asks. "I'm so sorry, you just want to get where you're going."

"It'd be my honor," I answer with a smile.

The driver nods, looking like she might burst into tears. I know the feeling.

This is exactly the kind of reminder that I needed. If I do right by listeners like her, none of the other details matter . . .

Right?

♦ ♦ ♦

I really wish I didn't, but I do love the rental that UWU and Zahra moved us all into. My house in the valley is lovely, but it's your standard suburban three-bedroom fare. This Beverly Hills mansion boasts six en suite bedrooms tucked away in a secluded canyon, all furnished with Spanish villa perfection. Everything is warm wooden beams and crisp white linens and glittering Moroccan lanterns, plus a backyard with the most gorgeous sunken pool and cabana setup I've ever seen. My own bedroom overlooks the trees on the side of the house, since I didn't care about having a room with a view. I did, however, care about the room that had a bathroom with heated tiles and was closest to CeCe. Vinny and Dea took the biggest rooms, naturally, while Stern was fine taking the smallest bedroom.

Sitting on my enormous bed, I stare at my still-full suitcases. We moved in here yesterday, but I haven't felt comfortable unpacking yet, for obvious reasons. All this lifestyles-of-the-rich-and-famous stuff felt fun, but also like a pair of golden handcuffs. Especially when Zahra delayed our first official meeting until later this afternoon. I don't know about the rest of the group, but three days felt like way too long after the finale for us to all sit down and talk. Still, who can blame Zahra for being busy? Thankfully, the house is a nice distracting flex, calming our fears and separating us into our luxury corners for the time being. I'd bet that's part of why Zahra purposefully delayed—so we'd have time to adjust and absorb.

Breathing in the cool central air, I start to settle a little. *Everly*, I tell myself, *you're sitting in a mansion paid for by your record label, waiting to meet your manager. You met a stranger today who loves your music enough to steal it. Remember when you said you'd pay people to listen to your songs?* I take another breath.

While all of this is absolutely, enormously true, I can't shake the feeling that this isn't quite how it's supposed to be. My whole world changed around me overnight, but it feels like I'm still stuck in the same place. Is that the group's fault or just my brain?

"So this is what winning a reality show will get you, huh?" I hear Dad's voice just as Alanis bounds into my room to greet me, twenty pounds of vibrating white fluff. I would say hello to Dad first, but on the day that he decides to run at me with his tongue hanging and his butt wagging, he'll get priority hello hugs like Alanis.

"Thank you for bringing her for a visit," I say once I've thoroughly snuggled and scratched Alanis. "And for dropping off Jane Honda."

"The security guard at the community gate almost turned me away on sight," Dad says, taking his turn to hug me hello. "Everly Brooks, this is . . ."

Dad looks around the room, tears welling in his eyes. Really, I have him to thank for all of this. He has always been my number one fan, never doubting for one second that I'd make a life out of my music. Tuition for Berklee was just one of the many other gifts he was planning to give me, along with the privilege of deferring for a year. The truth is, I can feel like a self-assured or confident artist because of the unconditional love and the safety net Dad has always offered me.

"I have to admit, I thought your musical gap year would cost me a lot more," Dad laughs, wiping at the corners of his eyes. "You did good, kid."

I hug Dad again, wiping at my own eyes. I've pursued songwriting because it feels like something I *have* to do. In the back of my mind, I knew it could yield stuff like this—money, fame, a fancy mansion—but that was never really the end goal. Still, of all the exciting perks, making Dad proud is by far the greatest one.

"Are you sure you want to rideshare back home?" I ask. "I'm sure the label could spring for a car."

"No need! Mama V to the rescue!"

Suddenly, Vinny's mom, Gia Vecchi, comes sauntering into my room in all her faux-Versace glory. She even has a gold V belt to match her tight jeans, floral blouse, and mile-high hair. Vinny enters behind her, looking every bit her mini-me. I suppose it's like father like daughter, like mother like son around here.

"Sorry to interrupt. I'm just so grateful you all agreed to let me stay in the pool house so I can be close to Vinny," Gia gushes in her thick New York accent. "Until I find an apartment of my own, I'm determined to make myself as useful as possible. Want a riceball, hun?"

Gia holds out a tray of homemade riceballs, still warm from the oven, and I happily gobble one up. I think everyone said yes to Gia staying in the guest studio out of sheer politeness at first, but she quickly became the Italian house mom of our dreams. She's always cooking and cleaning and chauffeuring, wanting to stay in a constant storm of motion.

"I told Gia I could rideshare back home, but she insisted," Dad says, popping a riceball into his mouth.

"Nonsense," Gia replies. "If anything, you're doing me a favor. I hate sitting still."

She smiles and it's like the mother of all suns beams down with warmth. She's so unlike my own mom, who feels very cold and distant. She was never the right fit for Dad, but judging from the way he currently beams back at Gia . . . maybe she could be more of a match?

"Just make sure she drives somewhere in the general realm of the speed limit, Mr. Brooks?" Vinny chimes in. "Mom tends to have a heavy foot."

"You can call me Steve, Vinny," Dad says. "And something tells me no one gets away with telling your mom what to do."

"Damn straight," Gia says, smiling deviously. "Now come on, I made the rest of this batch for your first group meeting. The others are waiting by the pool, and it's better that us parents aren't here when fancy-pants Zahra arrives. I'll make sure your dad and Alanis get home in one piece, so you two get to stepping."

Vinny and I say our goodbyes before heading toward the backyard. Once we're out of earshot, I turn and give him a playful shove.

"Did you see that back there? You and I might be siblings before all this is through!"

Vinny groans, looking nowhere near as pleased.

"Yes, that's just what we need in this group: another source of drama."

I'm ready to rib Vinny back until I realize how genuinely upset he looks. It's only for a moment, then he catches and corrects himself. I remember, then, how he talked in one of his interview packages about his dad dying when he was younger. I might be ready to see my dad move on, but it's pretty clear that Vinny isn't ready to see his mom do the same— and for very good reason.

I'm about to say something potentially consoling, but I'm distracted as we step into the backyard. Not just by the scenery—which is striking with the blue pool glistening in the afternoon sunlight and the green lawn sloping down into the canyon beyond. Or by the sight of Stern sitting under the cabana wearing a tank top that reveals his ridiculously cut arms. Instead, I'm distracted by the intense look Dea hits me with the moment I appear.

"My mom made riceballs," Vinny says, placing the platter down on the cabana coffee table. He stares at them longingly for a moment, then asks, "Any word from Zahra yet?"

Dea simply holds up her phone in response. On it, I'm surprised to see a picture of myself from earlier, standing in front of that drab office building. Above the image is a gossip website headline boldly declaring: **CherriPop Exclusive: Over Before It Begins? Is Everly Brooks Abandoning Jeweltones? The DRAMA!**

"Everly took a solo meeting with a manager today," Dea says, her voice calm.

Crap.

"I don't know how that wound up online," I start, refusing to let Dea have the upper hand. "Or how anyone knew why I was there, but I won't lie, I did take a meeting to get informed about our options. And I'm sure you'd all like to know that the alternatives all suck. Either we do this group, we lawyer up, or we walk away and sit out of the industry for a year."

As soon as the words are out of my mouth, I realize how harsh they sound. So I turn and focus my gaze on CeCe, who looks slightly out of place poolside in her usual pop-punk attire.

"I'm glad I went because it made me see the value in giving this group a real shot."

"Sure, now that you know you can't leave," Dea replies. "But you obviously planted this article to create some options for yourself."

"Excuse me?" I respond, dumbfounded.

"Inside, the article talks all about how you want to leave the group because you feel 'bullied and alienated' by me," Dea explains, even-keeled as ever. "And that you feel 'artistically stifled and exploited' by the rest of us."

"I did *not* plant any article," I say, my jaw clenching.

"Well, someone did. A 'source close to the new band' is cited. Who else here is convinced I betrayed you and that you're a better artist than the rest of us?"

My blood boils and I can't seem to think clearly enough to craft a coherent response. Dea is threading so many half-truths through her accusations that I don't even know where to start defending myself—especially because this article *did* obviously come from some inside source.

The photo I can understand; anyone could have snapped that on their phone—even if it's surreal that someone cares enough to now do so. And anyone could have figured out why I was at that building by looking up its occupants. What remains puzzling is how someone could assemble all of this so quickly, along with the very not-public information about the falling-out with Dea. Plus, I've never said to anyone else out loud before today that I feel artistically compromised. I'd suspect Benni, but she doesn't know a thing about the stuff between Dea and me. That leaves someone close to the show—or the group.

"I do not think I'm a better artist than any of you," I say with all the conviction I can muster. "And I am staying here because I believe some compromise is possible."

"Because your article backfired," Dea presses. "You wanted me to come off looking like the villain to set up your heroic solo exit."

CeCe and Vinny both open their mouths to jump in, but I wave them off.

Because enough is enough.

✦ "You're the influencer who loves talking to the press, Dea. If anyone is behind this leak, it's you trying to set me up and **sabotage things**."

TURN TO PAGE 77

✦ "I would never do that. However, there are a dozen people close enough to the show who could've talked, to generate buzz for a possible second season or whatever. But with you **attacking me**, whoever did this is getting exactly what they want."

TURN TO PAGE 79

Dea stares back at me, stiff and expressionless for a moment. Then she takes a breath. "I wasn't going to say anything, but Warner Music offered me a solo deal the day after the finale," she says. "They even offered to buy me out of my contract, but UWU refused. So I'm sorry, I don't need to feel or do anything about your manager meeting, except when it messes with my public image."

The cabana falls so silent that I can hear the warm breeze rustling the canopy and rippling the pool water. Dea might appear calm, but she clearly lost her cool. It takes her just a beat before she realizes the effect this news has not only on me, but on all the others as well. Suddenly it's like we can hear each other's thoughts: *Why her and not me? Does this mean Dea was supposed to win the show originally?*

"I wouldn't have taken the deal even if I could," Dea lies, and poorly at that. "I just hate that Everly pretends she doesn't want to be famous or successful as the rest of us. Like she's somehow purer as an artist."

Staring at Dea, I suddenly remember us in our joint hotel rooms on the second night of the semifinals, still awake at 2 a.m. I agreed to teach Dea some chords on my keyboard. She said she always wanted to learn, but was too afraid of being bad. I told her everyone is bad at any instrument at first, that you just have to work through the mistakes. I could see it so clearly then, how Dea might be fine with hard work, but she can't tolerate fumbling with piano key mistakes. Instead, she convinced me to do some silly dance moves with her to help get me out of my head. We both were so bad, we ended up laughing and giving up, falling onto the bed.

Snapping back, I look at her now and only feel my disappointment harden into a sharper edge. How stupid we were then as friends, giving each other endless fuel to burn each other now as enemies.

"Well, I hate that all you seem to care about is your 'public image,'" I reply. "That article is bullshit and you know it."

"We can agree on that much," Dea says. "I just wish you'd be honest about thinking you're too good to be here."

"And I wish you'd be honest about being terrified to be in a group where everyone else can actually sing."

I watch the tears spring to Dea's eyes and I close my own. Again, I'm the one who took it a step too far. I wish that if Dea were going to pick these fights, she'd at least hold her goddamn own. That she'd look back at me and say, *well, you're terrified of being in a group where everyone else can actually perform.*

Instead, Dea says, "Nice, Everly. Really nice."

TURN TO PAGE 81

"Of course I'm questioning whether this group is right for me," I say, testing the waters. "I can't be the only one wondering whether Jeweltones will play to their strengths or just expose their weaknesses? If they should go with their solo instincts or the group flow?"

Looking around, the others all nod one by one—except Dea, of course.

"This was *so* not the plan," Vinny says. "But, then again, I didn't really have a plan anyway. I don't know if this is the best or the worst thing to happen to us, but it's happening either way."

"You know I'm here for groups," CeCe replies. "But the divisions and dynamics can ruin our careers much faster than as solo artists, trust me."

"I still don't know how we're all going to shine here," Stern follows, placing a hand on top of Dea's. "But I do know the solo thing never got me a house in the Hills and a hot girlfriend."

Vinny laughs while CeCe rolls her eyes and I offer a tight smile. All Dea offers is silence. Which tracks because she is incapable of being anything other than a cold, picture-perfect, curated persona.

Staring at Dea, I suddenly see us in our joint hotel rooms on the third night of the semifinals, still awake at 2 a.m. She was obsessing over the filter for some photo, so I snatched her phone away. I told her she needed to care less about being who she thinks everyone else wants her to be. She told me I needed to care more about everyone else's feelings than my own. We laughed, then I turned our little exchange into a jingle. Dea made up a mini dance routine and we agreed to post it to her stories instead of her original photo.

Now that story has been lost forever.

I feel that loss sink deeper as I look at Dea now. Really, only former friends can become the kind of enemies capable of eating you alive.

Once it becomes obvious that Dea isn't going to take her turn to speak up, I speak for her.

"We do have to be extra careful, I think. Now that we're famous—at least for the current moment—this kind of leak could happen again. Stuff like that will make this situation a toxic minefield when what we need is a safe space."

Dea stares back at me with that cold look, sharp as ever.

"You know, Everly, you have a talent for making me look like an awful bitch when you're really in the wrong."

A dozen comebacks stampede through my mind, each one more cutting than the last. Still, I bite my tongue because all I can really think is: for once, we share the same talent.

TURN TO PAGE 81

Already needing a break from this exchange, I turn to CeCe—just as Dea turns to Vinny. I don't know what expression Vinny offers Dea, but CeCe offers me a sympathetic look. Still, she doesn't exactly rush to my defense. I can't decide if it's smart or cowardly of the others not to choose sides, but either way, it's mildly annoying.

"Am I really the only one freaking out that we are suddenly celebrities?" Stern says. "I mean, that article might not be great, but you're both featured on a major gossip site! Besides, does anyone else have more DMs than they could possibly find time to read?"

I try to smile. Bless Stern, attempting to find some common ground for us.

"That's what you're focused on?" CeCe asks.

Stern looks crestfallen. I can tell he obviously wants to say something to make it better, but he doesn't want to say the "wrong" thing again. I guess this whole Dea-Everly feud has sucked up so much air that no one has really given much attention to the potential CeCe-Stern issues that have been bubbling right under the surface.

"We can't even sit together for five minutes without ripping into each other," I say. "How are we supposed to collaborate and perform together? Or live and tour together?"

"By establishing some boundaries, maybe?" Vinny tries. "I mean, we're going to have to find a way to make all this discord work for us, not against us, right?"

"Vinny is absolutely correct, as usual," Zahra says, suddenly emerging through the door and onto the patio. She clacks across the stone pathway toward the cabana in her signature designer heels, looking impossibly chic and professional. "Sorry I'm late, but I hope you're at least liking the house?"

We nod like badly behaved schoolchildren as Zahra takes a seat and looks us over.

"I can't stay for too long, but I wanted to get the ball rolling," she continues. "I assume you've all seen the article about Everly. I'm afraid that's going to be par for the course now, so I suggest you all let it go. Addressing rumors and allegations will only fan the flames. That said, I am looking into who this potential leak might be. I suspect it's someone from the show. Still, we don't need anything hitting too close to home."

Zahra rolls on, not even bothering to single me out with so much as a sharp glance about meeting with another manager. Clearly she's not intimidated in the slightest.

Or she knows I can't go anywhere.

"Now, I come with some actual good news," Zahra continues. "I got Jeweltones booked tomorrow morning on *Wake Up America* to perform 'Press Diamonds' and do an interview!"

Stern nearly falls out of his chair, while beside him, Dea tries to hide her shock. A feature on *Wake Up America* is about as big as it gets. Across from me, Vinny looks thrilled one second, then visibly terrified the next. CeCe appears just as worried. This is indeed a career-making opportunity, but it could prove to be equally career-breaking if we aren't ready for it.

And everyone, despite their excitement, knows we aren't ready.

"Zahra, that's amazing," CeCe begins. "But we aren't even close to being on the same page. Can't we go on in a week? Maybe once we've had some time to sort this all out?"

"*Wake Up America* wants you tomorrow, and I can guarantee that if we delay even a day, the chances of anyone still caring will plummet," Zahra answers. "Jeweltones is hot off the viral finale, but given the news cycle we live in, that momentum will vanish very soon. We have to keep you all out front while the center holds. Plus, visibility like this will buy you exactly the time and credit with the public you're asking for.

"Listen, I know this train is moving very fast, but you can't slow it down now, not before we even reach the first stop," Zahra continues, her tone shifting somewhere more sympathetic. "I have you booked for the rest of today with a label-approved PR coach, stylist, and choreographer to get you prepped for tomorrow. So today, you put on your professional adult pants and you work for this once-in-a-lifetime opportunity.

"Of course, I'm not oblivious and I know you all have a lot to work out, personally and creatively. This weekend I cleared my Saturday and booked us a retreat, complete with team building and group therapy experts. In that spirit, I'm giving you some homework. I ordered vision board kits, so

I want each of you to prepare one for the retreat. You'll have all day after *Wake Up America* tomorrow to prepare. I want you to put everything down that you want out of your career, your music, and this group. Then you'll present them to one another at the retreat, and we'll start to find some common ground to stitch this group together.

"So, what do you all say? Can we make it through the next two days without killing each other?"

We're all silent for a beat. It's obvious that none of us are really sure we can, but it also sounds like we're going to be so busy that we won't have much time to do anything but work. At least we've had a crash course in how TV appearances work from being on the reality show.

All five of us nod slowly, but the word "choreographer" continues to ring in my mind like an alarm bell. I don't want to be difficult, but I have to say something before Zahra moves on.

"Zahra, when you say choreographer, you mean—"

"—They are going to work out the rhythms of how to feature all five of you in a more polished way, to elevate from the finale performances," she answers. "Don't worry, no one wants to scrub you all into one monochromatic form. We just want a streamlined rainbow: one unit with five lanes for you all to shine through. However, we don't want you to veer too far from the 'Press Diamonds' format, so that means no choreographed dances, but also no playing instruments yet. We'll leave the discussion on how you all potentially evolve as a group for this weekend. In the meantime, there's something else you all should see."

Zahra dips into her Hermès bag for her phone, and I can already tell she's reaching for another glittery carrot to dangle in front of us. So far she has talked a very good game, so I guess we need to give her the chance to keep delivering on her promises.

Zahra scrolls for a second, then holds up her phone for us again. On the screen I see a light stick like the ones K-Pop groups create for their fandoms. This one is topped with the glowing letters *JT* and adorned with our five signature gemstones. The American music industry must be paying attention to the K-Pop phenomenon to try making this a trend here, or at least UWU is.

"This prototype was put up on the Jeweltones shop one hour ago," Zahra begins. While she speaks, I'm busy analyzing the shapes they chose. A standard diamond, a heart-shaped ruby, and a teardrop-shaped sapphire are all straightforward, but I have to guess at the other two. Vinny's amethyst triangle probably stands for a crown, while Stern's emerald circle probably stands for the well-rounded center, maybe?

"Your Gemstones fandom has already bought out the preorders."

My brain reels at the fact that so many people actually care about this group. Then it clicks that Zahra said we have a website and an online merch store. Who makes all the money from . . . ?

But I stop myself. We all sold our souls to UWU to the tune of our first album, so why not merch too? We'll obviously be living an all-expenses-paid life as long as we remain profitable, so it's no surprise that monetizing our own creations won't be an option for a while. Though come to think of it, I bet Dea has already begun monetizing our fame. If I know her, the social media collabs are probably already piling up.

Before I can fall down the rabbit hole of wondering if I should do that too, I squash the thought. It's like Zahra said: we all have our lanes. Let her worry about merch marketing and let Dea worry about brand partnerships. I can't forget that all of this goes away if we don't have a bedrock of excellent music our fans want to hear. Creatively controlling *that* process needs to stay my main concern.

"I'm guessing that means the name Jeweltones is set in stone?" Vinny asks. "It's just a little . . . I don't know, derivative?"

"Band names are always either derivative or nonsensical, trust me," Zahra answers.

I run through a quick mental list and she is mostly right.

"Besides, with the branding and merch tie-ins, the name is set in stone. Learn to love it." Zahra offers a tight smile and stands to leave. "Now, I have to run. I promise in the future when your own tour jet gets stuck on the ground in Tokyo before a show, you'll be my first priority too."

As she waves goodbye, I try to take this all in. Today, I'll be rehearsing for my debut performance on America's number one morning show.

Looking around at the others, I can tell they're all trying to absorb this same reality—and probably wishing they could hit this milestone on their own terms too. Still, something tells me this exact sentiment is the cornerstone of the adult lives we're rapidly entering. I guess I just never thought my dreams coming true would feel so . . .

Complicated?

CHAPTER SIX

EVERLY

TURNS OUT I WAS RIGHT ABOUT AT LEAST ONE THING: WE WERE
so busy for the rest of the day, we barely had time to eat, let alone argue.
One stylist fitting bled into the next PR prep rundown into the next
rehearsal—wash, rinse, repeat.

Lying on my bed, it's like I can feel each individual muscle throb from
standing all day. I have to give it to Zahra and UWU though; they really
did hire the best of the best. And Zahra did live up to her promise, because
the choreographer didn't force us into any routines. Instead, she worked
with each of us to find some stylistic signatures for our "Press Diamonds"
solos, then showed us a few stances and marks to hit while singing
together. In fact, I was kind of surprised that we all got more attention
individually than as a group, at least in terms of our talking points and
retro-futuristic styling.

I look at my phone and see it's midnight, and another wave of exhaustion hits me. The only thing that hits me harder is that I didn't have
any time to write a single lyric or correspond with a single fan-listener-
collaborator—my newly nicknamed "FLCs." I know I should get some
sleep before our fast-approaching 4:30 a.m. pickup for *Wake Up America*,
but I refuse to waste the creative runoff from such an intense day.

I sit up with a groan and decide to log ten minutes trying to connect
to as many FLCs as possible. Then, while everything still feels fresh, I'll
write. Both are way more important than sleep anyway.

I pop open the email app on my phone first, hoping to find a response
from Kree Duski. I was dying to hear her opinion on how I should navigate

this whole group thing, so I got her email address from Zahra and sent her a message the day after the finale. However, still nothing. Sighing, I open TikTok next. I already spent way too much time the last few nights scrolling through the #PressDiamonds challenge, so I head to my inbox instead.

I'm happy I landed on the name FLCs for now. I really needed a new word to capture this relationship that feels even more vital than sleep. It's so hard to describe, but I feel like there is something very real that happens when I connect with all these strangers online. It truly feels like a partnership, an intimate alignment of tastes and emotions and experiences. While I'm the one lucky enough to be given the privilege of a platform, it doesn't make me feel separate from my FLCs at all. Instead, it's their messages that always remind me what matters in all this—just like the girl I met in the car earlier today.

I generally try to avoid reading the comments, since anyone writing anonymously in a few seconds usually has nothing valuable to contribute. However, my DMs always managed to be a place for more personalized love and questions—okay, and the occasional sliding creepshow. However, as I scroll open my first few DMs, I realize that I must have struck a new nerve. These messages are *very* different.

I used to love you, but you sold out. You obviously abandoned all us original fans. You haven't posted a new song in months. You don't give a shit about us or your music, you just care about being famous in that group, you dumb sellout bitch. (From OOut678)

I can't help the tears that well in my eyes. No one cared enough to hate me before, so this message hits me like a punch in the gut. I guess if FLC support feels real and perfectly aligned with my tastes, then hate like this can align just as easily with my most insecure thoughts.

I look over the next few messages and it's a real mixed bag. There's some more hate about how ugly I am and how bad I am onstage, a few "I love you" notes, some questions about a feud with Dea, some threats not to mess with her, and a lot more "why haven't you posted new music in so long?" The fourteenth message, however, bowls me over once again.

> Everly, I don't usually write messages like this, but I just wanted to say your songs helped me through a really hard time. My dad recently passed away and your song about your own dad literally is the only thing that makes me feel better. Hope you can keep writing songs like that in Jeweltones. Your fan for life, Genny. (From GenGen99)

More tears spring forward.

How the hell am I supposed to absorb the meaningfulness of helping another human process their grief, but do that without absorbing the heat of someone calling me a sellout bitch? Don't they know I'm just another person, lying on my bed and looking at my phone before I fall asleep?

I try to remind myself this is the job of the artist: to be vulnerable, entertain others, and exist in an industry where we're criticized more than the average human. But sitting here now, I wonder how I'm supposed to access all my pain, all my sensitivity for my art in public, then shut it off in moments like these?

Through the exhaustion, a defensive anger seeps into my thoughts. Everyone wants me to post new songs like it's some right they are owed for having discovered me. Don't they know the energy it takes? Besides, it's not like I don't want to release new songs, but being contractually bound to not own anything I post right now makes it impossible. I'd love to scream about that publicly, but then I'm probably damned to scandal if I do. And I'm clearly damned to seem like a sellout if I don't.

If I was charged with emotion before, now I'm feeling supercharged. At least I know exactly what to do. I close my phone and roll out of bed, because sleep would be impossible now anyway. What I need to do is replace these messages with words of my own. I head into my new walk-in closet and go to the very back, where I've hung a few scarves to create a curtain that covers one large cubby. Pushing this veil aside, I exhale as I return to my private wonderland.

When I was a kid, I turned a part of the hall closet into my secret songwriting space—hidden in the empty nook behind the hanging coats. I then kept a portable version of this closet setup with me in my *SYWBAPS* hotel room. Now, with an enormous closet at my disposal, I've recreated a fuller version in my room once again. In fact, it's the only part of this new home I've actually settled into. Looking over my songwriting corner, both brand new and yet completely familiar, I feel myself relax. Here, *I am home.*

I use two elements to help inspire my songwriting and work through my process, but I usually only focus on one at a time during my sessions.

✦ Tonight, I am most drawn to the locked carrying case, which contains the trappings of the fictional town I love writing songs about: **Brooksville**. Right now, I need to get lost in this escapist world.
TURN TO PAGE 90

✦ Tonight, I am most drawn to my favorite guitar and the satchel of notebooks and creative tools—**pens, paper, picks**—that help me capture my creative moods. I need to channel my feelings into words and notes right now.
TURN TO PAGE 97

I have always written songs in the nerdiest and most private way possible. And usually in the early hours between midnight and morning, when everyone else is asleep and the residents of my secret town can spring awake, uninterrupted.

I snatch the key to the carrying case from its secret hiding spot, then slide it into the lock. Turning that key is still one of my favorite sounds of all time, unlocking my own little wonderland with a satisfying *click*. The case is the size of a big backpack, which means I can bring it with me everywhere. I'm sure Dad thinks I just keep more of my custom-matched collection of notebooks, pens, and picks in there, which is partially true.

Inside the central case rests a hidden town, complete with miniature plastic buildings and dollhouse replica props. The folded-map walls of the case fall gently to the floor and I unfurl them carefully, laying out a board-game-style spread of various terrains: parks, forests, and lakes. This is Brooksville.

I might have gotten this playset when I was younger, but I've spent years customizing it like a prized historical war scene recreator. Inside this diorama, I spin the tales of the residents of Brooksville like my own game of *The Sims* mashed with a daily soap opera. I usually only write for five or ten minutes, drifting from character to storyline as it feels right, writing whatever flows to mind and entertaining myself. Really, if there were a vision board I'd like to present to Jeweltones, this would be it. Of course, I've never told another living soul about Brooksville. *Ever.* And I doubt anyone would understand it. Even if they did, it might ruin the magic. This is the only place where I can create for the pure sake of creating, unencumbered and without pressure.

It's also one of the secrets behind my songwriting. Once the story has progressed a bit, I see if there's anything interesting enough to mine for a song. How does an eighteen-year-old without much experience with love or travel write about discovery and heartbreak? Through her beloved fictional characters, of course.

Sure, my own life bleeds into the stories of Brooksville, but usually it's easier to filter my dreams and emotions subconsciously through the townspeople, writing about them like real people with some mix of empathy and objectivity. Take, for example, the town's newest resident. Lucy Diamond is a teenager who suddenly moved to town because her mom needed to move in with her semi-wicked aunt. Lucy's first cousin has recruited her into their friend group, The Rings. She doesn't like them, but she feels the need to stay loyal in order to make new friends. Unfortunately, the only person Lucy truly connects with happens to be her cousin's long-time boyfriend, Blake.

Looking over the little figurines I chose for Lucy and The Rings, I have them all currently sitting outside the makeshift high school. While this echoes how I never really found the right social groove in high school myself, I actually introduced Lucy to Brooksville when I made it onto *SO YOU WANNA BE A POP STAR?*

I reach for my latest Brooksville-specific notebook, which is always marbled in different colors, and realize it's time for Lucy to decide what she wants: popularity and acceptance, forbidden love with Blake, or the brave authenticity to seek a different friend group in this strange new town. After all, witchy covens are very real in Brooksville, along with tribes of talking animals. My world, my rules.

As my pen hits the ruled paper to capture this exact thought, I realize that before I decide on a path for Lucy, writing a song about her crossroads feels appropriate. Immediately, a chord plays in my mind, very minor, along with an eerily comforting note progression. Before I know it, a discordant song begins to assemble itself, one I title "Damned If You Don't."

Songs never really come to me in any usual order. Sometimes it's lyrics first, other times it's a concept and a sound. The only pattern I recognize? Brooksville always delivers me something, as long as I deliver myself to Brooksville.

What would anyone—Jeweltones, Zahra, the label, all those new listeners—think if they knew this was how I wrote "Press Diamonds"? To be honest, that song is really about Lucy and The Rings, about me trying to understand my peers and our fishbowl existence in the reality competition through fiction. What would they do if they knew all this life-changing fame and money for everyone started in a closet with plastic playsets and little painted figures? All I do know is that throughout this group experiment, Brooksville needs to remain pure. It's my safe space, my creative well, my source of sanity.

Remembering this, I plunge back in. Looking over the characters, I think of the perfect way to force Lucy into making a choice. It's about time in the fictional season for the annual Fall Formal at Brooksville High. It's a spooky event, vampiric and witchy, where every student must choose which infamous afterparty to attend—assuming they're invited in the first place. This single decision cements everyone's social status for the upcoming year. It's the perfect encapsulation of the decision Lucy must make—who is she going to afterparty with?

As I scribble all this down, that grim fairytale melody replays in my head. I begin to play with some lyrics to match the story and the dissonant chords, editing myself as I go.

DAMNED IF YOU DON'T

All dressed up for the ~~dance~~ ball
~~Mask~~ Masquerade or wrecking
It'll be your call
Crimson lip, blood red fire
Ocean eyes, frost blue ice
They'll know if you're naughty
They'll know if you're nice
So which version of ~~Lucy~~ you will rule this night?

Before I contemplate a chorus, I feel like Lucy Diamond needs to seal her fate.

❖ Lucy needs to strike out to find some enchanting new friends. She should go to the **Rebel** Rabbit afterparty and be done with The Rings. Even if that means she also needs to leave Blake behind.
TURN TO PAGE 94

❖ Lucy should become the **HWIC** (Head Witch in Charge) of The Rings, using the power and popularity they offer to take what she wants—including Blake.
TURN TO PAGE 96

If Lucy follows the path of The Rings, many social doors might open for her, but she'll never get to be the hero in her own story. She deserves to chart her own path, even if she has no idea where it might lead.

However, actually forging down this path will be a story to write another day. I've learned that the best way to get any writing done is to set realistic expectations for myself. If I'd told myself I needed to come in here and write a whole new chapter for Lucy and finish her entire song, I'd have felt too overwhelmed to even start—especially after a full day of meetings and rehearsals. Part of creating art is to just keep moving, and tonight making this huge decision for Lucy feels like enough. When I have more time and energy, I can dive into what the Rebel Rabbit afterparty looks like—and just what magical things it means to hang with them.

But before I close my notebook, a line for the chorus to "Damned If You Don't" occurs to me. My pen glides across the paper, feeling like the words flow out of me:

> Some days, you need ~~to know when~~ to throw in the towel
> Some nights, you need ~~to know how~~ to push through the pain
> Some days, you need to hold ~~your ground~~ the stillness
> Some nights, you need to blaze a new ~~trail~~ path
> Some times, you'll be damned if you do
> But every time, you'll be damned if you don't

Reading over this new chorus, I like it, but I'm not sure it fits the spookier first verse I wrote. I'll probably have to decide which I like better and rewrite the other. As I pack up for the night, I think the core of this song just revealed itself to me. Being an artist is truly just about staying in the game. Even when you fail or things don't go the way you wanted them to, it's not a loss.

The only way to lose is to quit playing altogether.

Taking one last deep breath, I jot this latest thought down, thinking it might make for a good replacement verse or even a bridge. I'm probably also going to have to change the discordant melody if I stick with this new direction, since the tone might now call for something more acoustically warm.

With these notes made, I force myself to leave the closet. I need to power down my brain. If I keep going on this track tired as I am right now, I'll only run myself around in circles.

Sometimes, it's a thin line between inspiration and obsession.

TURN TO PAGE 105

So what if Blake is Lucy's FBF's BF (fake best friend's boyfriend)? Lucy is going to put a spell on everyone until they belong to her.

The music for "I Put a Spell on You" then begins to roll through my mind, so I instantly decide that "Damned If You Don't" needs some witchy energy. Because in Brooksville, covens are real—and Lucy is about to build her own from the ruins she'll wreck amidst The Rings.

> Say this, wear that
> Sing what they ~~say~~ want 'til ~~I~~ you scream
> It only feels like ~~I'm~~ you're damned if ~~I~~ you do
> So say that, wear this
> Scream what ~~I~~ you want in ~~my~~ your wildest dreams
> Because ~~I~~ you know ~~I'll~~ you'll be damned if ~~I~~ you don't

I finish jotting the lines, editing the lyrics and perspective as I go. Then, looking them over again, I realize I didn't achieve any actual witchy vibes. Which means I'll need to bring that spookiness through in the vocals over my hauntingly comforting melody instead.

Shifting gears, I scribble a few sentences chronicling Lucy's decision, then I force my notebook closed. Writing the consequences of her choice can wait for another night. Standing to pack Brooksville, I feel the familiar pang of guilt that maybe I should do just a little bit more. But then I tell myself I should be proud of tonight's work. One crucial story beat and a song's chorus is far more than enough—especially after the grueling day I've had. Besides, if I tasked myself with more than that, I never would have sat down in here to begin with.

Songwriting, like any art, is like mining or a marathon. You only get the big milestones completed if you chip away inch by grueling inch, step by digestible step.

And I deserve to feel like today's steps have been enough.

TURN TO PAGE 105

Reaching for my leather satchel, I notice how heavy it's getting, crammed with my entire collection of notebooks, pens, and guitar picks. I keep the archive of all my filled-up notebooks in a lockbox at Dad's house, but I suppose this heavy satchel of supplies is one of the perils of my songwriting practice remaining so tactile.

Ever since I was little, I've loved collecting unique notebooks and pens. I never really kept a linear journal, but I always captured things on paper: emotions, experiences I want to remember, phrases, drawings. Pretty early on I began scattering this all through different curated notebook and pen combinations, picking up a design and style out of my collection that felt right—and I'm always on the hunt for new additions. Once I started writing songs and playing guitar, I transferred the habit to new sets of notebooks.

Sometimes I mine material from my fictional world of Brooksville first, but anything worthy of a song eventually ends up in this expansive notebook collection. Adding in my keyboard and my guitars—along with a capo, tuner, extra strings, and a canister of picks—I'm like a one-woman caravan. Somehow, I find that the physical trappings help my brain focus my many inspirations into the confines of a song.

Feeling the way I do right now, I know exactly which notebook to reach for. The cover is plain black with gold letters on the front reading **To Be Continued . . .** This is the notebook where I keep all my works-in-progress, appropriately worn and frayed at the edges. I'd already paired it with a sleek, golden pen, so I slide both out of the satchel along with a black guitar pick from the canister. This notebook rests against one of my newest additions, the one I bought in the hotel gift shop the first week of *SYWBAPS* filming: a white spiral notebook covered in black geometric diamonds.

I wrote the lyrics to "Press Diamonds" in this spiral notebook since it obviously has lots of physical thematic stuff to work with. I had already named a Brooksville character Lucy Diamond, after the Beatles song and this geometric notebook design. Who knew those little decisions would inspire a song that sparked this entire Jeweltones phenomenon?

Really, I wish I could just present these notebooks as my vision board to Jeweltones, but I've never told another solitary soul about the truth behind this part of my songwriting process. My loved ones know I write mostly in the middle of the night, and Dad knows about my secret closet space and my notebooks obsession, but no one really knows the full picture. Writing in these notebooks has always been my way to become aware of my thoughts before I choose which ones to let pass and which ones to empower. This externalization isn't just a creative process, it's also like therapy and prayer rolled into one—the only time I feel completely present and lose all sense of time. I guess that happens for other musicians onstage, but for me that kind of zone-flow only happens here, tucked away in a closet. This is probably why I reach for the black **To Be Continued . . .** notebook—to get back to my own roots.

I know exactly where to flip to find one of the first songs I ever started, about what I imagined heartbreak would feel like. I have the guitar chords and the melody locked in my head because that part of the song, lilting and aching, hasn't changed much. However, I've fiddled with the lyrics for years, never quite finishing it. I think it's because I want to fall in love for the first time before I can begin to even fathom heartbreak. Then again, another part of me thinks I just want the comfort of leaving this song unfinished so I can slip back into it like an old hoodie whenever I want.

I look down at the page now, where lyrics are written with doodles of all kinds of abstract hearts in the margins:

HEART TO RAGE

It didn't happen yesterday
But it sure does feel that way
You wore a backpack
For you that was new
Until I realized it was full
Of the stuff I had given you
Faded novels
Cracked-edge picture frames
You gathered every scrap

For the flames
I didn't know why
Still don't think I do
All I have is this shattered heart
Devoted to you

Tale as old as lie
Song so old begs why
All the clichés in the world
Don't add up to much
Except this broken trust
This hollowed husk
A pen on the page
A voice on the stage
Just wish I could find
The heart to rage

It didn't happen yesterday
But there is where I stay
Trying to find anger
To move my bones
Just not ready
To throw the right stones
I blame myself
It keeps you around my head
This long after
You proclaimed us dead

Suddenly, one more lyric occurs to me, hitting like a lightning strike. *Ocean so dark, didn't see the wave 'til it crashed. Water so deep, can't tell swimming up from down.* I jot it down, knowing this is the line I wrote that night on the finale party roof, the night before everything changed. The night I learned about Dea and . . . Stern.

Instead of unpacking that thought, I start doodling. I used to think this kind of thing was just procrastinating, but I started realizing that sometimes my best creative instincts would surface while sketching. Apparently, it's a thing and it happens to people while showering or driving or going to the bathroom. For me, doodling helps settle my creative gut more than anything else.

I draw a crashing wave in the upper margin over a beach made of heart-shaped sand. There's enough room under the rest of the wave to fit a figure, so I've started drawing a person there. The outline is getting to the point where I need to decide who is caught under this wave of heartbreak.

Staring down at this doodle, it suddenly strikes me who belongs there.

❖ I see **myself** standing under the wave. The only heartbreak I've ever known has come from my career.
TURN TO PAGE 101

❖ I see Stern **Green** standing under the wave. He's the one bound to break my heart.
TURN TO PAGE 103

All along, I've been waiting to finish "Heart to Rage" because I've been waiting to fall in love for the first time. But sitting here in this closet, it suddenly hits me: I've always been in love—it has just been with music. And if there's more than one type of love, that means there's also more than one type of heartbreak.

And being pulled into the riptide of Jeweltones certainly has the potential to crack my songwriting heart.

Looking over the lyrics I have rewritten on the page, another wave suddenly overtakes me. My pen moves like it's possessed, editing certain parts so the song can take on this new meaning.

> ~~You~~ I wore a backpack
> ~~For you~~ That wasn't new
> ~~Until I realized it was full~~
> ~~Of the stuff I had given you~~
> Then you stole
> What I already planned to give you
>
> I blame myself
> It keeps you around ~~my head~~ this abyss
> This long after
> You ~~proclaimed us dead~~ broke our promise
> Ocean so dark
> Didn't see the wave 'til ~~it crashed~~ the pound
> Water so deep
> Can't tell swimming up from down

I finish this first pass and immediately feel strange. Did I just evolve this song to the next level, or did I just abandon something vital? That question seems to be plaguing me quite a lot lately. Either way, I certainly feel . . . uncomfortable.

As an artist, sometimes it's impossible to tell if that's a sign of growth or danger.

I decide to call it a night and close my notebook. Part of getting writing done is setting realistic expectations. If I'd told myself I needed to finish this whole song after a full day of photo shoots and rehearsals, I'd have felt too overwhelmed to even try. I'll sort out what this potential edit really means when I have more time and energy.

For tonight, this step was enough.

And for tomorrow, the question I need to answer feels a little bit clearer.

TURN TO PAGE 105

The thought hits me with such a splash of clarity that I have to put my pen down. *I have real feelings for Stern.* I can try to deny it or hide it all I want, but the feelings are there.

And not being able to express them has the potential to break my heart.

I was trying to write this song about being broken up with, but what if this is really about unrequited love? No, that's not right. Stern has shown he has some kind of interest in me too. This is different. This is about being two worlds apart, about being next to each other but forced apart, about . . .

Forbidden love.

With this new lens, I then begin poring over the lyrics I've written and watch as these familiar words suddenly charge with new energy. I pick up my pen to shift the framework, changing certain parts so the song can take on this new meaning.

~~You wore a backpack, thought~~ You met me on the roof
~~for you that~~ That was new
~~Until I realized it was full~~
~~Of the stuff I had given you~~
But quick as you came
I just withdrew
~~Faded novels~~ Guitar strings
Cracked-edge picture frames

All I have is this ~~shattered~~ aching heart
Devoted to you

I blame myself
It keeps you around ~~my head~~ this abyss
This long after
~~You proclaimed us dead~~ We lost all our promise
~~Ocean so dark~~
~~Didn't see the wave 'til it crashed~~

~~Water so deep~~
~~Can't tell swimming up from down~~
Standing beside you
We looked at the ocean
~~Unable to~~ Couldn't see the wave coming
To ~~steal~~ crush our ~~devotion~~ emotion

Finishing my edit, I have no idea yet if I've just made this song better or worse. I'm tempted to give it another pass, but instead I close the notebook. It'd be easy to feel guilty about not doing more right now, but instead I force myself to feel proud. I came in here to take a step forward in my longest-running song, and I just took a major leap. Even if I don't know whether this leap was in the right direction, I've done my job for the night—especially after the day I've had.

Songwriting, like any art, is just about taking that next step. Most days feel like you're crawling inches, until one day you turn around and realize you've run an entire marathon.

As I pack up my things and put the closet back the way it was, I try to focus on this thought. Somehow, unbelievably, these songwriting questions are way easier to swallow than the realization I've just had about Stern. I guess, these days, neither is totally under my control.

But at least in this safe space, I can pretend I'm the master of some universe.

TURN TO PAGE 105

Suddenly, a pang of dread hits me. *How can I write more authentic songs for Jeweltones without compromising this deeply personal process?*

I'm not sure I can.

As I sit with this thought, it opens another door in my mind. *Fine, I can't write my own songs for Jeweltones. But what if I tried writing* with *them?*

Just then, there's a knock at my bedroom door. I carefully leave my songwriting corner, pulling the scarf-curtain as I go and making sure to close the walk-in closet door behind me. I don't need anyone wandering into my secret lair.

I wonder who it could be at this hour as I open the door to my room. I'm quite surprised to find Stern standing there. He wears pajama bottoms and a giant hoodie along with tousled hair and an apologetic smile.

"I hope I'm not bothering you. Yours was the only other light on in the house," he explains. My eyes catch on the large ice cubes in his glass of whiskey. "Could it be that this group has another insomniac?"

"Sorry to say, but you might be the only one," I answer, suddenly feeling the weight of the day and my aching muscles all over again. "I sleep fine, I just get my best songwriting done around now."

Stern looks at me then like I'm some mythical creature. I mean, I'm probably playing the part with my oversized nightgown and my hair in a messy bun.

"I don't mean to interrupt the magic . . ."

"I was just wrapping up," I say. "But tell me, what keeps Stern Green up at night?"

He hesitates a moment, like he's used to providing some rehearsed answer to this question. Then something in his face shifts.

"If I tell you the truth, will you promise to keep it a secret?"

My ears flash hot, despite myself. I nod, afraid my words might betray me.

Stern proceeds to lift the bottom of his hoodie and my breath catches in my throat. I get a whiff of him as he does—rain and oatmeal and tea tree oil. Then my eyes catch on his stomach, his skin dusted with blond baby hairs and rippling with individual muscles. Until I see what Stern really means to show me. There is a long red rash along his torso covered with some homemade-looking ointment.

"I have pretty bad eczema," Stern says before dropping his hoodie. "It's always worse at night and the itching wakes me up."

"Every night?" I ask.

"It comes and goes, but most nights, yeah. Do you mind?"

I follow Stern's eyes as he looks into my room at the corner with my guitar cases, which never all fit in my songwriting closet. It's probably not a good idea, but I nod and let him in anyway. He walks over and unearths one of my favorite guitars, a dark mahogany Fender. Surprising me yet again, he then begins strumming some chords.

"I didn't know you played."

"I'm just okay," Stern replies. "It's not something I wanted to advertise in a music competition. Especially one with you in it."

I can't help but smile, even though I shouldn't.

"Maybe I should start devoting my eczema nights to songwriting instead of whiskey and wandering? Or instead of reading what everyone writes about me on social media?"

"Ah. I'm not the only one?" I walk over to grab my second guitar, a folk acoustic Yamaha. I guess of all the things I should start unpacking, this is a good place to start.

"Mostly I have lots of spam from teen girls. And adult gay guys," Stern says. "It's weird, feeling like this object to them."

"Says the guy with the perfect shirtless selfie game," I reply. I mean to be playful, but Stern seems barely able to fake a smile.

"Do you know how much time I spend filtering out and color-correcting red spots? That image helped me make it here, so now I need to keep the perfect image up."

A dark look clouds Stern's face, so I try to think of the right silver lining.

"Do you really have to, though? Now that we have this platform, what if you were transparent about showing your real skin . . . and maybe people would embrace the real you?"

Stern laughs, then catches himself.

"Sorry, I don't mean to be rude," he says. "It's just, social media is brutal enough already. The hateful stuff . . . they all think I'm only in Jeweltones because of the way I look and perform, not because they see me as an artist. Not like you. If I take away the one thing people love about me, what do I have left to offer?"

Stern's honesty knocks me back a little. My brain feels foggy, so I'm not sure what to say. Over my silence, Stern stops strumming and takes a sip of his drink.

"It's a little ironic, maybe?" Stern continues. "I use my looks to get what I dreamed of, but that dream is messing up my looks. I mean, the eczema definitely gets worse when I'm stressed, and well, hello, the last few months. I'm just thankful it tends not to show on my face, but I haven't had a full night's sleep in . . . I can't even remember. I scratch in my sleep and don't usually wake up until I'm already bleeding. The cleaning staff back at that hotel had to throw out so many sets of my sheets, I started sleeping on a towel to spare them the trouble."

I want to ask Stern if he has tried night gloves or something, but judging from the homemade ointment I saw, I'm sure there's nothing I can suggest offhand that he hasn't already tried. It's just . . . that sounds so awful. I hate to think he has been suffering in silence all this time.

"I'm sorry, I don't mean to unload," he says with an apologetic glance. "It's just strange being here. Isolating?"

A part of me is tempted to remind Stern he has Dea here if he feels alone. But there is a larger part of me that doesn't want him to pull back.

"I guess I'm not sure how to keep up with this Jeweltones explosion yet," he goes on. "Even though it's literally all I've thought about having every day since I moved to LA."

"I guess you came here thinking you'd be discovered right away?" I say, trying not to sound too judgmental.

"Well, can you blame me? Some of us *do* get discovered right away," Stern replies, smirking at me.

I smile at the floor where Stern has placed his drink. He starts strumming again, and it makes me think maybe I should practice what I preach.

"Yeah, but maybe that's not such a good thing?" I finally say. "What if I'm just not ready for all this like I thought I was? I mean, you've seen how I lock up onstage. I know I can channel emotion into my performances in more intimate settings, but why do the stage lights make me freeze?"

"That's just a matter of experience. You'll get the hang of it."

Stern doesn't mean to, but his dismissal nudges me.

"But what if I don't?" I push. "I'm just as afraid of not meeting expectations as you."

"You're right," he says, straightening up and stopping his strumming. "It's just, I don't think you know how lucky you are to be sitting here on your first try. Or what it's like to be told no over and over. To be overlooked, undervalued. That silence is . . ."

Stern searches for the word but can't seem to find it. Then he looks at me, fear burning in his emerald eyes.

"I just have to get this right, Everly. I can't go back to living in a shitty apartment with three other guys again, task-building furniture to afford enough gas to drive to another audition I'll be rejected from anyway. I tried everything before. No one believed in me as a laid-back singer type, but if they believe in this boy band slick face, then that's who I'll be."

Staring at Stern, hearing the hurt in his voice, I can practically see the pressure sitting on his shoulders. It tightens that familiar knot in my chest.

"You're good at building furniture?" I joke.

"Yeah, IKEA is my jam," Stern laughs. "Though I actually got an awesome gig as a manny earlier this year. I love kids. I think I'd be the ideal stay-at-home-dad. Someday."

Stern pauses, picking up his glass to drain it.

"I had to quit that job to stay on the show."

There are so many things I want to say to him. *Stop numbing yourself out. You're perfect the way you are. You should be telling all this to your girlfriend.*

Unless, of course, he already has.

"I'm sorry, there I go again," Stern says, focusing back on the guitar. "I get like this at night when everyone else is asleep. I'd talk to Dea if she were awake."

I try not to let it show on my face, the ice that suddenly freezes my body. Stern stares at me, a softness settling in his eyes. I just wish I knew what he sees when he looks at me.

"It's just, I keep wondering . . ." he starts again. "What do you do when the thing you love is burning you out faster than you can outrun?"

Hearing these words, something inside me clicks. I might not know how to say all the things I want to tell Stern out loud, but it's like they bubble through my fingers, spilling out across the guitar I hold. Pretty quickly I find a minor chord progression that matches what I'm feeling right now.

Stern seems a little surprised at first, but he also looks down at his guitar strings. Then, to my own surprise, he starts improvising a melodic line over the chords. Whatever else we might be losing in translation, somehow this . . . fits. It doesn't take very long for us to lock in together.

Then, staring back at Stern, I sing the question he just spoke in his simple melody.

"What do you do when the thing you love,
Burns you out faster than you can run?"

Stern is so startled that he loses the melody for a moment. He quickly readjusts, finding our rhythm again. Then, once the moment comes back around, Stern sings these new lyrics with me in harmony.

Our voices sound *right* together. Like honey and apples, or caramel and salt.

Then Stern looks back at me, amazed.

And I know exactly what he sees now.

❖ I **lean forward** to kiss Stern.
TURN TO PAGE 110

❖ "I don't think Dea would be too thrilled about this," I say as I **stop playing**. Too many things would break if we decide to cross this line.
TURN TO PAGE 111

Deep in the recesses of my brain, a scream bubbles up. It tells me to stop, to not make this particular mess. That it might be too much to come back from.

But in this moment, my feelings for Stern overwrite all of that. I don't care if this is going to sabotage everything. Not if there's a chance he wants to kiss me back.

"Everly, we can't," Stern says, leaning away from me.

I pull back too, instantly mortified.

"It's not that I don't want to," he says quietly, looking pained. "It's just, the group. And—"

"—Dea," I finish for him.

"Yes, of course," Stern answers. "But I was going to say I don't want to ruin things between us. What we just wrote . . . that was like magic to me. And you matter to me, Everly."

I know he means well, but these words cut like knives. I know I'll feel embarrassed later, but right now all I feel is the pressing need for armor.

"Then you probably shouldn't have come to my room in the middle of the night," I say, standing up.

"Everly, I—"

"—You should go."

I turn away before Stern has a chance to see the involuntary tears filling my eyes. Then I make a beeline for the closet. My songwriting corner is the only place that might make any of this bearable.

I don't know if it's better or worse, but I hear Stern leave my bedroom instead of coming deeper inside to check on me.

At least, shut away in here, I know exactly what to do.

TURN TO PAGE 112

I force myself to think about the group. About Dea. About my own relationship with Stern and the song we just started.

I hope that if I focus on these things, I won't think about how Stern's struggle feels like a mirror of my own, or about how full and perfect his lips look, or how good he sounds playing one of my guitars.

Stern takes a deep, heavy breath.

"No, she wouldn't. But Dea and I don't . . ."

Stern trails off, leaving me dying to hear him finish that sentence. *You and Dea don't what? Connect like this? Write spontaneous songs together? Have a real relationship yet?*

"I remember when you and Dea were inseparable back at the beginning of all this," Stern says instead. "How did you end up here? It all happened so fast."

I don't want it to, but I feel my guard fly up anyway. I'm too . . . a lot of things this late at night to fight it.

"Dea has proven over and over what her priorities are. And that she can't be trusted," I answer, sounding more tense than I intend.

Stern looks down at the guitar. "So where does that leave us?"

"Us, the group?" I ask. "Or us . . . you and me?"

Stern's gaze rises to meet mine. He doesn't need to speak any words for me to know exactly what he means.

We sit like this for a beat before Stern stands to go. I want to stop him. I don't want to leave things like this. But I also don't have any idea what to say.

Which is why I let Stern leave without a single word.

TURN TO PAGE 112

CHAPTER SEVEN
VINNY

WASHING MY HANDS IN THE BATHROOM SINK, I HARDLY RECOG-
nize myself. Not because of the makeup left over from our *Wake Up America* performance earlier this morning—I'm clearly quite fond of a full-face beat. No, what I don't recognize is how puffy my face looks or how the purple bags under my eyes already start to show through the concealer. My body seems to be rebelling against me the exact week I need to look my best.

Forcing myself to scrub this thought along with my hands, I try to be thankful my stomach held out all morning in the first place. It might be angry with me now, but at least I didn't have to run offstage in the middle of our "Press Diamonds" performance.

Walking out of my gorgeous bedroom suite—which I haven't even had proper time to personalize yet—I head to the stairs to rejoin the group. After getting dropped off from taping the show, we all took ten minutes to gather ourselves before watching our segment together. I feel both exhausted and emptied, but also giddy as hell. The whole morning was a surreal blur of dressing rooms, famous strangers, and shining brightly. Yet it all felt weirdly familiar after the competition show grind.

Entering the lavish den now, I find everyone else already arranged along the sectional sofa—including Mom and Everly's dad, sitting far too close for comfort.

"Vinny, finally!" Mom proclaims. "Steve has to get to the office soon, but I skipped to the Jeweltones segment. I also made a spread. You kids must be starving!"

I smile at her, but have to fight a frown when I see the brunch she has lovingly assembled: a frittata, sausage and bacon, bagels and lox, and a fresh fruit platter. All of which looks delicious—and almost none of which I'm supposed to eat. Turns out, when I finally got to my food allergy blood test results after finale night, I understood why the nutritionist had been calling me nonstop. My delayed-reaction allergy count came to forty-five out of the one-hundred-fifty foods they test for.

Most people only get three to five.

I used to hate that LA stereotype of gluten-dairy-joy-free nonsense, but now I have become that nonsense based on the nutritionist's elimination diet. I'm supposed to not eat any allergens for three months to give my inflamed stomach time to heal, then I'm supposed to reintroduce allergen foods one by one to see what really affects me. The idea of cutting out so many foods at once is equal parts devastating and daunting—I've never, *ever* had the discipline to control what I eat before. Food has always served as too much of a comfort blanket—too much of a source of joy.

But as I've learned these last few days, being handed a piece of paper detailing foods that are somewhat proven to make me feel sick is pretty proper motivation. Plus, I've felt enough constant stomach woes to know I have to change something. Now cut to me having eaten nothing but rice, potatoes, meat, and vegetables cooked in avocado oil for the last few days.

Naturally, I thought this depressing diet would at least make me feel better, but nope. According to every inflammation influencer ever, it takes several days for the body to detox from eating years of allergens. And boy, is my body detoxing: fevers, chills, nausea, diarrhea, cramps—all topped off with the most vivid nightmares I've ever experienced. It feels so counterintuitive to be healing myself in the long term by doing something that makes me feel infinitely worse in the short term. The only thing keeping me going is seeing that my body is quite obviously expelling some shit it doesn't like—literally.

Of course, this unexpected food journey doesn't make catching my bearings during this surreal Jeweltones week any easier. My LA pop star life suddenly looks unrecognizable from my former New York high school existence. How could I have known walking into that one audition would lead me here, just like venturing to take one simple blood test would be equally life-changing?

The only familiar feature is Mom, who scrounged together enough for a one-way flight to LA after the finale. It feels invaluable to have her here, but at the same time she refuses to accept any of this food allergy stuff. It's like it hurts her Italian heart, or maybe she just feels guilty for not helping me figure this out sooner. Either way, not having her come around on this restrictive diet—like not even putting out one fully allergen-free brunch item for her only son—makes me feel super frustrated. Oh, and there's another wonderful side effect of this food withdrawal: mood swings like you wouldn't believe.

I try to push this all down for now, telling myself that the sudden flush of accompanying sadness I feel over seeing Mom with another man is also just the hunger talking. Instead of wallowing in my feelings, I pick out some approved fruits from the platter and settle on the sofa. Then I try not to cry thinking about all the waffles and pancakes and croissants I miss so desperately, averting my eyes from everyone else's full plates as they get settled as well. Just one week ago, none of us could have fathomed that our breakfast club would take so many dramatic turns.

"Who wants to be a morning show star?" I sing-shout operatically. I might be forcing it, but I refuse to let my stomach woes turn me into a full Debbie Downer.

"Not me," CeCe says through a mouthful of bacon. "Anyone else feel like it's none of our business how we perform? I just do what feels right."

I turn to Everly and Dea, but neither one jumps to agree. Which tracks. Dea is all rehearse-until-seemingly-effortless, while Everly still has no idea what to do with herself onstage.

"I'm with you, CeCe," Stern replies. "I hate watching myself back. Anyone else want a mimosa? Celebrations and distractions in one fizzy glass?"

"None of us are twenty-one yet," CeCe says, her eyes flashing to the parents here.

Stern's spirits seem to collapse with his shoulders. I'd feel bad about how hard he tries to be our cheerleader, but like CeCe, I cannot bring myself to weep for our six-pack poster child. Although, judging by the look on Stern's face right now, maybe I really should give him a break. I'm sure there's a world where he feels alienated here—the straight, cis-white dude in a gaggle of girls and gays. Darling, imagine that! Still, maybe it's time I tried a little harder to bond with Mr. Green Eyes, for the sake of the group?

Mercifully, Mom hits play before any more tension can build. Hushed by the sudden appearance of our HD selves, we all stare up at the flatscreen. I feel both mortified and mesmerized. There we are, the brand-new Jeweltones, being introduced by America's morning sweetheart.

"Do I always look so . . . intense?" CeCe asks, watching herself open our repeat performance. "That's a lot for 7 a.m."

"Yes, and yes," I answer, shooting CeCe a smile. "Be still our beating ruby hearts, dear."

CeCe smirks and shrugs as the pre-chorus arrives, with my belting voice booming loud as ever. Hopefully it's enough to drown out how puffy my face looks from all the detoxing.

"You sound incredible, Vinny," Stern says. "That's nothing new, but damn."

Flashing Stern a grin, I see the rest of the den has fallen into awed silence at the sound of my voice. I *do* sound particularly good. Could it be that something I was eating before was affecting my throat? I look over at Mom and find she has actual tears streaming down her cheeks. Sometimes I forget how much freaking fun it is to have a killer voice, so I thank my Britney Jean "Lucky" stars for that, despite everything else.

The chorus arrives and my eyes shift to Everly onscreen. It's such a shame—she might have written this song, but her presence still recedes into the background when she's next to the four of us. I really should find a way to help her come out of her shell onstage. Maybe I'll go through some of the standard musical cast exercises to loosen her up?

I glance at her, expecting to see red cheeks and a pained expression. Instead, I find Everly looking at Stern, then looking away immediately when he turns to her. I thought something weird was going on between them this morning, but I just assumed it was 5 a.m. pre-show jitters. Watching them now, I wonder if there's something extra brewing there like I always suspected. Divas above, I hope not. The last thing the group needs is a love triangle between Stern, Dea, and Everly.

To my relief, Stern turns away from Everly to watch Dea with pride as she works it on the stage. She really does dazzle a little more than the rest of us . . . which is probably good, because Dea barely hits her notes today. I'm sure it doesn't help that Everly wrote such a shady verse for her, but still.

"Dea, you're freaking iconic," I tell her, seeing that she's already picking her performance apart. She smiles over at me gratefully, but I still see the critical harshness in her eye.

Whatever our next song is, I wonder if Dea would ever consider fully committing to rap-singing? Unfortunately, the little vocal lessons I tried to give her back on the show never yielded much. She does have a cool cadence and smooth tone when she sings, and I can teach pitch or breath control, but she'll still need to work within her limited range. We need to find a way for her to lean further into her strengths instead of grasping to adapt to Everly's twisting melodies.

I catch myself mid-thought as all these ideas and instincts run through my mind . . .

Do I actually want this group to work?

I don't even know when this mental switch flipped, but sitting here watching our performance, I find myself suddenly hoping Jeweltones isn't a lost cause. I mean, despite our behind-the-music woes, we did turn out yet another killer performance when it mattered most. That's got to mean something, right?

Looking across the room again, I catch CeCe's eye. She raises an eyebrow at me as if to say, *see what I mean about our potential?*

I give her a small shrug and a wink.

I may not be completely convinced we can really make this all click, but I do know one thing: I like what we've done so far. Not to mention that I don't have much of a life or a career to return to if this all suddenly goes south. So maybe this really is where I'm supposed to be for now, while I figure myself out?

"Kids, that was wonderful," Steve says once the performance ends, beaming.

I turn to look at Mom, who is clapping beside him and still crying. Seeing Everly's dad so proud, then seeing Mom right beside him . . . out of nowhere, something about it suddenly turns my stomach. Literally.

"You all finish watching the interview without me," I blurt, unable to hold back. "Nature calls again."

♦ ♦ ♦

It must be ten minutes, but when I walk back into my room feeling exhausted and emptied, I find Mom waiting there for me.

"You feeling okay?" she asks, looking worried.

"The usual," I reply.

"Vinny, are you sure this elimination diet—"

"—Yes, I need to see it through," I snap. "And what I need from you is to be supportive, not questioning it every step. It's already hard enough."

"I'm sorry, you're right," Mom replies, surprising me. Usually she's much more the clap-back, tough-love type. Do I really look so crappy that she'll let me get away with this?

"You know, your dad would be so proud of you."

Ah, there it is. Now it's my turn for tears to well up.

"I know."

Mom and I stare at each other for a long beat, dancing this hauntingly familiar dance. I'm afraid if I hug her now I'll just melt.

"You all did well in the interview after the performance too," Mom pivots, and I'm thankful for both our sakes. "Though that seems to be where Stern comes alive, little charmer he is."

"Yeah, it felt like he was glowing a little brighter there," I say with a sigh. "The rest of us also felt a little rehearsed in person. Did it seem that way on camera?"

"A little. But rehearsed is better than everyone being honest right now, yeah?"

"Yeah," I sigh again. "Did you hear how many times they asked us about our next song? And our first album? It's like, it hasn't even been a week, and everyone is already looking for our next hit."

"That's only because they are," Mom says. "But Zahra has that retreat planned for you tomorrow; you'll sort yourselves out there. In the meantime, I have my glue stick hands fully prepped for your vision board. I took off my nails and everything."

As Mom waves her acrylic-free hands, I finally lean forward and hug her. Thankfully, the detoxing loss-of-impulse-control isn't all bad.

When I release her, however, she has a strange look on her face.

"What?" I ask.

"I have something I need to show you. Before you see it on your own."

Mom reaches into her back pocket, giving me a moment to populate conspiracy theories about potential on-camera sweat stains or nostril items. Then she shows me an article from the gossip site *CherriPop*—the same one that reported Everly's manager meeting yesterday. This time, the headline features just about the last story I'd expect:

New Romantics in Jeweltones! Move aside Stern and Dea, things are heating up between Everly's dad and Vinny's mom in the band's brand-new mansion!

Underneath the headline is a photo of Mom getting into her car with Steve outside of a Beverly Hills restaurant, both laughing and looking very happy.

Seeing this, I can't help the tight knot my throat twists itself into. With all the force in my body I try not to let my sadness show on my face. It's not just about Mom dating again, it's also that I don't want any of my own private business leaked this way. Been there, done that, darling. Luckily, Mom is too giddy to notice how clenched I've become.

"Can you believe I'm in a tabloid? I wanted to show you because Steve and I did get lunch together. I want to check with you before it goes any further—to make sure you're not uncomfortable."

I stare back at her for a moment, wondering if she means uncomfortable with her dating my highly sensitive groupmate's dad, or uncomfortable with it being out in the gossip mill? The answer is both, but I haven't seen Mom this excited in years. Plus, she did fly across the country to support me and take care of this group of teenagers while their own parents remained in their regularly scheduled lives. How could I deny her this, even if it makes me want to tear my hair out?

"I'm comfy-cozy as can be," I lie, forcing a smile.

Mom claps, still keeping her fingers apart even though she has removed her usual nail art. "Vinny, that's so great! I can't see why a man like Steve would be interested in me, but I guess I'm pretty different from these LA women. And he's not like anyone I've ever been with before, I'll tell you that much. They do say Jewish men make the best husbands . . ."

I want to scream, and only the thinnest thread of decency keeps me from doing so.

Because, no, Steve is *nothing* like Dad.

"Just try not to let it interfere with the group, okay? I think we're on thin ice as it is," I say instead. I look over the article again. "And how do you think *CherriPop* even found out? It's the same site that reported the Everly meeting and her feud with Dea yesterday."

Mom shrugs. "I'm sure some photographer recognized us from the show and made up a good story that happens to be true. You know how these scavengers can be."

While she might talk like she's a pro at all this, it really doesn't make sense. Mom and Steve were only in family photos and video messages during our interview packages on the show, plus I doubt paparazzi are roving the three-mile-zone for photos of just-arrived pop stars' parents. I take another look at the article, and it reeks of a potential leak again. Only someone who has been around the house post-show would even know there's a . . . whatever there is between Mom and Steve.

"Anyway, I'm glad you're on board," Mom continues, "because I'm going to start seeing if any of the *Wives* or *Moms* shows are casting. Your big break could be mine too, the way we always dreamed!"

This time my smile is genuine, if a bit weak. Mom has wanted to be on reality TV for as long as I can remember, hoping to become the next Kardashian-Hilton momager figure. That was part of the reason she came out here to be with me, and it's partly why I suggested she do so in the first place. She deserves to have something for herself, a purpose outside of taking care of me and Nona, especially now that I'm out of high school and Nona finally agreed to eventually move into an assisted living community. I do want this for her, to give her this shot at LA den-mother reality stardom . . . but there's no way *she* could be the gossip leak, right?

I push the thought down with a twist of guilt. I know my mother. She might be a little over the top, but she's also selfless to a fault. She'd never leak anything if she thought it'd hurt us. However, if she thought this kind of press would help keep Jeweltones relevant?

Well, *maybe*?

Either way, asking her about it now would only be an insult and probably wouldn't yield an honest answer anyway. Especially if she is leaking information because she thinks it's helpful.

"I should get back to the group," I say, knowing everyone has probably already dispersed by now. "But I'm thrilled for you, Mom. We'll scout for potential producer meeting outfits later, yeah?"

Mom gives me a bear hug, and I'm enveloped by her usual floral perfume. I absorb as much love as humanly possible from this hug, because I know I need strength to do what comes next.

❖ I need to prioritize figuring out who this **gossip leak** is. Dea is our resident influencer expert, so I should pay her a visit to start my internal investigation.
TURN TO PAGE 121

❖ I need to prioritize keeping my mom away from Everly's dad. Once they realize how different they are, their breakup will just create more drama for us all—plus, Mom doesn't deserve another broken heart. I should pay Everly a visit and see if we're on the same page about this **parental breakup**.
TURN TO PAGE 125

I stride down the hall toward Dea's bedroom with purpose, but I already doubt my conviction by the time I'm halfway there. As I walk, a little voice pops into my head. *You're focusing on the wrong thing. You should be building group unity, not obsessing over a wild goose chase to distract from the bigger problems that need solving.* But I quickly silence this voice, because what this group needs is a baseline of trust—and exposing the gossip leak will help create a safer space. Plus, it might even give us a common enemy to rally against, or at least get us to a more honest place. If I really do want to help make this group work, this is a good first step.

I've reassured myself by the time I knock on Dea's door, but then another thought hits me sideways. Dea is the influencer expert—what if she really did do this to sabotage the group so she can go solo? No shade, but Dea has the deepest incentives and connections, plus the drive to do whatever it takes to make it. It would be kind of an iconic villainess move, honestly.

However, I pull on a big smile as Dea opens the door. No matter what, I've come to the right place.

"Oh, am I interrupting something?" I ask, seeing Dea's cheeks looking unusually flushed.

"No!" Dea replies, a little too sharply. "I mean, CeCe was teaching me how to play *League of Legends* and I just got super into it."

Dea opens the door a little wider and I find CeCe inside, sitting with her laptop on Dea's enormous light-pink bed.

"Just doing my part to get Dea invested in this group," CeCe explains, waving me over. "The only group she likes is BLACKPINK, so I introduced her to K/DA, the game's animated girl group voiced by influencers. They're all glittered out, so I thought it might inspire Dea, but then we got to actually playing."

Dea closes the door behind me with a near slam and I jump. Why is she being so weird about this? Then I look between CeCe and Dea and realize how furious Everly would be to know her best group friend is bonding with her worst group rival.

Still, it's a good sign CeCe is trying to subtly build some bridges. This further convinces me that exposing the gossip leak is important, so stuff like this doesn't get out and cause more unnecessary cracks in the group.

"CeCe was right. I'm obsessed with the whole model. The music, the social media campaigns, their futuristic fashion in the music videos," Dea says, clicking back into her usual mode. "This really might be my angle in Jeweltones."

"But it turns out getting Dea into video games was a bad idea," CeCe adds with a smile. "Guess who's hyper competitive and hates losing?"

I laugh as Dea's cheeks flush red once again.

"I couldn't love this for you more," I say, flopping down on the bed beside CeCe. "Dea, are you going to put K/DA on your vision board now?"

"That's the idea," she answers, sitting cross-legged beside me.

"Whoa," I say, suddenly feeling how tired I am after our early morning media blitz. "Lying down was a bad idea."

"Take a nap," CeCe says. "We can work on our vision boards together later."

"That's probably a good idea," I say through a fat yawn. "But I came here because I actually think there was another gossip leak. About my mom and Everly's dad."

"Wait, is that really a thing?" CeCe asks. I must have a sour look on my face, because she immediately follows up with "I don't mean to sound too excited; it's just that they're kind of adorable. My parents are like the same person, so I love the whole opposites attract thing."

"Don't look at me. I was raised by nannies while my parents raised their surgical careers," Dea sighs. "But wait, was it also *CherriPop* who reported your parents?"

I nod and Dea scowls.

"Another leak involving Everly, on the same site."

"Oh, come on, Everly isn't the type," CeCe replies automatically.

"I don't know why everyone thinks she is some innocent, naïve mouse," Dea continues. "She grew up here in LA. Her whole pure-as-the-driven-snow songwriter vibe is carefully cultivated. She wants to be a mainstream pop singer. Not to even speak about her mean streak."

Dea's argument does more to convince me that she might be the leak, but I can't say that out loud. I give CeCe a quick cautionary look and she nods back, encouraging me to take this one.

"Okay, I hear you, diva. But let's say Everly is leaking the stories. How would she even do that?"

"Easy," Dea answers. "Establish a relationship with one reporter, then promise them a steady feed of inside scoops in exchange for anonymity, or money. It's a win-win."

I glance over at CeCe again, but Dea reacts faster.

"Oh, come on, just because I know how it's done, that doesn't mean I did it," Dea says. "Besides, I prefer sponsored posts I can control. This whole *Gossip Girl* vibe screams early 2000s."

Well, if I came here looking for clues, I just got some. The old-school vibe does shout mommy dearest, but maybe Dea has a point about Everly. Honestly, though, the fingerprint-free attack is kind of her MO, so I wouldn't put it past Dea either. Then again, there is still a high chance it could be someone from the show or Zahra's camps trading stories for money. While I might have gained a few clues, I definitely didn't narrow down the list of suspects.

"Well, at least now I know what my next step is," I say. "Find out which reporter wrote these articles, then reach out to them to see what I can learn."

"I can help," CeCe says, nudging me with her shoulder. "We can strategize about what to offer to get them to talk, because we don't want to become a leak ourselves. Maybe a juicy, very-fake story as bait?"

"Thanks, dear. We can figure that part out later," I say, pushing myself up. "But right now I need some beauty rest. Vision board date later?"

Dea nods, biting her lip like she wants to say something more. She doesn't need to.

"And don't worry, our resident sapphire need not hear about you two hanging. At least, not from me."

"A true queen, as always," Dea replies, looking relieved.

"I'm going to tell Everly, though. Just maybe after she's had her own nap," CeCe says, suddenly looking less sure. "Or maybe at the retreat tomorrow? Yeah, that'll be better."

I nod at CeCe and give her a wink. It is probably better to wait. The last thing we need is another best friend falling-out at the heart of this already-fractured jewel.

TURN TO PAGE 129

I stride toward Everly's bedroom with purpose, but by the time I'm half-way there, I've already begun to doubt my conviction. *You're just afraid of not having Mom all to yourself,* says the little voice that pops into my head. *You're fighting for control outside of yourself.* I silence this voice, however, because I know what's best for this group and for my mom.

Her intense NYC self will eventually be too much for Everly's chill LA dad, especially if she's angling for reality TV fame. Once her novelty wears off, he'll break her heart all over again. We both deserve better. I'd rather act to stop this trainwreck today before it falls to me to pick up the pieces in some horrible tomorrow.

Plus, I reassure myself, this also gives me a unique opportunity to bond with Everly. Outside of our little breakfast club exchanges, we haven't had much one-on-one time. I don't really know the deal with her own mom, but this is clearly my chance to learn.

After a few knocks, Everly answers her door looking about as tired as I feel. Now that the residual adrenaline buzz from our appearance has worn off, we all must be feeling the entire week catching up with us. A fat nap will be my next order of business, for sure.

"Hey, sorry to bug you," I say, "but I wanted to talk to you about something."

"Sure, come in," Everly replies, opening her door. She has the curtains drawn like she was preparing for a nap of her own, but I can still see all the fully packed suitcases in her room. The only things that seem settled in here are the open guitar cases in one corner. Then I see what Everly was really doing in bed. Her laptop sits open, displaying *Wake Up America's* YouTube page on our performance video.

"Oh, Everly, please tell me you weren't reading the comments?"

"I usually don't. But I assumed everyone ran to their rooms to read what the internet was saying about us."

"I ran to my room because my stomach is still rebelling against me. But no, I don't have any desire to read the comments. If it were up to me, I'd have a full-on flip phone."

Everly looks at me like I'm some unicorn. I give her a quick shrug.

"I mean, I'm not super in love with social media either," she says, "but how else are we supposed to share our music and connect with listeners?"

"Tell me, are you sharing music and connecting in those comments?"

Everly frowns, glancing back at her computer.

"Don't you want to know what they're saying about you?" she asks instead of answering.

"Hell no," I reply. "What other people think of me is none of my business. I think we pulled together that performance under incredibly last-minute conditions, and my warped stomach cooperated long enough for me to belt some killer notes. I probably looked puffy on top of already being thicc AF, and my purple outfit probably looked queer AF. I think there are lots of jealous, sheltered people out there taking their fear out on me in comments instead of living their own dreams out loud. No troll—and no diehard fan, for that matter—could ever understand the full truth of what went into that performance. So why factor in their opinions?

"Now, as a trusted and respected peer, *your* opinion of my performance does matter to me," I conclude. "What did you think, comment queen?"

"I thought you were perfect," Everly says, finally smiling. "And that you out-sing me on my own song."

"Bigger isn't always better, love," I say, smiling back. "But if you're looking to be bigger onstage, the answers aren't on that tiny screen. You know that, right?"

Everly looks unsure, but she still nods.

"Let's make a deal?" I say instead. "Every time you want to look at the comments, call me and I will teach you some performing tricks I've learned from my theater days, okay?"

"I dunno. That's so sweet of you, but my problem isn't faking it onstage. It's how to be present and authentic."

"Precisely. But you can't have the confidence to be vulnerable onstage until you feel comfortable there. Take it from a former musical actor and a future drag queen: sometimes the best way to get comfortable on a stage is to pretend to be someone else."

This advice seems to resonate with Everly, as if she'd never thought of performing this way caught in her folksy singer-songwriter bubble of "authenticity."

"In exchange for my services, you must give me little songwriting lessons," I add. "That way everyone wins. Except the trolls."

Everly smiles again, seeming finally at ease. "How did you know this is exactly what I needed to hear?"

"I wish I could say I was that witchy of a bitch, but that's not why I came here to talk," I say, heading to Everly's laptop. A few commands later, I pull up the *CherriPop* article about our parents dating.

"Oh, wow," Everly says, taking in the headline.

I wait for the anger or sadness to set in, but instead Everly turns to me with a look full of earnest conviction.

"I promise you, I'm not the leak," she says. "I know this looks bad, but—"

"—Oh, I know," I interrupt. "Honestly, the leak is irrelevant to me. It's probably some PA from *SO YOU WANNA BE A POP STAR?* trying to make a quick buck. This is noise, just like the comments. I actually wanted to see how you feel about our parents potentially dating."

"Oh," Everly says, surprised. "I think it's great."

Now it's my turn to be surprised. "Wait. You do?"

"Totally. My dad always dates these intense women, but that usually just means they're possessive or vindictive—my mom included. But your mom is so different. She's intense, sure, but in this bright, loud, loving way. I've never seen my dad light up like he does around her. She is the best, just like you."

I try to smile, because what she just said is so genuinely sweet.

And so genuinely *not* what I wanted to hear.

"But hey, shit, I forgot about your dad," Everly adds. "Is it too much, your mom dating someone who hits this close to home? I mean, literally your new housemate's dad?" She pauses and looks down at her hands. "Sorry, I'm rambling."

"It's fine. Dead parents make people do the verbal ramble dance," I deadpan. I know I have to keep it light. If I uncork that particular bottle right now, I will drain myself empty. "I'm glad you're cool with it. I just didn't want it to be another thing working against Jeweltones, you know?"

"Well, it isn't a thing for me," Everly says. "But hey, have you ever tried writing about this? If we're going to work on a song together, the deep end is usually the best place to dive."

"I don't know . . . the shallows feel safer to start with. Maybe a nice diva pride bop?"

"Okay, if I trust you that unlocking my performing starts with acting exercises, then you have to trust me that unlocking your artistry starts with emotional exercises."

This time, I don't have to force my smile. "Touché," I say.

Then, after a beat, I stand to go. While I trust Everly's songwriting instincts, I obviously can't trust her to understand why our parents dating is such a bad idea. Doing the work of protecting my mom is going to have to be a solo venture after all.

"Okay, nap time," I say. For good measure, I close Everly's laptop. "The library is closed, love, because that reading is not remotely fundamental. Now have yourself a rest. Take it from someone who knows: we could both go shopping with the bags hanging under our eyes."

Everly chuckles.

"We are definitely going to do a deep-well song, Vinny," she says, walking me out. "But if I ever need a catchphrase hook, I'm coming right to you."

"Damn straight you are," I respond, catching myself. "Strike that: damn queer you are."

TURN TO PAGE 129

CHAPTER EIGHT

VINNY

WELL, TODAY WAS SUPPOSED TO BE THE DAY WE HAD OUR BIG retreat with Zahra, but—surprise, surprise—she had to push it back to Monday because something else came up. I maybe should be worried about where Jeweltones really falls on Zahra's priority list, but I'm too excited by the prospect of an entire weekend off. After the full-out sprint that has been this week following the marathon of the competition, we all could use some precious time to recharge. Especially before this big make-or-break creative conversation happens.

I decided to spend most of my Saturday catching up on sleep. Then after a full afternoon of vision boarding, I decided to treat myself to a night binging the latest season of *Drag Race*. It's definitely what I wanted, but I was surprised when everyone else made grander plans. Dea and Stern were off to some premiere party, while CeCe and Everly put together a slumber party at Everly's childhood home. Even Mom and Steve went out to dinner. Meanwhile, I ended up sitting at home alone, sipping bone broth and trying not to cry in front of the flatscreen.

I also had grand plans of maybe testing out Grindr here in the Hills, but my stomach felt too bloated and cramped to do much of anything. Maybe I wanted a hookup, but maybe I also wanted not to be seen or touched? I really thought I wanted to be alone, but maybe I also wanted to be invited to one of these group activities? Maybe I wanted to relax in sweats, but maybe I also wanted to deck myself out for a night on the town? This bundle of contradictions was starting to feel particularly heavy, sitting alone in this brand-new city—where I suddenly realized I have no actual life beyond Jeweltones and my elimination diet.

So after finishing an episode of *Drag Race*, I decided it was time to do something about it. Back home, I always volunteered at the LGBT Center, mostly in the homeless programs. I discovered, thanks to a quick internet search, this work is even more vital in Los Angeles, a homeless capital of the country. Where I learned that the underage homeless population numbers in the thousands, with forty percent usually identifying as queer.

Stepping out of my rideshare now, I pull my hoodie tighter over my head. I know I'm probably being melodramatic with this incognito act, but I've heard tales from the others that we're maybe kind of famous now? Opening the main entrance doors to LA's central LGBT Center, a sprawling complex on Santa Monica Boulevard, I'm hoping things will be kind of slow on a Saturday night. I just want to slip in at a quiet moment and find out how I can best volunteer without causing a ruckus.

Unfortunately, as soon as I enter the lobby, I encounter a group of teens wearing incredibly festive formal wear. My heart begins to race as I realize that there must be some kind of dance happening tonight, and I certainly do not blend in with my jeans and hoodie. At least there are some sequins sewn in the crown emblem on my chest, thank divas above.

"Oh my god, that's Vinny V! From Jeweltones!"

The shout happens so quickly, the next thing I know I'm surrounded by a gaggle of queer teens in bright tuxedos and dresses. This close, I see that most of the formal wear is being rocked outside of the traditional gender expectations, which is so cool.

Even cooler? I'm being swarmed by a throng of fans like a freaking rock star.

Though I'll admit, the experience is also slightly unnerving. Being treated like a famous thing instead of a normal person, plus the complete lack of personal space? It's thrilling—but, it turns out, it's also a little claustrophobic.

"I love you all too!" I struggle to yell over the flood of declarations and questions. "I'm just here to volunteer, but maybe we can find some flyers or something for me to sign?"

The sea of teens ebbs and flows around me as I try to walk further inside. Of course, I want to give everyone some personalized love and attention, but I'm starting to wonder if maybe a queue system is in order. This is truly *wild*. However, before I've gone more than a few steps, a hand grasps my wrist. I turn to find a young teen—they can't be more than thirteen—looking up at me in full drag. My eyes lock onto theirs with laser focus.

"You're my new idol. Thank you," the young queen says.

In those six words, an ocean of meaning is conveyed. The wave of gratitude bolts me in place while nearly knocking me over at the same time.

"Do you think you'll ever perform with Jeweltones in drag?"

This simple question hits like another lightning bolt to my heart. Honestly, I assumed that Jeweltones drag just wasn't an option. After the *SYWBAPS* mandate against me performing in drag, I'd given up hope that the music industry wanted to embrace that side of me. But standing in this swarm of peers, looking at this young queen, the question suddenly seems vital once again. *Would I ever?*

"Okay, okay, let's give our guest some breathing room," a luscious voice calls out, full of authority. "The first shuttle will be here any minute."

At this request, the teens slowly disperse and reveal possibly the most commanding drag queen I've ever laid eyes on. She isn't particularly tall, probably only five-foot-eight with stiletto boots. But the teens still listen—not because this queen is mean, but rather because of the warmth and elegance she radiates. This is even more impressive since she wears an electric blue wig and Trixie Mattel meets Crystal Methyd clown-couture eye makeup. Black fringe swings from her metallic bodysuit, which hugs every swerve and curve of her thiccness.

"I'm The Hand Made," the queen says, extending a manicured hand to me. "Now, who do we have here?"

◆ ◆ ◆

Even ten minutes later, I cannot take my eyes off The Hand Made. I still feel breathless, and not just from the impromptu autograph-signing session we arranged in the lobby. Afterward, The Hand Made brought me back to her office and sat me down on a sofa beside her drag vanity in the corner. I look over the compacts and colors and brushes and try not to drool. I still feel light-headed, but I'm not sure if it's from this rush of an experience or from the lack of carbs. Either way, I beg my stomach to keep cooperating for this visit.

"We should be safe from your adoring fans in here," The Hand Made says as she settles in front of me. This close, she smells like coconut and campfire smoke. I also notice through the flawless makeup that she's probably somewhere in her thirties.

"Trust me, that was quite a new thing for me," I say, forcing some deep breaths to slow my hammering heart.

"Vinny, you said it was? Are you big on TikTok or something?"

I smile. The Hand Made doesn't know who I am—which feels much more normal.

"I just won a singing reality show. They funneled us into a group called Jeweltones. Have you heard a song called 'Press Diamonds'?"

"Oh, I heard that on the radio!"

I didn't even know people still listened to the radio, but I guess everyone in this sprawling, diffuse city does spend a lot of time in their cars. Divas below, I never thought I'd miss the subway.

"I didn't realize that was a reality show song," she adds.

"I guess it isn't anymore, if it's on the radio. I didn't mean to cause a fuss, Ms. Hand Made. Like I said, this is all very new."

"Oh, you can call me Made in drag, pronouns she/her. Out of drag, I'm Marg, pronouns they/them."

"You got it. I'm he/him out, and she/her in drag too."

Made's eyes go wide, and she serves me a tongue pop. "Not a pop star drag queen! No wonder the kids love you. What brings such royalty here on a Saturday night?"

"I think you're the royalty here, the way those teens treated you. Not to mention this slay of an outfit," I say, snapping. "But to answer your question, I used to volunteer at the Chelsea Center in New York all the time. Since LA is looking like home for now, I figured I should start back up here. I mainly focused on homeless youth programs and outreach. Mental health and support systems for queer youth, especially for those who are forced to leave their homes, is a huge passion of mine. I mean, the support systems are my passion, not the disowning."

Shut up, Vinny! I scream in my head, to stop myself from rambling more.

"Well, it just so happens I'm one of the youth mentorship coordinators here," Made says, smiling again as she blots her overdrawn lips in the mirror. "And you actually *just* met some residents from our youth housing complex program."

"Oh, I read about that! The apartment building opened by the Center, plus the Liberation Coffee House as a job pipeline? Incredible stuff. Is there a dance or something happening tonight?"

"Yes, but we're calling it a ball, naturally. I usually don't show up to work in drag, but the kids insisted I perform for them tonight." Made pauses, looking a bit distant before she continues. "Once upon a younger time I was homeless myself, so I actually listen to what they want. In turn, they listen to me, as you saw."

Then she looks back to her vanity, fluffing her wig.

"If you don't mind, I have some more finishing touches to settle before we shuttle to the space hosting us. But I am dying to hear all about you while I do, Vinny the drag-pop queen."

"I wish there was more to tell on that front," I say with a sigh, feeling a flush of embarrassment. "I was training myself to become a full queen after I graduated, then I got on the show, and they wouldn't let me perform in drag. Then we got unexpectedly turned into this group."

"So why don't you do drag in the group?" Made asks.

There it is, that question again.

"It sounds stupid now, but I just assumed the label wouldn't let me," I answer. "So far they want us to stay in our existing lanes."

"It's never stupid to assume people want to hold drag queens back, love. But that doesn't mean you shouldn't try. Who is your queen?"

I feel my cheeks flush red again as I answer. "Honestly, I'm not sure yet. My plan was to start figuring that out once I was old enough to work at one of the New York bars and start collecting some coins. Now that feels like a stupid excuse."

"Honey, drag ain't cheap!" Made says, cackling and unfurling a mascara wand. "And you're still a zygote from the looks of it, so don't be so hard on yourself. Who's your drag mother?"

"I don't have one yet."

Made looks at me in her mirror, then turns to me with a matter-of-fact look on her face.

"Well, there's your real problem, darling. Want to join the House of Made?"

I nearly fall off the edge of the sofa.

"Just like that?" I ask.

"Just like that," Made replies. "You'd be my fifth drag daughter, but I warn you, you're probably already the most famous."

"Oh, I don't care about that as long as you don't," I gush, my veins feeling like they crackle with fireworks. "It would be my honor!"

Made gives me a big, warm grin, then turns back to her vanity mirror to finish touching up.

"We'll figure out a time to talk drag, but for now, what's your pop star gig?"

I exhale and some of the sparkle leaves my body. Another question I wish I had a clear answer to.

"I'm still sorting that out too. But I can sing like all the great divas, and I love listening to queer artists."

"Okay, werk. I guess I should've asked first: What do you want to *say* as an artist?"

I open my mouth to respond . . . until I realize I don't actually have an answer to that question either.

"I guess I never thought of it that way before," I reply, feeling low and lifted at the same time. "I always focused on my looks and sound, but starting with what I want to say is . . . kind of genius."

"Mother always knows best," Made says with a playful look. "But ruminate on that question a while—don't force it. In the meantime, let's think of it like this: Which queer artists inspire you most? You don't want to be derivative, of course, but it never hurts to start with existing idols. Work out what they do well and reverse engineer it for yourself."

Listening to Made, I begin scrolling through the stars I want to emulate most, focusing on the gender-bending queer male and nonbinary artists.

❖ "Deep down, I really feel excited about going more **slick pop**, using my voice to feel edgy and pushing the boundaries of sound."
TURN TO PAGE 136

❖ "Deep down, I really feel excited about going full **glam rock** and letting my voice rip like a classic diva."
TURN TO PAGE 138

"A cool queen, okurr," Made purrs. "Who do you have in mind?"

"I mean, Sam Smith is one of my idols," I answer. "But I love when they go more dance vibes than diva. Like fitting in with Troye Sivan or Years & Years."

"Have you listened to much George Michael?"

"No," I admit a bit shamefully.

"Give him a try, he'll have some moments for you," Made offers. "And have you thought about someone like VINCINT?"

"I'm obsessed. I covered VINCINT on the show, actually."

"Werk! Well, you should check out Tia Kofi and Frank Ocean too. We can't only focus on our white queer idols," Made adds, hitting me with some literal side-eye. "Don't worry, I'm not throwing shade. You probably can't tell when I'm wearing ten pounds of makeup and a full bodysuit, but I'm half white myself. I'm Irish, but I'm also half Mexican, and one hundred percent full of lapsed Catholic guilt." She gives me a knowing, playful look before continuing, "But it sounds like I've given you quite enough to think about, already."

I sit back on the sofa in awe. Talking with Made makes me feel like a whole new part of my brain opens, full of light. Just as soon as that sense of excitement sets in, however, the questions begin to fire up. Do I perform as Vinny the boy with only diva and drag touches? I do identify as male, after all. Or is that binary nonsense just a box?

Then, pushing through the cloud of queries, a new face pops into my mind—the young queen I just met downstairs. I see that hope in their eyes, their question ringing in my ears. *Do you think you'll ever perform with Jeweltones in drag?*

I know what I need to do. I need to start showing exactly who I really am. If not for myself, then for that kid.

I run a hand through my hair, trying to process this new step. If I'm limiting myself with half measures by not going full drag, is there a way I can funnel all this slick pop energy into my queen alter ego? Maybe I can shift between both, depending on the Jeweltones mood?

I stop myself, once again getting sucked into the whirlpool of my thoughts. Just when I feel like I take one big step toward defining myself, I take two steps back.

TURN TO PAGE 140

"Hit me with your best shots," Made responds.

"Well, obviously Freddie Mercury and Adam Lambert, duh."

"Right, and have you listened to much Elton John?"

"No," I admit a bit shamefully.

"Well, let's give him a try. I think he'll have some moments for you," Made offers. "And have you thought about artists like Lil Nas X or Todrick Hall?"

"I mean, I'm obsessed with both. I guess I just never really thought of either as glam rock?"

"Probably because they're not white," Made says, hitting me with some literal side-eye. "Don't worry, we all have our blind spots. You probably can't tell when I'm wearing ten pounds of makeup and a full bodysuit, but I'm half white myself. I'm Irish, but I'm also half Mexican, and one hundred percent full of lapsed Catholic guilt." She gives me a playful, knowing glance before continuing, "But it sounds like I've given you quite enough to think about, already."

Somehow, this conversation with Made has already helped open my brain to so many new ideas. Could I really fuse R&B, classic rock, and diva antics all together in one package? If I can, should I just go full force as Vinny and infuse drag touches into my act, like most of these artists? I do identify as male, after all. Or is that binary nonsense just a box?

A face then pops into my mind, pushing all my questions aside—the young queen I just met downstairs. I see that hope in their eyes, their question ringing in my ears. *Do you think you'll ever perform with Jeweltones in drag?*

I think of them and wonder if I'm just limiting myself with half measures, not going full drag. What if there's a way I can funnel all this glam rock energy into my queen alter ego? After all, what's that saying? *If you want to see someone's truest face, give them a mask.*

Then again, what do all these things even have in common except isolating and breaking me down into different parts? The diva, the voice, the drag, the queer . . . all queens, no crown. All the colors in the rainbow bleeding outside the prescribed lines.

I stop myself and take a deep breath because there I go again. Just when I feel like I take one big leap toward defining myself, I take two steps back.

TURN TO PAGE 140

"Whoa, what just happened?" Made asks, leaning closer to me. "You just went from sunny to stormy in the flutter of an eyelash."

"It's just..." I say, trying to find a way to articulate this familiar struggle. "I always get so overwhelmed when I try to decide where I belong. Does that make any sense?"

"Vinny, that makes all the sense in the world. Especially for us queer folks who defy the easy conventions. But it doesn't make any sense to get so down about it." Made stands up, towering above me in her heels and wig. "You're a pop star and a drag queen. Isn't it time you had some fun?"

She reaches down and takes me by the hand, guiding me to stand up. Just then, I feel like some of the heaviness lifts right off my shoulders.

"You know, you're absolutely right," I say, straightening and giving her a smirk.

Made spins me under her arm with a dramatic flourish. "Of course I am. Now come with me."

"Where are we going?"

"Why, to the ball, my dear! I have to join the other chaperones and perform for the children. And if you're going to join my House, you'd better come see what I'm made of."

As The Hand Made sashays away, I can't help but feel like my week of living in a fairytale has just magically found its godmother.

I cannot imagine a better happily ever after.

♦ ♦ ♦

A few hours later, I sit in a roped-off booth in the heart of West Hollywood's latest gay bar-lounge and finally feel like I'm living my best life. I never usually get to be somewhere like this, but the lounge donated a few exclusive hours to host the Center's Youth Ball, which means the bar is serving its fiercest mocktails. I wouldn't need a drink anyway to feel high right now, sitting here with music thumping in my chest and watching The Hand Made slay on the main stage. She's currently lip syncing to "Confident" by Demi Lovato, and there is no better word for her performance. She has the crowd in the palm of her hand, playing between dramatic bravado, earnest emotion, and bitchy attitude. It's literally *everything*.

Looking at the crowd of fellow queer teens gathered around the stage, I eat up how much they cheer for Made. A less buzzy version of myself might worry if I could ever channel as much command as her, but right now I just feel lucky as hell to have stumbled into this night. I try to focus on basking in the glow of finding a mentor and being surrounded by my people.

Looking to my left, I'm also thrilled that those people now include CeCe and Everly.

"Thank you for calling to invite us!" CeCe shouts over the applause as Made nails a catwalk moment onstage.

I beam back at CeCe, knowing exactly how she feels. Beside her, Everly smiles and waves. I could tell she wasn't totally thrilled I interrupted their sleepover night, but she came for CeCe—and for me, I guess, which is nice. Especially since Dea and Stern weren't even answering their phones. This would have been an epic bonding night for all five of us, but I'm happy at least CeCe and Everly could come share it with me.

Just then, Made's performance begins to reach its final beats. I almost expect her to death drop, but she doesn't even need to. Instead, she lip syncs the last booming notes with her legs confidently spread and her hands clapping above her head, commanding the crowd. It's absolutely iconic behavior.

And everything I want to be.

"That was amazing," CeCe says once we've sat back down from our standing ovation. I insisted we didn't need to sit in this VIP section, but Made said it was the only way we wouldn't get ambushed all night. Of course she was right, but that's also probably because we spent our first hour here posing for photos and signing autographs. Then the three of us danced a little when they played "Press Diamonds," but it felt wrong to perform fully without Dea and Stern.

"I know, right?" I reply, still vibrating. "I need to do something like that in Jeweltones."

"You mean in drag?" CeCe asks, also buzzing. "Why don't you?"

"You heard Zahra. The label wants us in our lanes from the show."

"Well, that's exactly the kind of thing we need to discuss at this retreat on Monday," CeCe says. "Assuming Zahra doesn't reschedule again."

"Yeah, about that," I say, having to shout a little less now that the music has returned to a lower decibel. "I'm starting to worry Zahra might not have the kind of time we need from her. She's the best—obviously I'm her biggest fan—but I double-checked, and we're the only group on her roster. She's a pro with solo acts, but I'm worried she might not have the bandwidth for us. Pun intended."

"Well, let's see how Monday goes," CeCe replies before taking a sip of her lemonade. "I'm worried you're right too. But if that's the case, you and I might have to take the lead on getting this group together."

I smile back at CeCe and we clink our glasses together. Who knew we'd make such a dynamic duo?

After taking a drink, I look over at Everly and notice that she seems to have folded in on herself in the booth.

"You K, hun?" I ask, turning to Everly. I wait a beat and then try again. "Um, earth to Everly?"

Hearing her name, Everly snaps out of whatever trance she was in. "Yes, sorry. I'm good."

Except she doesn't look good . . . she looks completely freaked. Not about being here—she strode inside like she's been in a hundred LA queer spaces. If anything, it seems about the conversation CeCe and I just had. I guess I can't blame Everly, since nothing about any of our energies screams folksy acoustics. I lean over to try saying something to comfort her, until The Hand Made suddenly saunters up to our table.

"I can't stay long, but I wanted to come say hello," she says. "And thank you for coming. It really made the night extra special for our kids."

"Are you kidding? This is heaven," CeCe says. "And you were incredible."

"I do what I can," Made replies, winking at her. "Now, while I have you captive and mesmerized, I have a favor to ask. We have a charity drag brunch coming up soon. Think your new group would have any interest in performing? Or maybe just appearing? The donors would go gaga.

Plus, you're going to make me look very cool to the kids. And very good to my boss."

"It would be our honor," CeCe answers, beaming, before I can say the same.

Next to her, Everly nods and smiles genuinely. It's actually sweet how she's letting CeCe and I soak up this moment. I just hope she doesn't make too big a habit of fading into the background.

"Maybe I'll even debut a certain queen there?" I say with a mischievous grin, turning back to Made.

"That'd be a gag for the ages! Now I have to run, but you have my number. Don't be a stranger, love!" Then, with a flurry of hand-blown kisses, The Hand Made twirls off into the night.

"It's official," CeCe says. "I'm obsessed with her."

"Good, because she offered to be my drag mother tonight," I reply, not even trying to hide my excitement. "And I think you're right. I need to push to be the full artist I want to be in Jeweltones. No boundaries."

I take a sip of my drink and nudge Everly's leg under the table. When she looks up, I say, "And girl, we need to find a way for you to do the same."

"I know," she replies, playing with the straw in her drink. "But how are we actually going to do that?"

Her question quickly bursts my bubble. I look at her and then at CeCe, because as much as I don't want to think practically right now, this remains a major stumbling point. It's so easy to think big—it's my specialty, in fact. Getting into the focused details has always been my weak point.

And it's about to be the biggest problem facing Jeweltones too.

Everly has every right to be worried, but I don't say so out loud for some reason. The more I think about it, the more the reason starts to crystalize. Maybe it's because out of all of us, Everly has the safest launching pad. A well-trodden musical path is laid out before her, backed by her dad's support, her songwriting ability, and the entire existing music industry.

I guess the same could be said for Stern, but we all know he doesn't have the same family financial support. Dea might have that support, but she and Stern have both been fighting to make it in music for years already, so they *need* this Jeweltones break, whether they like it or not. Then you have CeCe and me, who need this more than anyone, really. With a few exceptions, no one in the mainstream is looking for curvy drag divas and Black pop-punk rocker chicks. We'd both exist on the fringes, at the best of times. However, Jeweltones is as main-stage as it gets right now. It's a platform none of us, especially CeCe and I, might ever reach otherwise.

I wrap my hands around my glass and think, *sorry, not sorry, Everly.*

Of course, I wouldn't just say this out loud. I need to find a gentler way to say this—preferably by the time our retreat rolls around on Monday.

"I have to tell you both something," CeCe suddenly says.

Everly and I turn to her and, seeing the serious look on her face, I wonder if maybe she just had some mini epiphany like mine.

"I've been keeping a secret, but being here tonight, it makes me realize I shouldn't have to hide," CeCe continues, looking like she gathers steam with every word. "I've been hooking up with Dea. And I think I'm falling for her."

My jaw nearly falls off the bottom of my face.

Across from me, Everly looks like she might faint.

"It just . . . happened one night after taping a results show," CeCe continues like she can't hold back the words any longer. "I thought it was a fluke. I mean, Dea shut me out after it happened, and we were never supposed to see each other again after the finale. But then Jeweltones happened. We moved into the house earlier this week and . . . it just started again."

"Why didn't you tell me?" Everly asks, looking like she barely holds back an avalanche of emotion.

I can think of nearly a dozen reasons why CeCe couldn't tell Everly this, but I bite my tongue.

"The first time was after you two fell out, before you and I got close," CeCe says. She stops and runs her hands over her face with a sigh. "But since then? Because Dea isn't ready to come out."

This much is obvious since Dea—my supposed closest friend here—hasn't told me any of this either. Meanwhile, I have practically spilled my guts out to her . . .

"Don't be mad," CeCe says, turning to me. "Dea isn't sure what her sexuality even is yet. She's afraid of what it might do to her future career, especially overseas. Plus, she didn't want to cause more problems in the group. Especially because of her thing with Stern. She made me swear I wouldn't tell anyone."

"Then why did you?" I ask. I feel a bit queasy as the implications and consequences begin to stack in my mind.

"Being here tonight, I just . . . I don't want to live my life back in the closet," CeCe answers. "And you both are becoming my real friends. We're the only ones in this together. It felt right to me, in the moment." CeCe slows down and takes a shaky breath, as if what she has done with her heart is finally catching up with her head. "But oh my god, I absolutely *should not* have told you."

Everly and I watch as her expression falls into shadows.

I try to think of the right words to say.

❖ "You shouldn't have to lie, but it wasn't right outing Dea either. And it's not right for her to keep cheating on Stern. Now that we know, we have to **talk openly** about it before the retreat."
TURN TO PAGE 146

❖ "I'm so glad you felt comfortable sharing this. But, for now, we have to **keep** this a **secret** between us. At least until we figure out how to work together as a group and set our creative direction."
TURN TO PAGE 148

"We can't bring this level of messiness in front of Zahra," I continue. "She'll drop us."

"That's exactly why we can't tell Dea and Stern yet," CeCe reacts. "There's no way we'll sort it out in time for Monday. Dea might never forgive me, and Stern might never forgive her."

"So it's fake, their relationship?" Everly asks.

That's what Everly is focused on? Her best friend has been sneaking around with her frenemy and she cares about Stern? Or is this just more ammo for Everly's "Dea is totally fake" campaign? Either way, neither of them seem particularly impacted by my bystander opinion.

"Stern thinks it's real, and Dea wants it to be," CeCe answers, looking even more defeated as she does.

"I'm so sorry," Everly says. "That must really sting."

For a few moments, we sit in silence amidst the thumping music.

"You don't hate me for being with Dea?" CeCe asks.

"Not if you really have feelings for her," Everly answers. "Especially not after you didn't judge me for crushing on Stern."

CeCe reaches out to take Everly's hand to thank her. It's a nice moment, but hearing about Everly's crush—even though I already suspected it—just goes to show the level of messiness we have achieved. Messiness I am excluded from, yet again.

"If we really do see something special in them," Everly says, "maybe we've been wrong about both?"

It's the only sentiment from the last few minutes that gives me any hope.

"Vinny, I know it's asking a lot," CeCe says, turning to me. "But can you give me some time to see if this . . . thing with Dea is even real? Maybe it's just a fling that'll end soon, and then we tell Stern when things cool off. If not, maybe Dea will be ready to come out about it on her own? Either way, we owe her some time."

I clench my jaw and look away. As much as I hate it, when CeCe puts it as a way to protect Dea, how can I argue? Besides, maybe there is a world where these secrets might help soften some of the edges between us, like what just happened with Everly.

Maybe.

As much as I want to believe in that thought, I know these secrets are far more likely to tear us apart the longer they are kept. Then again, who am I to say anything at all? Dea didn't trust me enough to tell me any of this in the first place, and it's not like I'm our leader. I'm just an extra, the backup singer, someone in the chorus line. I already know that unless I put in the maximum effort, I'm the one who is overlooked, the one who is forgotten.

I feel that familiar sting in the center of myself. I might have grown up in the relatively accepting NYC scene, but there's no protection anywhere from being a chubby and queeny little kid. Not even from the other gay guys in high school, who were the ones to teach me the term "skinny fat" the first time I lost some weight after a growth spurt. I've always gotten along better as one of the girls, but even then, always from the outside. I've never fit in as one of the guys and definitely not as one of the shiny, cool gays. I thought I was leaving all that high school stuff behind, but it's becoming clear I don't quite fit into this new group either.

As these thoughts spiral, I start to tread into the scary place. I wonder whether I'll ever find where I belong without constantly having to try so hard. What if Jeweltones isn't really where I belong after all?

I suppose if that's the case, then what do these secrets really matter anyway?

I don't know how I could go from feeling so high and so assured to feeling so low and so unsure in the span of a few songs.

So I finally give CeCe the nod she wants, agreeing to her terms.

No one needs me to speak up anyway.

TURN TO PAGE 150

"If this all comes out now, we'll break up for sure," I continue. "We need more time to find a rhythm and click as a group."

"Even if that's all based on more lies?" Everly asks.

I stop myself and look down at the table. I can't blame her for that. I know I shouldn't, but I feel hurt that Dea didn't trust me enough to tell me any of this. I can only imagine how hurt Everly feels as well.

But the fact remains: regardless of how we feel about it, this has always been Dea's secret to tell.

"Dea deserves the time to decide what feels right," I answer. "Maybe that means being with CeCe and coming out. Or maybe that means things with CeCe fizzle and she stays with Stern. It's her call, not ours."

"That may be," Everly says, "but is it fair to Stern?"

"He thinks their relationship has a real shot," CeCe adds. "Dea wants it to work too."

These words look like they hurt CeCe as much as they hurt Everly. Which is . . . troubling.

"Dea doesn't want it enough to stop cheating on Stern," Everly says, hotly. "It's not fair for her to use him for publicity. And what if the gossip leak finds out about this?"

"That's exactly why it needs to stay between us," I say, jumping in. "Everly, you were friends with Dea once. Now that you know what she's really been going through, could you maybe find a way to see her differently again? And if not, CeCe is your friend. She made a mistake, so don't punish her for it."

The words sound reasonable in my ears, but I'm not sure I even believe them. I sigh and lean back in the booth. There I go again, twisting myself into whatever shape best serves the moment. Vinny . . . always so willing to shift. After all, I'm the voice without a voice, so it's easy to compromise. I hoped Jeweltones would help me define myself, but all it ever seems to do is force me to play nice.

As I watch CeCe and Everly, I also realize that these pairs keep cropping up between the other four, friendly and feuding and romantic. What if everyone suddenly realizes I don't fit in, that I'm expendable?

My stomach turns. I'm reminded yet again how much harder I always have to work just to reach the baseline everyone else operates from—in my body, in my brain, in society, and in this group. Vinny: always too much, yet never enough.

Even with my own doubts swirling, I watch as Everly nods, agreeing to keep quiet. She turns to CeCe, who looks tearful and thankful.

"I just want you to be happy," Everly says, taking her hand.

This is definitely a silver lining in this otherwise ominous cloud, but it gives me a moment to play back the lowlights in my mind. Dea is seeing CeCe behind Stern's back. Everly and I know about it now because of CeCe, but Dea doesn't know we know. Meanwhile, Stern knows nothing at all. Everly probably despises Dea more than ever and, if my hunch is correct, she has a secret flame burning for Stern. Then there is the fact that we're all mildly famous, in the tabloids thanks to a likely internal leak, and under a ton of pressure to make more musical magic to stay in the spotlight. And, of course, we don't have a single clue how to do all of this, and our manager keeps hurrying us up only to make us wait.

How can it be that only minutes ago I was so sure that Jeweltones was the answer to all of my problems?

Now, I see the group for what it has always been . . . a ticking time bomb.

And CeCe just lit our fuse.

TURN TO PAGE 150

CHAPTER NINE
EVERLY

THE SPRINTER VAN TURNS ONTO A SECLUDED ROAD, AND ALL five of us sway to the left. We've been passengers for an hour or so, with no real idea where we're headed for Zahra's big retreat this morning. Honestly, Monday couldn't have come soon enough. After the wrecking ball with CeCe and Vinny on Saturday night, I slept in as late as possible on Sunday. Then I mostly hid in my room to avoid the others—which, as far as I could tell, was the general trend.

This continues as we all sit in silence listening to our respective headphones and soaking in the views on this drive through Malibu. We left the glistening coastal beaches ten minutes ago and are now being driven through a winding canyon. I'm thankful for the quiet time to process things. I had hoped to sort out my feelings yesterday, but I didn't even know where to start. I've been avoiding any alone time with Stern since our close encounter of the guitar kind, but this new Dea layer has me completely paralyzed around him, even in the group. I have no idea what the right thing to do is—other than to not betray CeCe's confidence. Even though doing that feels like a betrayal to Stern and the promise of Jeweltones.

I'm fighting very hard not to resent or judge CeCe, because she was put in an impossible position with Dea . . . even if it's a position I'm having a hard time wrapping my head around in the first place. I am trying to find some empathy for Dea, to understand how isolating and scary this must feel for her. That said, it's almost impossible not to blame her for creating all this drama, for once again being hellishly self-centered. I don't know how personal Zahra wants us to get today, but I just hope someone speaks up—for all our sakes.

Since I couldn't find a way to feel settled about any of this group drama yesterday, I instead focused on the one part I actually can control: my songwriting contribution. I did decide exactly how to handle this aspect, so I just hope everyone understands when I deliver the news today. Assuming we even make it to the creative direction portion.

After another ten minutes or so, we pull up to an ivy-covered cottage beside a small pond. The place is lovely, but I was expecting more of a sprawling ranch-style retreat spa, not a cozy hideaway. Still, this must be the place, because Zahra steps out the front door in a fitted blazer and wide palazzo pants. She looks like the most glamorous professor ever. In fact, this whole day kind of feels like a field trip—and this whole fame explosion kind of feels like a continuation of high school. *Go here, do this, complete homework, pass tests.* Really, it's like we've been assigned the most dysfunctional group project ever.

"So, change of plans," Zahra says the moment we exit the Sprinter. "You can leave your overnight bags on the van. First, I have good news: Jeweltones was such a hit on *Wake Up America* that sales and streams for 'Press Diamonds' are through the roof. The label wants to promote your next single ASAP, so I booked us the day here at my favorite studio. We'll still do the vision board exercise, then we'll use that momentum to record your second song. Isn't that exciting?"

I freeze.

Sure, that might sound like more amazing news for our careers, but I thought today was meant to be about getting on the same page. If we just keep wrapping bandages around our broken bones to get to the next thing, this is all going to fall apart—and much sooner than later.

"That's unreal news," CeCe says, looking around to take the temperature of the rest of the group.

Vinny and Dea seem to be feeling the same trepidation that I am, while Stern just looks plain excited. It makes my heart ache. If only he knew...

"But Zahra, I think your idea to have the retreat was the right one," CeCe continues. "We really need to sort through some core issues. Maybe after the vision board and recording sessions we can have a more . . . personal conversation?"

"Preferably with a trained moderator present?" Vinny jokes.

Zahra does laugh, but she also seems unable or unwilling to absorb any of the subtext happening here.

"Unfortunately, my schedule blew up and I have to be in London later tonight. But I hear you. Let's get to work now and maximize the time we have together?"

Uninterested in second opinions, Zahra turns and clacks back toward the studio. I look at CeCe and Vinny, but they both wear the same expression. *What choice do we have?* That sentiment is starting to become a troubling refrain in this experience. Obviously, Vinny and CeCe were right to worry that Zahra might be too big to have the time Jeweltones really needs.

Regardless, the five of us march reluctantly forward once again.

◆ ◆ ◆

I suppose if there's anything I can't fault Zahra for, it's her curation and access. Everyone she has arranged for us to work with has been top-notch, including this very A-List Swedish pop producer who greets us inside the cozy-yet-glamorous studio. Half of me is thrilled to work with a proven hit-maker, but the other half of me feels creatively terrified. At least Zahra has sent the producer to get set up in the recording suite so we can get settled in. Now we find ourselves gathered in the quaint living room overlooking the lush pond, ready to present our various visions.

Dea and Stern decide to split an oversized armchair, an intimate arrangement that makes my skin feel like it's on fire. I look away and force myself not to visibly react, even though all I really want to do is look at CeCe to check if she's okay. Instead, I meet Vinny's gaze, and he looks just as frozen as I feel.

Thankfully, Zahra has Dea present her board first. However, it offers exactly zero surprises, idolizing J.Lo and Britney Spears, listing Dua Lipa's

Future Nostalgia as her favorite album, then BLACKPINK and K/DA as her favorite groups. Dea winks at CeCe over K/DA, which sends another chill through my body. I try with all my might to keep my face forward and repeat over and over to myself: *don't react.*

"Okay, that couldn't be clearer, which is fantastic coming from our resident diamond," Zahra says. "We know who our lead will be when it comes to social media, product branding, and fashion styling. Music-wise, I'm thinking of all the BLACKPINK duets with Dua, Cardi, and Selena. Or the Britney-Madonna moment. Okay, CeCe! You're up next."

I fight to keep my mouth from falling open. That's it? I seriously hoped that Zahra was going to share some game plan or provide some guidance, but is this all just hollow lip service, having us present what we've already clearly defined about ourselves? I try to calm down and tell myself that maybe she'll have an exercise for us to stitch all these disparate parts together after. I look across the room at Vinny, and I can tell he's thinking the same thing. So I bite my tongue and try to stay present.

CeCe's board, while amazing, also offers no surprises. Her focus is on making the group work and features zero images of products, fashion, or achievements. She might personally channel a more emo-rock sound, but she highlights pop-punk artists like Olivia Rodrigo, Demi Lovato, and Fefe Dobson, who I make a note to look up later. CeCe finishes her board with a section devoted to collaborative sounds to emulate: in lieu of Fifth Harmony, she lists a duet between Camila Cabello and WILLOW, followed by an older duet between Tina Turner and Bryan Adams.

"I think you're on to something here, CeCe," Zahra says once CeCe is done. "If we can find a way to marry diva-pop with rocker-heart, we'll have cracked the code. 'It's Only Love' is a genius comp, especially if we modernize its eighties sound."

"But hey, CeCe," Stern says, causing every muscle in my body to tighten. "I love your board, but I'm worried you're focusing too much on fitting into the group. Is there anything you'd put on there if you were going totally solo?"

Woof. I know Stern means to be helpful and empower CeCe somehow, but it has the exact opposite effect. She looks at him like she's ready to rip into him for his unsolicited feedback, but she manages to keep it cool, knowing Zahra is present.

"That's thoughtful, Stern," I quickly butt in. "But CeCe knows exactly who she is as an artist, and we aren't going solo. That's kind of the whole point, right?"

As soon as I say this, I see Dea's lips tighten. *Crap.* She must think I was taking a dig at her own board. Meanwhile, Stern's entire face falls.

"Of course. I didn't mean—"

"—Why don't you just present next, Stern?" Zahra interrupts, pointedly.

We all sit in silence while Stern gets ready to present, but that's all it takes for one thought to crystalize in my brain. It's exactly like CeCe and Vinny feared—Zahra does mean well, and she probably does believe in us, but she doesn't have the time to get us on our feet. For Zahra to do her job, she needs her hottest act of the moment already in sprinting shape. Maybe a rookie manager could be our babysitter or our therapist, and maybe Zahra even wishes she could do that for us. However, what we truly need to do is stop and sit in the uncomfortable stuff simmering between CeCe and Stern, between all of us—not just keep brushing it under the rug.

But what are we supposed to do about it now?

My mind chews on this question while Stern presents a board filled with images of One Direction, Grammys, stadium tours, and big houses. I want to shake him, now understanding that everything on his board is only what he thinks he's supposed to want. However, that's yet another thing I can't say out loud without sending a new wrecking ball crashing through the room.

At the very least, the real Stern does seem to crack through listing his favorite collaborations: "Man of the Woods" by Justin Timberlake and Chris Stapleton and "I Don't Care" by Justin Bieber and Ed Sheeran. Stern looks to me as he wraps up on this note, and I try to give him the most private of smiles possible, so as not to set off more alarm bells.

It all makes my heart hurt.

"I know people just write off One Direction as another boy band," Stern finishes, "but I think they actually managed to combine super different categories of pop in one fused style, the way we hope to. Classic rock Harry, like CeCe. R&B Zayn, like Vinny. Dance-pop Liam, like Dea. And folk-pop Niall, like Everly."

"Well, Stern," CeCe says with a tight smile. "I love your board, but I'm worried you're focusing too much on fitting into the group. Is there anything you'd put on there if you were going totally solo?"

I know CeCe only means to give Stern a dose of his own "helpful" man-splaining, but repeating his words exactly back at him comes off way harsher than she intends. We all shift in our seats uncomfortably.

After a beat, CeCe looks apologetic. "Sorry, that wasn't the best way to make my point."

"You don't need to apologize," Stern replies, without a hint of edge. "I get it."

"Actually, I think Stern has a little country-folk singer-songwriter in him," I add again. "We started writing a song together on guitar the other night."

The moment the words leave my mouth, I regret them. I was only trying to defuse the tension, but who is going to like that news? Certainly not Dea, who now refuses to look at me. CeCe appears completely surprised, while Vinny looks pained over this new complication. Meanwhile, Stern turns about three shades redder.

"That's fantastic!" Zahra exclaims, remaining either willfully or blissfully oblivious to the straining undercurrents. I guess that's one person who likes this news. I can only hope that means she's going to like the songwriting news I'm set to deliver with my own board.

"I think One Direction is another great comp," Zahra continues. "It's the kind of vibe Everly created on 'Press Diamonds.' But before we get to our grand finale, Vinny, you're next."

I try not to visibly wince at these final words. I do not like the idea of being considered some kind of MVP in this group. From the looks of it, neither does anyone else.

Still, Vinny manages to be graceful as he stands to present. His board feels by far the most vibrant, but it's also the most unfocused. Instead of homing in on any one musical style, it creates an entire energetic mood and features a spectrum of gender-bending queer artists and drag queens.

"I know I'm a bit unbridled here," Vinny says. "But I do feel like, since everyone else has such a defined focus and role, I could maybe be the flexible glue that holds us all together?"

Vinny tries to project his usual confidence, but I swear I can sense some definite . . . *unease* beneath his sunny surface.

"Vocals, moves, lewks, styling, performing—I can pinch hit wherever I'm needed," he continues. "But I was hoping you'd all be open to me potentially doing so in drag?"

"Hell yes," I say, though only a split second before CeCe, Dea, and Stern all chime in with a version of the same. It's the first thing we've all instantly agreed upon, which is somewhat reassuring. Though not as reassuring as the smile of relief that spreads across Vinny's face.

"I love the energy you're bringing," Zahra replies. "And you know I'd fully support drag in Jeweltones, but we do have to check with the label and be sure it all jives with branding. Do you have a specific drag identity in mind?"

For some reason, this looks like the last question Vinny wanted to hear. He freezes completely, which is so unlike him.

"I was hoping Vinny might help teach me some stage tricks," I offer, hoping to buy him some time. "So maybe I could help hone the artistic intent behind his drag debut?"

I worry right away that I've just totally overstepped, like I have some monopoly on artistic intent, the straight cis girl telling Vinny who to be. However, he instantly exhales and sends me a thumbs up.

"Great. Let me know when you have something specific to present to the label on that front," Zahra says. "Which brings us to you, Everly."

I try to take a deep breath of my own as I stand for my turn. Not because my vision board is going to present any surprises. It's a bit more abstract than anyone else's, but still representative of my expressions so far. I've painted a mirrored disco ball and neon bar sign, very *folklore/evermore*, underneath a setting sun and a cracked jewel heart, very "Dimming of the Day" and "One Big Love." I also pasted in some magazine spread glamour shots of Maggie Rogers and HAIM, trying to flex to a more current indie-pop place. But it isn't the front of my board that I'm worried about. It's what I have written on the back that might not go over so well.

"HAIM is obviously another great group to emulate, especially their collabs with mainstream dance-pop acts," Zahra says after a moment. "I'm curious if, after seeing everyone else's boards, any new inspirations have struck for you, Everly?"

Translation: *Are you going to write more potential hit songs for Jeweltones?*

"Right. This brings us to the elephant in the room," I reply. "Obviously, I wrote 'Press Diamonds' for us on my own, and so far it has worked out. I don't know what everyone expects for our next song, or a whole album, but I've thought about it a lot." I pause, taking a moment to build my courage. "This quote is from Jewel when she was on my favorite podcast, *Song Exploder*, and it sums up how I feel better than I can myself."

I then flip over my board to reveal the quote I have written on the back:

> You're not allowed to do anything that's inauthentic as a songwriter. Part of me always knew it was an incredible longshot, but I also sang every night, and I saw what and how people felt when I sang—it could be only three people, but I could tell what I was doing was working. So I didn't want to give up on that music and being sincere and folky.

"In this spirit, I've made a decision," I continue, after giving everyone a moment to finish reading. "I want to give this group a shot, truly. However, I also can't compromise my songwriting authenticity or give over my favorite existing songs. Still, I do see that I stand to learn so much from everyone here . . ."

✦ "I want us to try to **collaborate**, writing new songs together as a group. I'd even be happy to take the lead on that process, if that's what everyone wants."
TURN TO PAGE 159

✦ "I have to keep this part of myself separate from the group, even if that means we need to work with **producers** like the one Zahra hired today to find new songs for Jeweltones."
TURN TO PAGE 163

I finish and try not to hold my breath as I wait for the group's reactions.

"I think that makes total sense," Vinny says. "I would love to collaborate, especially because I have the most to learn about songwriting."

"Everly already knows I mess around with sound-mixing software on my laptop," CeCe adds. "If she's in charge of keeping one creative direction, I think we could all find ways to shine."

"I love this for us," Stern says, grinning from ear to ear.

Next to him, Dea simply nods. I tell myself it's because she'd rather have creative control elsewhere and hope it's not something deeper.

All the same, my heart fills up. We might still have mountains of personal mess to sort through, but if we can at least find a creative groove together, maybe we can begin to build some trust. No matter what, we certainly have plenty of material to write from, even if we only stick to the surface stuff at first.

I turn to Zahra next, expecting to find her looking pleased. Instead, she looks at me like a golden goose who has suddenly refused to lay more eggs. My heart sinks.

"I think that sounds like an ideal step in the future," she begins, tapping her nails on the arm of her chair. "But I'm afraid the label has some short-term plans we need to satisfy first. Of course, I was hoping Everly would come ready to give the group another song today, but I respect this choice. It's a good thing I also came prepared.

"The label has put significant advance money behind you all, including today's very-expensive studio session. They expect us to deliver a second single to start promoting ASAP. We also booked Jeweltones last minute in the lineup at the Popella music festival for a two-song set!"

The way Zahra slips in this announcement, it's obvious she hopes to get us all excited instead of focusing on these latest label mandates. However, little bubbles of panic still begin to creep up my throat, because I realize that this "group retreat" has already come to an end. We resolved absolutely nothing, personally or creatively—we just conformed so we can replicate our viral success from the show. And that seems to be all Zahra really wants, or all she and the label have time for, at least.

"The next two weeks are going to be jam-packed, so we need to hit the ground running today," she continues. "I promise after that, the five of you can have more time to start putting together your debut album. I love the idea of Everly leading the songwriting. First, I'm afraid you need to keep earning that runway to launch from with a smash second single and viral Popella performance, since it will be streamed live to millions."

I look at CeCe first to see what she thinks, but I find her eyes locked on Stern and Dea as they lean in for a celebratory kiss. Catching this sets my own insides on fire, so I can only imagine how CeCe must feel. I turn to Vinny, and he looks just as anxious.

"I know this isn't what you all expected, but I promise this is a good thing," Zahra concludes. "Just hang in there a little longer. In the meantime, the producer and I have selected a song from his catalogue that we feel will be the perfect follow-up to 'Press Diamonds.' The label agrees."

Zahra stands as I slide back into my seat. I'm thankful I do, because that's when Zahra writes the title of our second single on the back of my vision board:

Reignbow.

I try not to panic even more.

◆ ◆ ◆

I can't count the number of times I've dreamed of standing in a recording booth. A professional one, not the makeshift tour bus studio that production brought in for us to record "Press Diamonds" the day of the finale. Standing in this booth now, I want to feel inspired.

Instead, I look at the music and lyrics to "Reignbow" and feel nothing but anxiety.

Absorbing the generic pop beat and bland lyrics, it all feels as semi-problematic as the title. Made only of phrases like "We got that Reignbow royal flush, all our tones make you blush," at best the song borders on pandering, and at worst it veers from queer representation into appropriation. But no one else has said a word—not even Vinny or

CeCe—so I resolved not to be the problem child again. Especially since it's kind of my fault we're stuck with this song in the first place.

That's also why I don't suggest any edits to the lyrics, aside from fearing that doing so will only anger this very successful, very expensive mega-producer. Who am I to suggest rewriting him? Will Zahra—who already left—be pissed if she hears that I slowed this process down? Will the other Jeweltones be annoyed that I'm being difficult, or feel that my "songwriting authenticity" is still "too good" for them?

I'm pretty sure rocking the boat now isn't the best way to save this sinking ship. Then my mind flashes back to that moment earlier, to the celebratory kiss between Dea and Stern, and my throat closes up. Which isn't the best feeling when standing in a recording booth.

Maybe Zahra is right. Maybe we need to earn our right to creative freedom. Maybe we should just be grateful for all the money and opportunity the label is throwing at us. Maybe a couple weeks on the grind is just what we need to gel and settle.

Then again, why do I feel like if we fall in line now, the day we finally get creative control will never come? It felt so good to have the support of the group for once, but is it a mistake to not just suck it up and offer to write more songs for Jeweltones? Now that we're here, will there always just be another festival, another appearance, another producer, another benchmark lined up for us?

I'm finally about to say something, but then I look through the studio glass. I see Stern looking like a little kid in a candy store. Next to him is Vinny, studying his lyrics. If anyone should disagree to the vaguely pride-related messaging of this song, shouldn't it be our self-professed "queen"? Shifting to CeCe, I see her sitting alone on one of the sofas and watch as she steals another secret glance at Dea.

I suddenly feel stupid, thinking we all could ever write together. What everyone needs from me right now is to behave, even though all I really want to do is scream.

As the producer cues me to start recording, I close my eyes and try to think of the song we *could* be creating . . .

The one we'd sing if we all started speaking our truths.

TURN TO PAGE 166

"And you're just assuming none of the rest of us want to write songs for Jeweltones?" Dea says right away.

"Of course not," I respond. "I'm just saying 'Press Diamonds' was a one-time thing."

I want to explain myself further, but there's one thought that wedges itself in front of everything else like a dam. *The secret between Dea and CeCe will probably rip us apart someday, one way or another.* I can't give myself to something that I can't fully trust, that I know is destined to fail.

"Well, I have some experience mixing songs," CeCe offers, an unusually sheepish look on her face. She has told me she is really good with home studio software, but she has refused to share her work with me, claiming none of it feels finished enough. If one good thing comes out of this retreat, at least it's getting to hear her announce this to everyone.

"I want to start learning how to craft originals, too," Stern adds.

Taking all of this in, Zahra sighs. "I love the enthusiasm, but I'm also disappointed to hear Everly's decision. It does simplify things today, at least. The label expects another single to promote. Now is the time for you all to bring your individual styles to the song that today's producer has created, which was modeled after 'Press Diamonds.'"

Zahra stands and grabs a pen off the table, so I scoot back to my seat. She writes something on the back of my board, then steps to one side so we all can read it.

Reignbow.

"It's the perfect second song for Jeweltones," Zahra says proudly. "And it's pre-approved by the label."

I try hard not to visibly wince. I guess I shouldn't judge the song until we've heard it, but that *title*. Still, I think the real reason for my unease is realizing that Zahra's "group retreat" has already ended. We resolved absolutely nothing, personally or creatively—we just conformed so we can replicate our viral success from the show. And that seems to be all Zahra and the label really want, or all they have time for, at least.

"There's another reason the label needs a second single from you ASAP," Zahra says. "It's some news I've been saving as a reward. We were officially able to add you to the lineup for a two-song set at the Popella music festival, which will be streamed live to millions."

Little bubbles of panic begin to creep up my throat as Zahra lets this latest news sink in. Unfortunately, her carrot-dangling tactics have become a little too transparent. Plus, performing a song called "Reignbow" at the world's largest pop festival, when Jeweltones is barely hanging on by a thread, does not sit well with me.

I turn to CeCe to see what she thinks, but I find her eyes locked elsewhere. I follow her gaze and find Stern and Dea, so thrilled by this news that they lean in for a celebratory kiss. This sets my own insides on fire, so I can only imagine how CeCe must feel. I glance away to catch Vinny's gaze, and he looks just as panicked as me.

Who is going to lead us out of this mess?

◆ ◆ ◆

I can't count the number of times I've dreamed of standing in a recording booth. A professional one, not the makeshift tour bus studio that production brought for us to record "Press Diamonds" the day of the finale. Standing in this booth now, I want to feel elated and inspired. Except all I feel when I look at the music and lyrics to "Reignbow" is disappointed and embarrassed.

Absorbing the generic pop beat and bland lyrics, it all feels as semi-problematic as the title. Made of phrases like "gems of every color shine bright under our Reignbow," at best the song borders on pandering, and at worst it veers from queer representation into appropriation. But since no one else has said a word—not even Vinny or CeCe—I've decided to keep my mouth shut. Especially since it's kind of my fault we're stuck with this song in the first place.

As I wait for the recording to begin, I can't help but wonder if I've made an enormous mistake not giving original songs to Jeweltones. Even if we don't have time to write another one on our new deadline schedule, I could have given over one of the dozens of songs I've already written.

Honestly, even the most amateur among them would feel more heartfelt than lyrics like "Not throwing elbows, we're crowning reignbows."

But then, the thought of giving away one of my songs still feels horrific. They feel so personal; how would the others navigate the lyrics? What if they hate them? And how might this mega-producer twist and bend a song to fit a potentially radio-friendly mandate? No. I couldn't do any of that.

Before I start singing, I wonder if the producer would mind if I suggested some lyrical edits or some melodic shifts. But would that just be stepping on his super successful toes? And would the others just be pissed at me for being difficult and backseat songwriting after refusing to take the driver's seat?

My mind flashes back to that kiss between Stern and Dea. There are so many fault lines forming in this group, I can barely even track the cracks. Hell, we could probably get an entire album of incredible songs if we were even halfway honest with each other. But how am I supposed to advocate for anything with both hands tied behind my back? It's up to CeCe to set us free of our secrets now. Or Dea will have to decide to tell the truth about what's been going on.

These are the thoughts that swirl through my mind as the producer finally cues me to start recording. I just hope some of this turmoil comes out in my vocals instead of making me sound defeated. The only thing keeping me from walking right out of this studio is the same thing keeping me silent: loyalty to CeCe, respect for Vinny, and . . . whatever I feel for Stern.

I try to tell myself that has to count for something.

Because right now, Jeweltones doesn't have much else to rely on.

TURN TO PAGE 166

Just once, I'd love to wake up naturally, feeling fully rested, and not be late for something. Unfortunately, as I startle out of bed this morning, I'm losing on both fronts. I "slept in," which only means I missed the breakfast club, but I still feel like I could sleep for another several hours. Tired and late and just trying to keep up: the Everly Jeweltones story.

In the days since our ill-fated studio "retreat," our schedule has been brutal. There was the promotional shoot for Popella, which had to be rushed given our last-minute addition. Dea was able to take the lead on that, steering us away from some truly hideous and borderline-homophobic rainbow outfits. Instead, she curated a jewel-toned series of looks, then arranged us in rainbow order for the promo as a compromise.

Then there was the day of label meet-and-greets and radio interviews, when Stern charmed his way out of some probing questions about the creative direction for our debut album by describing his ideal date with Dea. Then there was the very high-intensity music video shoot for "Reignbow," which was our first, since they used the finale performance footage as our video for "Press Diamonds." CeCe was the one to talk the director out of a romantic-partner storyline and instead feature us in a more organic, performance-centered direction. Finally, we started our first ten-hour Popella set rehearsal, where Vinny tried to start coaching me on ways to come out of my shell onstage.

I feel especially bad for Vinny. During all of this we learned that the label was fine forcing us to sing a song about royalty and rainbows, but was "tabling for now" the idea of him performing in drag. He shrugged it off, saying it was like so many major brands selling rainbow pride merchandise but ignoring or funding anti-LGBTQIA+ legislation locally. He said he was at least happy that the label agreed to let Jeweltones host the LGBT Center's fundraiser drag brunch after Popella, but I think he and CeCe deserve better. Dea too, I guess?

Lying here in bed contemplating "Reignbow," it makes me feel like I failed on the front that should have fallen to me. But then, I've been failing at songwriting all week. I haven't had one spare shred of energy to return to my songwriting closet. This is the longest I've ever gone without creating, and it's killing me. Especially because I've been bottling up my emotions all week—and not just creatively.

Being around Dea and Stern, America's newly cemented sweethearts, has just gotten more and more difficult. Our schedule keeps us so busy that we're either fully on as a group or off in our own corners, which means that I've barely had the time or bandwidth to talk to CeCe one-on-one about the whole mess. Part of me does wonder if she might actually be avoiding doing so . . . or if she's spending that precious solo time behind closed doors with Dea.

I try not to get lost down that particular rabbit hole. At the very least, there hasn't been another gossip leak from *CherriPop*. We've been all over the celebrity news, but mostly because of Dea and Stern's romance and rumors about which queer stars Vinny might be sleeping with. There's been some speculation on the feud between Dea and me as well, but nothing real from the inside. Maybe that's because things have cooled off with Dea. Well, frozen over might be more accurate. We just don't speak at all unless we absolutely have to.

I yawn and try to focus on pulling myself into some presentable form for our impending pickup, taking us into another day of promotional blitz. It's New Music Friday, so we have meetings at iHeart Radio, Spotify, Apple Music, and YouTube to promote the "Reignbow" single and music video drops. Then tomorrow it's back to a week of full-time Popella rehearsals and promotion before the festival starts next weekend.

I might be running behind, and everyone might be annoyed that I'm constantly five minutes late to everything, but I refuse to start the day without Gia's homemade breakfast and approximately one gallon of coffee. Brushing my teeth and combing out my frizzy mane can wait until after I hit the kitchen. Walking through the sunlit hallways of the house, I must admit that I do love this place. It feels equal parts tranquil and luxurious, but perhaps most importantly, it's spacious. When we're here, we can all truly recharge completely apart from one another—for better or worse, I suppose.

Which is why I'm startled as I enter the kitchen to find the unexpected sight of my own father cleaning beside Gia.

"Everly, you're up!" he reacts. "I was just about to bring you the plate I saved you."

"Um, thank you," I say. "But I didn't know you were coming over before work?"

"I'm afraid I'm to blame," Gia cuts in, approaching me with a full plate and an even fuller coffee mug.

"Your dad and I had a movie night, so I made him a bed in the den. You kids got in so late from your rehearsal last night, we didn't want to bother you."

Taking the plate from Gia, I suppress a smile. There is exactly a zero percent chance that my dad didn't stay in Gia's room last night, but I respect the attempt. I couldn't be more thrilled things are progressing between Dad and Gia, but I can tell Vinny definitely does not feel the same way. I decide Dad and Gia's discretion is probably a good idea, given all the Jeweltones fractures that are already under strain.

"Gobble up in the breakfast nook, hun," Gia says, returning to her cleanup efforts.

I could kiss Gia. To have these basic needs met by such a thunderstorm of caretaking love feels vital in the middle of all this. Glancing at Dad, I can tell he understands. I give him a side hug before I go, leaving him to enjoy the full brunt of Gia's hurricane-force love before work.

However, I'm almost blown away myself as I turn into the breakfast nook. I find Dea sitting there, nibbling on a fruit plate and already wearing a full face of makeup. Before I can turn back, she looks up, and we both freeze in the most awkward standoff. Leaving now would be beyond hostile, even for me. But zero part of my drooly, frizzy, pajama-wearing self wants to eat beside Dea's latest head-to-toe athleisure curation. She looks perfect as usual, while I look like a full mess.

I feel the usual storm of emotions, seeing her like this. Loyalty to CeCe, along with concern. Contempt for Dea's fakeness. Sympathy for her situation. Jealous of her access to CeCe and Stern. And finally, a flush of anger . . .

Because if I really break it all down, Dea Seo is the one standing in the way of *everything* I want—in every way.

"I'm almost done," she says, tipping her half eaten fruit plate.

Well, I guess there's no turning back now.

I fake a half smile and make my way over, too caffeine-deprived to think of an adequate excuse. Once I sit, I take the largest possible gulp of coffee, hoping it will kick-start my flailing brain. It's way too early for this minefield. My guard isn't anywhere near up.

"They pushed the SUV pickup back fifteen minutes," Dea offers. "Everyone is moving a bit slow this morning."

I nod, trying to ignore the way vegan-influencer Dea judges my plate of meat and eggs. Instead of speaking, I shovel a forkful into my mouth. Dea will probably think I'm being dismissive, but really I just feel blank as hell. *Come on, Everly. Surely you can find something inexplosive to talk about?*

However, all the usual small talk topics also fail me—we don't have any time to watch TV, and the weather in LA stays mostly the same. And now, despite my best efforts, all I can think about is secretly sitting in my room with Stern. No one has talked about that nugget, either.

But I refuse to feel guilty, given all the secret nights Dea has hoarded CeCe for herself.

"How are you feeling about all this?" she asks, her eyes glued to her halved grapes.

I'm thankful for the effort, but this isn't exactly a softball question. Still, it's a start, so I try my best to respond with a topic that Dea and I might actually be able to agree on.

❖ "It's weird, being **suddenly famous**," I say. "But not at all in the ways I would have expected."
TURN TO PAGE 170

❖ "I just wish I liked 'Reignbow' as much as 'Press Diamonds,'" I say. "I keep thinking of ways I could have fought to make it **fit us better**."
TURN TO PAGE 173

"Right?" Dea says, hooking into my response with relief. "I thought being famous would feel crowded or overwhelming, with all the attention. But it just feels . . ."

She searches for the right word, but I already know the perfect one. "Isolating?"

"Yes," Dea replies, spearing her fork through a triangle of pineapple. "Everyone I meet or interact with feels like they know me, but they don't. Not really."

I mean, that's a mouthful. I'm not sure anyone really knows Dea, but I'm not about to say that out loud.

"Absolutely," I say instead. "Or they treat me like an actual jewel, some precious trophy. I thought it was just because we're mostly around industry people. But something tells me interacting with the public would be even worse?"

"Don't even get me started on social media," Dea sighs. "The girls who come at me for being with Stern are relentless."

Oh, no. *Nope.* I am not going near that one, given everything I'm not supposed to know. And how I really feel about Stern or about how Dea is treating him. And CeCe. A pulse of anger snaps across my chest, but then I feel guilty. I should really be feeling bad for Dea, that she feels so much pressure to hide her real feelings.

Then again, I guess I should welcome her to the club.

"I will be avoiding social media like the plague today," I pick up. "I definitely don't need haters telling me what I already know about 'Reignbow.'"

"I know. It's like, this level of phenomenon, you can't create it, right? It has to happen on its own. And the way Zahra and the label are trying to sustain it feels . . . futile? It's like, now that this spotlight is shining on us . . ."

Dea trails off, but once again, I can easily fill in her blanks.

"You're afraid it will suddenly go dark?"

"Exactly," Dea says with a sigh. "Even though, like we said, the fame has felt super alienating."

"Part of that has to be our nonstop schedule, but I also think that has protected us?" I offer. "I bet we'd probably have a hard time going to get groceries or seeing a movie. This house is such privilege, but it's also a bit of a gilded prison."

"I'm also more afraid to post than ever," Dea goes on. "It's like, every move I make now carries all this extra weight. Between Zahra and UWU and all these new eyes and the press . . ."

This time, I can tell Dea trails off for a different reason. But it's still too early to start setting off any bombs, so I keep things moving.

"Have you gotten a sudden flood of DMs and texts?" I ask. "Long-lost cousins and randoms from elementary school suddenly want to know me again."

"Yes! And have you gotten any money requests yet? The really hard ones are the cousins or friends asking me to post about their products or businesses. To them it seems like nothing, but diluting my brand or posting for free would be an awful business move. Still, no one sees it that way, so then I'm just the bitch again for saying no or not responding."

I'm not sure I relate to that particular issue, but, then again, none of our new fame-induced issues seem relatable in the slightest.

"None of this is easy to understand from the outside, I guess," I try.

"Definitely not. I've tried to talk to my LA friends from before about this stuff, but I can tell it just makes them angry," Dea says. "I don't want to think they're jealous, but I know I would be, if the roles were reversed."

"My friends are all in college now," I reply. "In so many ways, Jeweltones wiped the slate clean. It's refreshing, sometimes. But other times it feels—

"—Unstoppable?" Dea finishes for me. "Like a gorgeous, glittering wrecking ball?"

I smile as Dea takes a sip of tea. That was a good line and she knows it.

Mostly, I marvel at the fact we just managed to have a civilized conversation. Not just that, but we actually connected like we used to when we first met. Right now, there are only a handful of others on the planet who can understand what this feels like . . . and four of them happen to be living under this very roof.

Maybe that's going to start counting for more than we ever could've anticipated?

For now, I try to be grateful that, for a few shining minutes, things felt like they used to between Dea and me. *Easy.*

How is it possible we made things between us so difficult?

Taking a sip of coffee, the memory of Stern leaving my bedroom the other night suddenly pops into my brain. I feel a wave of guilt burn its way through me . . . until I think of Dea potentially doing the same thing, leaving CeCe's room. And how through this entire conversation, Dea has concealed the truth without flinching. Without considering my feelings. Or Stern's feelings.

Unfortunately, I think that's probably what's going to end up counting more than anything.

TURN TO PAGE 175

Dea places both hands on the table, hooking into my response with visible relief.

"I thought I was the only one," she replies. "I mean, it's not that the song is bad—"

"—It's just that it sounds like every other song on the radio right now?" I finish.

"Exactly. I know Swede-Pop and K-Pop both love these chopped up English phrases, so they have global appeal. But what does 'true reign bow now' even mean?"

"I know, right? It all just sounds like some broad copy of 'Press Diamonds.' I know that was the point, but we have five unique styles. Shouldn't we be using that to push music forward, not blend into some generic sound of the moment?"

I can tell Dea agrees with me, but I can also tell the most obvious answer occurs to us both at the same time: we wouldn't even be in this position if I agreed to just keep writing songs for Jeweltones. Well, I can also think of a few compromising positions Dea has put Jeweltones in.

We sit in silence for a moment as a new layer of unease settles between us, but Dea tries to push through.

"I know the whole rainbow theme is supposed to relate to Jeweltones, but shouldn't CeCe and Vinny be the lead vocals or something, as our queer members?"

I instantly feel bad. How awful, to think that Dea might feel this way herself, but can't speak up about it.

Then again, I guess I'm in a very similar position—one she helped force me into.

"I've been wanting to say that too," I say, treading as lightly as I can. "But I don't want to make any more waves."

"I know. I've been wanting to say something about doing more advanced choreography—or any choreography," Dea says with a sigh. "I came up with a dance routine for the bridge of 'Reignbow,' but I've been too scared to pitch it."

"Well, I can't say I'd be excited about that," I reply, "but if this week has proven anything, it's that we can all play to our strengths in so many different artistic settings."

"Right," Dea replies. "But is that just because Zahra has pushed us to delay any creative resolution, so we're forced to fit into the mold demanded by the label?"

I mean, now Dea is speaking my language.

"So maybe instead of fighting so hard to blend, we can find a way to fight to protect each other as artists?"

Even though I say the words, they sound a bit like a fairytale. And Dea's face says it all, *That would be nice, wouldn't it?*

Unfortunately, that would require a level of honesty that might decimate us.

An awkward layer of silence settles between us once again, and we both pick at our breakfasts. We might all be in the same boat, but none of us trust it enough to remove our life vests just yet. No one more than Dea. I don't know what she's thinking, but I finally understand something about Dea and me:

We're magnets.

We repel just as easily as we attract.

I guess, if nothing else, we'd have a great hook for our first duet—if we can ever manage to get ourselves together.

TURN TO PAGE 175

CHAPTER TEN

EVERLY

I LOOK DOWN AT MY SONGWRITING SUPPLIES AND CANNOT
believe two weeks have passed since I've been in my closet corner. Well, I
can believe it given our nonstop schedule. Still, exactly what I feared at the
beginning of this journey has started coming true: Jeweltones has taken
me away from my songwriting. The only reason I'm even in here now is
because our Popella performance is tomorrow, and I can't sleep. Despite
being exhausted, I feel wired at the same time at this midnight hour.

I hoped freewriting a bit might calm me down, but my brain feels far
too sluggish and frazzled to produce anything. Instead, I've been scrolling
through my Instagram, reading new comments. My inbox has hundreds
of messages I should be responding to, but I don't feel capable of anything
more than tapping out red hearts. As I keep scrolling, I start to notice
something strange. All the notifications start to appear from the same
account: OOut678. The name sticks out because it's the same user who
sent me one of those first awful messages about selling out. A few days
ago, they started replying to every single comment on my posts. I focus on
one from a young girl who commented about how much one of my songs
helped inspire her, and OOut678 has replied:

Everly doesn't care about you, she only cares about being
famous.

My heart sinks. A quick survey makes it clear this troll has replied to
tons of comments, bashing me to my own followers. They're bullying not
just me, but all the listeners who go out on a limb to support me. It feels

like my blood drains out of my body. Something tells me that if I open my other socials, I'll find more of the same.

What do I do? I want to defend myself, but reacting to this hateful stranger would only be giving them exactly what they want. I definitely don't want to start getting in internet fights with anyone, so I lock my phone and close my eyes.

Why does doing the right thing lately always just involve staying silent?

I push myself off the floor and head toward my door. I'm not usually one to eat in the middle of the night, but maybe some bites of Gia's latest amazing pasta leftovers are exactly what I need to fall asleep.

I make my way to the kitchen, feeling awful. It's not just the guilt over neglecting my song world, it's this *feeling*. Like I'm frozen where I once was flowing, like I'm a plugged-up fountain. I worry if I keep holding everything in, that . . .

This thought fades as I enter the kitchen and find Stern there, enjoying a different kind of nightcap. Except "enjoying" isn't exactly the word I'd use. He actually looks kind of miserable, like the whiskey in his tumbler is bitter medicine.

"Oh," Stern says, straightening up once he spots me. The pained look on his face suddenly vanishes, replaced with more pleasant composure.

Neither of us knows what to say next. We haven't spoken alone since that night in my room. Or since CeCe told me about Dea's secret. My heartbeat suddenly explodes in my chest. I want to turn and run back to my room.

Except, I'm so tired of running.

"Can we just pretend that night in my room never happened?" I ask. "Or at least agree that it can't matter?"

Stern stares back at me, his green eyes still picking up bits of ambient light in this dimmed kitchen. There's a moment of silence between us as we just stand watching each other.

"I'd rather we talk about it," he responds. "I've been wanting to ever since, but I didn't want to overstep again. Still, I guess I'll do whatever helps us get back to normal."

I laugh. I can't help it.

"There is nothing remotely normal going on in our lives. Plus, you're still with Dea. There's nothing to talk about, really."

It's a little cruel, taking this tactic. But if Stern keeps reminding me how wonderful he is, I'll never be able to keep my distance.

"Fair enough," he replies, looking equally exhausted.

Instantly, I regret bringing Dea up. She is the last person I want to talk to Stern about, for too many reasons.

"Is your eczema acting up again?" I ask instead.

Stern sighs. "Worse than ever. I'd show you, but—"

"—You don't have to. Anything I can do to help?"

"I wish. But thanks for offering. Did you come in here for a snack?"

I nod, heading for the fridge. The motion is a relief, because I don't know how to talk to Stern. How to be his friend or what space to keep between us. Let's hope linguini will help.

While I fiddle with plastic containers, Stern takes a gulp of his drink, downing nearly the entire thing. I don't want to judge, but as far as coping mechanisms go, this one obviously isn't great.

"I haven't been doing this every night, I promise," he says, catching my eye. "I'm just so nervous about tomorrow. And today, the stylist for our performance must think I'm such a dick. I insisted on wearing a turtleneck under my jacket."

Stern turns toward me and pulls down the neck of his hoodie. Even in this dim light, I can see there's a dry, scaly patch of red running along his neck down his chest. Little blisters dot the rash, where Stern must have been scratching and bleeding.

I don't fully understand it, but seeing this massive blemish on Stern's otherwise perfect body . . . it makes me even more attracted to him. I wish I could show someone the wounds I'm nursing right now. Mostly, I'm just touched Stern trusts me enough to show me his.

"It never usually climbs that high," he says. "But I'm afraid that having the makeup person cover it with some heavy artificial concealer will only make it worse."

"You're still resolved not to let it show?" I ask, my eyes returning to the pasta I fork into a bowl. "I still think it would mean a lot, to a lot of people."

Stern pauses. "I'm not strong enough to do that. The social media stuff has gotten really intense lately. And the things they're writing in articles and on Reddit. It's already a lot."

"You shouldn't be reading all that," I say, instantly feeling like a hypocrite. As if I wasn't just doing the same exact thing when I was supposed to be writing songs. Why is this online feedback like an irresistible black hole, like picking a scab even though we know it will scar?

Stern smirks, seeing the storm that likely plays across my face. "And what are they saying about you?"

I smirk back. "For starters, that I'm a nervous wreck onstage. That Jeweltones would be nothing without me, but that I'm also the one destroying the group. That my nose is too big, that I'm too thin, that I'm too thick. That I'm a selfish, entitled bitch who thinks I'm better than everyone. That I'm a sellout and I don't care about my original listeners."

Saying it all out loud, these awful things I've been absorbing alone— suddenly it all sounds so absurd. Ridiculously, unquestionably absurd.

I start to laugh. Stern does too.

"Why do Vinny and Dea make this part look so easy?" he asks.

I turn to the microwave, needing a second to process my answer. Once my plate is spinning, I turn back to face him.

"I'm not sure comparing ourselves to anyone else is the way out of this."

Stern has something else he wants to say, I can tell. But first, he heads toward the bottle of Maker's Mark to refill his glass. He goes to pour, but then stops. Instead, he turns back to me with the full intensity of his emerald eyes.

"They say I'm a washed-up high school prom king who has already peaked. That I'm the pretty boy, lucky to get a second shot standing beside actual musicians with talent. That I should shut up and just take my shirt off. The problem is, I don't think any of it would hurt so bad if I didn't already believe all that about myself."

I stare back at Stern, my mouth hanging open just a little. I want to tell him he is none of those things. I want to tell him his star would burn so much brighter if he showed the world the darker sides of himself. But then I think of everything I've been hiding and, once again, I don't say anything I truly mean.

The microwave dings behind me, and when I turn to grab my reheated pasta, I wipe the tears from the corners of my eyes. This is too close, too dangerous. I need some air.

"Want to join me out in the backyard?" I ask, plate in hand, nodding toward the door.

We settle beside the pool, sitting cross-legged on matching lounge chairs. For a while we stay silent, just the sound of me eating and the breeze rippling moonlight across the chlorinated water. I know what I want to say, but I try to think of CeCe. I try to think of something meaningful to discuss that won't break everything. I focus on words that might help Stern.

"We all think that making our dreams come true will solve the other stuff, that the noise of success will drown out the bad thoughts," I say, feeling like I pull these thoughts out of nowhere. "But making your dreams come true only makes those voices louder, doesn't it? The success, the scrutiny—it all just amplifies what you already hate about yourself."

Stern keeps his gaze on the pool, but I can tell by the way he straightens that my words move him.

"And it's so much worse because you've got the thing you've been dying for," Stern picks up. "You're supposed to be happy, you told yourself you would be. And a lot of the new things do make you happy, for a little while. The house. Being onstage. The fans screaming for you. The clothes, the money, the social media attention. But it's all a sugar rush, like it has no substance. You get addicted to that sugar high, but then nothing actually feels different inside when things go quiet. Which makes it all feel . . . so much worse."

I nod. I knew Stern wouldn't try to hide. Or judge.

"I've been trying to figure out why I can't just embrace this opportunity," I add. "I've been blaming the group for stopping me from being the kind of artist I really want to be. But hearing what you said back in the kitchen, about only believing the bad stuff . . . I keep giving these external things all this power over my perspective. I want to change so much. But maybe the only thing I should try to change is how I see myself? Maybe until then, no version of success will ever feel like enough."

I'm still not quite sure where these words come from, but for now, I just try to be thankful I have any words to share.

"I think you're right," Stern says. "But how the hell are we supposed to change how we see ourselves?"

It's a good question. I don't have the answer.

At least, not for myself.

"Well, let me ask you this, mister golden boy," I say, putting down my plate. "You were always told you were the one destined for success, right?"

Stern nods.

"So you got to LA expecting just that. Then they told you that you were nothing. That had to be unbearable. Most people turn around and go home; they decide it's just not worth it. What kept you from giving up?"

It's a genuine question, not a leading one. I really want to know how Stern did it.

"I needed to make everyone proud," Stern answers. "I couldn't go back empty-handed. I just . . . *couldn't.*"

I turn over Stern's answer. As I do, I try to think of him like one of the characters I'd write into a song.

"Right," I say, working it out in real time. "And now here you are, you made it happen. But this new success depends on four other people. To keep it, you need to make us all get along. And to have value in the group, you're told you need to remain the heartthrob. It's no wonder you're bending over backward to be all of that."

Then something clicks in my brain, the same way it does when I've cracked part of a song. I follow this strange new flow, curious to see where it goes.

"But Stern, when we're not working, you always have a drink in your hand. Your body is fighting itself. You can keep going like this for a while, numbing with these coping mechanisms, living up to what everyone wants from you. You can go years even, but someday the wheels are going to come off. I mean, we've all seen it, especially with the twenty-seven club. So what if you changed the tune?"

"What do you mean?" Stern asks in a whisper.

"What if you told yourself you didn't stay in LA because you were afraid to fail, but because you love music too much to do anything else? What if you told yourself people want something deeper from you than the surface stuff you've been offering? What if helping the group meant speaking your mind, not always trying to make it nice?"

I say these words and they hit me like punches, over and over. I stun myself into silence, but I'm so tired of that too.

"It's terrifying how clearly you see me, Everly," Stern finally says.

I smile, but I don't look at him. If I do, I'll ruin everything.

It is pretty obvious that we both need to make some changes.

I try to think of someplace else we can start.

❖ If I'm asking Stern to share his most embarrassing secrets, to open himself up to judgment, then I need to do the same. I should show him my songwriting **closet**.
TURN TO PAGE 182

❖ If I'm telling Stern he needs to change his perspective to make Jeweltones healthy for him, then I need to change my own. We should **co-write** a song about this exact conversation.
TURN TO PAGE 185

"I have to show you something."

I meant these words back at the pool, but now on the long walk back to my bedroom, I feel the violent urge to take them back. *This is a mistake*, a voice screams in my head. *Your songwriting closet is too weird for anyone to accept. Stern shouldn't be in your room again.* It is so loud that it makes me feel light-headed . . . but then why do my feet keep moving?

"What am I looking at?" Stern asks.

It's only then that I realize we've reached the scarf curtain inside my walk-in closet. I feel like part of me is floating outside of my body, the adrenaline and exhaustion mixing to make everything feel like a dream. For now, this is as far as I can stand to go.

"Behind there is the secret to my songwriting, which I have never told a single soul about," I force myself to say. "It's kind of embarrassing, but I have this collection of pens, notebooks, and guitar picks—I'm kind of obsessive about matching perfect trios. I write all my songs in a closet like this wherever home is, in the middle of the night, all alone."

I take a deep breath, winding up for the next part.

"I also have this kind of dollhouse board-game setup in there, where I write about different fictional characters. And sometimes—a lot of times—I use it as inspiration to write songs. It's . . . how I wrote 'Press Diamonds.'"

I finish and my mouth feels parched and I still can't look at Stern. There's so much more I could tell him, but sharing this much feels like dangling myself off a steep cliff. I have no idea if he will reach out his arms to save me.

He stands quietly for what feels like forever. I think I might puke.

"I'm sorry, it's just . . ." Stern says. "Everly, you're the coolest, most creative person I've ever met. And all you do is fight to keep it to yourself."

I lose my breath. I don't know how to accept Stern's compliment and his acceptance along with his honesty. Because he is absolutely right.

"Mostly I'm jealous," Stern continues. "Or, no, I'm inspired. It makes me want to finish writing that song we started. It makes me want my own version of a songwriting closet."

Wow. Not only does Stern not think I'm a freak, but showing him this hidden part of myself actually inspires him? Has it really been a mistake to withhold this part of myself from Jeweltones?

"Hold on, I have something for you," I say, riding this impulse.

Sneaking behind the curtain, I reach into my notebook bag and open a side pouch. I always keep some bookmarks in there to hold the right place in my alternating notebooks. I've taken to writing different quotes about songwriting on each bookmark, and there's one I know Stern needs to see. I might not be ready to share everything in my songwriting corner with him just yet, but this much, he deserves.

Reemerging from my curtained corner, I offer Stern the bookmark.

"It's one of my favorites," I say. "It's a quote from Sara Bareilles. It always takes some of the pressure off."

Stern looks down and I watch him read the words I've transcribed, his green eyes ticking back and forth as his hair falls perfectly across his forehead.

I have an allergy to people taking too much ownership even over their own work. I have always felt as writers, we're channeling something, we're connecting into some greater network that has been around long before we were here and will continue to be around. It's like Martha Graham wrote, it's our job as artists to keep the channel open, not to judge what comes through. And to keep marching on the blessed unrest to the next idea.

Rereading it over Stern's shoulder, it makes me feel so stupid. Who am I to hoard my songs like they somehow belong only to me?

And who am I to keep lying to Stern about what's going on right behind his back?

"Everly, this is . . ." Stern says, but his voice falters. Instead, his gaze lifts to connect with mine.

For one perfect moment, it's like we really see each other.

I hold Stern's gaze and can't help it. My whole body feels pulled to him, like my cells are sizzling. A crackling heat rises through my entire body, threatening to consume me.

"There's something I need to tell you," he then says. "Something no one else knows."

"No, Stern. I know," I say, feeling my insides burst open. "CeCe told me about her hooking up with Dea weeks ago. She made me swear not to out Dea, but it's been killing me. Stern, I think you belong with—"

The words die on my tongue the moment I see the expression on Stern's face. He is in complete and utter shock.

"What?"

"You were about to tell me your relationship with Dea is just for show," I say, fumbling for the words. "Weren't you?"

Stern shakes his head, and the relief I felt suddenly curdles into dread.

I want to ask him what he was going to tell me. I want to explain everything to him. Most of all, I want him to stay.

"I can't," he says, the words faint as he backs away from me. "I need to be alone."

I want to stop Stern as he turns to leave . . .

But I'm terrified I've already said far more than enough for one night.

TURN TO PAGE 187

"You know, there's a quote I think about a lot, especially lately," I say. "It's from Sara Bareilles, who is obviously a songwriting legend. She once said, 'My spiritual practice was writing songs. And then as my business grew around it, that sort of pure seed of it started to have to hold a lot more complexity.'

"I never really got what she meant about the complexity, but I think I'm beginning to now," I continue. "What I'm really trying to ask, Stern, is do you want to grab some guitars and finish writing that song we started?"

I don't think I've ever seen Stern's eyes light up any brighter.

♦ ♦ ♦

We probably shouldn't be back in my bedroom, but making noise out in the open felt far more dangerous. Stern and I sit up against my guitar corner wall. I realize the other side of this wall houses the songwriting nook in my closet.

That feels fitting.

Stern draws my attention back to him as he starts playing the tune we came up with weeks ago. I'm impressed he remembers it, but doubly so at how light the guitar sounds under his fingers. I start playing the chords, my own guitar feeling technical and sturdy against his nimble sound. It's a nice effect, kind of opposite to the way our voices blend.

Stern then starts singing the melody with his buttered honey tone:

"What do you do when the thing you enjoy

Starts to feel like no fun?

What do you do when the thing you love

Burns you out faster than you can run?"

Stern blushes as he finishes. "I added some words since last time."

"I love that," I say, meaning it.

Then another line occurs to me, springing out of our poolside conversation. I start singing it in the same melody line, building out the front end of this potential chorus.

"They only see what I decide to show

And I hate them for thinking it's the whole scene.

They think the grass is greener up here,

But the weeds only grow more mean."

It's not perfect, but it's a decent start. Plus, the act of writing lyrics in this way, out loud and on the fly with someone else, feels really strange and a little terrifying.

But also *liberating.*

"That's good, I like that," Stern says, still strumming. "But I think it doesn't fit as well on the chorus melody. Maybe it'll fit better on a first verse?"

I instantly agree, nodding. I have an urge to start writing this all down, to get it under my control, but I fight that urge. Maybe this collaborative, organic process is exactly what I need to start embracing, instead? Could this be exactly the kind of thing I'd excel at if I let down the walls protecting me from Jeweltones?

I look over at Stern and can tell he's thinking the same exact thing.

"There's something I need to tell you," he says after a beat. "Something no one else knows."

Suddenly, a flood of relief washes through me. *He knows.* We can finally be honest with each other, the way we always deserved to.

"Stern, I already know," I reply. "CeCe told me about her and Dea a while back. But you shouldn't have to fake your relationship anymore."

Once I finish, whatever relief I felt suddenly curdles into dread. The only expression on Stern's face is complete shock.

"What?" he asks. "Dea and CeCe are a thing?"

I think I might puke.

"I thought that's what you were going to tell me," I whisper. "So you and I could . . ." I don't finish the sentence. I want to ask Stern what he was going to tell me. I want to explain everything to him. But most of all, I want him to stay.

"I can't," he says as he places the guitar on the floor. "I need to be alone."

I want to stop Stern before he leaves . . .

But I'm frozen in place.

TURN TO PAGE 187

◆ ◆ ◆

Hours pass, but I can't sleep.

Playing the scene over, I wonder how I could be so stupid. What was I even thinking?

After a while I work up the courage to go to Stern's room and try to explain myself. However, after knocking on the door, I realize that Stern isn't there. And his phone goes straight to voicemail when I try to call.

I think about going to talk to CeCe, but it occurs to me that, in the middle of the night, she might be with Dea. This causes a spike of anxiety so fierce, all I can think to do is return to my bed.

So here I lie, staring at the ceiling and hoping Stern comes back before the sun rises.

◆ ◆ ◆

The sun does rise, but I don't see Stern until I step onto the Sprinter van that will take us to perform at Popella. Vinny and CeCe are already seated and waiting, as well. I want to say something, anything, to Stern. But Dea already sits beside him, leaning her head on his shoulder. I can't even send him a text without her potentially seeing it. Besides, the moment he sees me, he avoids eye contact.

He doesn't want to talk.

"Are you okay?" CeCe asks as I sit beside her.

Every fiber of my being screams at me to tell CeCe what happened, about this awful thing I did. But how can I? We're about to give the biggest performance of our lives—on a stage in front of thousands of people—that will be broadcast live to millions. During the last week and a half, Zahra made it sound like our entire Jeweltones future relies on us proving we can take this next step. I can't be selfish again. I can't sabotage us now. This has to wait until tomorrow.

I look out the window and wonder if this is exactly what Stern is thinking.

I don't know.

It doesn't feel like I can trust my thoughts right now.

"Everly," CeCe says, nudging me. "Seriously—you okay?"

"I think I'm spiraling a little bit," I manage to say.

"Yeah, I could tell," CeCe replies. "But we're ready for this. *You're* ready for this."

"Just think of the theater exercises we've been running," Vinny says, leaning over the aisle. "You're ready."

I can't even bring myself to nod. I'm so thankful for Vinny's help, but I've been able to see it in his eyes all week—I'm not a natural. I'm still awkward and self-conscious and stiff. The only good news? I'm so full of guilt right now that my stage fright is the least of my worries.

"Vinny is right, Everly," CeCe adds. "You're not going to be perfect in a couple of weeks, but you are getting better. And you're good enough to make this work. If you let go."

I look at CeCe and I fight back tears. If only she knew what happens when I really let go. But I've been faking it until we make it for so long already, what's one more day? Who knows, maybe my sleepless night and supercharged emotion will actually help me break through onstage this afternoon. It's just, why do I have to find out in front of a few million people?

This is the very definition of *be careful what you wish for.*

I'm not sure I'd wish this on my worst enemy. Except, I guess, glancing at Dea sitting pretty beside Stern, I've certainly wished something on her?

At least, once the Sprinter van gets moving, sleep finally finds me.

♦ ♦ ♦

Hours later, I look at my reflection in a window in the Popella backlot. I hardly recognize the person staring back at me, and not just because of the face full of frosted makeup or my blue metallic dress. This is the first second I've gotten to be alone all day, and it's a moment stolen twenty minutes before we're supposed to go onstage. I told the others I was going to get some air, so I stand in the dry heat in the parking lot outside our trailer and try to pull myself together enough to do what I have to do. The only trouble is, I'm having a hard time catching my breath. I feel a little bit like I'm suffocating. I thought some air would help, but now all I can think is *how the hell did I end up here?*

"There you are."

I hear Stern's voice behind me and it does nothing to help me relax.

"I wanted to make sure you're okay."

I turn around and give him a look because he is a *lot* late for that.

"I know," he sighs, approaching me. "I just . . . today is such a big day. We've worked so hard. And I can't understand some of the choices you made."

"You're right; we shouldn't do this now," I say, feeling my pulse start to race.

"Listen, wait," Stern says, coming closer as his voice drops into a whisper. He glances at the trailer where the others are just inside. "I'm sorry, but I can't be the reason you're not okay. I need to be the reason you always feel okay."

These words aren't exactly lyrics for the ages, but they roll through my body like thunder.

"I don't know what to do without breaking things." The words just tumble out of my mouth. It's like I barely register that I'm speaking. "What were you going to tell me last night?"

Stern pauses, weighing something. Then he meets my gaze. "I was going to tell you that I was the gossip leak. I was the one to feed the stories to *CherriPop* in the beginning. I thought it would help keep us relevant like Zahra said we needed to. But I realized how fucked up that was and I stopped. I would have told everyone sooner, but I was afraid you wouldn't forgive me. That you'd look at me differently. But keeping the secret was killing me. So trust me: you don't have to feel like the only bad guy."

I see the earnestness, the purely apologetic look on his face. But I can't stop my body from stepping away from him.

Stern was the one to leak all that awful stuff about my manager meeting? About me being some artistic snob? I suddenly think of Dea speaking to that reporter, telling them all about me and my weaknesses. How could Stern?

How could this be happening all over again?

"You didn't tell anyone about Dea and CeCe hooking up, did you?" I ask.

I don't know if this question is fair or if it's an attack, but I have to know. I only wish I had looked behind Stern before I asked, because I now see CeCe standing frozen beside the trailer.

"Everly. No."

My breath catches in my throat.

Just then, Vinny also comes around the trailer, followed by Dea. Stars begin to fizzle and burst at the edge of my vision.

"What are you all doing out here?" Vinny asks. "We're on in . . ."

Then he stops, catching the expressions on our faces and understanding.

"Wait, what's going on?" Dea asks, looking from CeCe to Stern, then finally to me.

"We should talk about this after we perform—" Vinny tries.

"—Someone tell me what is going on," Dea insists, giving Vinny a bewildered look. "Right now."

"Actually, I think you're the one who owes me an explanation," Stern says. "Were you ever going to tell me you were just using me for the cameras? How long were you going to force CeCe to lie about being with you? Did you just do it because you know I've had feelings for Everly from the start?"

Stern's questions ring across this parking lot, sinking into the baked asphalt. Dea doesn't answer. Instead, she turns to look at CeCe like her trust—and her heart—have just been broken into a million pieces. I know it's the same look CeCe would give me if her eyes weren't fixed on the ground.

"Oh no."

I hear Vinny's voice and think of how he must feel, watching the group drive off a cliff with him stuck in the backseat. I realize that he isn't talking about us, however, as I follow his gaze behind me and Stern.

Standing there is a young guy wearing a badge that reads **Influencer VIP Access** and holding up his phone to record us.

In the same moment, a young woman wearing a headset comes around the trailer and waves us over.

"Jeweltones, come with me. You're on next."

◆ ◆ ◆

Standing on the darkened stage, I have trouble feeling my body. The last ten minutes were a blur of shuffling and getting set and simmering in silence. Jeweltones all stand on our marks, waiting for the lights and the music to fire up. We wear outfits in our genre styles, but with a uniting theme Dea pitched earlier: mirrored mosaics. It seems morosely fitting now, each of us dressed in the shattered shards of a disco ball.

We are a detonated bomb. A jewel that has finally fractured.

And somehow, we have to shine brighter than ever.

I look out at the crowd, and it stretches as far as my eye can see, punctuated by a galaxy of flashing phone cameras. It feels like the ocean at night, ebbing and ominous. The crowd sways and screams, but I hardly register it over the sound of my own heartbeat pounding in my ears.

The terror seizes me just as the lights and music blast on.

I'm vaguely aware that somewhere across the stage, CeCe has started singing. It feels like I'm underwater. The wave of cheers from the crowd drowns me and the cameras circling the stage feel like sharks, out for blood. My vision blurs.

My hands go numb.

I can't feel the microphone.

It's all too much.

❖ I'll try to **channel the emotion** into my performance. Maybe the fact that I'm not in control is exactly what I need.
TURN TO PAGE 192

❖ I refuse to put myself through any more of this. I **walk offstage**.
TURN TO PAGE 194

I need to pretend nothing just happened. Pretend like no one is watching me. I have to remember what we rehearsed. I need to let go.

Despite my best efforts, I still can't get my bearings. Somewhere in the background I think I hear Stern singing, which means the chorus of "Reignbow" must be coming. I have a mark for the chorus across the stage. We've practiced this a hundred times. I know where to go.

I cross the stage and a little bit of weight shifts off me as I think I'm in the right place. Except when I look up, all I see is Dea's face coming toward me. She's too close.

What is she doing on my mark?

Then I look down and realize I must be on her mark, and she bumps me out of the way with her hip. I know it's an accident, that she doesn't see me. I stumble a bit, but I don't fall. Which is good, but now I don't know where I am onstage.

This is a nightmare.

How many people are watching this? Why can't I feel my feet? I'm sure I could pull it together if I could just find . . .

My mark.

I find it and I ground myself in place.

Get it together, Everly, I scream to myself.

Somehow that helps clear the fog a little. The stage suddenly snaps back into focus, and the sound rushes in at once. I'm surrounded by the chorus, the one I'm supposed to be singing along with, and I hear how jumbled it sounds. No one is on the same page. No one can hear themselves.

Before I can join in, Dea is on to the new verse. I don't know if it's because I threw her off before, but she misses every note. Who am I kidding? Of course it's because I threw her off. *This can't be happening,* I tell myself. Millions of people are watching and they're all going to think Dea and I brought our feud to the stage.

Except, didn't we?

The second chorus winds back around and, mercifully, we manage to sound a little better. I even succeed in singing my part by some miracle. But we aren't out of the woods yet because the bridge is coming.

They engineered "Reignbow" to mirror the structure of "Press Diamonds," so I have a solo there again.

Except as the bridge arrives, my throat tightens and my mind goes blank.

I can't think of a single lyric. I can't even remember the melody to fake it.

All I can channel, here onstage in front of the world, is . . .

Absolutely *nothing*.

TURN TO PAGE 195

I'm in the grip of the riptide. I don't know what to accept or reject, what to fight for or fight against. Until I get my bearings, I just need to get off the ride.

I need to stop.

This is the worst possible timing, but the pressure has finally burst our glittering lies and exposed the ugly truth.

Just as the others begin to sing "Reignbow," I turn and walk offstage. I don't know if this is me trying to destroy the group or trying to save it. All I know is that if I fake it for one more solitary second, I don't think I'm going to make it. Especially not when who we really are in private is about to be exposed for the whole world to see.

As I step out of the spotlights, I see Gia. I knew she and Dad were here and that they'd be watching somewhere from the wings, but I didn't think she would be right there. I think Dad is standing beside her, but for some reason my vision tunnels. I can only focus on Gia's worried face.

"Can you take me to the trailer?" I say, my voice barely registering over the speakers blaring our song.

From there, I only feel Gia clutching my hand as she clears a path for us. There are a lot of people asking a lot of questions, but I don't hear any of them.

All I feel is Gia's hand, guiding me out of this nightmare.

TURN TO PAGE 195

CHAPTER ELEVEN

VINNY

IT'S SUNDAY MORNING ON THE PATIO OF WEST HOLLYWOOD'S
most iconic gay bar. I'm seated as the lone guest of honor at this charity
brunch for the LGBT Center. I watch as the famed drag queen Mother
Lake lip syncs across the stage to none other than "Press Diamonds."
It's all just so impossibly glamorous, darling. I should be feeling like I'm
inside my heaven.

Too bad everything feels cracked under that shiny surface.

It was just a few nights ago that Jeweltones detonated on the Popella
stage. But before that, standing on that platform in front of all those
people—I've never done anything that massive before. I guess not many
people on the planet have ever gotten to feel what it's like to have thousands of eyes focus their energy on you that way. The rush I felt . . . it was
the closest I've ever come to pure bliss. And in those sacred moments, one
thought crystalized:

I could never have gotten to a stage this big without Jeweltones.

Then, just as quickly, Jeweltones stole that same rush away.

I still don't know what possessed Everly to tell Stern the truth about
CeCe and Dea right before the biggest performance of our careers—or why
she brought it up in a backstage lot swarming with press and influencers.
We were obviously a hot mess before going on. Then Everly panicking
pushed down a domino that toppled the rest of us. We tried our best to
regain our balance, but let's be real—we were never really a cohesive unit
to begin with. I don't think I've ever been more mortified than when
we slinked off that stage. They literally turned off the lights on us after
"Reignbow," cutting us off before we could perform "Press Diamonds."

I still don't know if it was a blessing or a curse. But to go from that sky-high to that rock-bottom . . .

I half-expected fireworks to erupt between us backstage. Instead, we were immediately shuffled outside into separate black SUVs. All our post-performance press was canceled. I just found myself sitting beside Mom, after Everly's dad said he was taking her back to their house in the valley. I tried calling Dea, but instead of answering she just texted that she was going to her apartment in WeHo. I tried CeCe next, but her phone went straight to voicemail.

I had no particular desire to talk to Everly or Stern yet, but Stern was the only other one of us to return to the house that night. He told me what happened, including the extra grenade that he had been the gossip leak all along. It was all too much.

After assuring Mom I didn't need anything to eat, I hid in my bedroom until this morning. I half-hoped to hear from the others, but I understood why each one of us hid away. Not only did the footage of our performance fail get covered everywhere, it was also bolstered by the video of our pre-show trailer fight. Though, of course, the only part of the fight that cursed influencer captured was Stern's list of questions incriminating Dea. It included nothing about Everly's loose lips or Stern's own gossip-leaking habits. Jeweltones went viral for the second time in a month, but this time for all the wrong reasons.

I tried calling Dea again, but her phone was still off. Which was probably for the best, since my only glimpses of the coverage have questioned our collective talent, shipped the new coupling of "EverGreen," and completely villainized Dea in just about every way possible. Everyone from hopeless romantics to Stern-gazers to die-hard Gemstones to homophobe haters to queer advocates could find a reason to hate Dea, having only heard Stern's side.

I wanted to march over to his room and chew him out for not owning his part publicly, but I wasn't sure what good that would do—he probably felt guilty and betrayed enough on his own. The only call I did get was from Zahra, saying she would talk to the label and get back to us. But since then, there has only been radio silence on the Jeweltones front.

Sitting here at this brunch now, playing this all over in my mind, I don't know if it would have been better or worse for the others to show up today. I'm not sure if any of them have talked to each other, but as usual, no one has involved me. I can't help but feel like I didn't do enough to prevent this. Like I should have worked harder to force us to communicate. Divas below, I didn't even follow through on the investigation I promised to start. I did do some digging, but I got nowhere before prep for Popella took over our entire lives. I suppose I can't blame myself too much. We were always just hitting our marks and shutting our mouths. And if there's anything the world loves more than a meteoric rise, it's a catastrophic crash.

How far we'll fall, nobody knows.

The worst part is that only four other people on the planet know what I'm feeling right now, but I can't seem to talk to any of them about it. Even if we somehow miraculously find a way through this, I don't know if I'd even want to stay in Jeweltones.

I'm used to feeling lonely, but this seems like a unique brand: famous AF with no one to talk to. I'm part of a unit that refuses to function, sitting on the sidelines watching a real drag queen perform my song. It all makes me feel like an empress with no clothes.

A frown tugs across my face as Mother Lake reaches the bridge, but I force myself to put on a smile. I might as well try to be here and now while I can still use my fifteen minutes for a good cause. Looking around the patio, I'm relieved to find that most eyes remain fixed on Mother Lake's swinging fringe instead of rubbernecking at this mostly empty table. Though, I do find one set of lovely eyes on me.

The guy I find staring is quite cute. Short, super thin, and stylish. I match his gaze dead on, but it doesn't seem to intimidate him. Instead, he keeps on cruising and nods toward the bathrooms, a sexy grin on his face. I smile and nod right on back.

I try to stand as discretely as possible, noting that I leave a full table of food behind. It wasn't easy ignoring the voice that screamed at me to eat the stack of fluffy, gluten-filled pancakes in front of me the last hour. But after sticking to my elimination diet these past couple weeks, I'm actually starting to feel fantastic. Not only have my withdrawal symptoms stopped, but I haven't had a stomachache in days—which has never happened. *Ever.* I've also suddenly de-puffed, dropped some inflammation weight, and my skin is doing this kind of dewy glow thing. That doesn't all matter to me as much as suddenly feeling healthy, but it's certainly a nice set of perks—along with the realization of how much power food used to have over me. How eating whatever I wanted, whenever I wanted, was far more important to me than feeling healthy.

Sure, food still has power over me in a way, I guess. I might not be able to eat most things at this table yet, and I have no idea how I'm going to start navigating ordering without seeming like a nightmare diva. But the point is, I have stuck to my guns on the allergy-elimination diet against all odds, during the most stressful period of my life, and it has paid off. I'm not sure I'm meant to avoid foods like this forever, but for now, I enjoy the clarity the limitations have given me.

I know some rogue gay is probably going to take a picture of this table of uneaten food, saying I have an eating disorder. Dea told me last week that plenty of blogs already claim I'm on a crash diet to try losing weight now that I'm famous, the same way they ripped at Adele and Sam Smith and too many others. Which is absurd, because my body is always going to serve curves and swerves—I'm just far less inflamed. Not to mention that they keep on digging into my sex life, finding old hookups or trying to catch me with new ones. Someone will probably post about the guy I'm about to follow into the bathroom—more slut-shaming to add to the fat-shaming.

But then I think: It's a very good thing I don't care. It's a good thing I've always loved my body, at every size. It's a good thing I genuinely love being young and single. And it's the best thing that I'm never going to let their hang-ups stop me from doing me.

So I sashay into this bathroom with zero shame in my fabulous game. After all, straight rock stars have been promiscuous with their fans forever—now it's about time this queer star evened the score.

Besides, after this weekend, I might not be a pop star much longer.

♦ ♦ ♦

Coming out of the bathroom, I feel a bit more relaxed. The guy—Marcos, as I learned—asked if he could hang behind another minute so we wouldn't be seen exiting together. Obviously I don't care if anyone knows, but neither of us wanted to fuel any more gossip that might distract from this charity event. I don't know if it's a good thing or a bad thing, then, that the first person I see upon emerging is The Hand Made, in full brunch-food-themed drag.

I brace myself for some kind of disapproval, but instead, Made smiles from ear to ear.

"You go, girl," she says. "Now, come with me. You've put in far more than enough face time, and we have quite a bit of tea to spill."

A few quick turns later, I follow Made into a dressing room behind the bar. There are a few vanities covered with makeup products and the floors are dusted with stray feathers, glitter, and rhinestones. Made sits at one of the vanities and pulls up a highback chair for me. I get a better look at her drag now, which features a sunny-side egg bra and coffee cup earrings.

"Now, my dear, forgive me for being a doting mother," Made begins, "but I always need to make sure you youths are being safe when it comes to the birds and the bees."

"I'm on PrEP and keep condoms in my bag," I answer, smiling.

"God, I love how sex- and body-positive your generation can be," Made replies. "I'm still battling the closeted Catholic shame and Abercrombie body mess that ruined us as teens. But then, the children always have something to teach we who preach."

"Amen. I figured I deserved a snack after the weekend I've had," I joke. "By the way, I'm so sorry the others didn't attend."

"Please, I totally understand. Besides, you are more than enough pop star for us. We've already raised a ton for the homeless youth programs. Plus, we did get a nice donation from one Dea Seo."

Without any messages from Dea since Friday, this feels like a really lovely one. Especially because the label has only given us our prize money, which doesn't amount to much split five ways and saved for taxes. Which means Dea must have donated from her pre-show money. I wish I were able to donate too, but now I find myself wondering if we'll get paid again at all, if Jeweltones gets dropped or breaks up. Suddenly, all I want to do is talk to Dea about everything. She really has become one of my best friends . . . but will I lose her too if this all ends?

"Aw . . . here, babe," Made says, snatching a tissue. I barely even realize that I've started crying a little. "You can let it out here. You're in a safe space."

Hearing this from Made, I really believe her. It's like the words then tumble from my mouth, falling with my tears.

"I forced myself to try and fit in with Jeweltones, to become what they needed," I start. "I tried my absolute best and it still wasn't enough."

Then I feel it, bubbling up my throat like bile: the voice of my inner saboteur.

⊛ "I work so hard to fit in everywhere, but I don't end up **belonging** anywhere. No one wants the real me."
TURN TO PAGE 201

⊛ "I don't know who I really want to be, and I'll never be **enough** until I do. But every time I try, I fail."
TURN TO PAGE 203

I speak the words and they make me sound so small. Like even this, my deepest and darkest, isn't enough. Found wanting. *Oh, is that all? Don't be so silly, you ungrateful brat.*

I expect Made to say as much, to snap me out of it.

Instead, she reaches out and takes my hands in hers.

"Vinny, listen to me. I know we haven't known each other that long, but you remind me so much of myself at your age. And from where I'm standing, I see how you have handled an extraordinary experience and a boatload of stress like a goddamn pro. You're only human, and you've been shot out of a cannon. It would be a lot for anyone."

Made's words wash over me, and I can feel them start to soak in, just a little.

"I might not be half as smart as you kids these days, but I have lived twice as long. So let me tell you something you'll probably learn later: you'll never meet a harsher critic than yourself. But you'll also never find a better friend. Sometimes you gotta get outside your own head and think of yourself as someone you love. Think of how you accept that person, even at their worst, how you forgive them their flaws, and apply that to yourself. All I'm really trying to say, Vinny, is that you gotta learn to go easy on yourself."

I look back at Made, knowing in my bones that she is right. I just wish I knew how to do what she says.

"And if you can't do that for yourself at first, then do it for all the queer kids who now look up to you," Made adds. "You belong to them, to us."

She lets go of my hands, probably able to tell how embraced I'm starting to feel.

"Now, it sounds to me like you already know who the real you is . . . and she is a queen," Made finishes with a smile. "Stop fighting to fit in and start fighting to stand out."

I sit back and let her words sink in: Can I really be a drag queen and a pop star? All the usual answers spring to mind, the limitations and restrictions and excuses. I open my mouth to speak them, then I stop myself, suddenly realizing something: that voice belongs exclusively to my inner saboteur.

"Now, honey, I don't know if Jeweltones is done for. And, honestly, it doesn't look good from where I'm sitting," Made says. "But if the group is really on the rocks, what do you stand to lose by doing things exactly the way you want? If you ask me, you all owe it to yourselves to at least see if you can come up with something better than that dreadful 'Reignbow' garbage."

I laugh, because she is so right.

Made gives me a grin and a quick pat on the knee. "Besides, if you can't make it work, then fine. We'll just have to find you someplace else to shine."

TURN TO PAGE 204

"I don't deserve all this talent if I don't know how to use it," I say. "It's why I never really win."

Hearing the words out loud makes me sound, and feel, so small. Like even this, my deepest and darkest, isn't enough. Like I'm somehow still found wanting. The voice echoes in my head, *Oh, is that all? Don't be so silly, you ungrateful brat.*

"Honey," Made says, reaching out to grasp my hands. "If this is what failing looks like, then I'm not sure I'd know what winning was if it walked up and kissed me."

Made gives me a dazzling smile and I can't help but laugh, just a little.

"Vinny, we haven't known each other that long, but let me tell you— the things you've accomplished already, they're incredible. I know when you're young it can feel impossible to know how you're going to make your talents count. But look where that talent, however raw, has already gotten you.

"But no one said it would be easy. The stress and the pressure, they're real. It would be strange if you weren't feeling overwhelmed. But I need you to hear me on this next part, because I wish someone would've said it to me when I was your age. You are never a waste of anything, Vinny. You are Superman. You are Wonder freaking Woman. It's just gonna take some time to learn how to use all your superpowers. And that's perfectly okay. Okay?"

Looking back at Made, even though I'm still crying, I also smile wide.

"The moral of the story?" she goes on. "You're allowed to be every freaking color you are, Vinny. And if Jeweltones won't let you shine, then let that ship sink. Honestly, it looks like that's happening anyway. But if you ask me, I think this group thing could still give you a place to let all your talents shine, collaborating with your peers. You could be one of the first drag queens to do it in the mainstream pop world. It will be a hard road to travel, but you can't walk it if you're afraid."

TURN TO PAGE 204

Made winks at me, so I wipe the tears from my eyes and wink back.

"You know, that reminds me of exactly something my mom would say," I say with a small laugh.

"She sounds like a smart lady."

"You two would really get along. Actually, you'd probably make a pretty terrifying team."

"Then I *definitely* have to meet her," Made says, standing up from her chair.

I move to follow, but she motions for me to stay.

"The other queens won't be back for a while; we have hosting duties," she says. "I'll come get you when we need you. For now, take a moment. Feel the fantasy. *Play.* You've earned that much."

Made plants a lipstick kiss on my cheek, then clacks out of the dressing room. I experience a full-bodied burst of gratitude. Of all the people who have come into my life through this surreal LA experience, Made ranks as one of my absolute favorites.

Sitting in this space alone, soaking in the wig stands and makeup brushes, I turn Made's words over and over in my brain, like a song on repeat. It starts to crystallize things, sharpening them in my mind. Jeweltones might already be doomed. There isn't any sense in trying to run from that. However, if it has any chance of surviving, it won't be because we keep doing as we're told. The way to save Jeweltones might be the same way I start to save myself.

By embracing the ugly.

Because we're prettiest when we do.

After all, isn't that what being a real artist is all about? Externalizing your demons to inspire something stunning? It's certainly what drag is all about, at its heart.

If I'm looking where to belong as my own artist, then that feels like the place to begin.

◆ ◆ ◆

Before I know it, I'm twirling around the dressing room like I own the place. I've borrowed a long black wig and plugged my phone into a set of speakers to play my favorite queer anthems. Someone could walk in or overhear at any moment, but I don't care. I just want to let them all *have* it.

So I finally just sing.

I belt at the top of my lungs with abandon just for the joy of it. It's preposterous that I can't remember the last time I did this. At some point in these last few years, my voice became a tool, a way to get the things I want, or a reason people are drawn to me. I guess I just got used to preserving it for professional posterity.

But today, I embrace my voice for what it is:

A gift from the divas above.

Right now, singing along with my favorite queer artist inspiration like a pro, my voice feels like the greatest gift anyone could possibly receive. I need to give it away more freely, more fearlessly. It's the debt I owe for possessing the talent.

Sashaying into the next verse, I start improvising and freestyling some of the words. It sounds like a hot mess, but I still sing the words of my inner saboteur loud and clear. Belting the words out this way, it feels like I sap their power and use it to supercharge myself instead. Mostly it all sounds so much less scary, sung aloud.

Why was I taking it all so seriously? I'm a fucking pop star. Isn't it time to have some fun?

I wish I could feel this light, this free, all the time, but I know our inner tides always turn. So it is okay that I need a reminder, every day, of how I feel right now. How I want to feel all the time. Maybe that's where I can start to craft my queen?

My brain begins to whir again, processing all the different parts of myself. My voice, my look, my stage stunts. I try to make some singular sense of it all, but the moment I feel anxious again about defining it, I stop myself. I rewrite the narrative. I play Made's words in my mind, sounding so much like my own fabulous mother.

Then suddenly it hits me, hard and whole.

My queen, she exists at the push and pull between being undefined and branded, excluded and included, too much and not enough. She lives somewhere between breadth and focus, between my diva voice and my drag voice, between my heart and my head. Most of all, my queen needs to be the living embodiment of these motherly words, a physical reminder of how to embrace and overcome my inner saboteur.

❖ My queen embraces her traumas and turns them into strengths, wearing them like badges of pride. My queen is **Dame** Made of Reignbow.
TURN TO PAGE 207

❖ My queen is always two things at once. She is all of me and all my divas above. My queen is Made **Via** Gia.
TURN TO PAGE 209

Dame Made of Reignbow reclaims and reappropriates. She can take a bland song and make it a banger. She takes sad tales and transforms them into origin stories. She takes terrible tumbles and turns them into elegant recoveries.

She is the rainbow, the queerest and boldest icon out there. But even rainbows are made of individual colors—and Dame Made intends to use them all, both inside and outside the lines. This new queen will reign as pop royalty. She will challenge the status quo. And she will shine, especially when it rains. She will always wear bows, and she will always be ready to throw some too.

Most importantly, Dame Made of Reignbow can take Jeweltones' greatest flop, our cracking pressure point, and turn it into a precious gem. She will exist because of Jeweltones' success and despite its failures. Her queendom will show everyone this group will be forever a part of me, even if it only ends up being for one bright flash.

My queen will strive to always be authentic, but to show out at the same time. Once the elusive chanteuse, now the charismatic chameleon. She will focus on flawless performance and presentation, on balance and compromise. The fact that she can be everything doesn't mean she fits in nowhere. It means she can fit in anywhere.

And when this queen feels excluded—because, on some level, she always will—she will remember to feel proud. Because Dame Made is an enigma. You'll know exactly what you're going to get from her—but she'll still surprise you every time.

As the Sam Smith song ends and there's a beat of silence before the next begins, I feel settled myself. And suddenly I know why I never defined my queen before today.

I just wasn't ready.

Of course, there will be plenty else that I'll need to keep sorting out in the future. I can already tell it's going to take consistent work to rewrite my personal narratives, to rewire my perspectives. And that when I forget myself, my inner saboteur will scream even louder than before.

But now, at least my outer drag queen will be there to scream right back and remind me exactly who I want to be.

TURN TO PAGE 210

It's all right there in the name. I am a daughter of the House of Made, but I'm also the son of my mother, Gia, who is of her mother. Everything I am proud of most, I got from my matriarchs.

And they are freaking queens, all.

However, I am also made via my idols, the queer artists and diva mentors. And even via my peers in Jeweltones—forged in their fires, cracked open by their pressures.

I see her so clearly now. Made Via Gia lives in the space between, flowing in the push and pull for balance. Above all else, she is a vessel for talent: the voice, emotive and acrobatic. She is less flashy than I might have expected, but always still fabulous. She calls upon the right skill at the right moment, understanding that her full arsenal is always at her disposal. She sets the course because she knows how to lead the way. Most of all, when this queen feels overwhelmed—because she will from time to time—she will remember to feel inspired. She won't try to transform into something she's not. Instead, she will channel the emotion she is feeling, be it good, bad, or ugly.

And that's what will make Made Via Gia the most beautiful queen in all the land. The fact that she can do anything will not reduce her to nothing, but will open her up to everything she ever wanted.

I feel more settled as the Adam Lambert song ends and there's a beat of silence. Suddenly, I know why I never defined my queen before today.

I just wasn't ready.

I also know there will be plenty more for me to keep sorting out in the future, but that makes sense. Epiphanies eventually give way to the ordinary. I can already tell it's going to take consistent work to rewrite my personal narratives, to rewire my perspectives. And that when I forget myself, my inner saboteur will scream even louder than before.

But now, at least my outer drag queen will be there to scream right back and remind me exactly who I want to be.

TURN TO PAGE 210

With this regal and renewed power surging through me, I realize it's time to boss up.

If there is any hope of saving Jeweltones, then we need to get our real issues out in the open. After that, we'll see if we can actually create something honest from the mess and pull some beauty from this disaster.

But first, there are some enormous demons we need to face.

Good thing I know exactly where to start slaying.

CHAPTER TWELVE

VINNY

I'M IN DEA'S APARTMENT NOT EVEN AN HOUR LATER. IT TOOK A few phone calls to get the address, but it turns out her condo is walking distance from the brunch bar. I sit on a firm white couch in a pristine living room that's light, airy, and full of prisms and plants. I even hear the faint squawking of birds from the bedrooms down the hall.

It's not lost on me that this is probably where I'd be living if Jeweltones had never been formed. Then again, there's still a high chance that I might need to take Dea up on her offer anyway . . .

I shake the thought from my head and try to focus on what I came here to do.

"I wasn't sure you were home," I say as Dea hands me a seltzer can and sits in a silver armchair across from me. "Or that you'd buzz me in, if you were."

"Of course I'd buzz you in," Dea says. "It's really good to see you, Vinny."

"Then why haven't you returned any of my calls?"

"I took a page out of your book. I put my phone on *Do Not Disturb* and I haven't gone near it. But honestly?"

Dea looks away, out the nearest window.

"I was afraid you were mad at me. I don't know how to say sorry for what I did yet."

"You have absolutely nothing to be sorry about," I say, my voice forceful enough for Dea to turn back to me.

"You're not mad I didn't tell you about CeCe?"

"You're not mad I didn't tell you CeCe told us weeks ago?" I return.

Dea almost cracks a smile at that. Almost.

"I just wanted to respect your space," I continue. "You deserve all the time you need to figure out who you are and to come out on your own terms. I'm sorry that was taken from you. I know exactly what that's like."

Tears glisten in Dea's eyes, but she blinks them back. This is one of the few times I can ever remember seeing her without a full face of makeup, just some eyeliner and lip gloss. She still looks gorgeous, but something about her energy feels so . . . defeated. It breaks my heart.

"Thank you, Vinny," she says. "I should have known you'd understand. I wish I had the courage to tell you sooner."

"That means a lot, but I get why you didn't. The drama in the group . . . I guess CeCe ended up putting us in that position, anyway. It obviously wasn't a good idea."

I notice Dea flinches a bit when I say CeCe's name.

"Have you heard from her?" I ask.

Dea shakes her head. "I tried to call, but I never got through. I just hope she's . . ."

She doesn't finish, but I can see it in her eyes.

"You really care about her, huh?"

She nods. "I didn't expect to feel this way. I didn't expect any of this to happen. I thought I could just control it all until I understood what I really wanted from everything. But you know how it's been. There was no time to think. I guess that was selfish, looking back . . . but I'm certainly paying the price for it now."

"You did the best you could, but it's like we were pulled into the middle of a tornado," I say. "I hope you've been staying off the internet?"

"Yes, once I understood what the narrative was going to be. Dea, the ice queen. Unfeeling. Calculated. Manipulative. Trying too hard. Untalented. Too much and not enough."

Dea's final words cut into me. I feel her pain like it's my own—because it is my own. Part of me is just so touched she is finally sharing it with me. Even if she's so wrong about herself it literally hurts.

"'A glittery, reflective, beautiful fake,'" she says with a heavy sigh. "Everly really called that one, didn't she?"

"No, absolutely not," I reply. "Dea, I need you to hear me on this. The fact that you felt pressured to hide your feelings for CeCe *does not* make you fake. Or a liar. It means you understand that we still live in a world where it's not fully safe to be queer. And that being 'out' requires an inner strength you need to be sure you've built up, especially if you're in the public eye. And that this is all ten times harder if you come from a family that might be less than thrilled?"

Dea nods. "Just one more disappointment to add to my parents' list—"

"—Oh, fuck them," I blurt out. "Fuck literally anyone who doesn't accept every ounce of how amazing you are. I know I haven't been so good at feeling that myself lately, but I'm trying."

"Really? You don't seem like you struggle with any of this," Dea says. "You're always above the drama. You have so much talent. You're out and proud. You don't care what anyone thinks."

I laugh. I can't help it.

"If you really believe that, then we're both very good at projecting and camouflaging. Because I have felt like an imposter this entire time, one who doesn't fit in or know who they want to be."

"No offense," Dea says, smiling, "but that's absurd."

"Well, I've very recently—like, very recently—come to understand that. So can you believe me when I tell you the same exact thing?"

"Maybe. I want to," Dea tries. "I wish I could be more like you. I mean, I was so impressed with the way you handled that last *CherriPop* story."

❖ "I don't know about that. I did try to investigate and find out who the **gossip leak** was—for all the good that did us."
TURN TO PAGE 214

❖ "I was just trying to protect my mom. It wasn't like I was doing anything selfless by pushing for a **parental breakup**."
TURN TO PAGE 215

"I never even figured anything out," I say before pausing to glance at her. "Did Stern ever tell you it was him?"

"He sent me a very long text, but I stopped reading right after I got to that part," Dea says. "But that's not what I meant. I was impressed how your first instinct to the leak was to be proactive, to defend and protect. My instinct is always to hide."

Dea pauses and I give her time and space to finish.

"After that whole Dame Gloves outing in high school, you could have chosen to hide too. And after . . . losing your dad, you could have totally shut down. But with that gossip leak about your mom and Everly's dad, you were instantly ready to fight back. To protect the people you love. Even today, showing up here. All I've done is hide behind some curated image, then shut the world out when it gets torn away."

I absorb Dea's insights, trying to accept her compliments. I've never seen myself like that before. It's nice, but I really think Dea deserves to feel the same.

"Thank you for seeing me that way. Truly. But Dea, you should know, there's a reason I fight to protect you. You're such a good friend and you give without a second thought. Plus, you're talented as hell." I give her a gentle look before continuing. "Why do you think CeCe tried her best to keep your secret?"

Dea is silent for a moment, looking at her hands folded in her lap. "CeCe told me that she didn't want to go back in the closet . . . but that I was worth doing anything for."

There's a heaviness in Dea's voice that tells me it's hard for her to say this out loud, even if it means the world to her.

"Well, there you have it," I say, grinning.

Dea looks up and grins too, so I leave it at that. As we sit in comfortable silence, I make a mental note about the connection Dea drew between my gossip leak reaction, Dame Gloves, and Dad. I guess I never quite saw it all that way . . . but leave it to your best friends to see you in ways you never could before.

TURN TO PAGE 217

"But that's my point," Dea says. "After the whole Dame Gloves thing in high school, the idea of a gossip leak could have shut you down. Instead, you brushed it off and focused on protecting your mom. But me? It feels like all I've thought of lately is myself."

I absorb Dea's words. While they are kind, I'm not quite sure they're fair.

"Dea, this just happened to you a few days ago in front of the whole world. Mine happened years ago and in one school. Besides, I wasn't just protecting my mom . . . I think I just hated the idea of her moving on. Of her . . . replacing my dad."

I'm surprised by the words that bubble up, but I feel a little relieved that I finally say them out loud.

"Oh, Vinny," Dea says. "I can't say I know what that's like, but I obviously know how it feels to have your world change overnight. Thinking about it this weekend, I think each of us tried to hold on to something familiar. It makes total sense you'd want to hang on to your mom that way. And the memory of your dad."

Tears spring to my eyes again, but I've cried enough today.

"Still, moving on doesn't have to mean losing anything, does it?" I ask, hoping it's true.

"I don't know," Dea says with a sigh. "Change is terrifying, even when it's exactly what we ask for. I mean, we all like to fool ourselves into thinking we have control. This career move, that relationship. Withhold this, dig up that. Really, we control very little. Plus nothing is ever stable in an artist's life . . . but maybe that's to obliterate our illusion of control even more often than the average person? And maybe it's our job to remind everyone of that?"

I stare back at Dea, a little shooketh.

"And you let people say you're not a writer at heart?" I say, grinning.

Dea just shrugs, grinning back.

"Well, that actually reminds me of something my dad always used to say," I continue. "'When you're afraid of losing something in the future, let it be a reminder of something you're grateful to have in the present.'" I smile another second before feeling sad again. "But what if you've already lost something?"

Dea looks back at me, knowing exactly what I mean.

"I think the same solution applies?"

I feel a smile grow on my face. Once again, Dea is absolutely right.

TURN TO PAGE 217

"Well, you are right about something else," I say. "I *am* here to fight for you. I actually just came from that charity drag brunch—and your donation was much appreciated, by the way."

Dea just gives me a gracious nod, so I continue.

"I got my own dose of wisdom there, and I'm now here to deliver the gospel to you. I think us Jeweltones owe it to ourselves—and to each other—to come together for one honest conversation."

"Vinny, I don't—"

"—Hear me out. This is probably the end for Jeweltones, which I will accept if that's really the case. But I'll only accept it if we all bring our full selves to the table once, holding nothing back."

I can tell Dea still isn't convinced. So I try to channel my new drag queen power to help her conquer her own inner saboteur.

❖ "We can't leave things this way, with you taking the fall. We don't need another diva cat fight or pop princess fall-from-grace storyline. Even if it's our final act as a group, we should take the opportunity to **change** the **narrative**."
TURN TO PAGE 218

❖ "You don't need to have your presentation perfectly figured out. It's okay to **discover yourself** as you go. But it's not okay to give up."
TURN TO PAGE 219

I give Dea a few moments to absorb my words.

"I guess a joint statement with the others could help shift public perception," Dea says.

"Sure," I reply, knowing that's not quite the point. "But I think girls of every kind out there need to see you stand up for yourself, no matter what people try to say about you. I think the group will get behind you on that, even if it's our last act."

Dea thinks another moment. "We could be pretty revolutionary, if we could get out of our own way . . ." she says, mulling it over.

"Hell yes. And I don't know about you, but I'm not ready to return to obscurity just yet. Not when I've just finally figured out what I want to say as an artist."

"I don't exactly love the idea of losing all I've worked for either," Dea replies. "But do you really think we can get past our issues?"

I think of how CeCe and Stern must be feeling right now. I think of all the new layers now separating Dea and Everly. And I honestly don't know.

"That's up to you messy bessies, not me," I say. "But I know this much—I'll stay with Jeweltones, even if it only ends up being you and me."

"Don't tempt me," Dea laughs. "Do you think the label or Zahra would go for that? Do you think anyone would give us a second chance?"

"I really don't know," I answer. "But I do know there's only one way to find out. So what do you say, is it time to come out of hiding, my dearest diamond?"

Dea considers this a moment, then takes a deep breath. "I'm in. But who do we call first?"

"Oh, I have some ideas," I reply, standing to hug Dea. "Hold on to your wig, because this queen has some serious tricks up her sleeve."

Giggling, I release Dea. Because after this moment, whether this truly is the end for Jeweltones or not . . .

This is just the beginning for Dea and Vinny.

TURN TO PAGE 220

"Well, you're not wrong," Dea says, mulling this over. "I've only been projecting what I think will get me what I want. What everyone seems to expect. The perfectly curated pop star . . . But the people I've been trying to please just ended up tearing me down for it. What's the point of hiding, of trying to appear perfect anymore?"

Then it's like a light bulb goes off in Dea's head.

"This is the worst thing that has ever happened to me. The world hates me. But I've also never felt more liberated in my entire life. I'm . . . free to be me."

"Exactly," I say, smiling wide. "So now the million-dollar diva question: Who is she?"

"I don't think I know for sure yet," Dea answers. "But I'm very ready to find out."

"Now that's the spirit!" I reply. "I still think Jeweltones could be a place for us all to come together and do just that. But I think we should stop taking orders and asking for permission. We have to come back to the label and Zahra on our own terms."

"You really think we can all forgive each other?" Dea asks, looking down at the floor. "And even if we can, will our audience give us another chance?"

"I have no idea," I sigh. "But I know I want to find out."

Dea considers this another moment, taking a deep breath of her own. "Okay. Where do we start?"

"Dea, my darling," I reply, standing to hug her. "I thought you'd never ask. This queen has some serious tricks up her sleeve."

Laughing, I release Dea. Because after this moment, whether this truly is the end for Jeweltones or not . . .

This is just the beginning for Dea and Vinny.

TURN TO PAGE 220

CHAPTER THIRTEEN

EVERLY

IT'S SUNDAY AFTERNOON AND I STILL DON'T FEEL ANY BETTER.

Maybe it's because I've only left my bedroom to eat with Dad. I've been too afraid to even go outside to walk Alanis around the block. Popella is all I can think about, but I still don't feel ready to face what happened yet.

I'm still not even sure what happened. The term "panic attack" has been mentioned delicately, but the sensory overload I experienced seemed to fade once I got off the stage. From what I understand about anxiety attacks, they tend to have lingering effects. It felt much more like my body was rejecting the stage—rejecting the very reality of Jeweltones. I guess I should have seen it coming after that trailer lot blowup.

After it all happened, the next thing I knew I was sitting in an SUV beside Dad, being shipped away to LA like a crate of damaged goods. We had the driver take us back to our house in the valley, then I locked myself in my room the second we got home. I turned off my phone and my laptop, knowing that my onstage shutdown and that influencer video were both bound to go viral. The next morning, I was still too freaked to approach my phone, so I sent Dad to the Jeweltones house to pick up my songwriting cases. Even though I haven't had the energy to use them for weeks, I just wanted them close.

It wasn't until Dad returned, handling my cases from the closet and instruments with care, that I finally cried. Dad never once questioned me. He just showed up to take care of me after the most spectacular fall of my life without judgment.

"I know I don't say it often enough," I said, sniffling as Dad hugged me. "But thank you. For everything."

"Aw, sweetie. You never have to thank me for a thing. Do you want to talk about any of what happened yet?"

All I could do was shake my head as I stepped away to return to my room.

"Well, go easy. You've done your best," Dad said. "And no matter what, I know you. Think of the songs you'll mine out of all this."

I had to close my eyes to stop from balling. Leave it to Dad. No "it'll be fine" or "this happened for a reason" or even to "suck it up." Instead, he knew that what matters most to me is always the songwriting.

After that, I went back to my room to do just that . . .

But I only ended up staring at the wall for an hour.

It was like my emotions were in a bubble, hanging over my head and floating just out of reach. So maybe it was time to burst that bubble?

Once I turned my phone back on, the first thing I did was try to call CeCe. It went straight to voicemail, which left me to see all the messages I had from Stern. What happened between us, the things we both did to each other and the group in that hellish lot—I was not ready to unpack that quite yet.

Ignoring the mountain of additional text messages in my inbox, I took a deep breath and ventured a dip into the internet instead. I braced myself for a blast of hate, but I was surprised to find that, while everyone was indeed talking about the epic Jeweltones meltdown, somehow my onstage flop was totally eclipsed by the takedown of Dea. Everyone believed she was the cold-hearted bitch who kept apart America's sweethearts, EverGreen. That absurd nickname aside, everyone blamed Dea for my spinouts, both behind the scenes and on the stage. Even my archnemesis OOut678 commented everywhere that Dea's sabotage probably explains why I've been so awful in Jeweltones. Seemingly in the blink of an eye, all the hate and blame I'd ever felt was directed at Dea, casting me as the helpless damsel in distress to her wicked stepsister.

It all made me want to scream.

How many times had I dreamed of people caring enough about my music to make me famous? A tingle crept up my spine, returning the sneaking suspicion that this was somehow the secret definition of adulthood. *This is what I've always wanted—just not like this.*

Feeling disgusted and relieved and overwhelmed all at once, I turned off my phone again and crawled into bed. And that is where I stayed until now.

It's like my body caught up on all the sleep it had been missing in one epic shutdown. I still feel tired, but in a different way. Mostly I'm tired of feeling trapped and silenced. The problem is, I still don't know what I want to say. Do I want to apologize to all the listeners for how I handled everything? Do I want to make amends for inadvertently outing Dea? Do I want to scream at Stern for the way he makes me feel? Do I want to call CeCe and make everything right with her? Do I want to call Zahra and quit? Or do I want to fight to rebuild Jeweltones into something better from our ruinous ashes?

This last question surprises me. I thought I would feel free, knowing we are probably breaking up and getting dropped. So why am I mourning the way things *could* have been?

Why do I suddenly feel like fighting back?

Well, if I'm looking for a fight, at least I know one place I can start. I grab my phone and turn it back on. Why not start by taking down my most vocal hater, OOut678. Wouldn't that surprise everyone, if my first response since the Jeweltones meltdown is targeting a troll? The instinct for that instant satisfaction builds like an itch that needs scratching. Everyone wants me to say something? Well, they're about to get an earful.

Except, as my phone lights up with banner notifications, there's one in particular that catches my eye—an email from Kree Duski. My heart was already pounding in my chest, but now it sets off in double time. *She finally wrote me back?* I open the email, beyond eager to devour it.

Everly,

Sorry I didn't write back sooner. I wanted to let you find your own way through this. But after Friday night, I'm guessing you could use some words of wisdom.

I'll try to keep this brief. Unfortunately, no one can tell you what's right for your art, and by extension, your career. It'll always be up to you to balance setting a course against the opportunities made available. You'll never be in full control, and nothing will ever feel perfect, but you'll have to trust yourself to know what feels right enough.

We already talked about this, but what has always served me is having a mission statement. You know my biggest song, "Going 'Til You Know," those last lines in the chorus? "Can't know where you're going/'til you know where you're coming from"—that's not about history. It's really about intention. I've always wondered why people are drawn to storytelling in all its forms, as creators and consumers. We all need entertainment and escapism, sure, but I think the connection runs deeper than that. I think it's a harsh reality that people only grow through suffering. Growing pains are unavoidable, at least if you're living right. But I think the real key to storytelling is that, sometimes, stories allow us to grow without enduring the hardship.

That's invaluable.

So like we discussed, I write songs to soothe and transport people, sure. To express myself, to heal, and so that if someone is suffering the same pain, they don't feel alone. But the real goal is to translate the hardest-earned lessons so that someone else may not have to struggle the same way. And in doing so, maybe we shift the cultural consciousness forward an inch?

What you need, my dear Everly, isn't an answer about this group. You need a mission statement of your own. If you have that, everything else—the platform, the collaborators, the fame, the hate, the riches, the rejection—it all becomes secondary. Or, better yet, it all becomes tools at your disposal.

To put it more poetically, songwriter to songwriter: you gotta set the current, not ride the waves.

Yours,

K.D.

PS—For what it's worth, judgment is cheap and easy. Participation is costly and valuable. I've bombed on more stages than I can count. What matters, always, is playing the next song.

I read this email. Then I read it again.

I turn on "Going 'Til You Know" and read it again.

I read and reread her email until I can finally feel some tides turning inside me.

Because Kree is right.

I don't need reactions, I need *intentions*.

Then I realize the impulsive mistake I just dodged. No matter what, I don't want to be the kind of artist who gets in pointless fights online. Especially because when I picture OOut678, I realize I see the kind of listener I want to reach most, and I think of failing them. But really, they could be a bitter middle-aged man or a rejected peer or an eight-year-old with a crush. Ultimately, they're just a troll doing the cheap and easy thing. In the end, it doesn't matter who they are or what they have to say. It doesn't matter what anyone calls me.

It matters what I answer to.

And I choose to answer Kree's call.

If I need a starter mission statement, I'm sure Kree won't mind if I borrow hers. Why fix what isn't broken? Goddess knows I have plenty more to fix.

I still don't have the answer for how to disengage with social media while engaging with my dearest FLCs, how to filter the hate and embrace the love, how to share transparently while setting boundaries. And I still don't have the answers about songwriting and Jeweltones, about the line between collaboration and compromise, about separating my anger from my passion, my authenticity from my ego. Or about what to say when I finally have to face CeCe and Stern, or Vinny and . . . Dea.

But that is part of the gift Kree has just given me. I don't always need to know the exact directions at every turn, as long as I have an internal compass. I don't need perfect creative conditions as long as it feels right enough. I don't need to crash with every wave, rising and falling, if I become the current.

All I need is my intention: to write songs that matter, for the people who need them. To express myself so well that it empowers someone else.

So after all this lost time, that's exactly what I'm going to do.

❖ The last time I wrote, I turned to **Brooksville** for inspiration.
TURN TO PAGE 226

❖ The last time I wrote, I used my **pens, paper, picks**.
TURN TO PAGE 231

It takes a few minutes to get Brooksville properly laid out on the floor, but it gives me a chance to remember where I left things.

When I was last with Lucy, she was attending the annual Fall Formal at Brooksville High. She had just made a huge choice about who to go to the afterparty with. Was she going to cling to popularity and her cousin's boyfriend who she crushes on, or find some new and enchanting friends?

Stretching out in a corner of my room, I realize this is actually the perfect place to pick back up.

So I prepare to let the words flow.

❖ I decided Lucy would attend the **Rebel** Rabbit afterparty.
TURN TO PAGE 227

❖ I decided Lucy would become **HWIC** of The Rings.
TURN TO PAGE 229

I know my next step is to forge a new chapter for Lucy, so I set one attainable goal for this mini-session: to decide what makes the Rebel Rabbits special, then write the next section of "Damned If You Don't." Any more than that and I might feel too overwhelmed to even start.

Eager to channel this surge of inspiration, it immediately becomes clear to me who the Rebel Rabbits need to be. I press my pen down to capture the thoughts as they churn.

> The Rebel Rabbits are a group of outcast teens who don't fit in anywhere else and have befriended a coven of rabbits from the Brooksville enchanted forest. When a teen pairs up with the correct misfit rabbit, it grants them both secret magical potential. Naturally, everyone at the high school finds them weird and childish for befriending bunnies, but the Rebel Rabbits don't care about popularity or haters. Why would they when they have wondrous powers no one else knows about? The Rebel Rabbits only have one rule: to never judge anyone unfairly, the way they have been judged.

As I finish scribbling this, it suddenly occurs to me how I can fuse this idea into new lyrics for "Damned If You Don't." Quickly, I press my pen back to the page.

> The power to create
> Is the ~~power~~ strength to alleviate
> The ~~power~~ will to empower
> Girl, it'll make 'em cower
> When you've found
> Where you belong
> ~~You'll finally understand~~
> ~~My song~~
> The group that's been waiting
> All along
> That's when you'll ~~start singing~~ sing
> The right ~~kind of~~ song

I finish writing and read over these new lyrics. They feel like the song's bridge to me, a kind of culmination. Looking over the first verse and chorus I constructed, I realize this new bridge would be a potential way to connect the haunted-magical first verse with the more-grounded chorus. I can switch back to spooky on the second verse, repeat the same grounded chorus, then weave those threads together retroactively with these lyrics as the bridge. It'll be about songwriting as a superpower, a creative career as a dangerous quest.

I'm not sure it'll fully work, but it could at least open some interesting avenues for instrumentation. For now, it's enough. Because no matter what, when I read these lyrics, and when I hear that potential bridge, it will bring me right back to this moment in my childhood bedroom after the Popella disaster, feeling bleary-eyed and full-hearted.

Back to when I finally cut through the clutter and the chatter.

TURN TO PAGE 236

Lucy decided to steal her cousin's throne and her boyfriend with witchy, dazzling spells.

Reading this now, it's wild how obviously this applies to my own perspective on Jeweltones. Looking back, what Lucy lacks is the very same thing I lacked: purpose. Why does Lucy want to be beloved and popular, why does she even want to be with Blake? Is it because it's what she's told to want? Or is she just reeling from the changes in her life and trying to find some control?

If Lucy really is going to disrupt things, she better find some better reasons for doing so.

I scribble down these exact notes and, as I finish, I don't know what the answers for Lucy should be just yet. But I suddenly realize how I can translate all of this into the next lyrics for "Damned If You Don't."

~~Invited to the party~~
Invited inside
They'll tell you what to covet
Fame, money, fans, haters, ~~influencers, followers~~
They'll tell you to only love it
Influence that
Leverage your platform
Because there's only one way ~~for you~~ to perform
~~But do you know~~ But I know the secret
The one they don't share
All the distractions in the world don't matter
When intention ~~should be~~ is your only care

I finish writing and read over the lyrics. I don't love them yet, but they'll serve as a nice foundation for the second verse. Then the bridge can be about defining what this intention really means. This is enough for now, though. Because no matter what, when I read these lyrics, when I hear that potential verse, it will bring me right back to this moment in my childhood bedroom after the Popella disaster, feeling bleary-eyed and full-hearted. This moment when I remembered what really matters—and realized how easy it is to lose sight of that.

I take one last look before closing my notebook, reviewing my little burst of work.

And I can't help but feel proud.

TURN TO PAGE 236

I zip open my backpack and pull out my **To Be Continued . . .** notebook and its accompanying gold pen. With both in hand, I walk over and get settled in a bucket chair in the corner of my bedroom, getting cozy under a throw blanket. I turn to the last page I wrote for "Heart to Rage."

I look over the words of this all-too-familiar song, one of the first I have yet to finish. I look over the two verses and a chorus that I've reworked yet again. In this moment, I instantly know what the bridge needs to be about. It should be about my realization sparked by Kree's email.

I grip the golden pen like my sharpest weapon and get to work.

❖ I last reworked "Heart to Rage" to be about **myself** and my career.
TURN TO PAGE 232

❖ I last reworked "Heart to Rage" to be about the heartbreak Stern **Green** could cause.
TURN TO PAGE 234

Reading feverishly over the lyrics I generated last time, I feel renewed inspiration flood through me. Because if the crux of this song is about career heartbreak, then the bridge needs to be about the inevitable healing that comes after.

Got crushed under this wave
Tumbling
The riptide pulled me apart
Crumbling
~~Got~~ Swept out to sea
Scattered into a thousand
Shimmering shards of me
But in the calm
I began ~~regathering~~ to regather
~~Floating along,~~ Started seeing
The heart of the matter
I became my own ocean
Flowing
Queen of the current
Always knowing
That now I make
My own waves

I finish writing and reread my words. I don't know if it's a perfect fit, but I know these words will always remind me of sitting in my childhood bedroom after the biggest failure of my life so far—and finding my voice again.

And being able to find a kind of peace I never even knew existed.

For now, that is so much more than enough.

I swipe at the tear that rolls down my cheek and smile, because I think I just finished "Heart to Rage." I just closed a chapter that I opened at the very start of my songwriting journey. And it feels a bit bitter . . . but so much sweeter.

Looking at the song now, I realize I didn't know then what I know now: that hearts only break so they can heal back together stronger. That's why I could never finish it before.

Sounds like I've got a new song to start.

TURN TO PAGE 236

Reading feverishly over the lyrics I generated last time, I feel the same complicated emotions wash over me. Since then, Stern and I have both broken a lot of things, beginning to admit our true feelings. But maybe this bridge needs to be about the hope we can salvage from the wreckage?

> Our fire burned
> This place to the ground
> But babe
> I think we can turn
> This wreck around
> Use the ~~fire~~ same flames
> To light our way
> Look forward
> To a brighter day
> We thought we ~~had~~ got
> What we always wanted
> But those were just ghost stories
> That kept ~~to keep~~ us haunted
> Old waves they used
> To ~~crash~~ keep us small
> But now we've found
> Our wrecking ball
> I've got a pen
> You've got the page
> Together we'll mend
> Our hearts to rage

As I finish writing and reread my work, I don't know if I love everything yet, but I know that these words will always remind me of this moment. I'll always remember sitting in my childhood bedroom after the biggest heartbreak of my life so far and finding my voice again.

And finding a kind of peace I never even knew existed.

For now, that is so much more than enough.

A tear rolls down my cheek as I realize that I just finished "Heart to Rage." I'm closing a chapter that I opened at the very start of my songwriting journey, all by mending my own heart.

Even though I've now written about it, something still tells me I haven't even begun to understand true heartbreak. But I will someday.

And that pain will be the fuel for another song to start.

TURN TO PAGE 236

The doorbell downstairs rings, breaking me out of my thoughts and nearly stopping my heart. Alanis, who has been sleeping on my bed, springs to life. It could be anyone, but I'm overwhelmed with a very sudden desire for someone specific to have come to my doorstep. As Alanis starts barking, I know it's time to stop hiding. Taking a deep breath, I stand up and head out of my room.

I'm halfway down the stairs when Dad opens the door . . . And I see Stern standing there, flowers in hand.

"Mr. Brooks," he says. "I know Everly's phone has been off, but—"

"—It's okay, Dad," I say as I descend the stairs. "I got it."

Dad turns and nods at me, scooping up Alanis as he turns from the door.

Next thing I know it's just Stern and me, standing face-to-face. It feels both comforting and surreal at the same time.

"Come in," I say, gesturing toward the living room.

"These are for you," he says, stepping inside and holding out the flowers.

Hydrangeas. How did he know those are my favorite?

"That's remarkably cheesy of you," I say, accepting them. "But still, thank you."

"My mom taught me never to show up at someone's house empty-handed," Stern says with a laugh. I also laugh, inexplicably.

Then we sit on the couch and I'm not sure where to start.

"I'm sorry to just show up, I'm sure you need space," Stern says after a moment. "But I needed to see you. I've been . . . I haven't seen any of the others. But I needed to apologize to you first."

"It's okay. And I owe you an apology too," I reply. "Not just for what happened on the stage, but for the position I put you in. It was wrong of me. But I just felt so . . . stuck. I think telling you when my defenses were down—that was maybe a cry for help."

Stern exhales, then he laughs again.

"You have a habit of taking the words right out of my mouth. I was going to say the same thing about everything I messed up at Popella. Just far less eloquently."

I resist the urge to smile. "I haven't talked to any of the others, either. But I bet we would all agree we're not proud of the ways we handled things."

"Maybe. But what happened . . ." Stern starts, pausing to find the right words. "I was just trying to do right by the group. By Dea. But there was always this wall there. Now I know why. Still, I never meant to hurt her. Or you."

"I know," I respond. "I don't know if Dea would agree, but wherever she is, I hope she is staying off the internet. Still, she did use you and cheat on you. I'm not saying she deserves any of this backlash, but—"

"—I was just as bad, Everly." Stern's voice is firm, and he looks at me with a seriousness I've never seen in him before. "I started to sense that Dea didn't feel anything for me, but we both liked the attention the relationship got us. I mean, I liked the attention so much, I fed those stories to *CherriPop* at first."

It's not like I'd forgotten, but that breach of trust still stings more than I thought.

"Is that why you did it?" I really want to ask him what the hell he was thinking, but I shouldn't throw stones from my own glass house.

"I don't have a good answer. Except that I really thought that I was helping us. That it was important to keep us in the spotlight while we figured it all out, like Zahra said. And that I was only giving up small stuff. I actually thought I was being selfless, not offering any stories about myself. But then they made such a bigger deal of the little details I gave them and added all this speculation and photos I didn't even know about. So I stopped."

Listening to Stern, I can't help but think back to that first group meeting beside the pool, about the fight between Dea and I over the first *CherriPop* story. How Stern stayed silent, how he just let us dig at each other instead of owning up. I know he was probably terrified or that he thought he was doing the right thing, but it doesn't lessen the hurt.

"It was so wrong, and it was even worse that I didn't speak up about it sooner," Stern continues. "But I really thought about it the last few days, trying to understand why I did it. I realized that it was partly to help save the group, but I also wanted to save Jeweltones because *I* needed to stay famous and successful. Without that, I felt like nothing. I couldn't go back to feeling worthless. So I was reckless. I don't know, that sounds so . . . simple now."

Stern's eyes fall to the floor and his face twists like he might cry. "Obviously I learned enough to stop weeks ago, but I should have told everyone sooner. I was just . . . acting out. On instinct, but it was the wrong one."

I understand what Stern is saying, but I also feel the familiar sting of someone betraying my trust, talking about my weaknesses behind my back to gain something. Still, if things really are going to be different, I know I have to start letting that sting go. Especially if I expect the hurt I caused to ever be forgiven too.

"I wish you would have told us sooner," I say after a moment. "And I definitely wish it didn't happen outside that Popella trailer. But I was the queen of bad timing in my own way, so I forgive you. It just . . . might take a minute to build some trust back?"

Stern looks like he doesn't know whether to smile or frown, but there is a little bit of relief there as well.

"That means a lot. More than anything, I want us all to have a clean slate," he says. "Do you think we can find a way to just start over?"

I look away, because I know what Stern is hinting at. He wants to know if I'll give Jeweltones another shot. If I'll want to give *us* a shot.

But even after all I've resolved today, I don't have those answers yet.

"Remember what we talked about the night before Popella?" I say instead. "About success feeling empty until we learn how to see ourselves differently?"

"Of course," Stern says. "But honestly, I still have no clue how to do that."

"Well, Kree Duski just answered an old email of mine. And it made me realize just one person saying something to you can change how you think about yourself, good or bad. But only if it's the right person, and only if you're ready to believe them. And you know what else can sometimes do that?"

"What?" Stern asks, hanging on my every word.

"Songs," I answer. "And Stern, I hope you're ready to believe that you're a singer-songwriter, too. Because I see that in you so clearly."

Stern takes his turn to look away. I can practically see the lump in his throat, his lip quivering. Once that passes, he turns back to me.

"Hearing that from you is way better than a stadium full of screaming fans," he says.

"Well, then," I say, standing up. "Let's finish that song you started?"

❖ I've already shared my songwriting **closet** with Stern, so I need to keep sharing more of my creative secrets.
TURN TO PAGE 240

❖ Stern and I started to **co-write** a song together to try changing our perspectives. Now is the perfect time to finish.
TURN TO PAGE 243

"After what you showed me, I created my own setup back at the house," Stern replies. "It's just a corner in my room that faces a window and has a coffee table with a notebook, pens, and some candles. I keep my guitar there. And I spread out this little collection of keychains, one from everywhere I've traveled, for inspiration. Nothing too elaborate, but it's nice to have a space to sit and write. It kind of grounds the whole process. But you already knew that."

Listening to Stern, my heart swells. I obviously intend to share my songs with listeners who need them—but it's still a revelation that sharing my process with other artists could help inspire them too.

"I also finished that song," Stern adds, sounding a bit nervous. It makes me realize I haven't said anything in response yet.

"Do you think you could teach me so we can play it together?" I ask.

Maybe the best way to share my songwriting isn't pulling people into my private world . . . maybe it's opening myself up to create in a new way?

From the way Stern smiles ear to ear, I think I have my answer.

◆ ◆ ◆

It feels scary, but I let Stern come up to my bedroom. Even though it's a mess and filled with embarrassing childhood things. Even though my songwriting stuff is still laid out on the floor. I let Stern see all of it while I grab my guitars, then I hand one to him and we sit cross-legged in the corner under my favorite window.

It only takes Stern a few minutes to teach me the chords he came up with, since they're based on the same progression we riffed on that first night. I tell Stern I'll try to find harmonies under his melody, but mostly I just want to hear him sing—and hear what he wrote.

I start strumming the chords, facing out so we're not looking directly at each other. Stern begins to sing the melody we crafted together, his syrup and honey voice humming with tenderness.

"We all dream the same
Hearts in one beat.

Chasing the damn thing
Fingers grasping to clutch.
Then it happens
The impossible becomes yours.
Until you see the finish line
Is just where the trouble starts."

"What do you do
When the thing you enjoy
Starts to feel like no fun?
What do you do
When the thing you love
Burns you out faster than you can run?"

"Everyone around shines so bright
It makes your star seem dull.
Rebel hearts and dancing queens
Royal voices and crystal chords.
Paling in comparison feels not enough
So you become glue to fill the cracks.
But the shiny package
It crumbles all the same."

I stop playing before Stern can repeat the chorus.

"What?" he asks, turning to me with a worried look. "That bad?"

"No, Stern. It's good," I say, because there's something so simple and straightforward about what Stern has done. My own lyrics are twisty, and I can't resist a good rhyme, but Stern's crafting feels . . . sturdy.

But that's not why I stop. "Is that really how you see yourself in Jeweltones?"

Stern sighs. "What other way is there to see it? I'm not the best at anything and I'm definitely not the leader. How am I supposed to keep up?"

Words stick in my throat. I can't get them out fast enough to stop Stern.

"Sometimes I think I'd have nothing without Jeweltones," he continues. "But then sometimes I think the pressure would be off, not having to compare myself to you four."

I watch as Stern slumps. I take a moment to gather my thoughts, because I really want to get this next part right.

"I understand," I begin. "But I hate that you feel that way, because in a room full of soloists, you're a true team player. Do you know how special that is? I'd kill to be like that. The solution instead of the problem."

"I definitely haven't been the solution," Stern says. "And you're definitely not the problem."

"That's sweet, but I have been. And I want to do better. But I also think maybe we're both too hard on ourselves?"

"Who isn't?" Stern replies. "Still, hearing you say all that . . . I've never thought of myself that way."

I can't help but smile at Stern. What Kree did for me, I may have just paid forward to Stern. And maybe that's the key to . . .

Everything?

TURN TO PAGE 246

"I wrote down what we came up with last time," Stern says, pulling a folded sheet of paper out of his pocket. "I've been carrying it around with me."

"Why?"

"Well, I added some lyrics based on what we talked about. And I've been wanting to share it with you. But I've also been too afraid."

"Well, I hope you're going to show me now?"

Stern grins a little, blushing at the same time. He unfolds the paper, then he approaches me slowly, like he holds something precious and dangerous. I suppose, in a way, he does.

I take the paper and start reading.

BURNS YOU OUT

They only see what I decide to show
And I hate them for thinking it's the whole scene
They think the grass is greener up here
But the weeds only grow more mean

What do you do
When the thing you enjoy
Starts to feel like no fun?
What do you do
When the thing you love
Burns you out faster than you can run?

They always think once you hit that goal
Perfection sets in, it all just comes true
But when you live in that dream, when it's suddenly mundane
You just chase what comes next, wondering where the time flew

I read Stern's edits and his additions . . .
And I love them.

"It's about that question we asked," Stern explains, nerves rattling in his voice. "What do you do when you realize your wildest dreams coming true isn't enough to fill you up?"

I force myself not to chuckle, because Stern is so damn adorable.

"Yes, I know," I reply. "And this is really good, Stern. Seriously. Can we play it together?"

He beams. "It's our duet. Of course we can play it together."

Then it's my turn to beam right back at him.

◆ ◆ ◆

Once I've brought my guitars down from my room, we sit cross-legged on the living room floor. We position ourselves not quite facing one another, but side by side. We decided it might feel best to alternate verse lines, then sing in harmony on the chorus.

Feeling nervous, I begin strumming the chords we came up with last time. After the first eight-count, Stern starts singing the melody we crafted for the verses, his voice smooth and shimmery as ever. Then I pick up the second line, my own lilting voice floating across the melody more ethereally. It's a nice contrast, sturdy and airy.

We go on like this, finding a nice harmonic groove on the chorus. I'm relieved we aren't facing one another, because singing like this, on a song we both wrote together—it already feels wildly intimate. Then, somewhere in the second chorus, a thought occurs to me.

"Stern," I say, stopping. "I think I know what the bridge should be."

"Oh? I'm all ears," he says, turning to me.

"What if we asked that question directly, the one about what to do when dreams feel empty, when they warp into nightmares? Because I think, after today, I might have an answer."

"That, I am also dying to hear," Stern says, leaning in.

I take a breath, hoping this doesn't sound totally lame.

"I think the answer, instead of looking at what you want next, is getting yourself to value what you already have."

"Right," Stern replies. "But how?"

I pause another second.

"You imagine how you'd feel if you suddenly lost it all."

He takes a moment. After a few seconds, he frowns. "Is that what's happening now? Are we losing this before it even begins?"

I stare back at Stern and I can't help but wonder . . . Is he talking about Jeweltones?

Or is he talking about us?

TURN TO PAGE 246

Sitting beside Stern, something in my head clicks into place alongside my heart. If my mission statement is to make music that will reach people who need it, and if I can make music like this with Stern . . .

Why can't I do all of that without holding back in Jeweltones, on the platform we've been granted?

"I've been such an enormous idiot," I say. "I've been treating this whole Jeweltones experience like a trap, or an obstacle. But what if it's really the way we all become exactly the artists we need to be?"

Stern grins.

"I was hoping you'd say something like that, despite everything," he says. "But don't be too hard on yourself. None of us ever got the time to see what the group could really do, what we could really be."

"And we never had a mission statement. That's exactly what we need," I say. "But do you think it's already too late?"

I feel naïve to think we'll all suddenly be on the same page, that we won't keep disagreeing and feuding and being jealous of each other. Or that I won't act the fool again. But then I remind myself, it's okay to be a fool. To forget myself, to fight and struggle, to do the wrong thing, to listen to the wrong voices, to react, to be vulnerable—it's all inevitable. It will all be fine in the end, as long I eventually return to my center.

And maybe if Jeweltones can at least agree on our purpose, that intention could hold the center for all of us too?

"I don't know if the others will forgive us," Stern replies. "I don't know if the label or Zahra or our Gemstones will give us another chance. All I know is that I'm willing to try." He stares back at me, his green eyes turning from determined to soft. "Just like I know things with Dea and I are done. And that I should have always been with you instead."

My breath catches in my throat.

❖ If this experience has taught me anything, it's that holding back won't help us. Stern doesn't just feel safe—he also feels inevitable. I want to give this a shot as a real **couple**.

TURN TO PAGE 248

❖ If this experience has taught me anything, it's that Stern and I need to remain **collaborators** and friends for now, especially if Jeweltones has any hope of surviving.

TURN TO PAGE 250

Sitting with Stern, here in this safe space, I feel consumed. It's so over-whelming, my first instinct is to pull away. It feels so much safer to hide in the comfortable corner I know, to retreat into myself. To protect myself.

Telling Stern how I really feel is such a leap. I see it so clearly, how diving in could really end up with me shattered on the ground, lying in the rubble of Jeweltones. It's so scary, I feel the terror shaking into my hands.

Will me being with Stern be a non-starter for the others? And for the listeners, will this "EverGreen" thing eclipse everything? Will they embrace us or turn on us? Will Stern and I ruin this magic between us if we remove the tension that's been simmering?

I close my eyes as I remind myself of one thing. I can never know the answers to questions like these before I decide what to do. All I can do is find my own center and let that lead the way. Withholding myself, playing it safe—that's exactly what got Jeweltones off on the wrong foot. If I want to bring my whole self to this group so we can make the most authentic music for our listeners, then I need to be honest about my feelings.

All of them.

"Stern," I begin, surprised to find my voice trembling.

"I know," he says, turning to face me. "What if the others won't accept it? Or what happens if you and I can't make it work? The odds aren't in our favor."

"No, they're not," I say, leaning a little closer.

"And the fans, they're going to be obsessed," he continues, leaning in too. "What if the scrutiny is too much? Or what if we're no good at writing together once we're together?"

"All good points," I say, my lips now hovering inches from Stern's. "But honestly, none of it feels as big as my feelings for you."

Stern's gaze flickers from my lips back to my eyes. "They're all just going to have to deal, aren't they?"

I don't answer Stern.

Instead, I kiss him. Finally.

My eyes close and he kisses me back, with only my well-worn guitars between us. Kissing Stern feels like a lot of things. Bubbles fizzling over.

A warm blanket. Fireworks cascading. Plunging into warm water from the highest of heights.

And maybe it's the songwriter in me, but really, there's only one incredibly cheesy, infinitely appropriate way to describe what finally kissing Stern feels like.

EverGreen really works for us.

TURN TO PAGE 252

"Stern, I know there's something here," I say, feeling a knot tie in my stomach.

He can already see it in my face, so his own expression falls. "You don't feel the same way," he says, before I can finish.

As emotional as I am right now, I want to snap at Stern for naming my feelings instead of just listening. But then I force that reactive instinct to pass, because this moment—this entire group-repairing venture of mine—is going to require way more empathy and compassion. Besides, Stern's heart is on the line here, so I can't blame him for scrambling to salvage it.

"I'm not saying that," I continue after a deep breath. "I know there are feelings here, for both of us. But we literally just decided how important Jeweltones is to us too. How can we get everyone past another super-couple mess? Is it fair to ask the others to tie their careers to another romantic risk?"

"You're assuming we'd break up before we even try?"

Stern looks so defeated it nearly kills me, but I have to stick to my guns. Funny how this time I do so to try and save the group, not separate myself from it.

"Stern, come on. You know it's not that simple. Our relationship would be highly public. And tangled with our careers in a pop group. Do you know what kind of bond it would take to survive all that? I'm not saying it's impossible, but the odds aren't in our favor.

"Still, that's not even the biggest reason. I need to show the others I'm restarting on a selfless note. If we have any hope of fixing what's broken between Jeweltones, I don't think returning to the group as a new couple is the way to go. Not after how the press has spun this and treated Dea. It'd eclipse everything."

Stern wants to argue with me, but I already know him well enough to see he agrees. Even if he hates to.

"It's not fair to them. You're right," he finally says. "But it's not fair to us, either."

"Maybe. But it is a choice," I sigh before continuing. "Right now, I have to choose the music. I have to choose Jeweltones. I think that means not choosing us. Or what we might be."

"And if we do manage to get the band back together?" Stern asks. "Or if Jeweltones breaks up before we get the chance?"

I smile, just a little.

"Then that changes the choice, doesn't it?"

I watch as a grin begins to spread across his face. "So, you're not saying never? You're just saying not now?"

Looking back at Stern, I truly don't know if I mean what I say, or if this is just some excuse I'm making. All I do know is that, if there's really something there to explore, we'll find a way to do it when the time feels right. When trust is rebuilt, when we feel like we're on solid ground instead of dangling over another ledge. Or at least, until the pull becomes irresistible. Right now, for whatever reason, I can find it in myself to resist. Which should mean something.

"Never say never," I offer, trying not to sound too flirty.

"That, I can live with," he says, hitting me with that devastating smile. "Besides, it'll drive the fans nuts, the will-they, won't-they EverGreen shipping."

I roll my eyes. "That is so deeply not the point."

But then I think, whatever tension Stern and I do manage to keep between us, that's bound to be good for the music. So even now, sitting in my home, feeling surrounded by Stern's sound, feeling the longing of all that . . .

I still know I'm making the right decision.

The happily ever after I'm chasing here is with myself. With Jeweltones. And, most important of all, with the listeners still out there.

TURN TO PAGE 252

CHAPTER FOURTEEN

EVERLY

THE DAY AFTER STERN'S VISIT, I FIND MYSELF SITTING IN THE poolside cabana at the Jeweltones house, shielded from the late-morning sun. CeCe sits beside me. Being back in her presence, I feel a mix of comfort and anxiety that's so potent, I have to stop my knees from bouncing.

Once Stern and I settled yesterday, our first call was to Vinny. We asked if there was any chance we could all sit down together and come to a group decision before we ask Zahra or the label what's next. Vinny laughed, then said he was actually with Dea and they talked about doing the same thing. It was a relief to hear, but that was replaced with worry when he said they hadn't heard from CeCe either. Vinny told us he was "handling it, because he had some wild investigative oats to sow."

I wasn't sure exactly what he meant, but I was super happy when all five of us turned up today. Yesterday, Stern went back to the house after our talk, so I had all night to ponder ways why the group probably isn't going to work. I still have no idea what everyone wants to happen today, but I brace myself to find out.

CeCe takes a deep breath and pulls her eyes away from the shimmering pool. Whatever she might be feeling on the inside, she looks great on the outside. Relaxed, even, in her usual boots and an artfully tattered sweater.

"The others are waiting inside for us, but I asked if we could talk first," she says. "I already got to talk to Dea. She forgave me for telling you and Vinny, and I told her I wanted to keep trying at our relationship now that we don't have to hide. She wants to take it slow, but that's more than I expected, honestly."

I hate that my first emotion is sadness, feeling like CeCe has prioritized a relationship with Dea over our friendship. Then again, I hate everything about the way Dea makes me feel about myself. I swallow that emotion, because I want to do better.

"I'm glad to hear that," I lie, trying to pivot to the truth. "I was worried that I wrecked things between you two. I know you probably have a lot you want to say to me, but I was hoping you'd let me explain myself first. And apologize?"

"I don't have much to say to you," CeCe replies. "Other than you don't owe me any apologies or explanations. If anything, I'm sorry for the position I put you in and the distance it put between us. I told you that night because I felt silenced and trapped and you felt like a safe space. But I know you probably felt exactly the same way about telling Stern."

"Maybe. But I'm sorry, nonetheless," I answer, feeling relief flood my system. "I handled the whole Popella thing so selfishly. This whole Jeweltones thing from the start, really. Mostly I'm sorry you and Dea felt like you even had to hide in the first place."

"Well, it turns out I'm pretty damn good at hiding," CeCe sighs. "Which is why I need to quit Jeweltones, Everly."

The words knock the wind out of me. I'm surprised how much that idea cuts like a knife.

"My parents live by a lake, did you know that?" CeCe continues, looking back out at the pool. I shake my head.

"With so many siblings, I used to spend a lot of time out there. With them, but alone too. That's where I ran to hide after Popella, the closest lake I could find. I know you love Taylor Swift, so you know her song 'the lakes'?"

"Of course, it's about the artist cottage backup plan. Escaping to some remote lake where poets go to perish. Where you keep being an artist, but you don't subscribe to all the public business things drowning you."

I suddenly know exactly what CeCe means to communicate. She's so damn good at speaking someone else's language. Still, I want to hear her own.

"I hate to admit it, but I realized Stern was a little bit right, what he said about me at that vision board thing," CeCe continues. "I forced myself to blend into the group, like I've done my whole life. The middle sibling, the team player, the always-strong Black girl. And I literally put myself back in the closet for Dea. Then, instead of recognizing all that, I acted out by throwing a grenade in the middle of us. Basically, I did all the things in Jeweltones I promised myself I'd change in college. This group hasn't brought out the best in me, and that's no one's fault except my own."

CeCe takes a deep breath, then goes on. "I want to evolve, not regress. I'm hoping Howard will let me start in the spring semester. I'll stay in LA to see how things go with Dea, for now. I just . . . I can't do any of that until I know that you and I are good."

CeCe looks back at me, wanting my answer. I'm afraid I don't have the one she wants.

"CeCe, we'll be good no matter what you choose is best for yourself," I begin. "But I need you to hear me out on something, first."

❖ "Look how much Jeweltones has challenged us to learn about ourselves in its worst version. Imagine the potential if we bring that kind of **honesty** to our listeners, not holding back?"
TURN TO PAGE 255

❖ "I want us to all sort out how to create together as equals," I say, trying to **show** CeCe I've changed. "I'll even give all my songs to Jeweltones, if that's what we need to do."
TURN TO PAGE 256

"None of us have been our best selves," I continue. "But that's because we've been reacting to nonstop expectations. To cope, we fell back on familiar patterns. Knowing that, would you be interested in trying to build Jeweltones as a space for us all to potentially evolve?"

CeCe doesn't look convinced such a thing is possible.

"No, really," I say. "We've all been doing our own version of the same thing: prioritizing ourselves and repressing ourselves at the same time because we don't trust each other. And why would we, given our history? But what if, before anything else, we tried to build some trust? To find some common ground in a shared purpose?"

"You really think we can?"

I hesitate. I still don't know for sure.

"Listen, you and I both see something in Dea and Stern the other obviously doesn't. So I'm willing to keep an open mind, to give us the headspace to try. And if Jeweltones really is over, then we lose nothing by giving this a shot. If we can really work together, I think what we stand to gain is much bigger."

CeCe hears me, I can tell. However, she obviously also still sees the personal mountains we'll each have to move to get there.

"Honestly, we don't stand a chance without you," I finish. "Because even if you haven't felt like it, you've always been our leader."

CeCe tries to suppress it, but she grins.

"We all need to step out of the shadows," she says. "But the only way to do that is to step into our shadows, huh?"

I grin back at CeCe and reach out, grabbing her hand.

"No matter what, you're my priority in all this, now," I say. "We try to make it work together. But if either of us sees it becoming bad for the other's mental health again, we both walk away. Together. Is that enough to get you to keep an open mind today?"

CeCe pauses a moment, but it doesn't take her very long to say, "For you? I'll try."

TURN TO PAGE 257

"You'd really do that?" CeCe asks, looking genuinely surprised. "I don't want you to compromise your writing for the group. Or for me."

"That's the thing, CeCe. I see now that it's not a compromise. It's a privilege," I answer, easily this time. "I know I've had one foot in and one foot out, and that I caused a lot of drama. But we all did while we got our bearings. I think we owe it to each other to let that stuff go?"

CeCe looks emotional as I say this. Funny how, after all we've talked about, this is what really gets her.

"Think about what that could do for our listeners. The message we'd be sending if we found a way to unite," I add. "Especially with you as our leader. Because that's what you've always really been, CeCe."

This seems to hit her even harder.

"For me, that's worth risking everything for," I finish. "But only if we figure out how to do it the right way. We haven't been given a chance to make it work, not properly. Don't we owe ourselves that much? Just one shot to actually collaborate?"

"Stepping out of the shadows by stepping into our shadows," CeCe muses, mulling my words over. "That could be good." Finally, a smile reaches her face. "I'm not making any promises. But I am willing to see how today goes."

After everything, this single sentence sounds the most like music to my ears.

TURN TO PAGE 257

♦ ♦ ♦

Shortly after my conversation with CeCe, we all gather in Gia's temporary home: the guesthouse behind the pool. It's a spacious studio with a bedroom and living room, but Gia has already turned it into a cozy, glamorous wonder full of floral candles and animal print blankets. Vinny was the one to recommend we meet back here, to create the impression of some safe new space in lieu of the retreat we never got to take. It seemed like a good idea, since we need all the fresh energy we can get.

Though right now, sitting arranged around the couches and armchairs in silence, nothing feels particularly fresh. Maybe that's because Vinny disappeared into the bathroom the moment we got back here, asking us to wait for him to officially start. I know his stomach has been a challenge for him, but we've now been sitting here close to five minutes, pretending to be busy on our phones. Maybe it's just my imagination, but it's like I can feel invisible energy crackling hot and cold between Dea and me. Stern sits beside me while CeCe and Dea sit across from us, tangling so many unspoken lines. My palms sweat from the nerves. I know this meeting needs to start with more apologies, but now it feels like no apology will ever be anywhere near enough.

Then Vinny emerges from the bathroom, and I gasp out loud. I hear the others react similarly as we all turn to get a better view.

Because Vinny stands before us in full drag.

He didn't have much time to do his makeup, just wearing some mascara and lipstick, but the rest of his look is sensational. He sports a wig that is obviously inspired by Gia's own hair, then a dress made entirely of cascading, fringe-like rainbow flags. Noting our awed reaction, Vinny does one spin, sending his dress and hair twirling. Then he gracefully pivots into the nearest armchair, draping over it in a dramatic pose. We all find ourselves clapping. I mean, how could you not?

"Thank you. And thank you for waiting to indulge my dramatique entránce," Vinny starts, sitting up in the chair. "I know it's a bit extra, but I promise this lewk is a part of the point I want to make. And as the one among us least stirred up in the drama, I was hoping to go first, if that's all right?"

"After an entrance like that, you can have the floor for days," Dea says, looking delighted.

I don't blame her. Vinny has hit us with a blast of sheer joy. It makes me wonder: Why were we all feeling so dreadfully serious just a few seconds ago? I know there's obviously very serious stuff here to sort out, but Vinny has given us exactly the first break we needed—a reminder of the energy we can bring instead.

"Thank you, dearest," Vinny coos. "Okay, I'll try to keep this brief because I know each of us has a lot to say. I might not have any specific wrongs to right, but this group has made me feel a bit excluded and undefined. So I wanted to start everything with different energy. To begin, I'd like to preemptively forgive everyone. I know you all still will need to hash things out, but I understand everything that happened. On my end, I'm ready to move forward."

Vinny makes sure to connect eyes with each one of us as he speaks, then takes one final breath. Whatever he is about to say next, it's clear he has thought about it just as carefully as his heartfelt opener.

"The reason I want to move forward is because I've started to believe the five of us together, as Jeweltones, went viral for a reason. I think the world is starving for a group like us. A group that defies old pop conventions. And I don't just mean crossing genre boundaries. I mean how we're different genders, different ethnicities, different sexualities. We're different everythings, but with one shared dream. I mean, is there anything more all-American than that? Sure, we're also messy AF, but that's a part of the great experiment. So if we can really find a way to work together, I think we have an opportunity to set a new example here. Not just for us, but for pop stars that come after us. And our fans. If we can figure out a way to make this right, think of the message it will send."

Vinny's words reverberate around the room and I almost cry. This obviously echoes the kind of realization that also brought me back to the table. Suddenly, the idea of being in a group with Vinny, especially in this drag form, feels like even more of an honor and a privilege.

"All that said," Vinny continues, "hitting that wall on a stage as big as Popella, the aftermath made me see myself more clearly than I ever have before. If we decide to keep going with Jeweltones, I need to bring the most authentic version of my performance self. And here she is. I know we're going to have to make compromises to make this group work, but no one should need to make themselves smaller to fit in Jeweltones—we should need to make ourselves bigger."

All I want to do is give Vinny an enormous hug. He took the words right out of my mouth and said them more beautifully than I ever could have. Which is perfectly okay, because there are plenty of other words that I need to say when it's my turn.

Dea actually raises her hand next, indicating that she'd like her own turn.

"Vinny, I think I speak for us all when I say we'd be honored to have your full queen in the group if we decide to stay together," she says. "And while your forgiveness is appreciated, we can't keep sweeping things under the rug. I got to clear the air with you and CeCe yesterday, and then I got to chat with Stern just now, while CeCe and Everly were talking. We are good."

Dea looks at Stern and nods. I wish I could ask him what was said, but for now I'll have to settle with guessing.

"Which means everyone knows that Dea and I are giving our relationship a real shot," CeCe cuts in, looking at Dea. "You should also know it was my intention to quit Jeweltones today. However, after Vinny's speech and talking to Everly, I am trying to keep an open mind."

Dea flinches as she processes this new information. She looks conflicted, hearing CeCe take this step.

"Needless to say, Everly," Dea says, swallowing her reaction and turning to me. "I think you and I need to talk privately after this group session?"

I nod. Even though I'd rather pull out my fingernails, she is right.

"I am hopeful we can resolve the personal stuff happening here, because I think we're all genuinely sorry," Dea continues. "I certainly am, for the way I handled things. But still, as much as I believe in the vision

Vinny just pitched, I truly don't see the way we make this work creatively. Personally, if I'm going to stay, I need to leave today feeling positive we can collaborate.

"But as Vinny said, we need to build trust if we're going to do that. Which means we need to start being more honest. I think about everything I projected, being the perfect performer with the perfect boyfriend and the flawless looks and flawless posts. For better or worse, Jeweltones shattered that illusion for the whole world to see—and to criticize. It has made me ask why I felt that pressure to project in the first place, and honestly... I'm not sure I have the answer. But I should. And a huge part of me thinks this group isn't the place I should be figuring all that out.

"Then another part of me says to stop throwing walls up. So even though I don't know what it means for my identity yet, I do know I have real feelings for CeCe. I don't want either of us to have to fake anything anymore. Whether we both stay or go, Jeweltones has to be okay with that. *With us.*" Dea finishes, looking like that just took a whole lot out of her.

Despite myself, I'm impressed.

"Duh," Vinny says first.

"Of course," I say at the exact same time as Stern.

I turn to him and when I look into his eyes, I know what I need to say next.

❖ We need to tell Jeweltones that we are a **couple**.
TURN TO PAGE 261

❖ Stern and I need to tell Jeweltones that we are just remaining **collaborators**.
TURN TO PAGE 262

"Especially because Stern and I need to ask the same thing," I say, still looking at him. I take a breath and then turn to the others. "We know better than anyone how it might complicate things. But it's a risk I'm willing to take, just like Dea and CeCe."

"Same," Stern says.

"Then I guess we need to extend the same openness," CeCe says after a moment. "Though Stern, I think you and I also should talk one-on-one before we reach any group decisions?"

Stern nods, looking like he feels the same way I do about my looming conversation with Dea. Given all the revealing and cheating and tension between Stern and CeCe, it might prove to be an equally difficult summit.

"I obviously kept you two apart long enough," Dea says, looking particularly uncomfortable. For a moment I think she's going to say more, but she doesn't.

"Who am I to stand in the way of love?" Vinny says with a grin. "Though you monogamous messies do remind me how thrilled I am to remain a single Miss Independent. Just don't go pulling a Fleetwood Mac on me?"

"We could do worse," I say with a laugh. "But all I can promise to be is transparent, whatever happens."

Everyone nods in agreement. And I realize my own moment to speak up has probably arrived.

TURN TO PAGE 263

"I know you're all probably wondering about me and Stern," I continue. "There *are* feelings there, but we both agreed to focus on the group and building back some trust between us. So we're just friends."

"For now," Stern adds, which makes me want to sock him in the arm.

"What matters is that we want to put the group first," I say, shooting him a look. If I thaw too much, I know I'll melt entirely. "Anything else, we promise to be transparent about."

"That's fair," CeCe says.

Beside her, Dea nods, looking particularly uncomfortable about all of this. Even though it's slightly annoying, I can't say I blame her.

"Though Stern," CeCe follows up, "I think you and I also should talk one-on-one before we reach any group decisions?"

Stern nods, looking like he feels the same way I do about my looming conversation with Dea. Given all the revealing and cheating and tension between Stern and CeCe, it might prove to be an equally difficult summit.

"Who am I to stand in the way of love?" Vinny says with a grin. "Though you monogamous messies do remind me how thrilled I am to remain a single Miss Independent. Just don't go pulling a Fleetwood Mac on me?"

"We could do worse," I say with a laugh. "But yes, agreed."

We all sit for a moment, until I realize my own turn to speak up has probably arrived.

TURN TO PAGE 263

"All right, while I have the floor," I continue, "some of you have already heard me say this, but I owe everyone an apology. Not just for how I handled everything surrounding Popella, but also for focusing on the wrong things from the start. Getting thrown into this group, I just could only see myself and my career as a singer-songwriter going a certain way. I think in the rush of it all, I mistook artistic integrity for being inflexible. But someone I respect very much recently asked me to define what matters most to me as an artist. For me, the answer is to write and perform songs that matter to the listeners who need them.

"So even if this isn't the platform I expected, I'm seeing now that it's the one I needed. Not just to open up my creative process, but because I see how much I can learn from each of you. I wish I could have seen that from the start, but here we are. So I have two points to make. First, I want to share my songwriting with Jeweltones fully, in whatever way we decide best serves the group. And second, I hoped we could find a mission statement for Jeweltones, one that also serves our individual artistic intentions. But it already sounds like most of you agree with mine? Being authentic to represent our listeners."

"Can I get an amen?" Vinny chants.

I smile back at him, especially once Dea nods in agreement. Turning to CeCe, she looks deep in thought. I don't know if that's a good or bad sign, so I turn to Stern. He takes a breath and begins.

"This all sounds great to me. But then, I've believed in Jeweltones from the jump. Still, I've talked to Everly and Dea about how I probably believed in it for the wrong reasons. I wanted this group to work because it was my ticket to being a pop star, to being rich and famous and successful. But I've never really asked myself why I want those things in the first place, other than it's what we're all *supposed* to want.

"If I'm being honest, if I take all that away, I'm not sure I really even know why I want to be a pop star, other than to make music. So I guess that's why I still need Jeweltones—to figure out my purpose? I wish I had it more figured out, but I also think I'm here to learn from all of you, if that's okay?"

The others all nod at Stern and I'm really proud of him. However, we all know there's another elephant still left in the room, so he takes another breath and continues.

"I do know this much, though. What matters to me most is how I treat people, and how I can support them. I know I've been bad at that, especially with the whole gossip leak mistake. I know it seems like a betrayal. I guess it is one. I see that now. But it's like we were just talking about, Dea faking our relationship, Everly not sharing her songs, CeCe hiding away, Vinny not performing in drag—I was clinging to the wrong thing. No one else was fighting for Jeweltones, and Zahra kept saying we needed to stay in the spotlight. I was leaking stories to keep us relevant. I thought maybe if we had more time to work our issues out . . . Anyway, I see now how messed up that was. All I can say is that I'd never do something like that again. And I hope you can all trust me someday."

"I forgive you," I say, touching his arm. "Like I said, we all did things we regret to get to this place."

Stern turns to me, looking grateful. But then we all turn toward Dea, waiting.

"I wouldn't have done it, but I understand where you were coming from," Dea says hesitantly. "Still, I hope you at least now see the way the public is so quick to give you, specifically, a pass. And the kinds of crap female or queer pop stars have to deal with that you probably won't ever have to?"

"I do," Stern replies. "And I understand why you hid what you did, Dea. All I want to do is be a good ally. And a good group member."

"Then I forgive you too," Dea says.

"Well, I can only forgive you on one condition," CeCe adds. "If you make a public statement that Dea didn't keep you and Everly apart in some purposefully malicious way, that you both faked it in your own ways. Dea can come out at her own pace, but you need to take some public accountability to make this right, for me. Because Dea has been dragged through hell more than any of us."

Stern takes this in for a beat. I can tell he is resisting some urge to immediately agree to please CeCe.

"I'm nervous about saying the wrong thing again," he says carefully. "I'll do that for sure, but will you all help me write a statement that sounds right?"

CeCe looks like she wishes Stern knew how to be an ally all on his own, but she nods. It might not be perfect, but at least it's progress.

"I meant it when I said you're all forgiven in my book, for everything," Vinny says. "But still, I think for any of us to forget the last few weeks, actions are going to have to speak louder than words. We're going to have to prove we really mean the things we say today. And actually deliver on some of the promises. Me included. Okay?"

Vinny is right. Forgiveness is easy to say. Whether we can really live it out, really trust each other, remains to be seen. At the very least, our foundation is now secret-free.

Or I hope it is, anyway.

Once we settle and it's clear Stern has finished, we turn to CeCe. We all must be wondering the same thing—has any of this been enough to change her mind about quitting?

"I appreciate everything that has been said today. And you all already know I'm sorry for lying and forcing that onto you too," CeCe says. "And Stern, we'll talk, yes. But I have to say, I'm with Dea on one thing: I need to see how we actually collaborate to be convinced Jeweltones is worth fighting to save. However, what you've all said about intentions has also really struck me. I've never really focused in on a specific mission statement, but my own feels clear now.

"I want to break barriers as a queer Black woman, to represent and vocalize our experiences. And I want to be a part of something that pushes me out of my shell. Being in a big group or a big family, I'm always going to want to blend in. That's what feels safe. But I need people around me who push me to stand out. So far, this group has been about self-protection and survival. About our weaknesses showing. But I also think there's a reason we worked so well together onstage in the first place. It's because our unique strengths help cover those weaknesses. That version of Jeweltones, the one where fighting is inevitable, but no matter how much we feud or get jealous internally, we still present a united front to the public? That family version of Jeweltones I can get behind."

CeCe looks drained when she finishes, but I sincerely hope, from the bottom of my heart, she feels what a good look this is on her.

"Well, damn," Vinny says, wiping at his eyes. "If we need a leader, I vote for CeCe."

"Hell yes," Stern agrees.

"You know," I begin to work out, "having a person to settle ties and set direction, someone we all trust equally to hear our voices . . . that's not a bad idea."

"I couldn't agree more," Dea adds, her eyes on CeCe—and filled with more affection than I've ever seen.

"Oh, I don't want to be our actual leader," CeCe says, definitively.

The rest of us all look around at one another, clearly thinking the same thing.

"That's *exactly* why it should be you," I say, smiling wide.

Then it clicks on CeCe's face. Exactly what she asked for just played out in real time.

"Right," she says, smiling as well. "This is a start. But I need to have that conversation with Stern. And so do Dea and Everly?"

My stomach drops, because I know CeCe is right.

"The crown suits you, diva," Vinny says, standing and placing a hand on his hip. "Old Vinny would feel left out, but this is definitely one part of the roller coaster I'm happy to miss. I have some ideas on how to run our first-ever creative session. So assuming you four don't spontaneously combust, I'll be waiting to get started on our next mountain to climb."

With that, Vinny turns and sashays away. The rest of us probably wish we were in his high-heeled shoes.

This has been a better start than I anticipated, but Vinny is right—we still have many mountains to climb. Not just these difficult private conversations, but seeing if we can finally get on the same creative page. Even then, we still need to see if Zahra, the label, and the listeners will give us a second chance.

But as my eyes settle on Dea, I tell myself to just fight one battle at a time.

♦ ♦ ♦

Stern and CeCe agreed to talk in the breakfast nook back in the main house, which means Dea and I sit alone in the guest studio. In complete silence.

After several awkward beats of staring at each other, it's clear that neither of us knows where to begin.

Then it occurs to me: I don't know where to begin with Dea because I don't really know what I want from her. Resolution, sure, but what kind?

Before I say anything, setting my intention is probably once again the best place to start. I think about it, and it suddenly becomes crystal clear. I want us to work together and build trust in each other to help Jeweltones.

But given our history, how are we going to get there?

◈ The best shot I have at becoming an authentic performer in Jeweltones is to feel it's a trusting, safe space. I want to try rebuilding a genuine **friendship** with Dea.
TURN TO PAGE 268

◈ The best shot I have at maintaining my artistry and ensuring the survival of Jeweltones is to create some boundaries. To do that, Dea and I need to strive to become respectful **colleagues**.
TURN TO PAGE 271

I guess we're about to see if you can really put shattered glass back together? The only way to find out is by being brutally honest, the way we just promised. I don't want to just patch things up—I want to try resetting our broken bones.

"I know I should be sorry for telling Stern about you and CeCe," I say. "Part of me is. But I'm also not sure it was fair to be put in that position to begin with."

Dea sighs. "You won't believe me, but I never knew you had feelings for Stern."

She's right. I don't believe her, but that's not the point. "Would you have done anything differently if you had known?"

"There," Dea says. "*There it is.* That's what you really think of me."

"I know I haven't made things between us any better, but that first betrayal really hurt me," I respond. "I never recovered, so I've been fighting fire with fire this whole time."

"But Everly, there was no fire to begin with," Dea replies, looking frustrated as ever. "I was nervous—and yes, by the way, I get nervous—and I made one stupid slip about your stage fright. We'd talked about it a hundred times and it didn't seem like some big secret. Should I have done it? Of course not. But to me it was a thoughtless mistake, and you took it like I was intending some mortal wound. You bugged out on me at the scariest possible moment in my life, then you went on to make my dream coming true feel like a nightmare."

I watch as tears fill Dea's eyes. It's like an avalanche of emotion has shaken loose and now she can't stop herself. I expect anger to flare in me, but instead I just feel . . . mortified.

"I tried to understand, because I obviously hit a nerve in you," Dea continues. "But instead of listening to me, you chose to believe I'm some calculating demon who aimed to take you down. That's how you see me. Do you know how much that hurts? I only ever wanted to be your friend. I have so much respect for what you can do, how you can change people with your music. But you obviously don't respect me. And then you used your talent to make the whole world see me the way you do."

Dea wipes away the streaks on her cheeks, sniffling. "I do want to be your friend, Everly. I always have. But honestly, I'm not sure you deserve that, after everything."

I take a breath, because I want with all my heart to remain empathetic and honest instead of defensive. That has always gotten us nowhere, but I also can't ignore that I have a lot to say.

"Look, I have struggled to see your perspective in all this," I say, trying to keep my tone level. "And I wish I could have sooner, but I don't think I was in a place to hear you, even if you had said this same exact thing before. But you also need to give me a break. The stress we've been under, in the competition and then with this surprise group becoming famous literally overnight—it has all happened so fast. Each one of us has been knocked back on our heels. And no, I didn't handle it perfectly. But come on, Dea, neither did you."

"Maybe," Dea replies, icing up a bit again. "But you're the one who went for my neck at the slightest misstep. I mean, can you blame me for protecting myself? How am I ever supposed to trust you again?"

"Dea, you've been lying about who you really want to be for a while," I reply. "And I don't mean your sexuality, I swear. I mean the whole pop star influencer façade. Is it so impossible to understand that it was hard for me to tell when you were being genuine and when you were trying to sniper me from the side?"

"It is impossible for me to understand, yes," Dea sighs, looking exhausted. "I don't know if we're ever going to agree on this."

Dea is right. We aren't going to.

"That's fair," I say, trying not to seem exasperated. "But today, I can definitely see how I hurt you. I can see why you behaved the way you did more clearly. And I can accept that we both did what we felt we had to do in an extraordinary situation. So even if I still think you owe me an apology and some accountability, I can forgive you without either. And I can honestly say that I'm sorry. I'm not proud of any of my behavior, but I really did feel justified."

I stop myself there, because I could go around and around in circles on this forever. "Is that enough to start over with?"

Dea looks down at the floor, thinking.

"I don't think so," she finally says. "But I have to ask something else. Do you respect me as an artist?"

I consider the question. It's a tough one. It makes me realize that, while I respect much of what Dea has to offer, I don't think I'd call what she does "artistry." And she can absolutely tell. She has always been able to.

"I didn't before," I say. "But I was wrong. I have so much to learn from you. Seriously."

Dea shakes her head. Then she also lifts it, looking at me. "We're never going to stop fighting, are we?"

I'm not sure what's going on here between me and Dea. We're too similar and too different, bound together against our will, jealous and competitive, awed and awful, fearless and fierce—we're all of it at once.

But despite all that, can we ever be friends again?

"At the end of the day, I think I want Jeweltones to be what CeCe said: a chosen family," I reply. "If I know you really have my back, I can live with fighting."

"This is exhausting," Dea sighs again. "But I have no desire to hurt you. I never did."

"Me neither," I reply. "I want us to be friends again too. Not just for CeCe or the group. For real."

Dea seems to take this in. "I hear you. I hope that can happen. But let's take baby steps this time around?"

"Deal," I say.

Dea and I both stand, but don't hug. We don't need to. One way or another, we're both as ready as we'll ever be to face whatever comes next.

For today, that's not only enough, it's something take pride in.

TURN TO PAGE 273

I take a beat to let this intention soak in. It means that this conversation will require honesty, but nothing brutal. We need a bandage, not to break any more bones.

"Listen, I hate that we ended up where we did," I say. "But I think there's a reason. A lot got lost in translation in the middle of a stressful situation. I think we bonded so quickly because we're so similar when it comes to our work. But somewhere along the way, comparing our strengths and weaknesses turned into a competition."

Dea stares back at me, waiting until I've finished.

"Everly, we might have the same dreams, and we're definitely both stubborn as hell. But we have nothing else in common."

"That's not true," I return, but I try to check myself. I don't want this to devolve into another standoff. "We both regret how we handled the whole CeCe-Stern situation."

Dea shifts in her seat, glancing toward the door. Why can't we ever seem to communicate? I'm not sure I owe Dea an apology for telling Stern about her and CeCe, but I'm also not sure she owes me one for placing me in that situation either. I don't know what else to say.

"Listen, we don't need to be friends again to make this group work," Dea says. "All we need is a clean slate and some mutual respect. I don't understand the way you treated me, but I'm willing to let it go and give you a second chance."

"I don't understand the way you treated me either," I reply. "But I'm also willing to let it go and try to do better."

"And do you respect me as an artist?" Dea then asks. To my surprise, there's a sudden vulnerability in her voice, which I can tell she wishes she hid better.

In this moment, it becomes so clear to me what this has probably always been about.

"Not only do I respect you, but I have a lot I want to learn from you," I say, meaning every word. "And I'm sorry if I ever made you feel that wasn't true."

Watching Dea's reaction, I wish I had removed the "if." This is obviously exactly what I did to her, even if that wasn't my intention. I realize, on some level, she must feel the same way about everything she did to me.

"You know, you always think you can see right through me. And you can, which I hate," Dea says. "But you never realize I see right through you too."

I'm a little speechless. Dea is right on the money. It reminds me why I was drawn to her in the first place. For a moment, I second-guess myself. Is not trying to be friends again a mistake? Isn't life too short to keep people at a distance?

Then I remember that life is too short to waste keeping the wrong people close. I'm not sure I'll ever really know how to tell the difference, but right now my gut is telling me that it's better for both Dea and me to keep our distance.

And to never say never.

"So, yes. Colleagues," Dea concludes. "Especially now that we know what buttons not to push. We'll see where that takes us?"

"I really like the sound of that."

Dea doesn't exactly smile and neither do I. Still, it feels like we have reached some solid ground. I can only hope Dea is feeling what I do, right now . . .

A whole hell of a lot more hopeful.

TURN TO PAGE 273

CHAPTER FIFTEEN

VINNY

SIPPING SELTZER IN THE KITCHEN, I CAN'T HELP BUT FEEL GOOD.
Well, maybe not physically—this wig is a little itchy and the padding under
my outfit is quite tight. But you know what they say: beauty is pain.

I even feel a bit giddy, honestly. Because maybe, just maybe, this group
can actually deliver all the things I've always wanted? Not just the fame
and the stage, but a family of friends. A place to belong, in all our queer
and diverse glory. I'm also giddy because next comes the fun part—or at
least, I hope so. Next, we get to create together. I can't wait to see what
that looks like, when we're working with each other instead of against one
another.

I realize that the bubbly feeling I'm currently experiencing probably
has something to do with nerves too. While I might be free from the tough
conversations now happening between Stern, CeCe, Everly, and Dea, I
certainly won't be free of the outcomes, one way or another.

Just then, Mom walks into the kitchen carrying many bags of groceries. I move across the island to help her.

"Oh, Vinny!" she exclaims. "You look incredible!"

Taking a bag, I do a little curtsy in my quick-drag outfit.

"Does this mean the group conversation went well?" she asks.

"The first part, yes. The others are talking one-on-one now. If that
goes well, we'll use the songwriting space you set up for us last night."

After I told her the latest, Mom insisted on making a run to Home-
Goods to surprise the group with a converted songwriting space. I can't
wait for the others to see it—assuming we make it there to begin with.

"Well, that sounds promising," Mom says, beginning to unbag the mountain of groceries. We Vecchis might not have much, but what we do have always goes toward food. I try to ignore what that might mean for me, in this new space I occupy with eating.

"Not to be a narcissist, but is your drag queen supposed to be me?" Mom asks, trying to hide a smirk.

"In a way," I reply. "It represents all the queens that give me life."

As I speak, I pull out a sack of potatoes and avocado oil. Peering into the bag, I suddenly realize that every single thing Mom has bought fits within my allergy exclusion list. I glance at the pasta boxes again and do a double take. She even bought the gluten-free kind.

I could cry.

"What?" she says, brandishing a long spaghetti box like a sword. "I still think this stuff is sacrilege, but anything for my Vinny."

She softens a bit then, looking back down at the bags.

"I think maybe, since we got to LA, I haven't been the best mom. At least when it comes to your new stomach stuff. It's just, there have been so many changes so fast. You're a grown-up all of a sudden, getting a house for us from your career. I'm no therapist, but I think feeding you was always my way of showing love. And I suddenly couldn't do that anymore, and—"

Before she can finish, I envelop her in a bear hug.

"Stop. You're the best mom on the planet," I say. "I get it. This was your way of holding on to a piece of something familiar. Turns out there was a lot of that going around in this house."

Speaking the words, I realize that now is probably the time to fess up to my own past-clinging path. Especially while the others are engaging in their heart-to-hearts.

"It really means a lot to me, you coming around on the stomach thing. I have to admit I've been pretty slow to come around on the idea of you and Everly's dad. I even . . ."

I pause, not sure I want to tell Mom about my reaction to the gossip a few weeks ago. Luckily Mom grabs my hand before I can go on.

"Hun, you can tell me, really. Do you not want me to date Steve?"

"I didn't, before," I finally admit. "But not because of the group or anything. I just don't want to see you hurt again. And . . . I don't think I'm ready for us to let go of Dad yet."

Saying the words out loud brings tears to my eyes, but I don't want to smudge my makeup. Mom squeezes me into a hug before I can have much of a reaction anyway.

"Vinny, listen to me. I'll never be ready to let go of your dad either. But at some point, I had to decide that freezing ourselves in place doesn't honor his memory. Carrying him with us into the new chapters does that, okay?"

"Okay," I reply.

"But losing a husband isn't the same as losing a father at the age you did. I'm always here for you, but maybe we should find someone who might understand more? A support group? Maybe even at the LGBT Center?"

I smile. That's not a half bad idea. Not remotely.

"You know, it's funny, I was just reading an article in this issue of *Oprah*," Mom says, pointing to the magazine she unpacked on the counter. "I was going to show it to you because I thought it would help with the Jeweltones group therapy, but I think it applies to more than that. It's all about how when we're afraid of something unknown, there are two options we resort to: control or trust. If we can't trust, then we try to control. But there's so much we can't really control, so it just spins us right around. It's better to just learn to trust."

"But trust what?" I ask.

"I don't know, I'm not Oprah," Mom says with a laugh. "I think she means trust in some higher power. But you can always trust me. And trust that you can be honest with me."

Then she pauses, considering something else.

"You know, I never want to influence your memories of your dad. But you were so young when he passed, he got to show you the best parts of himself. Me, I'm a human megaphone, so you were always going to see the good and the bad. But your dad, he kept a lot in. He was a bit of an anxious mess, under it all. Just like you, he put on a good show. And I hate to break it to you, kiddo, but you've got a big ol' slice of both of us in you."

Tears finally slide out of my eyes. She is right—I was too young when Dad died. I never got to know him as a whole person the way I know Mom now. Part of me never wants to tarnish the legend of him that exists in my memory. But another part of me is so damn thankful to know I carry more of him with me than I ever even realized.

"There was so much I think he never said out loud. And there's so much I wish . . ."

Mom stops a second, wiping away some tears of her own.

"I just wish I knew how to say some things to him, back then. I'll say them to you now," she says, pressing on. "You don't have to be fun and light all the time. It's okay to go dark sometimes. That never makes you a burden. And I am so stinking grateful to have you in my life, even when you're not feeling your best. Or if your stomach is complete garbage."

We look at each other for a moment and then burst into laughter.

"Thank you, Mom," I say, grabbing a napkin and folding the corner to blot my eyes. "I think I really needed to hear all of that."

She gives me one last squeeze, then we get back to unpacking. As I sift through these fresh groceries, a new feeling settles over me.

"You know, whatever happens with Jeweltones, I am going to have to deal with my appearance changing in the public eye eventually," I say. "And I think I just figured out how I want to handle it, when the time comes."

❖ "This whole transformation I'm experiencing, especially with my stomach sensitivities, needs to stay private. If it's going to stay a source of **personal** strength, I can't let it be affected by outside voices or opinions."
TURN TO PAGE 277

❖ "This whole transformation I'm experiencing, especially with my stomach sensitivities, needs to be shared as part of my **public** persona. Being vulnerable might open me up to haters, but it might also inspire others."
TURN TO PAGE 278

My main goal with these new dietary restrictions has always been to feel healthy in a way I never have before. But it's also important to me to make sure these restrictive needs affect as few other people as possible. I refuse to let this stomach stuff make me a demanding diva.

The fact that this moment of transformation converges all at once—physical and mental, inside and out, career and life—is not lost on me. After all, sometimes being a chameleon means evolving—changing shape in the best way.

That said, I can't be naïve about the reaction I'll likely receive now that I'm in the public eye. How many female and gay pop stars have endured body shaming? Just look what they said about Adele and Sam Smith and Jennifer Hudson. *Fame went to their heads, they betrayed their body-positive personas, they think they're better now.* Everyone will have an opinion about my body changing, and no one will understand the full truth of my transformation. Or that I loved myself then just as much as I do now.

Most of all, it'll be hard for anyone to understand that these seemingly limiting food restrictions have actually started not feeling like a trap at all. Sometimes too many options can feel as crippling as no options at all. If anything, I feel a bit liberated by the boundaries rather than restricted. But that all feels . . . impossible to explain. And highly likely to evolve, when I'm ready to start reintroducing foods. Which means I'd better prepare for lots of noise—and to not be overwhelmed by it.

"Hell to the yes," Mom replies. "If anyone asks about your body, just tell them your health is none of their business. It'll set an excellent example."

I smile. Maybe someday I will feel comfortable being public about my journey with food, but for now, inspiring myself feels like way more than enough.

I guess now the question is: Will it all still feel like enough tomorrow?

TURN TO PAGE 279

That's the thing about being a leader, or in the public eye, or trying to belong to anyone or anything—you can't open yourself up to love, connection, and inspiration without also being vulnerable to hate, rejection, and judgment.

But to find your people, doing so is worth the risk every time.

My dietary transformation will just be another dimension to add to my pop star, drag queen, queer advocate life. If it inspires anyone else to tackle these issues with confidence and pride instead of fear and doubt, I'll have done my job.

"I love that for you," Mom says. "Raising awareness is starting to feel like your calling card. It's a good look on you, hun."

Hearing these words out loud as well, they sound absolutely right.

For today, finally knowing what I want to say feels like an enormous win.

Tomorrow, this social media nonfluencer can start working out how to say it all best.

Maybe with a little help from my suddenly famous friends?

TURN TO PAGE 279

◆ ◆ ◆

We all reset in the unused sixth bedroom on the first floor, hopefully to start writing the next chapter together. Stern and CeCe finished talking first, emerging from the breakfast nook with actual smiles on their faces. It was easy to know how that went, but when Dea and Everly finally finished, they both looked exhausted—but also calm, in a way.

"Dare I ask how that went?" I ventured, as they rejoined the group.

Dea turned to Everly before answering, like they hadn't worked out exactly what to share from their conversation. With a silent nod, Dea seemed to understand Everly.

"We're starting over on a new page," Dea said.

"For now, that's enough," Everly added.

So miracles do happen. I'm dying to know more about what everyone talked about in private, but I'm sure Dea and I will download on that later. For now, I'm just grateful Jeweltones survived our emotional crucible relatively unscathed. Now it's time for the creative one.

This spare bedroom has been transformed into a comfortable and cozy creative corner thanks to Mom. She laid out pillows in jewel-toned colors everywhere, along with clusters of candles. On the bed sits a huge whiteboard and set of markers, while the sitting area near the window has a coffee table full of notebooks and pens. Everly has brought her keyboard and guitars, and CeCe has her laptop. Now we sit around the coffee table in a hodgepodge of chairs, the tools of our trade surrounding us. But where exactly do we begin?

"I guess I can get us started?" CeCe says, still sounding a bit unsure—even though everyone nods at her eagerly. "Okay. We know we need to present something to Zahra and the label. A clear direction. Songs that represent who we are as Jeweltones. Why we're still special."

"Can I propose we all vote to scrap 'Reignbow'?" I ask. "That song was deeply meh even before we tanked it."

"Hell yes," CeCe replies.

"I honestly didn't think it was so bad," Stern says. "But I don't mind losing it."

"We can do way better," Dea says.

"I completely agree," Everly adds, nodding at Dea.

I shift my eyes to CeCe and Stern—*will wonders never cease?* Once upon a time, these two would disagree just for the sake of it.

"I'm learning you all have your own experience with songwriting," Everly continues. "I obviously want us to co-write, but I'm happy to lead or help as much as you all want."

Everyone nods at this as well, because we know Everly still has the most experience in the songwriting department.

"Awesome," Everly says. "I don't know if it's the best place to start, but Stern and I finished something together when he visited me yesterday."

I look at Dea and wait for her reaction, because I'm not sure a song powered by "EverGreen" is the best new look for Jeweltones.

"I guess it doesn't hurt to hear it?" CeCe asks.

"Sure," I follow up. "But maybe afterward you can lead a group vote on it?"

CeCe and Dea both consider this, then nod. We turn to Everly and Stern, who both look a little unsettled. Still, they turn to each other and shrug.

It seems we're in for a little show.

◆ ◆ ◆

"What do you do when the thing you love,
      Burns you out faster than you can run?"

Stern and Everly finish singing their song in harmony, playing their guitars perfectly in sync. As the last few notes ring out, I experience a full-body chill. The duet they sang, it's not just a hit, it's another potential *phenomenon.* The layers of tension and warmth and longing and passion in their delivery, paired with the tones of their voices and those lyrics? It would be a crime against music to not deliver this song to our fans, in exactly this form. I feel it in my bones—this will be huge for Jeweltones, even if we're not all featured on the song as lead vocalists. But could I convince CeCe and Dea to stand on the sidelines with me? Is that even a fair thing to ask in the context of a group?

Everly and Stern look a bit vulnerable once they finish, but they also glow a little. I start clapping as vigorously as my manicured nails will allow. CeCe and Dea quickly join in, to my delight.

"That's really good," Dea says, sounding both awed and annoyed. "Like, really good."

"I agree, but how would we make it work for Jeweltones?" CeCe asks. "Could Dea and I maybe sing half? Dea, are you even comfortable with that yet? And what about Vinny?"

No one has answers, until a new idea strikes me so hard and fast, I can't even contain myself.

"Wait, hold on. That duet is perfect as is. It still feels very Jeweltones to me, even without the rest of us. If we're really going to represent all the colors of pop in a new way, who says all of us need to be on every single song?"

I have no idea if I've just had a stroke of genius or madness, but I try to wait as the idea settles with everyone.

"Other bands have done it," CeCe finally says.

"Hey, it worked for Fleetwood Mac," Everly says, predictably.

"Little Big Town does this in country," Stern jumps in. "My parents love ABBA, I think they were similar. We could be the modern pop version?"

"I like that angle," Dea says. "But only if we still keep things equitable. If we do a Stern-Everly duet, then Vinny, CeCe, and I would need our own song."

The moment the words leave Dea's lips, her eyes connect with mine.

"Four-on-the-floor dance anthem," we both say, literally in unison.

CeCe laughs. "I could channel my inner Demi to get with that. But obviously we still do songs all together, like 'Press Diamonds'?"

"Totally," Everly agrees. "The full group songs can be our core sound, the 'Press Diamonds' Jeweltones signature. But then we can explore and flex into other pop genres in different combinations that feel organic. And always equally distributed?"

"I'm obsessed with that idea," I say, feeling sky-high. Because if this really works, we just cracked a code to making this group iconic—and to make room for us all to thrive.

"Same here," Stern says, grinning.

"If this means I can finally do some real choreography," Dea adds, "then count me in."

"It's decided," CeCe concludes. She walks over to the whiteboard on the bed, picking up a marker to begin a list: "Press Diamonds," "Burns You Out," and "TBD Dance Anthem."

"If we're presenting this, we should probably round it out with one more full group song in the same lane as 'Press Diamonds'?"

As CeCe writes, everyone nods in agreement. Looking around, I feel intoxicated by our momentum. It's a real thrill, feeling our abilities uniting instead of dividing.

"Good. We can break into groups later for these combo projects," CeCe continues. "I'm thinking maybe we make a short video reel to present to Zahra? We can discuss that later. For now, I think we should work on our full group song?"

Once again, everyone nods in agreement.

"Good," she picks back up. "If it's okay, I actually have an idea on where to start. But I need a few minutes to get something together."

"Girl, if these are the results you get us," I answer, grinning, "you can have a few damn hours."

"Wait, does this mean you're not quitting?" Everly then asks.

CeCe doesn't even pause to keep us in suspense. She can't help it.

"I guess not," she says, smiling. "But before we start celebrating, let's just hope anyone actually still wants us together in this form?"

Despite the sobering note CeCe tries to end on, our smiles still spread. We can't help it either.

◆ ◆ ◆

Ten minutes later, we all return from our various bathroom and snack breaks to see what CeCe has come up with. Once we're settled, she stands before us with the whiteboard facing down. Then she lifts it up to reveal a marker masterpiece.

CeCe obviously has a steady hand, because she has drawn an incredibly neat and clean presentation. Under the initial song list on the whiteboard, she has new notes and an empty grid drawn—all in blue, purple, green, red, and black.

"This is based on something Everly and I talked about earlier," CeCe says as we devour the board.

STEPPING OUT OF THE SHADOWS BY STEPPING INTO YOUR SHADOWS

- A song about honoring your truest self but also balancing your personal vision to find success.
- About how to redefine success in the first place.
- About following a dream and things not turning out the way you expected—but different actually being better.

"If we all like this direction, I figured out an exercise to help us also pinpoint the sound of the song," CeCe adds, pointing to a gorgeous kind of spiraling Venn diagram.

VINNY FLEX: Diva Pop to Glam Rock
CECE FLEX: Pop Rock to Group Anthems
DEA FLEX: Group K-Pop to Dance Classics
EVERLY FLEX: Pop Classics to Indie Songwriter
STERN FLEX: Country Songwriter to Boy Band Pop

"Looking at our flexes, I think we can find some common ground, the way Zahra tried to have us do," CeCe continues. "But I think I have an idea on how to get more specific. If we want?"

"Girl, we want!" I shout.

"I especially love the 'Shadows' song idea," Stern adds. "It's perfect for where we are right now."

"I can obviously sink my teeth into that, lyrically," Everly says.

"Okay, what did you have in mind next?" Dea says, flashing CeCe the proudest of smiles underneath her all-business focus. It's deeply adorable.

"Okay, cool," CeCe says once everyone has weighed in. "I think we should all pair up to find one collab that best personifies each particular duo. We do that with everyone until we have ten songs for this empty grid. Then we each vote for our two favorites. The song with the most votes becomes our template for this new group sound?"

"Methodical," Dea responds. "I like it."

"And having all ten will be a good list for the future, no matter what," Stern says.

Everly looks less sure. "Yes, but I still don't want us copying anyone. Or limiting ourselves."

"But we do need something recognizable and specific to point to for our Jeweltones core songs, right?" I counter. "A foundation, one we can build our other combo songs off of, like we said?"

Everly considers this.

"Like a solid tree trunk. And the combos are branches, changing with the seasons."

"Leave it to you to make it sound way more poetic," I say, laughing.

Everly laughs too, then we all turn back to CeCe.

"Okay. Then let's get to it," she says simply, but with an excitement that charges us.

I deeply love this direct approach, especially after all our time spent circling the drain. It's so clear now that instead of letting the label, Zahra, and the show tell us who we should be, we need to tell the world who we are. It's okay we couldn't catch our breath to do so earlier—because we're certainly catching it now. For the first time, this group has actually given itself the chance to really collaborate.

Could it mean that we actually do *work*, darling?

♦ ♦ ♦

Thirty minutes later, we all sit regathered in front of the whiteboard. Breaking apart in one-on-one pairs to find our ideal collabs was a lot smoother than most of us thought. The results of those sessions have already been neatly transcribed in CeCe's grid:

Everly	Dea	"Pray to God"		HAIM & Calvin Harris
Dea	Vinny	"Dancing with a Stranger"		Normani & Sam Smith
Vinny	CeCe	"I'm Ready"		Sam Smith & Demi Lovato
CeCe	Stern	"I Know What You Did Last Summer"		Camila Cabello & Shawn Mendes
Stern	Everly	"Everything Has Changed"		Ed Sheeran & Taylor Swift
Everly	Vinny	"Easy"		Kacey Musgraves & Troye Sivan
Vinny	Stern	"One of Me"		Lil Nas X & Elton John
Stern	Dea	"For You"		Liam Payne & Rita Ora
Dea	CeCe	"psychofreak"		Camila Cabello & WILLOW
CeCe	Everly	"Edge of Midnight"		Miley Cyrus & Stevie Nicks

I must admit, I wasn't sure this exercise would yield more than when we tried with Zahra, but I've been proven gleefully wrong. I don't know if it's our renewed energy or the specificity of our goal this time around, but this new list feels exciting instead of pointless. Especially given the way the votes have shaken out so far.

CeCe went first, setting an important precedent: she voted for one of her collabs, "I Know What You Did Last Summer," thinking its driving energy between a feuding couple would best channel our group sound. Then CeCe voted for a second song she *didn't* generate, "For You," based on the same big-hook sound. Both songs occupy the same anthemic space as "Press Diamonds," but CeCe also set a template for voting fairly.

Stern followed her lead, literally, putting his first vote on "I Know What You Did Last Summer." He then put his second vote on "Edge of Midnight," saying it better captured the moodier undertones of "Press

Diamonds." Everly agreed with this sentiment, but she put her first vote instead on "Pray to God," feeling it was a less eighties-sounding take on haunting-anthemic pop. For her second vote, Everly picked "One of Me"—one of my collabs. She liked the unexpected, retro-meets-future pop fusion energy there.

Naturally, Dea went the opposite direction, voting for the most bombastic song on the list, "I'm Ready." She said our group songs should go bigger, but she also conceded this might be a better template for the dance banger with CeCe and me. Then Dea surprised everyone by placing her personal vote on "Pray to God." She promised it wasn't to placate Everly, but rather because she loved the more club-EDM direction.

When it came time for my votes, I had to go for "Dancing with a Stranger" first, the perfect song for modern, genre-blending pop—even though I also could see how it might be too laid back. Which ended up being fine, as I then realized this put me in a tiebreaker position for casting my final vote. The only songs with two votes each so far have been "Pray to God" and "I Know What You Did Last Summer."

Right now, sitting here facing this decision, it really does feel like a sign. Me—the overwhelmed one, the undecided pioneer, the ultimate chameleon—being the one to decide our creative direction. Honestly, both songs feel like the organic evolution for Jeweltones and an excellent complement to "Press Diamonds." It's also not lost on me that both songs happen to be the collabs between our resident feuding pairs. Clearly, there's something essential about the tensions there.

Still, it falls to me to decide which will serve as the best fuel for our creative fires.

⟡ I vote for Stern and CeCe's collab, "I Know What You Did Last Summer," to be our foundational inspiration. Not just because I favor the driving, **upbeat** pop anthem, but because I can already see it shaping our performance style.

TURN TO PAGE 288

⟡ I vote for Everly and Dea's collab, "Pray to God," to be our foundational inspiration. Not just because I favor the discordant, **edgier** pop anthem, but because I know it will best fit our vocal styles.

TURN TO PAGE 289

"I Know What You Did Last Summer" encapsulates all the things that make Jeweltones charismatic: love and heartbreak, push and pull, friends and feuds, pride and compromise, secrets and truths. It's a buzzy bop with deeper darkness in the lyrics, written by an iconic pop couple. What could be more Jeweltones than that?

I might not be the true leader of this group, but each one of us is going to have to start taking the lead in different ways. I think it's fitting this group keeps putting me in the middle—it forces me to be inspired when my instinct is to feel overwhelmed.

I cast my vote, then glance at Everly and Dea. I'm worried I'll find them looking annoyed or disappointed I didn't vote with them, but instead they both look inspired too.

"It's not what I would have chosen," Everly begins, "but I can definitely still relate to that song. And we'll make our version distinctly our own."

"A hit is a hit," Dea adds. "And I want us to have more hits and less misses."

Dea and Everly avoid eye contact, because they already know they'll probably never be entirely on the same frequency about stuff like this. Thank divas above, we've at least started to prove today that we don't have to be on the same exact frequency in order to collaborate.

"I'm biased, but obviously I agree," Stern says. "Shawn Mendes is major goals."

CeCe shakes her head at this, but thankfully seeming more amused than annoyed. "Not how I'd say it, but I agree. Camila's career is also goals for us, minus the group splitting."

"Reality comps and forced groups and celebrity couples, oh my!" I exclaim. "Jeweltones to the core, darling."

We all laugh, but it occurs to me that's partly because of our nervous energy. Now we're all wondering . . .

"Okay, what comes next?"

TURN TO PAGE 290

I'm not the only chameleon in this group, so I believe this direction will fuse our greatest collaborative talents. With so many unique and stellar voices to serve, we're going to need songs with some extra depth.

I cast my vote for "Pray to God," then look toward CeCe and Stern to make sure they're good.

"You all know what you're talking about," Stern says, smiling. "And hey, maybe someday Calvin Harris will invite us to collab on a song?"

CeCe still rolls her eyes at Stern, but at least she seems more playful than annoyed. "HAIM are rock stars on the stage. That vibe works for me. Sharp edges meet smooth synths."

"And honestly, it has the same kind of steady guitar beat that the 'Summer' song does," Everly adds. "Just a bit edgier, like CeCe says."

"Edgy or not," Dea says with a smirk, "you all know I can get behind a club dance lane."

I look around the room and smile. Sure, our differences are never going to disappear completely, but at least we finally seem to possess some ability to smooth them over. It's a promising sign, along with this promising new sonic direction.

"All right, then," I conclude. "We're in agreement. What's next?"

TURN TO PAGE 290

It turns out CeCe has a clear answer to this question too.

"Well, I mentioned this a while back, but I'm a pretty decent sound engineer," she says, pointing at her laptop. "It's not a full studio suite or anything, but I can make us a basic track based on our new song template? Then Everly can lead us in some group lyric and melody writing?"

"Great. This is definitely the part I need to learn," Dea replies. "But maybe I can lead us when it comes to the reel presentation part?"

"Fine by me," Stern says and we all agree.

"Just give me a vocal solo and a spotlight on the stage and I'm a happy camper," I add.

"All right, Jeweltones," Everly says, standing to grab her keyboard and some pens. "Let's write our first song together?"

♦ ♦ ♦

Hours later, the adrenaline still pumps through my body so fiercely, I can practically feel it humming in my limbs. Because we did it—we actually wrote "Stepping into Shadows" together.

And it's good.

At least, we all really think it could be good, which feels like a small miracle.

Trying to ride the wave of this creative high, Dea, CeCe, and I have regrouped back in the pool house to work on our poptimism-fueled dance banger. We left Everly and Stern in the spare bedroom to polish "Burns You Out," because the three of us will need the space to move. Dea even changed into a pair of high-heeled boots for the occasion to finally dance. Meanwhile, CeCe brought a notebook, pens, and her laptop for recording purposes. She really has turned out to be a SoundCloud-style whiz, our own little Billie Eilish in the making.

"So where should we start?" I ask, stretching my legs out on the floor in my own heels.

"Let's make sure we're on the same page about the song first?" CeCe offers.

"I'm thinking we continue with the Sam Smith/Demi Lovato vibe we identified earlier?" I begin. "But like, a full Kelly Clarkson/Britney Spears 'Stronger' moment."

"I'm game," Dea replies.

"I was thinking something like letting CeCe go pop-punk rocker on the verses," I continue. "Then me belting the chorus on full blast. And Dea, how would you feel about a dance breakdown on the bridge? Maybe even over some . . . spoken word rap-singing?"

I've been meaning to make this suggestion for a while, and now feels like the right moment. There's no way Dea could match our vocal intensity on a song like this. And rap-singing would give her full range to slay –I just hope she receives my suggestion that way.

"What do you mean?" Dea asks, looking intensely unsure.

"Like Beyoncé on 'Formation,' or Madonna on 'Vogue,'" I try, thankful I brainstormed some ideas in anticipation of this conversation. "There are so many other iconic examples."

"Rap-singing is such a thing now," CeCe jumps in. "And it would fit with your diamond edge, plus give Jeweltones a new dimension. And honestly, it would take pressure off you keeping up with the vocal beasts. I know you hate that."

Woof. I don't know if I would've said that part out loud, but there are many dimensions between CeCe and Dea I don't yet know about—let's hope hearing this brand of honesty is one of them?

Dea considers all of this, looking troubled at first.

Then it's like a lightbulb goes off above her head, cascading calm down her entire body.

"I think that's a genius idea," she finally says. "It would give me an entire lane to myself, one that would also justify dancing. And I could still sing, adding melodies to the raps."

"If it's good enough for Doja and BLACKPINK and Nicki, it's good enough for Dea," I say, flooded with relief of my own. For the first time, I see some real sparkle in Dea's eyes.

"Good. But that's not the only question," CeCe says—and I'm pretty sure I know what's coming next. "Vinny and I are obviously out and proud. Dea, of course you need to go at your own pace addressing what's being said in public about us. But if this is going to be an uplifting anthem from the three of us specifically . . ."

CeCe doesn't finish, but her question is still clear: Are you comfortable with this potentially being taken as a queer pride anthem? It's also obviously a very loaded question for these two, way beyond our song.

"I know," Dea sighs. "I want to pretend I have the answers. That I know exactly what I'm doing. But the truth is, I don't. That makes me . . . uncomfortable."

Dea says the words in a small voice and I know how hard this is for her. Still, I'm proud she is trying to change.

"All I know right now is that I want to see where things go between us, CeCe," Dea continues. "I'm not going to hide who I am, but I also don't fully understand my own sexuality yet. I just know I'm not ready to be a full-blown advocate the way you two are. But I think I have to let exactly that vibe be a part of our art?"

I stand up and wrap Dea in a hug, because she looks like she could use one.

"I can't tell you how many people out there you'll represent just by being you, even if that means being unsure," I offer, feeling Dea hug me back stiffly.

I then release her so CeCe can have a turn—but it appears CeCe shares Dea's aversion to PDA. Divas above, what a match.

"Labels help some of us be out and proud," CeCe says. "But fluidity helps others. We need both in our song."

"The full spectrum, darling!" I snap.

Dea laughs. "Actually, that fits with the theme I was thinking of. Something about breaking things to build them back better. You know, breaking the band, breaking ourselves, breaking the expectations of society."

"Breaking Band," I say, the words snapping directly into my mind.

"That could be one hell of a title," CeCe says, reaching for a notebook. "It fits all those themes. And we can use 'band' for so much else. Disbanded. Bandaged. Wrecking Band. Band of Gold."

CeCe immediately starts writing this down, while more ideas pop into my head.

"Oh, and maybe there's something about regrouping?" I pose. "And if we go the queen route, something about crown jewels? The Crown Jeweltones, as the queer and questioning ones?"

"Ooh, I love that," CeCe says as she writes.

"I also have had this line in my brain, but it might not work out loud," Dea adds. "'Watch us cause some dischord/Watch us pull the ripchord.' But 'chord' spelled with an *H*, like the musical term."

"Oh, I love that as an Easter egg for a lyric video," I reply.

On the heels of this, CeCe begins playing a new track. I don't even know when she jumped onto her laptop, but suddenly we hear an epic drumline marching beat. Then she adds a blaring horn section, a full Beyoncé Homecoming moment. Underneath all of that, CeCe starts to experiment with the sound of a car crashing, with glass shattering.

A Jeweltones explosion.

"This is all stock stuff, but it can serve as a baseline," CeCe says, looking up. When she does, she freezes in place, seeing the expressions on our faces.

"What, no good?"

"No," Dea replies. "That's freaking perfect."

CeCe smiles, seeming to blush a little.

"Queens," I begin, jumping up and down in place. "I think we have the start of an absolute artistic *smash* on our hands!"

◆ ◆ ◆

Tomorrow, we will share our progress with Zahra.

Tomorrow, we will give our chosen performance presentation. It might have taken us another hour of debate to agree upon this chosen presentation, but we did eventually settle on one. No manifestos, despite Everly's pitches, and no vision boards, despite Dea's pitches. Instead, Stern, CeCe, and I presented an oddly unified front: a music video–style reel to showcase our clarified Jeweltones vibe, then a live performance of our three new songs. Even if it's all still new and unpolished, we need to show who we want Jeweltones to be in the way that always matters most—through the music.

Once we finally agreed on this, we also agreed that first thing tomorrow morning, Dea should take the lead on producing the video reel, while Stern and I should take the lead on the performances. Besides, CeCe and Everly did the most heavy lifting today. Then we'll see if this is all enough to convince Zahra to help us keep our deal, our house—all of it. If we're lucky, next will come the work of convincing the public to fall back in love with Jeweltones. That will no doubt require social media pushes and public statements and new releases and comeback efforts, hopefully all aided by UWU. I suppose there's a world where we can try to do all of that even if the label drops us, but we agreed we really do need deep resources to keep launching Jeweltones at this level.

Already, I'm terrified what we've done isn't enough. I'm still so proud of us and what we produced, but now that the creative rush has died down, the doubt has settled. What if the songs we started aren't that good? What if they don't click or pop? What if the label doesn't get our vision? What if it's all in vain, and this really is the end for Jeweltones?

These questions all feel so loud, so I try to force them out of my mind. But that never really works for long, does it? So, even better, I acknowledge these questions as perfectly valid. I thank them for showing up with their concern. Then I kindly dismiss them. Because we'll get all the answers soon, and doubt won't help us get the ones we want.

Tonight, we've earned the right to celebrate. Sure, it's nearly 10 p.m. and none of us have eaten a proper dinner yet, but one mustn't interrupt the creative flow, darling. Besides, when one has a mother like Gia Vecchi around, dinner at 10 p.m. is no problem at all.

Right now, the five Jeweltones sit around the dining room table. Mom was gracious enough to whip us up a feast and then retreat to her finally vacated pool house. We all thanked her profusely before digging into mounds of chicken broth rice, roasted herb potatoes, and three-meat vegetable stir fry—all on the approved gluten- and dairy-free list. In this moment, I couldn't feel more seen or nourished or grateful.

"Anyone else completely proud and completely terrified at the same time?" I ask, figuring I should share.

"Thank goddess someone said it," CeCe replies. "Very that, yes."

"It's nice, though, being in our little bubble for now," Dea says. "I am dreading dealing with all of this online."

"Hard same," Everly offers. "I think maybe our next battle will be working out some boundaries with social media, moving forward. I mean, assuming we get to move forward."

"Don't even put that energy out there," Stern shudders. "But there is something personal I think I want to share with our fans, when the time is right. It's a health thing . . . nothing that will affect the group, I promise. But I just need a minute to build up some more confidence around it."

Stern shares a private smile with Everly over this, but I smile too. This reminds me of my own stomach-sharing mandate—and it also makes me realize how little effort I've made to really get to know Stern. Maybe this can be a place for us to start to connect?

"My stomach hears you loud and clear," I joke, raising my now-empty plate.

"Oh, that reminds me!" Dea says, jumping up.

She disappears into the kitchen and then reemerges with a gorgeous-looking cake, one covered in crystallized candy jewels.

"Dea! What's that for?" I ask.

"I just wanted us to have something special to celebrate with," Dea says, looking sheepish. "It's no big deal."

"That's so thoughtful," Everly says. "But when did you have time to bake a cake?"

CeCe bursts out laughing. "Yeah, right. She ordered it when we were on one of our breaks this afternoon."

"It's from one of my favorite bakeries in LA. Vinny, I don't know if you can eat the candies, but the cake is baked with almond flour and coconut cream, so it's allergy approved."

Once again, tears spring to my eyes. Dea: privately thoughtful and generous as ever.

"Oh, don't cry!" she says, setting the cake down.

"No, happy tears, I promise," I manage, wiping at my eyes. "It's just, this whole stomach thing has been a lot, on top of everything else. This is really, really nice."

"Well, I'd just hate for you to feel left out," Dea says, winking at me.

Winking back, my only thought is that feeling left out is clearly a state of mind.

And from here on out, this queen aims to remain inclusive AF.

CHAPTER SIXTEEN

VINNY

THREE WEEKS. THAT'S HOW LONG IT HAS TAKEN FOR JEWELTONES to get here, gathered in this backstage dressing room. As usual, none of it came easily, but we're all just so thankful to have gotten here at all.

First, we presented our new group vision and songs to Zahra. She was impressed, but also hesitant—this new creative direction was a lot, especially my drag. She was initially worried our fans wouldn't give us a comeback chance in such a different form. But, to her credit, she said she always believed in us and that she wished she did a better job providing us space to work ourselves out. As proud as she was, she said that windows of opportunity can close quickly in the music industry. She was willing to fight for us—she just hoped our window hadn't already sealed shut.

From there, it was a whirlwind of presentations to the label, strategy sessions, and lots of internal creative arguments. Through it all, the new and improved Jeweltones managed to stick to our vision—and to stand up for each other. Things like genre side-collabs and me performing in drag became non-negotiables.

There was a moment when I thought we were finished, because many at UWU balked at our ideas. However, with some finessing from Zahra, the label eventually came to respect our bold direction for Jeweltones.

However, they were also quite clear about the need for us to make exactly the right comeback splash. Which is how we found ourselves booked for a four-minute performance slot at this year's mega-popular DVA Awards. We'd been radio silent ever since Popella, letting the noise around our meltdown die and hopefully building anticipation. In private we've been refining, rehearsing, and recording to prepare for our reintroduction. This is officially the make-or-break moment for Jeweltones, our final chance to shine on a national platform and in front of the entire music industry. This is where we'll learn if anyone will embrace our new vision or dismiss us as one-hit wonder flops.

Staring into the dressing room vanity mirror, I force myself to remember that this is my favorite part of the job. The quiet moments before a big performance, decked out in full glam, finding the calm center in the middle of a storm about to rage. I have to remember to enjoy this, because otherwise my nerves might ruin me. Add in the big onstage drag reveal I'm planning—the first of its kind on the DVAs—and I have every reason to feel anxious.

I currently present as glam-rock boy Vinny, but halfway through our performance, I will transform into my full drag queen glory. For this groundbreaking opportunity, I have so many queens who came before to thank. I only hope that tonight, I do them all proud.

Of course, there was an intense debate about how to use our allotted four-minute performance slot as we prepared. Most of us wanted to devote time to each of our new songs, but CeCe talked us out of that. She argued it would feel too chaotic and crowded, and she was probably right. In the end, we settled on two minutes of the expected "Press Diamonds" that everyone wants to hear, then a quite-dynamic shift to "Stepping into Shadows." And let's just say I'm not the only one with a stunt reveal planned.

Right after our performance tonight, the label plans to post our joint-group statement, drop our new reel-style music videos, and release the four-song EP we recorded—which also includes "Burns You Out" and "Breaking Band." One way or another, by the end of this night, we'll know where Jeweltones stands—and whether the fans are ready to embrace our next steps.

No pressure.

"You're all going to be great."

I hear Mom's voice across the dressing room and pull myself back into the present. We each sit in our own mirrored corners, joined only by Mom, Steve, and Zahra. Looking around the room, it's safe to say the others appear even more nervous than me—especially Everly. If she wasn't wearing so much makeup, I swear she'd look as green as Stern's bespoke blazer.

"Really, you are," Steve adds, no doubt sensing his daughter's amplified stage fright. "The people who matter all want to see you win. And you have to remember what a huge win it is for you to even be here in the first place."

He beams at all of us, but I watch as Mom turns and beams at him. It still tweaks my chest, but less than before. Besides, it's been a big week for Mom. Steve officially asked her to be his girlfriend, then she got a call from some reality casting producer for a meeting. I'm still mildly terrified all this change will separate us somehow, but how can I worry too much when I see how deliriously happy she is right now? And when I know a huge part of that happiness will remain being the biggest cheerleader of Jeweltones—and of me?

She catches my eye across the room. She offers me a private smile and a wink, then twists the ring on the new gold chain around her neck. I press my eyes shut, because I refuse to cry and ruin this sickening base makeup. Instead, I wink back and twist the gold band that now resides on my right index finger—Dad's wedding band. Mom gave it to me earlier this week when she told me about her and Steve becoming official. Apparently, she had been waiting until my own potential wedding to give it to me, but she realized I should have it now, as a reminder that Dad is always with me. With *us*, since the ring around Mom's neck is her own wedding band. She promised that whenever we twist these rings, it'll be because we're thinking of Dad. And reminding ourselves how proud he'd be of us.

I give the gold band another twist.

I need all the extra pride I can summon tonight.

Just then, the door to our dressing room opens and a PA appears—a very hot PA.

"Twenty minutes to stage," he says, flashing us all a smile under his headset. His eyes then fall on me and stick there a few seconds, brightening his smile before he ducks out.

Well, win or lose, I know what I'll be doing after the show. While everyone around me seems obsessed with monogamy, I am nowhere near ready to give up on the fireworks and butterflies provided by beautiful new boys. I'm an eighteen-year-old pop star. As long as I keep staying safe, I'm going to have all the fun I want. How else am I going to have big gay adventures to write songs about?

Speaking of big gay adventures, I'm equally thrilled when I realize who has just unexpectedly popped through our door. The Hand Made enters in all her glory, wearing a gorgeous gown and a backstage VIP pass around her neck.

"Oh my goddess," I shout, standing up. "How did you get back here?"

"I work in mysterious ways," Made says, giving me an air hug and a double air kiss. Can't risk the glam, darling.

"I'm afraid this was my doing," Mom then says, striding up to us. "Mrs. Made DMed me asking if I could get her backstage to surprise you with something. But selfishly, I was dying to finally meet this drag mother you keep raving about."

Mom extends her arms and gives The Hand Made a very real hug.

"Not Mrs.!" she cries. "Call me Made, or Marg if you're nasty."

"Well, I'm a lady, so Made it is," Mom volleys right back.

"Oh, we're going to be trouble, you and I!" Made laughs, snapping at Mom. She strikes a quick pose, then they both turn to me.

"But enough about us mothers," Made says. "I wanted to sneak back here to wish you luck, not that you need it. I know the stunt we planned will go flawlessly."

Made pauses, reaching into a pocket in her gown. Today, her queen is serving full red carpet realness.

"Really, I have something else for you. This is from the Center." Made pulls out a card, decked out with rainbows and covered in signatures. "It's from a lot of the youth at the Center. They wanted to remind you they're so thankful for the time you've continued to spend there. And that no matter how tonight goes, your queen always belongs with us."

I look up at the ceiling and blink rapidly, because I still refuse to cry and ruin my makeup. Weeks ago, I was officially cleared as a youth mentor for the Center. My time there has finally begun to make LA feel more like a home, like I have some semblance of a life outside Jeweltones. This card means everything to me—and reminds me exactly what matters about tonight's performance.

It's not about winning.

It's about representing.

Thankfully, both Made and Mom seem to understand what I'm feeling without the need for me to speak any coherent words.

"Breathe, darling," Made says. "Especially before I show you the back. This took some serious string-pulling, but . . ."

Made flips over the card to reveal a handwritten note.

My Queen!

I heard what I did in high school. I swear I didn't know you weren't out yet, but that's no excuse. I'm sorry for being a messy bitch. Can we kiss and make up on a duet sometime soon?

Your Dame, Gloves

Reading this, I see Made was right about remembering to breathe.

⊛ One of the world's most iconic pop divas just asked me to **duet**. Saying yes can be about rewriting an old wrong.
TURN TO PAGE 302

⊛ I feel like an old scar finally begins to **heal**. Saying no seems like the best way to close that chapter.
TURN TO PAGE 303

At the end of the day, pride is all that matters—and I don't mean the egotistical kind.

I can't think of a better way to boost my platform, and hopefully that of Jeweltones, than duetting with Dame Gloves.

More than anything, once the public knows our story, the gesture on both our parts will speak volumes about evolution, resilience, and forgiveness instead of rigidity, shame, and cancellation.

My next thought might be less important than this message, but it's like I can already hear this duet in my ears now. Step aside, Whitney and Mariah, Elton and George—Dame Gloves and the queen she accidentally Made shall be coming through.

It's going to be a legendary moment for the divas above and below.

TURN TO PAGE 304

Really, this feels more like an old scab finally falling away, because I healed that part of myself all on my own already.

If I really want to keep charting my own course and leading the way, then I will continue to do so on my own terms.

This apology is a meaningful gesture, sure—but not quite as meaningful as delivering it in person might have been. However, I will take this note for what it is: a shiny nail in the coffin of my high school life.

Right now, I've got a very fabulous new adult life to lead.

Not to mention four very good candidates for any duets I might want to sing.

TURN TO PAGE 304

"You really are too much, you know that?" I say, looking between Made and Mom.

They both just nod, knowing full well.

"Thank you," I say, extending my arms to hug them both. "It's just what I needed to turn out this slay today."

"All right, Jeweltones," Zahra calls out across the dressing room. "I have other artists performing tonight and we need to get everyone to their seats."

Made winks, taking this as her cue to go. Steve and Mom also wave, knowing it's time for us to get into our performance zone. Once they exit, Jeweltones gathers around Zahra.

"Before I go, I can say with full confidence that you all have truly earned this second shot. I'm proud of you for taking that initiative on your own. I wish I could take more credit, but I will say this. You might not have felt ready before, but you still managed to capture the world's attention. You're definitely ready now, so it's time to let them all have it. Good luck. And don't screw it up."

Zahra smirks at me while delivering this riff on the iconic *Drag Race* line. And it has exactly the effect she intended—it fires me all the way up.

It's show time.

Zahra then makes her own exit, leaving just the five of us. We all know we'll be called to the stage in a matter of minutes, so it's like electric energy crackles all around the room.

"I know this is scary," CeCe says, "but we have to let go of all that pressure. And remember who we're doing this for."

"For us," Stern replies. "The new and improved Jeweltones."

"And for the listeners who need us," Everly adds.

"We worked hard for this," Dea says. "And we really are ready, like Zahra said."

When it comes to my turn, all I can think of is one stupid line to get us fully ready. So I deliver it with all the warmth and attitude I can muster.

"All right, Jeweltones. Let's shine bright like a Reignbow!"

◆ ◆ ◆

I stand on the darkened stage and, for a few moments, all I can hear is the hammering of my own heartbeat. I feel supercharged, stuck in that surreal headspace before the lights fire up. I'm really here, we're really about to do this. It's enough to make my head spin . . .

Until I remember I was born for this.

The celebrity announcer calls our name and the speakers blare to life a moment later, just as we're bathed in our signature jewel-tone spotlights. For a second, I can hear the roar of the crowd. I can see thousands of faces flashing into existence, all their attention and energy focused on us. I can feel it surging through me, then surging through the cameras to the viewers watching live at home. I think of the millions who will replay this performance in the future.

And I have never felt more alive in my entire life.

Before I know it, CeCe is finishing the first verse of "Press Diamonds," charged with even more intensity than usual. It lights more fire in my veins—and in my vocal cords.

As the pre-chorus arrives, I begin belting. And even *I* feel startled by the depth and power of my voice suddenly booming all around. We've been rehearsing with in-ear pieces, but immediately I hear mine crackle and pop. In one graceful motion, I pull the pieces out, going rogue. I'll have to trust my ear through all the noise and auditorium feedback—but I've never missed a note onstage in my life. I'm not about to start now. Besides, every diva ever has had an in-ear dropout moment. It makes me feel slightly iconic, having my first.

Thankfully, when the chorus arrives, I can still hear the others enough to harmonize properly. I try to stay in the moment, but as soon as my singing part is over, I focus on the enormous hurdle I now have to clear.

Dea and Stern perform their usual solos next, sharper and more charming than ever. But I'm especially eager to see how Everly does. We agreed to cut the second chorus and roll right into the bridge to shorten the song, then Everly will be the one to transition us to "Stepping into Shadows." She starts singing the "Press Diamonds" bridge, and her warbly voice definitely sounds shaky on the first line. She takes a breath between phrases, and I see her turn to her right. With the subtlest of movements, Stern nods at her. Then when Everly turns left, the rest of us do the same. *We got you, girl.*

By the time Everly sings her second line, her voice sounds surer. Then by the third, she begins to sound comfortable. By the end, she might even be approaching . . . confidence? Maybe not—I can still feel her anxiety from across the stage, how it makes her vibe a little awkward and robotic. But right now, Everly channels something far more important than polish or perfection.

In her glittery blue dress, Everly seems fearless for the first time.

As the music shifts, so do the lights. The bright jewel-toned spots fade to a starker black and white as Everly takes us to "Stepping into Shadows." I need to run backstage for my own transformation, but I linger a few seconds to see this next part live.

Huddling with the other Jeweltones out of the spotlight, all focus falls on Everly bathed in a gray-blue hue. I watch as a stage producer dressed in black runs out to hand her the key to her transition.

❖ Earlier, Everly and Stern decided to give it a shot as a **couple**.
TURN TO PAGE 307

❖ Earlier, Everly and Stern decided to remain friends and **collaborators**.
TURN TO PAGE 309

Everly straps on a guitar covered in diamond-like rhinestones, scattered with emerald accents. She stands there wielding her greatest weapon, ready to wave it like a white flag. The symbolism behind these studded stones speaks louder than any public statement ever could.

"What am I to do
When I know exactly who I am
Isn't enough for you?"

Everly begins singing the verse she wrote, backed by the melody she crafted—but the music still somehow feels distinctly Jeweltones. A little moody while bolstered by the big-pop sound of our inspiration song. Dripping with crippling tension while soaring high all the same.

Music to cry to, and music to fly to.

That's Jeweltones, darling.

My time for such viewing indulgences has expired, however. With all eyes still on Everly, I finally scoot my tush backstage.

"What am I to say
When change feels impossible
But compromise is the only way?"

I can hear Everly finishing her verse as I make it to the team of stage producers waiting for me. We have about one minute to get me into my drag look and apply some quick makeup enhancements. As we frantically strip away my amethyst slick-glam outfit, my eye catches on a monitor featuring the live telecast. I watch in bursts as Stern steps forward to join Everly for the chorus we all wrote together.

"Finally stepping out of the shadows
But isn't it funny
Isn't it true
The only way out
Is stepping into my shadows
With you."

Everly and Stern sound incredible together as usual, blending like salted caramel. And this chorus—which features some epic guitar riffs and an ascending melody—packs the perfect amount of punch.

But not as much as Stern turning to kiss Everly in the moments before the second verse.

As they confirm the rumors of EverGreen for the world to see, I realize we're all going to have to brace ourselves . . .

Because the reaction from the crowd is almost deafening.

TURN TO PAGE 311

Everly straps on a guitar covered in crystals the color of emerald, diamond, ruby, and amethyst. She stands there wielding her greatest weapon, ready to wave it like a white flag—one completely devoid of the color sapphire. The symbolism speaks louder than any public statement ever could.

"What am I to do

When I know exactly who I am

Isn't enough for you?"

Everly begins singing the verse she wrote, backed by the melody she crafted—but the music still somehow feels distinctly Jeweltones. A little moody while bolstered by the big-pop sound of our inspiration song. Dripping with crippling tension while soaring high all the same.

Music to cry to, and music to fly to.

That's Jeweltones, darling.

My time for such viewing indulgences has expired, however. With all eyes still on Everly, I finally scoot my tush backstage.

"What am I to say

When change feels impossible

But compromise is the only way?"

I can hear Everly finishing her verse as I make it to the team of stage producers waiting for me. We have about one minute to get me into my drag look and apply some quick makeup enhancements. As we frantically strip away my amethyst slick-glam outfit, my eye catches on a monitor featuring the live telecast. I watch in bursts as Stern steps forward to join Everly for the chorus we all wrote together.

"Finally stepping out of the shadows

But isn't it funny

Isn't it true

The only way out

Is stepping into my shadows

With you."

Everly and Stern sound incredible together as usual, blending like salted caramel. And this chorus—which features some epic guitar riffs and an ascending melody—packs the perfect amount of punch.

Everly then leaves Stern onstage, a purposeful move to sidestep confirming any romantic rumors. However, given their pairing in the song, it doesn't exactly dispel any rumors either.

Feeding the fantasy, darling!

TURN TO PAGE 311

Now, stripped down to my shapewear undergarments, I half-watch as Stern takes the spotlight for his own solo verse. He looks like a full-blown superstar, sparkling in his slim-cut hunter green suit and crisp white t-shirt.

"What should I do?
The question I always ask
Wanting to please you."

As Stern sings, he begins to take off his blazer. I hear the screams amplify from the audience. Everyone must think he's about to pull some *Magic Mike* moment, but I know from our relaunch prep that what's coming runs so much deeper.

"What should I say
To make you see
Living an illusion isn't the way."

Stern lifts his t-shirt while singing these lines. It's not to show off his perfect six-pack underneath, though that is appreciated. Instead, Stern turns his torso to show an awful red patch of eczema, circled for emphasis with green body paint. Along the side reads: **Perfection = Illusion.**

As his verse ends, Stern drops his shirt, leaving room for CeCe to join him on the next chorus refrain. Stern's revealing moment might have passed quickly, but something tells me it's going to live for a while in news cycle infamy. Especially given the public discussion campaign on skin conditions of all kinds that Stern plans to launch tomorrow.

As CeCe and Stern sing the second chorus, I focus on getting strapped and zipped into the custom-made dress for my drag look. Still, I note with pride how much fun these two have interacting. This isn't a pair anyone would expect to have playful chemistry onstage, but something about their opposite styles contrasts nicely. Listening intently, I turn my head to the makeup artist just as I hear CeCe break into her solo verse.

"They told me what to do.
To get all I ever wanted
Simply kneel to you."

I catch a glimpse of the monitor to see CeCe singing directly into the camera. She looks like an absolute rock star, decked out in head-to-toe red and black faux leather. All she ever needs is her gritty, powerful voice and her direct emotional intensity to make it clear she is the one leading our charge.

"Here's what I have to say.

Things are different than I thought

But expectations aren't the only way."

The makeup artist finishes applying enormous fake eyelashes to my lids just in time for me to catch Dea joining CeCe for the next chorus refrain. I'm so glad I can see as they sing together like this for the first time in public, because I also know what's coming . . .

As CeCe turns to Dea and kisses her right on the lips.

And the crowd goes absolutely. Positively. *Wild.*

CeCe turns away with a smile, leaving Dea to do her thing.

Then, in the space before the bridge, Dea makes her solo moves. She turns to the spotlight and pulls off her bedazzled white skirt to reveal a glittering mirror-and-diamond bodysuit. She begins to rap-sing, dancing fiercely as she does.

I smile from ear to ear.

"Vinny, your lips."

The makeup artist whispers as she tries to apply some bright lipstick— the final touch to the quick exaggerations we planned. I nod and settle my mouth, adrenaline fizzling through me twice as fast now. Because once Dea finishes, it will be time for a grand entrance of my own.

But first, Dea has one more move planned.

❖ Earlier, Dea told me she and Everly resolved to rebuild their
friendship.
TURN TO PAGE 313

❖ Earlier, Dea told me she and Everly resolved to remain respectful
colleagues.
TURN TO PAGE 314

"Doesn't matter

If you're sad and blue

Or green with envy."

Once Dea makes it through this part of her bridge, there's a sudden pause in the music. She looks around the stage, pretending—very convincingly—like something has gone wrong. The crowd gasps, no doubt thinking they're witnessing another Popella-level meltdown. Especially as Everly comes walking back onstage, holding something strapped behind her back.

Dea freezes as Everly approaches, the silence making it all seem incredibly ominous.

Until Everly reaches Dea and reveals what she was carrying: a hanging keyboard that looks like it's made of diamonds.

Everly starts playing, and the music crashes back in. She turns around, so Dea also turns and leans back-to-back with Everly, rap-singing as she plays.

"Doesn't matter

If you're red with rage

Or white with grief.

We're all the same

Royal purple

Where it counts."

As these two finish this section together with a grin, one message feels very clear: drama queens are going to have to look for their next pop girl feud somewhere else.

TURN TO PAGE 315

"Doesn't matter

    If you're sad and blue

    Or green with envy."

Once Dea makes it through this part of her bridge, there's a sudden pause in the music. She looks around the stage, pretending—very convincingly—like something has gone wrong. The crowd gasps, no doubt thinking they're witnessing another Popella-level meltdown. Except, behind Dea, a massive screen begins to populate with headlines, all of them tearing her down or speculating the worst about her. The headlines begin to multiply and, as they do, Dea does a frustrated—yet fierce—dance routine underneath.

Until suddenly she stands bolt still. Staring at the nearest camera, Dea slowly drags her finger across her lips. And the moment she finishes, the headlines piled high behind her explode into a million glittering shards.

And the music drops back in with a crash.

"Doesn't matter

If you're red with rage

Or white with grief.

We're all the same

Royal purple

Where it counts."

Dea brings her message home with flawless precision, nailing every note and choreographed move like an absolute pro.

Then again, should we have expected any less?

TURN TO PAGE 315

By the time Dea finishes, I stand ready to reemerge for the second part of the bridge. As the music settles down, I take a deep breath.

Next, an acoustic gospel clap starts up, setting a breakdown lull to build to another crescendo.

Which means my time has come.

The world is about to meet my chosen queen.

⬥ Aiming to make the strongest statement possible, I went with simpler drag to focus on an elaborate, hopefully iconic **vocal**.
TURN TO PAGE 316

⬥ Aiming to make the strongest statement possible, I planned a straightforward vocal to keep the focus on my elaborate, hopefully iconic drag **lewk**.
TURN TO PAGE 317

I stand ready to retake the stage, wearing a fitted lavender gown. On my chest rests a simple-but-elegant broach, studded with amethyst, diamond, ruby, emerald, and sapphire, worn right over my heart.

An understated look that speaks volumes. Leaving me to bring the actual volume with my voice.

"I am a warrior
Unbreakable and aloft.
I am a river
Fluid and soft."

I step back onto the stage, belting in full voice at the top of my range. I can hear the crowd react with surprise to my drag butterfly reemergence at first, but then the noise quickly hushes under the weight of my voice. Everyone stops to listen, in awe.

I pause before my next line. The choir clap and background music start to amp back up with my about-to-rise melody.

"Someone tell me
Just how long
'Til I know
When to flow . . ."

On the word "flow," I perform the most acrobatic vocal run I'm capable of, with laser accuracy and intent. Then, on the next and final line, I punctuate each syllable in a rising melody, with my voice careening up into the stratosphere.

"And when to be strong?"

On "strong," I hold one final epic note over a bar of silence.

I close my eyes and let my voice churn like a locomotive . . .

Until the music finally crashes back in full force.

When I finish, I open my eyes to find myself surrounded by the other Jeweltones.

And the audience in front of us leaps to their feet.

TURN TO PAGE 318

Sometimes the best way to make people lean in is to speak with a whisper . . . especially when they expect you to scream.

Besides, as I stand backstage waiting to reveal my outfit, I know the deafening statement it will make, on every level.

A boy in a dress.

A queer in the spotlight.

A queen on the mainstream stage.

Literally, as the stage producer finally nestles a crown on my wig.

"I am a warrior

Unbreakable and aloft.

I am a river

Fluid and soft."

I sing the words with a low rumble as I step back out onto the stage. As instructed, they've lit me so that I remain semi-darkened, in silhouette. If all goes according to plan, the only thing the audience will be able to see right now is a figure creeping forward in a crown.

I pause before my next line. The choir clap and background music start to amp back up with my about-to-rise melody.

"Someone tell me

Just how long

'Til I know

When to flow

And when to be strong?"

I hold the final note out over a bar of silence, until the music suddenly crashes back in. Then, at the same time, the lights flash back on to reveal me standing in my best diva pose, radiant in a bejeweled gown cascading with rainbow stripes: in our five Jeweltones colors. I also wear a sweeping lavender wig under the crown that boasts gemstones in our signature shapes: sapphire teardrops, emerald circles, ruby hearts, diamond diamonds, and amethyst triangles.

Standing there, I finish my final resplendent note.

Then I look right into the audience, dripping iconic diva energy.

Once again, the crowd loses their freaking minds.

TURN TO PAGE 318

With the music racing to its absolute peak, stacking all these sonic layers at once, Jeweltones finally reassembles in our final form. We all begin to sing this song's chorus refrain *together* for the first time, our five voices blending in harmony.

We then break into a few ad-libs, in all our "Lady Marmalade" glory. CeCe rasps, Stern smooths, Everly floats, Dea punctuates, and I belt.

Until we reach the last line of the final chorus, which we rejoin to sing fully a capella. Our voices sing out together, sounding stronger than ever before.

For one glorious moment, we finish and stand triumphant.

Then I see it, alongside the others. At first it's just a few, but then the phenomenon quickly spreads. People all across the audience hold up lit Jeweltones glowsticks, the mark of our Gemstones fandom. I don't know if Zahra planted these prototypes or if these listeners brought their own homemade versions—either way, the message is clear.

We still have our fans.

I can just feel it in my bones. It isn't just this chill-inducing performance, but all the messages we packed in about our private lives and our public creative direction . . .

We're gonna go viral again, aren't we?

The crowd confirms this premonition as they give us an extended standing ovation, roaring louder than I've ever heard in my life. I look at the others and I can see it in their eyes, the same thought. In this moment, the future feels so vivid. It feels like recording an album and shooting music videos. Like going on tour and invitations to the Grammys. Like new ladders to climb and challenges to overcome.

Standing here reflecting the stage lights, I can practically *feel* the radiance.

And I cannot wait to see how bright we shine next.

We Jeweltones absorb all this for a few more seconds standing onstage, united and evolved. Then, inevitably, the lights go down and our turn in the spotlight ends . . . for now.

But divas above, what a spectacular turn it was.

ACKNOWLEDGMENTS

THANK YOU ONCE AGAIN TO BRITNY BROOKS-PERILLI, EDITOR extraordinaire, for choosing to adventure together again. You've now inspired me to write two books I always felt I was meant to, but didn't even know that I had in me. For your support and guidance, I remain eternally grateful. And while you might have a love-hate relationship with Everly Brooks, she still joins the ranks of Choices characters named after you!

To Lucy Carson, fiction agent extraordinaire, you are an absolute anchor in my writing life and process. I still can't believe how blessed I've been to have your belief in me. That gratitude extends to Amanda Burnett, stalwart television agent, whose resilience is only matched by her grace (and good taste).

To the team who helped bring this novel to life, I can't thank you enough for your tireless work. To Julie Matysik, for your iconic turn as interim editor. To Marissa Raybuck and Frances Soo Ping Chow, for your genius design work. To Jeff Östberg, for our glittering cover and interior artwork. To copy editor Duncan McHenry, for covering all our blind spots, your insightful, creative edits, and your heartfelt feelings toward the book—as only the second person to react to the final draft, you restored a lot of my confidence in this work after a fast flurry of rewrites. To Amber Morris, for once again handling the production of this second Choices novel puzzle. To Becca Mathson, Kara Thornton, Elizabeth Parks, and the rest of the marketing and publicity team for helping bring this experience to readers. And to everyone who worked on this book I might never even know about, thank you!

To all the booksellers out there, your work is meaningful and valuable beyond words. Same to all the librarians and educators. Getting to meet you through these books remains the privilege of a lifetime. In equal measure, thank you to all the book reviewers out there—your tireless work, done often purely for the love of books, means the world. Special shout out to @LGBTQReads, @TheNerdDaily, @ezeekat, @RachelMarieReads, @Aarons_Books, and many, many others for your support!

To early readers Chase Baxter, Chelsea Sanders, and Gen Chapin (and her secret singing weapon, Vince Peterson), your feedback and insight proved invaluable. To the community of Young Adult authors I am now lucky to be accepted into, it's a true dream come true. To Jessica Goodman, Adam Sass, Robbie Couch, Adib Khorram, Rex Ogle, Zoraida Córdova, Erik J. Brown, Emery Lee, and Steven Salvatore (just to start)—I thank each and every one of you for your guidance and friendship. To my longtime community of interactive writers, Jessica Delfanti, Jim Dattilo, Hannah Powell-Smith, Eric Moser, Natalia Theodoridou, and many others, I thank you for your endless inspiration. Special thanks to fellow writers Grant Ginder, Kate Myers, and Georgia Grace Hays for keeping each other sane (mostly).

To my Penn writing community, I thank you for the many cycles of support—Mingo Reynolds, RJ Bernocco, and Jessica Lowenthal, ultimate shepherds to all Penn writers. Extra shout-out to John Strauss, the ultimate TV writing mentor and friend.

To faithful readers like Saira Arber, Qymana Botts, Mercedes Petrilla, and many more like you—your additional support on Patreon (and social media) makes the struggle to remain in business as a writer a little less grueling. You are my own FLCs, now and forevermore!

To my third-grade self, who vibrated with excitement to receive a blank bound book and fill it with the epic tale of a diva dog entering a singing competition—we're all grown up now, and we did it for real. It is also said that every gay boy has a diva spirit animal, so I'd be remiss not to thank my lifelong idol of choice: Kelly Clarkson. To combine warmth and charm with such deep and insightful ache, covering such a breadth of genres—it's inspiration for who I strive to be as a writer and a person. No one's music has ever meant more to me.

To every musician mentioned in this novel, I adore your work. There are so many artists who inspire me every day, and I pay additional tribute to you in the enormous SO YOU WANNA BE A POP STAR? playlist on Spotify, which I played on loop while writing the novel. To all of you out there who help create reality singing competitions—I've seen every episode. If you ever need an impartial Simon Cowell–style judge, I eagerly await your call.

To Taylor Leigh Tasich, for your ergonomic expertise, and Krzysztof Pakula, for your physical therapy wizardry, I thank you for helping treat the sciatica I gave myself while writing this book. I quite literally couldn't have done it without both of you teaching me your ways!

To my immediate family—my parents, Stephen Sergi and Anne Prisco, my brother and sister-in-law and niece, Louis and Amanda and Everly Sergi—I couldn't do this without your support, figuratively and quite literally. To my husband, Kyle Goins, I can't even put into words all the wonderful impacts you've had on my life—and my whole job is words. Basically, you're the best human out there. This family knows I think of writing as an act of service, and if this novel touches anyone out there, it's because of their support and generosity. It takes a village, and I'm so grateful for mine.

To anyone who might seek to ban this book for its queerness, I ask you to read the words of Father Richard Rohr: "Religion is often one of the safest places to hide from God. Your ego always wants to feel separate and superior, and religion can enable this." I hope your capacity for spirituality—for love and kindness—someday outweighs your capacity for religious fear and condemnation.

Most importantly, to you, the reader: I thank you for picking up this book. Every novel belongs to the reader eventually, but in Interactive Fiction, the story really becomes yours to have and hold in a unique way. Handle it with care. I hope it will serve you as well as it has served me.

READING GUIDE

USE THIS SHEET TO KEEP TRACK OF YOUR CHOICES AND TO HELP calculate *your* unique reader personality profile at the novel's end. This sheet is an optional bonus feature, so no need to fill it out if you're just here for a good read. Each column can represent a new reread, but record your keywords however you see fit! I encourage you to write in this book, but if you can't, a PDF copy of the Reading Guide can also be found online.

CHAPTER ONE		
Mic drop *crawl* **or** *harmonize*?		
CHAPTER TWO		
Dea *dismiss* **or** *engage*?		
CHAPTER THREE		
Winning skill *voice* **or** *drag*?		
Trolls say *doesn't belong* **or** *waste*?		
CHAPTER FOUR		
Group start *fake it* **or** *compromise*?		
CHAPTER FIVE		
Favorite album *Hotel Paper* **or** *Rumours*?		
Dea leak *sabotage things* **or** *attacking me*?		
CHAPTER SIX		
Songwriting *Brooksville* **or** *pens, paper, picks*?		
Brooksville *Rebel* **or** *HWIC*? **or** Pens, paper, picks *myself* **or** *Green*?		
Stern crossing *lean forward* **or** *stop playing*?		
CHAPTER SEVEN		
Investigate *gossip leak* **or** *parental breakup*?		

CHAPTER EIGHT		
Made by *slick pop* **or** *glam rock*?		
Ball outing *talk openly* **or** *keep secret*?		
CHAPTER NINE		
Group songwriting *collaborate* **or** *producers*?		
Breakfast *suddenly famous* **or** *fit us better*?		
CHAPTER TEN		
Stern breakthrough *closet* **or** *co-write*?		
Popella *channel the emotion* **or** *walk offstage*?		
CHAPTER ELEVEN		
Made saboteur *belonging* **or** *enough*?		
Drag persona *Dame* **or** *Via*?		
CHAPTER TWELVE		
Dea *change narrative* **or** *discover yourself*?		
CHAPTER THIRTEEN		
Future *couple* **or** *collaborators*?		
CHAPTER FOURTEEN		
CeCe *honesty* **or** *show*?		
Deverly *friendship* **or** *colleagues*?		
CHAPTER FIFTEEN		
Stomach journey *personal* **or** *public*?		
Pop anthem *upbeat* **or** *edgier*?		
CHAPTER SIXTEEN		
Dame note *duet* **or** *heal*?		
Finale reveal *vocal* **or** *lewk*?		

EVERLY

CHAPTER ONE
CRAWL: Add 1 to *Expressive*, Add 1 to *Creative* **HARMONIZE:** Add 1 to *Innovative*, Add 1 to *Confident*
CHAPTER TWO
DISMISS: Add 1 to *Affected* **ENGAGE:** Add 1 to *Reactive*
CHAPTER FIVE
HOTEL PAPER: Add 2 to *Expressive* **RUMOURS:** Add 2 to *Innovative* **SABOTAGE THINGS:** Add 1 to *Reactive*, Add 1 to *Confident* **ATTACKING ME:** Add 1 to *Affected*, Add 1 to *Creative*
CHAPTER SIX
BROOKSVILLE: Add 2 to *Innovative*, Add 1 to *Affected*, Add 1 to *Creative* **PENS, PAPER, PICKS:** Add 2 to *Expressive*, Add 1 to *Reactive*, Add 1 to *Confident* **LEAN FORWARD:** Add 2 to *Reactive*, Add 2 to *Creative* **STOP PLAYING:** Add 2 to *Affected*, Add 2 to *Confident*
CHAPTER NINE
COLLABORATE: Add 2 to *Creative*, Add 1 to *Affected*, Add 1 to *Innovative* **PRODUCERS:** Add 2 to *Confident*, Add 1 to *Reactive*, Add 1 to *Expressive* **SUDDENLY FAMOUS:** Add 1 to *Expressive*, Add 1 to *Affected* **FIT US BETTER:** Add 1 to *Innovative*, Add 1 to *Reactive*

CHAPTER TEN

CLOSET: Add 2 to *Expressive*, Add 2 to *Confident*, Add 2 to *Centered*
CO-WRITE: Add 2 to *Innovative*, Add 2 to *Creative*, Add 2 to *Empathetic*
CHANNEL THE EMOTION: Add 2 to *Affected*
WALK OFFSTAGE: Add 2 to *Reactive*

CHAPTER THIRTEEN

COUPLE: Add 3 to *Centered*, Add 2 to *Expressive*, Add 2 to *Creative*
COLLABORATORS: Add 3 to *Empathetic*, Add 2 to *Innovative*,
Add 2 to *Confident*

CHAPTER FOURTEEN

HONESTY: Add 2 to *Empathetic*, Add 1 to *Expressive*, Add 1 to *Confident*
SHOW: Add 2 to *Centered*, Add 1 to *Innovative*, Add 1 to *Creative*
FRIENDSHIP: Add 3 to *Expressive*,
Add 2 to *Empathetic*, Add 2 to *Confident*
COLLEAGUES: Add 3 to *Innovative*, Add 2 to *Centered*, Add 2 to *Creative*

EVERLY STRENGTH TALLIES

Which one of the below has the most tallies? Choose your favorite if there's a tie. This is the first half of your **Everly Type**, the greatest strengths you gave Everly.

Confident Tally:			
Creative Tally:			

EVERLY INSECURITY TALLIES

Which one of the below has the most tallies? Choose your favorite if there's a tie. This is the second half of your **Everly Type**, the insecurities Everly struggled with most.

Affected Tally:			
Reactive Tally:			

Find your **Everly Type** combo of Confident/Creative and Affected/Reactive in this grid:

	AFFECTED	**REACTIVE**
CONFIDENT	The Soloist	The Supreme
CREATIVE	The Songwriter	The Teller

EVERLY GROWTH TALLIES			
Which one of the below has the most tallies? This is your **Growth Direction**, the way you guided Everly to overcome her insecurities.			
Centered Tally:			
Empathetic Tally:			

POP STAR TYPE TALLIES			
Which one of the below has the most tallies? Choose your favorite if there's a tie. This is your **Pop Star Type**, the musical expression you empowered Everly with most often.			
Expressive Tally:			
Innovative Tally:			

Flip to the page of your **Everly Type** and remember your **Growth Direction** and **Pop Star Type**!

THE SOLOIST

Clearly **Confident** and sometimes internally **Affected**, The Soloist always ELEVATES themselves . . . but that also means they sometimes SEPARATE themselves. When it comes to problem-solving, The Soloist doesn't hold back: they act on INSTINCT and do what they think is RIGHT, even if it's not their own first desire. However, when HURT or ANGRY, their first instinct is to bottle emotion and diffuse conflicts. The Soloist FEELS DEEPLY but can also FEEL ALONE. That's why it's crucial to let others in, even while leading the way for them.

BALANCES TO REACH
Don't let self-assuredness mean a lack of collaborative spirit. Don't let honesty mean cruelty. Don't mistake strength for a lack of vulnerability. Sometimes the best way to heal yourself is to focus on healing someone else.

GROWTH DIRECTION
CENTERED: Has recognized tendency to stew in emotions silently or try to sublimate them, but has learned what really matters and how to express themselves better.   **EMPATHETIC:** Has focused on putting the needs and emotions of others above their own.

POP STAR TYPE
THE EXPRESSIVE SOLOIST: As confident as they come, thrives in private creative situations. Knows how to channel their emotions into their craft. A true classic.   **THE INNOVATIVE SOLOIST:** Blending confidence and creativity, also balances the old school with the new school. Has learned that collaboration can be balanced against private expression.

THE SUPREME

Brilliantly **Confident** and often **Reactive**, The Supreme always WINS . . . even if that means TAKING DOWN others when they deserve it. When it comes to problem-solving, The Supreme doesn't hold back: they act on INSTINCT and do what they think is RIGHT, ever the fearless leader. Similarly, when it comes to conflict, their first instinct is to LASH OUT and certainly to never back down. The Supreme PRIORITIZES themselves and isn't afraid of being EMOTIONAL. That's why it's crucial to recognize the emotion in others, especially while leading the way for them.

BALANCES TO REACH

Don't let self-assuredness mean a lack of self-awareness. Don't let honesty mean cruelty. Don't suffer fools, but don't become dismissive. Sometimes the best way to heal yourself is to focus on healing someone else.

GROWTH DIRECTION

CENTERED: Has focused on processing the root of emotions, letting unproductive feelings pass, and weighing everything against core intentions.

EMPATHETIC: Has recognized a tendency to react emotionally, but has learned to let instinctive anger pass and find the emotion truly driving interactions, on both sides.

POP STAR TYPE

THE EXPRESSIVE SUPREME: As confident as they come, has learned to lead fruitful collaborations. Never threatened by the talent of others, and always willing to share themselves.

THE INNOVATIVE SUPREME: Blending confidence and creativity, incorporates many elements from life into what they do best. Professional to a fault and always focused on groundbreaking techniques.

THE SONGWRITER

Deeply **Creative** and often internally **Affected**, The Songwriter is the most BRILLIANT at what they do . . . but also the most ANXIOUS about it. When it comes to problem-solving, The Songwriter always seeks unique SOLUTIONS not always seen by others. However, when HURT or ANGRY, their first instinct is to bottle emotion and diffuse conflicts. The Songwriter FEELS DEEPLY but can also FEEL ALONE. At the same time, a walking contradiction, The Songwriter can be wonderfully COLLABORATIVE and even a bit of a ROMANTIC.

BALANCES TO REACH

Don't let creativity mean obscurity. Feel deeply, but don't get swept away by emotions. Trust others, but never more than inner self. Don't measure personal talent against the talent of others.

GROWTH DIRECTION

CENTERED: Has recognized tendency to stew in emotions silently or try to sublimate them, but has learned how to regain perspective and how to express themselves better.

EMPATHETIC: Has focused on putting the needs and emotions of others above their own.

POP STAR TYPE

THE EXPRESSIVE SONGWRITER: Blending confidence and creativity, knows how to get personal with others. Follows their heart above all else, even if it leads to trouble.

THE INNOVATIVE SONGWRITER: As creative as they come, always puts their work first. A consummate professional, focuses on the newest and best ways to do things.

THE TELLER

Extremely **Creative** and equally **Reactive**, The Teller always channels the TRUTH and AMPLIFIES their own voice . . . even if that means SHOUTING over others or riding a wave of ANGER. When it comes to problem-solving, The Teller always seeks unique SOLUTIONS not always seen by others. However, when it comes to conflict, their first instinct is to LASH OUT and certainly to never back down. The Teller RUNS HOT, which makes them PASSIONATE about everything. Their flame burns bright but is always in danger of burning out if they try to do it all themselves.

BALANCES TO REACH
Don't let creativity mean obscurity. Embrace anger when it fuels, but always examine its deeper root. Listening to self doesn't always mean ignoring others. Don't let honesty mean cruelty.

GROWTH DIRECTION
CENTERED: Has focused on processing the root of emotions, letting unproductive feelings pass, and weighing everything against a more selfless motivation.
EMPATHETIC: Has recognized tendency to react emotionally, but has learned to let instinctive anger pass and find the emotion truly driving interactions—certainly in self, but most importantly in others.

POP STAR TYPE
THE EXPRESSIVE TELLER: Blending confidence and creativity, knows how to communicate with others. A leader in all the ways that matter most.
THE INNOVATIVE TELLER: As creative as they come, knows how to forge new territory. Also knows how to pull the best work out of others with an eye on the best product possible.

VINNY

CHAPTER THREE
VOICE: Add 2 to *Talent*
DRAG: Add 2 to *Charisma*
DOESN'T BELONG: Add 1 to *Excluded*
WASTE: Add 1 to *Overwhelmed*

CHAPTER FOUR
FAKE IT: Add 1 to *Leader*
COMPROMISE: Add 1 to *Chameleon*

CHAPTER SEVEN
GOSSIP LEAK: Add 2 to *Overwhelmed*, Add 1 to *Leader*
PARENTAL BREAKUP: Add 2 to *Excluded*, Add 1 to *Chameleon*

CHAPTER EIGHT
SLICK POP: Add 3 to *Charisma*, Add 1 to *Leader*
GLAM ROCK: Add 3 to *Talent*, Add 1 to *Chameleon*
TALK OPENLY: Add 2 to *Excluded*, Add 1 to *Leader*
KEEP SECRET: Add 2 to *Overwhelmed*, Add 1 to *Chameleon*

CHAPTER ELEVEN
BELONGING: Add 2 to *Excluded*, Add 1 to *Chameleon*
ENOUGH: Add 2 to *Overwhelmed*, Add 1 to *Leader*
DAME: Add 2 to *Charisma*, Add 2 to *Chameleon*, Add 2 to *Excluded*, Add 2 to *Proud*
VIA: Add 2 to *Talent*, Add 2 to *Leader*, Add 2 to *Overwhelmed*, Add 2 to *Inspired*

CHAPTER TWELVE

CHANGE NARRATIVE: Add 2 to *Charisma*, Add 1 to *Leader*
DISCOVER YOURSELF: Add 2 to *Talent*, Add 1 to *Chameleon*

CHAPTER FIFTEEN

PERSONAL: Add 2 to *Inspired*, Add 1 to *Chameleon*
PUBLIC: Add 2 to *Proud*, Add 1 to *Leader*
UPBEAT: Add 3 to *Charisma*, Add 1 to *Inspired*, Add 1 to *Leader*
EDGIER: Add 3 to *Talent*, Add 1 to *Proud*, Add 1 to *Chameleon*

CHAPTER SIXTEEN

DUET: Add 2 to *Proud*, Add 1 to *Chameleon*
HEAL: Add 2 to *Inspired*, Add 1 to *Leader*
VOCAL: Add 3 to *Talent*, Add 2 to *Inspired*, Add 2 to *Leader*
LEWK: Add 3 to *Charisma*, Add 2 to *Proud*,
Add 2 to *Chameleon*

VINNY STRENGTH TALLIES

Which one of the below has the most tallies? Choose your favorite if there's a tie. This is the first half of your **Vinny Type**, the greatest strengths you gave Vinny.

Leader Tally:			
Chameleon Tally:			

VINNY INSECURITY TALLIES

Which one of the below has the most tallies? Choose your favorite if there's a tie. This is the second half of your **Vinny Type**, the insecurities Vinny struggled with most.

Excluded Tally:			
Overwhelmed Tally:			

Find your **Vinny Type** combo of Leader/Chameleon
and Excluded/Overwhelmed in this grid:

	EXCLUDED	OVERWHELMED
LEADER	The Example	The Giver
CHAMELEON	The Showout	The Emulator

VINNY GROWTH TALLIES			
Which one of the below has the most tallies? This is your **Growth Direction**, the way you guided Vinny to overcome his insecurities.			
Proud Tally:			
Inspired Tally:			

POP STAR TYPE TALLIES			
Which one of the below has the most tallies? Choose your favorite if there's a tie. This is your **Pop Star Type**, the musical expression you empowered Vinny with most often.			
Talent Tally:			
Charisma Tally:			

Flip to the page of your **Vinny Type** and remember your
Growth Direction and **Pop Star Type**!

THE EXAMPLE

Always a **Leader**, even when feeling **Excluded**, The Example PIONEERS new paths that no one else is capable of... but standing out can be LONELY and EXILING. When it comes to problem-solving, The Example sets a DECISIVE course, always doing what's best for their FLOCK. However, when it comes to these relationships and groups, they often feel like an OUTSIDER, causing them to FORCE their way into places they might not belong. The Example isn't affected by NOISE, but can also TRY TOO HARD if left unchecked.

BALANCES TO REACH
What makes someone different makes them strong. No one is meant to be understood or adored by everyone. Focus on those who do offer acceptance. Flowing works as well as forcing, usually even better.

GROWTH DIRECTION
PROUD: Has recognized tendency to feel like an outsider, but has learned to recognize self-worth. Is now less afraid to be authentically individual and emotionally honest.
INSPIRED: Has focused on channeling emotion to remain honest and positive as a confident individual and a force for others.

POP STAR TYPE
THE TALENTED EXAMPLE: Focused on vocals and raw talents, with an emphasis on expressing emotion and channeling deeply personal inspiration. Projects quiet confidence.
THE CHARISMATIC EXAMPLE: Focused on performance quality and elaborate presentation, with an emphasis on amplified personality and anthemic advocacy. Projects bold confidence.

THE GIVER

A heartfelt **Leader**, even when feeling **Overwhelmed**, The Giver PUTS OTHERS FIRST ... but sometimes putting others first means AVOIDING their own issues. When it comes to problem-solving, The Giver takes COMMAND for others, always doing what's best for their FLOCK. However, when it comes to self, can feel surprisingly DIRECTIONLESS. The Giver operates on their FIRST INSTINCT and can SHARE deeply personal things, but also later DOUBTS self and fears the LOSS of what's good.

BALANCES TO REACH
Turn fear of future loss into gratitude for the present. What makes someone different makes them strong. Containing multitudes is normal, but must learn when to apply personal tools. Cannot truly give to others unless first giving to self.

GROWTH DIRECTION
PROUD: Has focused on being less sensitive and trying less to fit in, instead standing up and speaking out more authentically.
INSPIRED: Has recognized tendency to feel overshadowed or directionless, but has learned to embrace full self while remaining a selfless advocate for others.

POP STAR TYPE
THE TALENTED GIVER: Focused on exposing raw nerves and healing through art, using voice in every way. A true classic.
THE CHARISMATIC GIVER: Focused on bold uniqueness and channeling empathy, utilizing all powers of presentation. Pushes boundaries.

THE SHOWOUT

Ever the **Chameleon**, often because they feel **Excluded**, The Showout possesses the BOLDEST and BRIGHTEST personality . . . but often PROJECTS from a place of NEEDINESS. When it comes to problem-solving, The Showout puts PERSONAL relationships first and usually balances the best COMPROMISES to find a way forward. However, when it comes to these relationships and groups, they often feel like an OUTSIDER, causing them to CHANGE to be included in everything. The Showout cares about ADVOCACY but struggles with issues of CONTROL and PERCEPTION.

BALANCES TO REACH

Molding self into what you think people want might attract more people, but the wrong kind. Staying true to yourself might attract less people, but the right kind. What makes someone different makes them strong. No one is meant to be understood or adored by everyone.

GROWTH DIRECTION

PROUD: Has recognized tendency to feel like an outsider, but has learned to recognize self-worth. Has learned to wear scars of trauma as a badge of honor.

INSPIRED: Has focused on channeling emotion to remain honest and positive, both as a confident individual and as a force for others.

POP STAR TYPE

THE TALENTED SHOWOUT: Honors idols by pushing abilities to the limit and never holding back. Nervy and swervy.

THE CHARISMATIC SHOWOUT: Honors idols by pushing boundaries and always evolving. Unique and unexpected.

THE EMULATOR

Ever the **Chameleon**, often because they feel **Overwhelmed**, The Emulator is a true jack of ALL TRADES . . . but perhaps a master of NONE. When it comes to problem-solving, The Emulator PLAYS THE GAME and is adept at SHIFTING strengths to fit the need of any situation. However, adapting easily can also mean lacking SELF-CONFIDENCE or FOCUSING on the wrong things. The Emulator can be more PRIVATE and draw from EMOTIONAL wells of strength, but this inner world can also be filled with ANXIETY and a need for CONTROL.

BALANCES TO REACH
Remaining flexible is a great gift, as long as you control the shifts. Containing multitudes is normal, but must learn when to apply personal tools. Controlling things never works as well as trusting you can weather anything. Emulating is a great place to start, but always grow into your own version.

GROWTH DIRECTION
PROUD: Has focused on being less sensitive and trying less to fit in, instead standing up and speaking out authentically. **INSPIRED:** Has recognized tendency to feel overshadowed or directionless, but has learned to embrace full self and channel the right skill or feeling at the right time, for self and others.

POP STAR TYPE
THE TALENTED EMULATOR: Honors those who came before by studying the greats and blending into own unique style. The voice of a generation. **THE CHARISMATIC EMULATOR:** Honors those who came before by synthesizing the fresh and the futuristic. A multi-hyphenate threat for the ages.

JEWELTONES SONG SORTING MATRIX

WHAT JEWELTONES SONG BEST REPRESENTS YOUR MOST IMPORT-ant choices and your spirit as a reader?

EVERLY KEY CHOICES	
CREATIVE PROCESS: Songwriting Focus (Chapter Six) **PERFORMING & GROWTH:** Stern Breakthrough (Chapter Ten) **GROUP DRAMA:** Deverly Resolution (Chapter Fourteen)	
If you chose songwriting *Brooksville*, Stern breakthrough *closet*, & Deverly *friendship*:	7
If you chose songwriting *Brooksville*, Stern breakthrough *closet*, & Deverly *colleagues*:	3
If you chose songwriting *Brooksville*, Stern breakthrough *co-write*, & Deverly *friendship*:	4
If you chose songwriting *Brooksville*, Stern breakthrough *co-write*, & Deverly *colleagues*:	1
If you chose songwriting *pens, paper, picks*, Stern breakthrough *closet*, & Deverly *friendship*:	8
If you chose songwriting *pens, paper, picks*, Stern breakthrough *closet*, & Deverly *colleagues*:	5
If you chose songwriting *pens, paper, picks*, Stern breakthrough *co-write*, & Deverly *friendship*:	6
If you chose songwriting *pens, paper, picks*, Stern breakthrough *co-write*, & Deverly *colleagues*:	2

VINNY KEY CHOICES	
GROUP DRAMA: Investigate Focus (Chapter Seven) **CREATIVE PROCESS:** Drag Persona (Chapter Eleven) **PERFORMING & GROWTH:** Finale Reveal (Chapter Sixteen)	
If you chose investigate *gossip leak*, drag persona *Dame*, & finale reveal *vocal*:	5
If you chose investigate *gossip leak*, drag persona *Dame*, & finale reveal *lewk*:	3
If you chose investigate *gossip leak*, drag persona *Via*, & finale reveal *vocal*:	8
If you chose investigate *gossip leak*, drag persona *Via*, & finale reveal *lewk*:	7
If you chose investigate *parental breakup*, drag persona *Dame*, & finale reveal *vocal*:	2
If you chose investigate *parental breakup*, drag persona *Dame*, & finale reveal *lewk*:	1
If you chose investigate *parental breakup*, drag persona *Via*, & finale reveal *vocal*:	6
If you chose investigate *parental breakup*, drag persona *Via*, & finale reveal *lewk*:	4

Add your Everly Number to your Vinny Number
to get your Jeweltones Sum: _____
Using your Jeweltones Sum, match to your spirit song below,
then flip to that song for your lyrics.

2: Stepping into Shadows
3–4: Damned If You Don't (Brooksville Rebel Version)
5–6: Damned If You Don't (Brooksville HWIC Version)
7–8: Burns You Out (Songwriting Co-Write Version)
9–10: Press Diamonds
11–12: Burns You Out (Songwriting Closet Version)
13–14: Heart to Rage (Pens, Paper, Picks Green Version)
15: Heart to Rage (Pens, Paper, Picks for Myself Version)
16: Breaking Band

2: STEPPING INTO SHADOWS

What am I to do
When I know exactly who I am
Isn't enough for you?
What am I to say
When change feels impossible
But compromise is the only way?

chorus:
Finally stepping out of the
    shadows
But isn't it funny
Isn't it true
The only way out
Is stepping into my shadows
With you

What should I do
The question I always ask
Wanting to please you
What should I say
To make you see
Living an illusion isn't the way

(chorus)

They told me what to do
To get all I ever wanted
Simply kneel to you

Here's what I have to say
Things are different than
    I thought
But expectations aren't
    the only way

(chorus)

Doesn't matter
If you're sad and blue
Or green with envy
Doesn't matter
If you're red with rage
Or white with grief
We're all the same
Royal purple
Where it counts

I am a warrior
Unbreakable and aloft
I am a river
Fluid and soft
Someone tell me
Just how long
'Til I know
When to flow
And when to be strong?

(chorus)

If this is your Jeweltones spirit song,
write the lyric that means most to you here:

_____

_____

_____

_____

_____

3-4: DAMNED IF YOU DON'T
(BROOKSVILLE REBEL VERSION)

All dressed up for the ball
Masquerade or wrecking
It'll be your call
Crimson lip, blood red fire
Ocean eyes, frost blue ice
They'll know if you're naughty
They'll know if you're nice
So which version of you will
    rule this night?

chorus:
Some days, you need to throw
    in the towel
Some nights, you need to push
    through the pain
Some days, you need to hold
    the stillness
Some nights, you need to blaze
    a new path
Some times, you'll be damned
    if you do
But every time, you'll be damned
    if you don't

All suited for the game
Win or lose
They'll know your name
Calloused fingers
Steady hands
Won't be judged
By those in the stands

(chorus)

The power to create
Is the strength to alleviate
The will to empower
Girl, it'll make 'em cower
When you've found
Where you belong
The group that's been waiting
All along
That's when you'll sing
The right song

(chorus)

If this is your Jeweltones spirit song,
write the lyric that means most to you here:

_____

_____

_____

_____

5-6: DAMNED IF YOU DON'T
(BROOKSVILLE HWIC VERSION)

All dressed up for the ball
Masquerade or wrecking
It'll be your call
Crimson lip, blood red fire
Ocean eyes, frost blue ice
They'll know if you're naughty
They'll know if you're nice
So which version of you will rule
    this night?

chorus:
Say this, wear that
Sing what they want 'til
    you scream
It only feels like you're damned
    if you do
So say that, wear this
Scream what you want in your
    wildest dream
Because you know you'll be
    damned if you don't

Invited inside
They'll tell you what to covet
Fame, money, fans, haters
They'll tell you to only love it
Influence that
Leverage your platform
Because there's only one way to
    perform
But I know the secret
The one they don't share
All the distractions in the world
    don't matter
When intention is your only care

(chorus)

You sang to validate
To prove your worth
But now you sing to liberate
Knowing you were worthy
All along

(chorus)

If this is your Jeweltones spirit song,
write the lyric that means most to you here:

_____

_____

_____

_____

_____

7-8: BURNS YOU OUT
(SONGWRITING CO-WRITE VERSION)

They only see what I decide
    to show
And I hate them for thinking
    it's the whole scene
They think the grass is greener
    up here
But the weeds only grow
    more mean

chorus:
What do you do
When the thing you enjoy
Starts to feel like no fun?
What do you do
When the thing you love
Burns you out faster than you
    can run?

They always think, once you hit
    that goal
Perfection sets in, it all just
    comes true
But when you live in that dream,
    when it's suddenly mundane
You just chase what comes next,
    wondering where the time
    flew

(chorus)

Dream, nightmare
Perfection, illusion
Reality, delusion
Beloved, beware

(chorus)

If this is your Jeweltones spirit song,
write the lyric that means most to you here:

_____

_____

_____

_____

_____

9–10: PRESS DIAMONDS

All that glitters isn't gold
That's the line we're always sold
Diamonds are a girl's best friend
Molds we fit to not offend

pre-chorus:
But these diamonds drip
    with blood
Sweat and tears pooling to flood
Your feed with shiny stories
Sure signs we'll edge your glories

chorus:
Put us in to pressure cook
Forever pressed, unexpressed
All the news that's fit to print
Marathon we're forced to sprint
Live rent-free to mine our
    lonely islands
But won't be turned into your
    press diamonds

Once before there lived pure coal
Stripped it down with just
    one goal
Upgrade, shift states 'til you break
A glittery, reflective,
    beautiful fake

(pre-chorus)
(chorus)

Diamonds are really just stones
Falling ruins and building homes
Marking tombs and trapping rings
Skipping lakes and breaking things
Throw your stones to my
    witch death
'Til stone coal is all that's left

(chorus)

If this is your Jeweltones spirit song,
write the lyric that means most to you here:

_____

_____

_____

_____

_____

11–12: BURNS YOU OUT
(SONGWRITING CLOSET VERSION)

We all dream the same
Hearts in one beat
Chasing the damn thing
Fingers grasping to clutch
Then it happens
The impossible becomes yours
Until you see the finish line
Is just where the trouble starts

chorus:
What do you do
When the thing you enjoy
Starts to feel like no fun?
What do you do
When the thing you love
Burns you out faster than you
    can run?

Everyone around shines so bright
It makes your star seem dull
Rebel hearts and dancing queens
Royal voices and crystal chords
Paling in comparison feels
    not enough
So you become glue to fill
    the cracks
But the shiny package
It crumbles all the same.

(chorus)

We are the problem
We make it wrong for ourselves
But what if that only means
We are also the solution?

(chorus)

If this is your Jeweltones spirit song,
write the lyric that means most to you here:

_____

_____

_____

_____

_____

13-14: HEART TO RAGE
(PENS, PAPER, PICKS GREEN VERSION)

It didn't happen yesterday
But it sure does feel that way
You met me on the roof
That was new
But quick as you came
I just withdrew
Guitar strings
Cracked-edge picture frames
You gathered every scrap
For the flames
I didn't know why
Still don't think I do
All I have is this aching heart
Devoted to you

chorus:
Tale as old as lie
Song so old begs why
All the clichés in the world
Don't add up to much
Except this broken trust
This hollowed husk
A pen on the page
A voice on the stage
Just wish I could find
The heart to rage

It didn't happen yesterday
But there is where I stay
Trying to find anger
To move my bones
Just not ready
To throw the right stones

I blame myself
It keeps you around this abyss
This long after
We lost all our promise
Standing beside you
We looked at the ocean
Couldn't see the wave coming
To crush our emotion

(chorus)

Our fire burned
This place to the ground
But babe
I think we can turn
This wreck around
Use the same flames
To light our way
Look forward
To a brighter day
We thought we got
What we always wanted
But those were just ghost stories
That kept us haunted
Old waves they used
To keep us small
But now we've found
Our wrecking ball
I've got a pen
You've got the page
Together we'll mend
Our hearts to rage

(chorus)

If this is your Jeweltones spirit song,
write the lyric that means most to you here:

_____

_____

15: HEART TO RAGE
(PENS, PAPER, PICKS FOR MYSELF VERSION)

It didn't happen yesterday
But it sure does feel that way
I wore a backpack
That wasn't new
Then you stole
What I already planned to give you
Faded novels
Cracked-edge picture frames
You gathered every scrap
For the flames
I didn't know why
Still don't think I do
All I have is this shattered heart
Devoted to you

chorus:
Tale as old as lie
Song so old begs why
All the clichés in the world
Don't add up to much
Except this broken trust
This hollowed husk
A pen on the page
A voice on the stage
Just wish I could find
The heart to rage

It didn't happen yesterday
But there is where I stay
Trying to find anger
To move my bones

Just not ready
To throw the right stones
I blame myself
It keeps you around this abyss
This long after
You broke our promise
Ocean so dark
Didn't see the wave 'til the pound
Water so deep
Can't tell swimming up from down

(chorus)

Got crushed under this wave
Tumbling
The riptide pulled me apart
Crumbling
Swept out to sea
Scattered into a thousand
Shimmering shards of me
But in the calm
I began to regather
Started seeing
The heart of the matter
I became my own ocean
Flowing
Queen of the current
Always knowing
That now I make
My own waves

(chorus)

If this is your Jeweltones spirit song,
write the lyric that means most to you here:

_____

_____

_____

16: BREAKING BAND

Disband
Call you out
Band-Aid
Bleeding out
Wrecking band
All alone
Band of gold
All jewel tone

chorus:
Think I'm gonna
Break down
Think I'm gonna
Break free
Think I'm gonna
Break rules
Think I'm gonna
Break you
Think I'm gonna
Feel I'm gonna
Know I'm gonna
Breaking band

Regroup
Crown this queen
Lead group
Mind this queen
See group
Storm the throne
Make group
Shine jewel tone

(chorus)

You don't understand
Not making the band
You must understand
We're breaking the band
Break us down
To build us up
Break your rules
To make our own
Cause some dischord
Pull the ripchord
We're breaking band
Are you a fan?

(chorus)

If this is your Jeweltones spirit song,
write the lyric that means most to you here:

_____

_____

_____

_____

_____